LILY UPSHIRE
IS
WINNING

WITH THANKS TO

Meredith Nason - editorial advice
B - beta reading
Teresa Holmes - initial cover design work
Maggie Harrison - patience and support

many writer friends in Brighton and Retford for
listening to extracts, providing advice and support

and:

HSP for making it all happen

and:

Nancy Mitford: 'Life is sometimes sad and often
dull, but there are currants in the cake, and here is
one of them.'

Don Van Vliet: 'If you want to be a different fish,
you've got to jump out of the school.'

A longer version of one of the 'corporate' scenes
appears in the anthology Night Bus to Speakers
Corner and was performed as a short play at the
North Notts Literary Festival

LILY UPSHIRE
IS
WINNING

by
John Holmes

LILY UPSHIRE IS WINNING

First Edition 2021

ISBN: 9798701747669

Published by Happy Self Publishing
www.happyselfpublishing.com

1

It was a typical day in the life of Lily Upshire. A typical schoolday.

It was typical because of the bullies, Lily's main preoccupation outside of her home life. In particular, there were the Bizzell twins. Lily, who was small for her age of twelve going on thirteen, was afraid of them, although not as afraid as some other girls were. Some were terrified. Although there were other distinguishing features, the Bizzell sisters were known as 'Blue and Green' because of their different eye colours. They strolled everywhere together, be it around school or about town, and they expected their victims to keep out of their way as a mark of respect, if not fear. They lived just a few streets from Lily, streets which in a sense they owned, and so she was used to crossing the road to avoid them. At school there were two other girls who hung around with the twins, and if anything, they were even more obnoxious, including their vicious younger sister, generally known as 'the Runt'. The Runt had been hardened through routine beatings from older kids who'd in turn been bullied by her sisters. She was Lily's nemesis.

On this Wednesday, Lily hadn't encountered the twins yet, but she did hear a familiar voice behind her in the corridor. It was the Runt's evil friend, a girl nicknamed Mitch: 'Hey Upshite, why are you even here?'

She did not turn round or reply.

'Upshite!' She wanted to turn but still resisted. She was staring at the ground, feeling depressed, and did not see the tall man appear in front of her. 'Hey, head up there, Lily!' It was Mr Heger, the Canadian science teacher—a kindly man but one of the teachers who she was sure had written her off. A concern not without foundation.

'I'm sorry,' she said. Behind her she heard the disgusting pair sniggering and imitating her. She was tempted to walk along with him, on some pretext she couldn't even think of, but he took such big strides she would almost have to run, and the Runt and her friend would get plenty of laughs from seeing that, as well as from her cowardice. So she turned to face her tormentors. She would take it, whatever it was going to be. They were itching for a scrap. She became aware that she'd begun sweating under her arms.

'Surprised to see you,' said Mitch, who had long straggly red hair and a hunted look that aroused sympathy but was deceptive. Mitch the Bitch they called her and she delighted in it.

'Why?' said Lily, though she knew why.

'We thought you'd be dead,' said the Runt. She was smaller than Lily, had blonde hair much shorter than hers, and a wide grin. She always moved fast, like a ball of bright energy, here one minute, there the next, wherever she could make trouble that she could just as quickly retreat from. 'We thought you'd have killed yourself like we talked about. You know it would do everyone a favour. When your grannie dies you'll have no-one, and you'll be a poor little orphan girl no-one cares about, except maybe a pimp.'

'Yeah. Or a trafficker,' said Mitch, savouring the word.

'So you might as well just do it. Tonight. There's websites to tell you how. You'll see your mummy again.'

'Shut up,' said Lily.

'Wouldn't that be nice? You might find out who your daddy was.'

Mitch joined in: 'That's if her mum even knows.'

The Runt laughed. 'Maybe he was a serial killer. How would you feel about that?'

'Or a rapist,' said Mitch.

'Yeah, that's right, a rapist.'

'No,' said Lily, determined to hold it in her face. She could let it out in tears later.

'Tell you what,' said the Runt with the delight of a thought occurring to her for the first time. 'Your friend Brian looks like a rapist. Yes he does. Just saying.'

'No he doesn't.' She was unprepared for this attack on her best friend and lost her temper 'Leave me alone, you bitch!'

The Runt gave that expression of fake shock beloved by bullies everywhere: *'Did you hear that!?'* She turned to her friend.

'Let's get her,' said Mitch.

In a fight she could deal with either of them but not both together. She would get a kicking which was their favourite form of punishment. And how it worked was that a dozy teacher like Miss Cotton would find Lily defending herself with her fists and see her at that moment as the aggressor. The one she wasn't hitting would say she was trying to protect her friend from being beaten up by Lily. And even at best, Lily would still get fifty percent of the blame.

Mitch rushed to grab her so the Runt could land some kicks, but they stopped on hearing the shout of someone approaching: 'Leave her alone, you filthy skank!'

It was a voice Lily recognised: it was of an older girl. She relaxed a little. There were a couple of girls, said to be lesbians, who intervened whenever they saw bullying. After being terrorised by the Bizzell twins for months on end, they'd taken up boxing and were now fearless and, when circumstances required, ruthless. Lily idolised them and wished either, but particularly the pretty Afro-Caribbean one who was so quick, could be the sibling she'd never had. The twins no longer messed with them, and if the Runt or Mitch saw them, they ran off, which is what they did now.

It was a typical day because of the teachers at Retingham High. Lily had a poor reputation as a student. She was, by her own admission, a dreamer. She was inattentive in class and indifferent to homework. She also had an unfortunate reputation for having 'attitude', in other words being rude, when it came to authority figures, but this was largely a misreading of her acute shyness, though not helped by her tendency towards bad language. The fact that she was bottom of the class in every subject except English (in which she was second to bottom, but the teacher, whom Lily adored, thought she showed 'promise') fuelled the narrative that she was thick and lazy, attributes that encouraged rather than appeased the detractors amongst her fellows.

On this typical Wednesday, the English teacher, Emily Hass, asked her for a word after class. Lily, distracted throughout the lesson thinking about what the bullies had said, was immediately worried the only remaining teacher she thought liked her might be changing her mind. Emily Hass was Lily's idea of a goddess: young and long-limbed as an Olympic high-jumper, encouraging in her class the same energy and quiet determination she believed vital for success in all things, passionate about her subject and her students' progress, and with a kindness Lily found addictive. Most of the other teachers were tired old crabs in comparison. Lily had no more interest in English than any other subject, but her desire not to disappoint the teacher was so strong it inspired her to something that at least looked like effort. Emily was now holding up Lily's latest essay in front of her with hands so elegant and beautiful they could be modelling the world's most luxurious skincare products. She handed the book to her. 'Lily I'm going to give you another chance to do this essay. I know you're capable of better. Just this once, I want to give you the chance to redo it. You're on the right lines with it, but I think you rushed it as usual.' Every few weeks they went through this same unacknowledged ritual: 'just this once'. And of course, being a goddess Emily knew exactly what was happening, and knew it was worth this student dashing off a below-par essay for all the attention it earned her. But being conscientious and concerned about favouritism, Emily knew she would need to address this in a different way in future, although not this once.

'OK. Sorry. How much more time can I have?' said Lily.

'How much do you need?'

'I don't know.'

'Friday, then.'

'Monday?'

Emily smiled, which for Lily was the most cherished part of the encounter. 'OK.'

'Um, while I'm here can I ask you something?'

'Sure.'

Lily moved closer. She always loved the subtle perfume Emily wore. 'Would it be possible for me to transfer to your form? I think Miss Cotton hates me.'

'Oh...' Emily struggled to hide her embarrassment. 'I'm sure she doesn't... and, I'm afraid, there's no...' She was silent for a moment, biting her lip, maybe for effect. 'No, I don't think that would be possible. Or even a good idea, if I'm honest. I'm sure at heart Miss Cotton believes in you every bit as much as I do.'

'No, I don't think she does, but thank you anyway. Can I ask you something else?'

'Go ahead.'

Lily screwed up her face for a moment to moisten her eyes. 'Well, when my grandma withdraws me from school—'

'Why on earth would she do that!?'

'Er, well, I'm working on it.' The tiniest flicker of a grin. 'Would you be OK to be my private tutor for English?'

'Oh, Lily, what can I say? I certainly hope it never comes to that, but, erm...' Lily caught her glance with a look of such wide-eyed waifish appeal that Emily blushed. 'Actually, yes of course, it would be... But I'll see your grandma at parents' evening, won't I?'

'I don't know.'

It was at this point that the head teacher arrived to see Ms Hass, and so the chat was over.

It was a typical day because of Brian. A year older than her, he was her soulmate. They often spent lunchtimes together. Sandy-haired, he was lean and lanky, and as a chaperon he was pretty useless when it came to dealing with bullies. He was the son of Ted Panker, a former professional boxer with his own gym, but Brian had no interest in that or any other sport. He was considered diffident and a bit weird like Lily, and indeed some of the older town gossips claimed they were biologically half-brother and sister. Although these gossips could not agree on who was the common parent, the Panker family insisted it was a myth anyway. Because of his father, Brian was rarely bullied; it was less the threat that Ted might appear at the bully's front door and more in recognition of the regard held for him within the local community. Grandma loved Brian, and he'd been round for tea several times, although to Lily's puzzlement this was never reciprocated, not that it much bothered her.

As on most other days, Lily met Brian after school to walk home together. The weather was pleasant, so they walked slowly. Brian told a rather boring story about his maths lesson and, soon sensing Lily's total disinterest, said, 'So how's it been so far this week then?' He meant the bullying.

'Let's see. Five "fat cows". Four "slags". And that's just from the teachers.'

'Yeah?'

'No - just me being silly. Only the usuals. And some "Upshite"s today from the Runt and that Mitch. And a couple of "weirdo"s. But no "gay"s yet.'

'No? OK.'

'But stuff about my mum and dad and why I should kill myself. That's pretty bad. That's their big thing right now.' She chose not to mention the comment the Runt had made about him.

'It can't go on like this, Lily.'

'I get used to it. I can't say I accept it—how could I? And after last week I know I'll get more of it.' They were silent, increasing pace as they crossed the end of the smart cul-de-sac where the Bizzells lived.

'Tell me again what happened,' he said when they were clear of it.

'I told you twice already, Brian.'

'I know but I love to hear it.'

'OK. You know where it was—where the corridors cross, there just past the art room, I was where those two steps are, she came hurtling round the corner like she does, shouted: "Out of my way, dyke!" And I just reacted: "Piss off, Runt!"'

'That'll do it.'

'Yeah, she hates it. And she threw herself at me like she was going to nut me but she tripped—maybe my foot or her shoelace—lost balance and hit the wall with her head and she swore at me and she was on the ground, confused, staring at me and I thought: This chance may never come again. I grabbed her by the hair and slammed her face hard into the wall, and next thing I know she's bleeding from the nose, and she gets up and just stares at me like she's shocked, and I notice her lip's bleeding as well as her nose, blood all down her shirt and everywhere—she just lets her nose bleed out—and then people come and the whole circus begins. And later I'm in with the head and I said it was an accident and I can tell she doesn't believe me, but all the witnesses said it was an accident...'

'Because they've had their own issues with her and the twins.'

'Right. But I don't think anyone even saw what I did. And the Runt even said it was an accident because of the shame of it. But although I shouldn't have done it, I don't care because they make my life miserable. And others' lives, even worse. And I know I'll pay for it. They'll get me and it will be bad. I mean, if the twins came round here—' she pointed ahead to where the pavement narrowed and it was hard to see round the hawthorn hedge that jutted out '—I would literally wet myself with fear. They'll ambush me one day, but they'll bide their time while then. I don't walk on my own by the canal any more. I don't like to go out alone. I'm always looking behind me in case one of them is following. But whatever they do is fine: I'll bounce back because I've got my mother's spirit.'

'It's a crazy situation with that family.'

'Isn't it? You've got the boys who are, like, the drug dealers for the town, then you've got the twins who are bullies, then you've got the Runt who's the most messed up of the lot. All five of them horrible. The dad's always away, and the mum's a school governor!'

'And she's actually quite nice.'

'She is nice—on the surface. And rich. And she's always donating stuff to the school. And she will know the truth because the Runt will have told her, and never mind what everyone said about it being an accident. And who's on my team? A grandmother who spends all day listening to Ravi Shankar, or whoever it is, and one day soon she'll be all chilled out from meditating and she'll find she's got a letter about it all. Maybe I'll be suspended. That would be cool.'

'I hope not.'

'It's alright. I just think of my future one day with Travis.' Travis had been her online boyfriend in New York for six months. He was ideal for her: tall, handsome, athletic, kind, romantic. And a keen surfer. She was looking forward to meeting him on Skype for the first time, whilst hoping he wouldn't realise she'd added a year to her age for him. He would soon be sixteen. Although she was twelve, she told him she was thirteen because it sounded better, making her a real teenager, and because she would soon be thirteen anyway.

'How is he?'

'I don't know. As I said last time you asked, he sent me an email saying he had to go offline for a while and I wouldn't hear, but not to worry. Back any day now, I'm sure. Maybe tonight.'

'I don't know, Lily.'

'What do you mean?'

'Are you sure about him?'

'Why wouldn't I be?'

'Well, for a start, there's no surfing in New York.'

'Yeah, there is.'

'Where?'

'Rockaway Beach. Know where that is?'

'No.'

'There you are then. If you must know, I asked him. But you're just so jealous you won't accept he's real. You think I'm too naive to spot someone who's fake.'

'No. I just don't want you to get hurt, that's all.'

'I know. You care about me. But I won't get hurt. Believe me, he's very sincere. And he's bright. His dad owns a successful fashion business, and Travis is going to make a ton of money one day, and I'll be there with him in New York.'

'But you know if—'

'I know, and it means a lot.' She turned to look him in the eyes, smiled and touched him on the forearm affectionately. It was at this point they reached the shop where they always stopped so Lily could buy her favourite drink, despite the fact the shopkeeper, Mr Bashett, was the most bad-tempered in the whole of Retingham and never hesitated to tell the world how much he hated children. Brian, who refused to ever go in the shop, gave her a couple of

11

pounds for a chocolate bar each. When she emerged she said, 'Shall we sit?' The early spring sun was warm, and they often sat on the wooden bench outside the shop, but on this occasion Brian declined. They walked in silence into Saviour Park, which was empty except for one man playing with a labrador retriever. She assumed Brian's sudden moodiness was because he was annoyed with her. 'I'm sorry,' she said, a bite of chocolate somehow giving her the impetus to speak. 'I've obviously upset you so I may as well apologise, even though I don't know what for.' Brian did not reply and, irritated, she stopped walking. He gradually slowed his steps and looked back at her. She said, 'If you're not going to talk to me, I may as well walk on my own, which would be entirely fine with me. What have I done now? I assume it's to do with Travis.'

'Surfer Boy? I don't care about him. He'll be gone in three months anyway, if that long. Oh Lily... why do you make stuff up?'

'What do you mean?'

'You never did that to that girl.'

'Yeah I did.'

'You've told me that story three times and every time it still makes no sense. The reason everyone says it was an accident is because it was. Why do you do this to yourself? Why do you lie? It's like you live in a different world which only occasionally, like the eclipse of the moon or something, corresponds with reality.'

'Brian, listen to yourself. Do you not realise what you're saying and how depressing it is for me? I know what I did.'

'You could not possibly have slammed her face into the wall in the way you described it.'

'You weren't even there.'

'If you did it the way you said, you'd have had to twist her neck off. There's no way. I even asked my sister about it. She's a paramedic. It would take Vera or Endeavour or one of those two seconds to pick your story apart. And I don't believe it happened at all. If you want, I'll sit myself against the wall where the garages are along there near the canal, and you show me exactly what you did. You can't because it never happened.'

'It did!'

'You made it up. Maybe you tripped her, but she crashed into the wall through her own stupid actions, and that's why she was bleeding.'

Furious, she marched past him and left him standing there. He called out, 'It doesn't matter!' But she walked on out of sight behind the garages and towards the canal. With a sad grin, he shook his head and sauntered along the path. He found her waiting for him, looking anxious, leaning against the garage wall. There was no row, no attempt to explain or justify. Neither said anything about it. But she'd been destroyed like a withdrawn child deprived of a toy held dear. He felt bad, but what he'd said had been necessary. Seeking reassurance, she reached out her hand for him to take. He held it tight in his for several moments and then gently released it. They began walking quickly. She said, 'Shall you come to tea tomorrow?'

'Am I invited?'

'I'll ask. It won't be a problem. She'd rather talk to you than me anyway.' Later, she said, 'I'm sorry I upset you. I never meant to.' He could have apologised to her, but he decided not to.

After they'd said, 'See you tomorrow' and he'd gone, she dawdled in the driveway to Grandma's small detached house as she thought it all through. The fact was, she hadn't lied to him. She'd believed every word she said. She went over the incident in her mind again. And then once more. She remembered it so clearly, and yet what he said couldn't be ignored. No-one seemed to believe anything she said. And when she'd consciously lied, it had turned out to be the truth. Was this what living in your own world meant? Not only that you lived in a world of the imagination, but that you saw real things differently to anyone else? That you believed things happened when they didn't? How terrifying was that? And yet, how magical. It was like discovering a power you didn't know how to use, or even whether it could be used. Thinking about this gave her a headache. It was altogether too much. Was she crazy, or just a bit weird like people said? As she approached the front door, how comforting it was! The feel of the edge of the keys and the sound of the metal. And hearing Grandma's laughing. How calming it all was.

It was a typical day because of Grandma. She had looked after Lily since the car crash that took her mum away from her when Lily was not yet two. Whoever her father was had left even before she was born. Grandma had been a hippie in the 1960s— Grateful Dead, dope, Oz and all the rest of it—and some of that era's ideas had influenced her upbringing of Lily. Or at least, that's what her sister, the fearsome Auntie Gwynne, was convinced of. She believed Grandma's laissez-faire approach had ruined 'the child' (she never referred to Lily by name) and, when combined with the youngster's unpromising academic prospects, she told her that, in the absence of 'strong measures' the child's bleak future potential would lie amongst one or more of: runaway, prostitute, drug addict, drug dealer, drug mule, thief, scammer, artist (or some other 'useless' creative pursuit) or, if she didn't cut back on the sugar, 'one of those people so big they can't get through their bedroom door'. More charitably, on the other hand, she did suggest that by strict weight management Lily could aspire to be 'a lower tier footballer's wife or something like that'.

Auntie Gwynne's own childrearing beliefs were based, not on personal experience, but on watching soaps and episodes of true crime shows with titles like *Evil Online, Killer Couples,* and *Blood Relatives,* which to her mind were replete with examples of the dangers of lack of discipline in the home, children being spoilt and indulged with the most unrealistic of expectations, as well as all the dangers of predators and perverts on the internet. On this typical Wednesday, she'd phoned Grandma as usual, asked after 'the child', and reiterated her belief that only through strict discipline and punishment for failure would Lily 'turn her life around'. 'I'm wondering if I should drive up there this Sunday. I'll have a chat with her myself if you like.'

This prospect filled Grandma with alarm. Perhaps it was all the TV Gwynne's brain had consumed, but her memory was clearly departing her. How could she not recall the three previous occasions she'd invited herself for Sunday lunch? In every instance, 'the child' had fallen ill for the three days before she'd arrived, recovered a little on the day of the visit, sufficient for her to make a rare appearance in the kitchen to 'help' Grandma just before lunch, and then Gwynne had suffered with a stomach bug for a week afterwards. How this sequence of events occurred three times in a row remained mysterious to Grandma, though not to Lily.

Gwynne said, 'You know, you do a wonderful roast. I wish I could get the Yorkshires like you do them. And the beef you always get... is it local?'

Like a footballer finding a route to goal through a thicket of players, Grandma suddenly saw a way out of this bind: 'I'm afraid I don't buy beef anymore. Lily's gone vegetarian and, well, it just makes it easier.' This was a lie—Lily had asked if they could both go vegan, and she'd said she would think about it. She hadn't, but now if going vegan or even fruitarian was the price for no more visits from Gwynne, it would be worth paying.

There was a long pause. Finally, with a sigh Gwynne said, 'Well, that just supports everything I've been saying, doesn't it? Who's in charge—you or her?'

'It's not about being in charge. It's about love. I love her. I want her to be happy. It doesn't mean I agree with everything she wants.'

'I'm afraid, it does. But don't worry, I get the picture. And I don't want to get into an argument with you, Grace, my dear, one and only sister. And you've always been a bit away-with-the-fairies yourself, so it's unlikely any child you bring up will be any different, but then of course they're always going to find some way to rebel. There'll be plenty of times in the future you'll want to have a chat with me, don't worry. As it happens, this Sunday I had intended to go through the planner.'

'Planner?'

'Yes, I've got a whole series of *American Monster* to go through.'

'What's that about? Sounds a bit... sinister.'

'It's all about home videos. So it will start off at, say, a wedding or birthday or baby shower or something like that—a family gathering with everyone happy and smiling and loving everyone else like a good American family—then as the story progresses all the tensions begin to emerge and, as it turns out, one of them is evil all along and they go and murder other members of the family, but of course at the start you're wondering who the monster's going to be. It's fascinating. And so true.'

'Well, it is true crime.'

'Yes. I mean, they're all the same really.'

Grandma was tempted to say that if they were all the same, why was there a need to watch a whole series of them? But that would have been counterproductive, so she let her sister wind down the conversation, culminating in a final, 'Just be vigilant over what she's doing.'

It was a typical day because the neighbours, Nancy and Fred Peacemaker, were visiting when Lily arrived home. They were an old couple, though not of retirement age and not as old and wrinkly as Grandma. Nancy was a member of the local council and with her military-style bun, businesslike demeanour, and smart, prim clothes, always conveyed the impression she should be elsewhere doing something more important but stayed talking to you out of kindness (Grandma heard Nancy was like this even at council meetings); whereas Fred, a creature of the indoors, was always pallid, like one of Grandma's pie crusts the moment she put it in the oven, and some of his teeth shifted when he talked which Lily found compulsive watching, especially as it was unpredictable since sometimes none of them moved at all. Usually it was Nancy on her own that visited, but at least once a week her husband would make a special effort to join her. Nancy, who made Lily feel seven years old rather than almost thirteen, found her obtuse and eccentric, which was the commonly held view amongst the neighbours. Fred, on the other hand, admired Lily's 'individuality' and quirkiness. She liked it when he asked her, as he did this time, 'So are you winning, Lily?' or on other occasions, 'Are you winning yet?' But she never liked to admit she was and so would reply after a contrived pause, 'Erm, not really,' or 'I don't know,' or 'Maybe,' or (on a good day) with a rising inflection, 'Soon'. This time she merely shook her head and then gave him a sad smile, keen not to encourage a follow-up question, although Fred never asked them anyway, not from disinterest but because he was not sure what to say next.

Neither of the Peacemakers worked full time, but Nancy 'helped out' at a friend's hardware shop three mornings a week. Fred's working career had been shortened by an industrial accident twenty years previous for which he'd received a lump sum in compensation and a pension. He still complained of 'twinges' in his back which often flared up, particularly when something needed doing. For example, lacking the strength to climb beyond the lowest rung of a ladder ruled out visits to the loft, DIY often required stretching and so was avoided entirely, and gardening was out because the bending played havoc. When in doubt, Fred took to his bed. Nancy believed everything he said about his physical condition, although others who knew the family were less understanding. Someone once suggested to Grandma that Fred was in reality a skilled professional conman, but Grandma thought she knew better; he lacked the requisite charm and, more importantly, the necessary cruelty, and besides, the work involved would have been far more than he could ever accommodate.

It was a typical day because Lily had bought a blueberry flip smoothie at Mr Bashett's shop on the way home from school. It was one of the high points of her average day. She was very particular: it had to be a 'flip' smoothie which meant it contained banana as well as blueberry. She never opened the bottle on the walk home these days, keeping it in her bag. This was because, in the past, bullies she encountered would seize the bottle from her and throw the contents either away, or over her, except for one occasion when she was able to fling the liquid into the bully's face.

But it was an untypical day because when she was in the kitchen and had twisted off the plastic lid, perhaps a little more easily than usual, and poured out most of the contents, she noticed there was something in the glass that shouldn't be there. She then searched in a drawer until she found a long-handled teaspoon. After initial difficulty she managed to catch the small round object with it. At that moment, Grandma came into the kitchen. 'Are you alright?' she said. 'What's the matter, Lily, love?'

'There's something in this smoothie. I don't think I can drink it.'

Grandma took the spoon from her. She peered at the object, then brought the spoon close to her face. She sniffed. 'It could be a garden pea,' she said and ran the spoon under the tap. The object fell into the sink. 'It looks like a pea but it has absorbed the colour, so I'm not sure. I can't see its—what do you call it?—radicle. How odd! Was it really in the drink? Not one of your little pranks?'

'Oh no, it was definitely in the smoothie itself—as if I'd do that with my favourite drink.'

'Well then, perhaps it will bring you luck. The right people are here at least; Nancy and Fred will know exactly what to do.'

'Do?'

Grandma put the spoon into the sink and eased the object back on to it. 'Don't touch that,' she said, indicating the glass with the smoothie in it. She took the spoon into the lounge to show the others, knowing they would make a big production out of it. The absurdity of it all was not lost on her. Such a fuss over a little pea or whatever it was. But then who knew what power lay in such a humble, ostensibly harmless, little object—perhaps the potential to alter a life's course, or to change many lives in ways not even noticed? But a pea, like any other seed, took time to germinate, took a while to manifest its power.

2

Nancy Peacemaker had not been her normally buoyant self when she'd arrived at Grandma's house. This was because she'd had a row with her daughter Sally. It had all started with a council meeting after which fellow councillor Julia Bizzell had told her 'that little monster next door to you' was going to get her 'comeuppance'. She'd complained to the school about the way it had handled an incident concerning her youngest, in which 'Upshire' had deliberately tripped her up and then pushed her face hard into the wall causing her a bloody nose and considerable distress, and the school was treating it as an accident even though they knew it wasn't, and what's more it had happened before. Nancy had told Sally about all this, adding that Lily was becoming a 'problem child' and a bully and Sally, who was old enough to remember Lily's mother, had told Nancy not to be so stupid and not to 'brown-nose' the Bizzell family who were financed entirely by drug money and, apart from Julia who was completely corrupt, were all violent. Sally had added that she had visited next door many times to cut Lily's grandma's hair and had many little chats with Lily and had found her sweet-natured, and if she seemed a little different, it was hardly surprising, given that she was an only child and had lost her mother so early in life and never had a father. To make matters worse, Fred, as if he knew anything about it, had weighed in, saying that if Lily had hit another child, it would have been in self-defence. Nancy had found this all too much to cope with, especially Sally's use of the term 'brown-nose', and it had shaken her confidence in her own ability to read people. Thus, the foreign object in Lily's smoothie was a pleasant distraction.

Lily did not wish to hear their opinions about the pea or whatever else it might be, so she stayed in the kitchen. Grandma sat down in her usual chair with the neighbours on either side, and she would now pass the spoon with the little purple ball on it to Nancy and Fred in turn, for their perusal in their respective fields of expertise. Nancy's field was in finding cause for complaint, whereas Fred's was in converting such complaints into cash.

Grandma presented it first to Nancy who stared hard at it as though it were a rare jewel, albeit not a very valuable one. 'If it's a pea, it's lost all its green colour. It could be a blueberry,' she said.

'That would be entirely logical,' said Fred professorially. 'Or a blackcurrant.'

'No, I don't think it's that,' said Nancy, determined to be seen as equally learned. 'It is soft, I take it, Grace?'

'Yes. It's not a bead or anything like that. It's vegetable matter alright.' Grandma now took the spoon from her and passed it to Fred.

'Ah,' he said with the air of a scientist finding a weakness in a rival's research. 'It may not be edible at all. Indeed, it may well be toxic. I am sure there are many hundreds, if not thousands, of apparently harmless fruits or legumes that are in fact poisonous to the very touch. Lily is very lucky. She may have had a close brush with death. I've always said that child was blessed.'

Nancy grimaced, seeing his comment as a dig related to their earlier argument, while her husband, determined to reach a conclusion on what the object was, screwed up his face tight, straining like a mandrill on a no-roughage diet to try to draw out its truth. Unfortunately, his expression was so extreme it prompted Grandma into a chuckle she struggled to hide, and as she at last took back the spoon her hand began to shake and the pea-like object wobbled. As she rose to her feet she could not resist another glance at his earnestness, enabling the little purple sphere to escape the spoon and fall onto the carpet, whereupon Fred, stretching his leg as he relaxed from his exertions, crushed it with his heavy shoe. It was now stuck to the sole and embedded in a small piece of mud.

'Oh dear,' said Grandma. 'I do believe it's now on your shoe.'

'Do you want me to take it off?' he said.

'No!' said Nancy sharply.

'Sorry about it,' said Fred. 'Don't want it causing a mess. Let's scrape it off and put in on a tissue if you've got one handy.'

Nancy was astute. 'It can wait till you get home.'

Grandma saw what her neighbour was up to. After finding a Kleenex she said, 'Fred, if you just hold up your foot for a moment, I can scrape the pea off.' He did so, and she used the edge of the spoon to remove the flattened vegetable. Holding his foot up played the devil with his back, however, and as a result his foot began to shake and the material, a mixture of 'pea' and mud, began falling everywhere, not only onto the tissue.

'It's making a terrible mess, Fred,' said Nancy. 'That's enough.' She turned to Grandma, 'I'm sure you've got enough there. Major crimes have been solved with less. Come along now, Fred, we should be on our way. Don't forget, we've got someone coming round.' The prospect of a visitor seemed to be news to Fred, but Nancy answered his quizzical look with a stern nod. He was glad for the opportunity to lower his leg.

Nancy was about to get to her feet, but it was at this point that Lily, who'd spent the last few minutes with an ice cube on her palm to calm herself while Grandma was safely out of the kitchen, appeared in the lounge to find her grandmother straining to look for something on the carpet. 'Lost an earring?' she asked.

'No.'

'Shall I get the vacuum cleaner?'

'No!' Grandma snapped, but then, embarrassed at her own uncharacteristic abruptness she added, 'No, dear, we're looking for bits of the pea or whatever it is.'

'Why?'

'Evidence,' said Fred firmly. Lily thought this ridiculous but did not want to offend him so said nothing and was about to retreat to the kitchen again when Grandma said, 'Bring your sharp eyes here.'

Lily returned.

'Don't touch anything, though,' said Fred. 'Could be toxic.'

Lily, concerned lest anything dangerous might stick to her feet, bent down and gave a cursory look but saw nothing. 'How toxic?' she said.

'Highly,' said Fred, hoping to impress her but not succeeding.

'Then shouldn't you take off your shoe in case of any residues on the sole?'

'Not that highly,' said Nancy, wincing in the face of the wild child's logic.

Annoyed but trying to hide it, Lily stood up and said, 'Can't see anything.' She turned to leave, picking up the tissue from the table on her way.

'I suggest you put it in a bag and seal it,' said Grandma. 'Be careful with it. Nancy and Fred know what we should do about it.'

'Really?' replied Lily, rather obviously disinterested.

'Yes. We should take a photograph of the smoothie bottle and the glass with some of the liquid in to show you drank it. Nancy and Fred know someone who can help us.'

'OK,' said Lily, not wanting to ask what was meant by 'help'. She was in the doorway when her exit was delayed by the inevitable question from Nancy: 'And how's school, Lily?'

She was tempted to reply that she hated every moment of it except for English, and that all of the teachers except for Emily Hass she'd be glad to read on the internet had been brutally despatched by a mass shooter, also taking out the Bizzell family and a few fellow students as well, and learn that crows had flown in to peck their eyes out, and wild animals (she couldn't decide which species) had violated their corpses, and pyromaniacs had burnt the place down to a pile of ash, but instead she merely said, 'Fine, thanks.' And she rushed out before any follow-up question could be asked.

In the kitchen she threw the tissue into the small blue box used for peelings and the like for the compost heap. She found some grinds from Grandma's coffee and threw them on top, adding compost from the pot of basil on the windowsill. She then returned to the lounge.

'So what do *you* think it is, my dear?' Grandma asked, a little alarmed at her granddaughter's abrupt removal of the 'evidence' from the lounge.

'Like you said: a garden pea.' Lily was aware of Nancy and Fred looking at her.

'Where's the tissue now?' Grandma said.

'I threw it away.'

All three adults looked shocked. 'You took a photograph, presumably?' said Nancy.

'No.'

Nancy gave a look of intense irritation which Lily noticed, but Mrs Peacemaker was nothing if not resourceful: 'It doesn't matter. We all saw it.' She turned to Grandma, 'And there'll still be residues on Fred's shoe. If all else fails, you could always put another pea in the drink.'

'But that would be fraud,' said Grandma, looking appalled.

'From a strictly technical point of view,' said Fred, keen to be seen as both deeply learned and supportive of his wife. 'But in my experience, allowing for the smaller petit pois—'

'I don't think it was one of those,' Grandma said.

'Indeed, that is my conclusion too.' He paused as his teeth shifted, to Lily's amusement. 'But my point is, there's not a huge amount of variation between individual peas. That is, if it is a pea rather than the fruit of some dangerous Amazonian plant. Certain tree species in Borneo and Sarawak...'

Nancy yawned and said, 'Give over with your Sarawak. Let the company worry about that when Grace makes the claim.'

'Claim?' said Grandma.

'Yes. You can make some money—can't she, Fred?'

Fred was like a dog let off a leash: 'She...' he glanced at Lily, '...They sure can.'

'It's a local company makes them, I think,' Grandma said. 'We wouldn't want to put a little family enterprise out of business.'

'You won't,' he said, amused. 'They'll have insurance. I bet they're not even local. Let's have a look at the container.' Lily went to the kitchen, emptied the plastic bottle, washed and dried it. She looked at the glass still containing the smoothie. Grandma had said not to touch it but that meant not to drink it, so she tipped it out down the drain and rinsed the glass. She then took the bottle to show the Peacemakers. She gave it to Fred who held it up to the light. He could not read it, however.

'Do you want the magnifying glass this time? I think I remember where it is now,' said Grandma.

'Maybe Lily could read it,' he said. He lowered it and passed it back to her. Even to her young eyes it was difficult to read, not assisted by the fact it was written in white on a background of the palest grey. She was successful, however, and read out an address in Peoria, Illinois. The name of the company meant nothing to any of them.

'There you are then,' said Fred triumphantly. The others sat silent and looked at him for elucidation. 'That'll be a huge corporation. Multinational,' he said.

'So has the smoothie come all the way from this Peoria?' asked Lily.

'Almost certainly not,' said the professor. 'That'll be their head office. Operations everywhere. And they'll be owned by someone else, and so on.'

'Fingers in every pie,' said Nancy.

'Whole hands, more like. In fact, the biggest pie in the world. I bet they're shelling out millions every day,' he said.

'Shelling out money like peas,' said Nancy.

'Exactly. Claims like this coming in from all over. They won't even notice. Say you've got allergies,' said Fred.

'But I haven't,' said Lily. 'I have peas at least twice a week. I like peas.'

'They don't know that,' the Peacemakers chanted in unison. Nancy added, 'The point is, it's obviously not supposed to be there.'

'I've never heard of pea allergy,' said Grandma.

Lily noticed Nancy's expression—it was the sort that adults liked to give to someone of her age. 'Think about it,' said Fred, so animated that, were it not for his back 'twinges', he could have sashayed around the room.'Peanuts, legumes, peas—all the same family.'

'I bet we're not the first,' said Nancy, bored with Fred showing off.

'We?' said Lily.

Nancy gave her a sharp look. 'So where did you buy it?' she said.

'I always get them from the same shop. That place where the post office is. Bashetts.'

'It's not called that now,' said Grandma. 'But everyone still calls it Bashetts after the family that's always owned it.'

'That man in there's so rude,' said Nancy. 'A really nasty piece of work.'

'Old Bashett? It's because he feels trapped in it. Never wanted to be a shopkeeper, so he takes out his anger on the customers, especially the kids.'

'I never had a problem there before this latest,' said Lily.

'Well we have,' said Nancy proudly. 'We had a smoothie from there once and it fair turned poor Fred's stomach.'

Lily glanced at Fred who looked uncomfortable, either at the memory of it or at not remembering it at all. 'I just want an apology,' Lily said. This prompted laughter from the others.

'Oh no,' said Nancy, 'that would be too selfish.'

'Selfish?' said Lily.

'Yes, think of your poor grandmother. She does everything for you, and perhaps it's time for you to put her first for once.'

Lily was mystified and Grandma felt embarrassed to an extent that she immediately changed the subject. She asked how Sally was. Sally, who visited every six weeks to cut Grandma's hair, was one of Lily's favourite people. She liked the fact Sally always asked her how she was and what she was up to, and it inspired her because the interest seemed genuine. She felt there was a mutual affection. 'When is she due to come next?' she asked her grandmother.

'A couple of weeks time. The twentieth, I think.'

'She's got a new boyfriend,' Nancy said, in a tone that could not hide her disapproval. Lily observed in Grandma's look a note of satisfaction, both at Nancy's discomfort and the prospect of a whole new subject to talk about when Sally next called round.

'What's his name?' Grandma asked.

'I don't even know,' said Nancy.

'It's Jim, isn't it?' said Fred.

Nancy glanced at the clock and mentioned it 'really' was time for them to leave. She said they would assist with any claim against the smoothie company, remarking to Grandma as they left, 'You'll need the money, you know.' Realising this sounded like an insult, she added, 'We all do these days, don't we?' As if to end the conversation, Nancy immediately stood up and then helped Fred struggle to his feet.

Lily looked over at Grandma, noting how she wore the same dress every Wednesday since she could remember. It was even frayed at the hem. Thinking further about it, she couldn't remember Grandma ever having a new dress, only clothes from charity shops. How could she possibly afford to withdraw her from school? On the other hand, she suspected Grandma had plenty of money, but her fear of falling into poverty was so great she was afraid to spend it. But why should they feel pressured to make a claim?

As soon as she saw their neighbours entering their own drive Lily said to Grandma, 'I'm not interested in making a claim against the company.'

'OK, my dear, but you should tell the shopkeeper anyway.'

'Why?'

'There might be a batch of dodgy smoothies. Someone else could get one and end up sick. Like Fred said, they might have allergies. People could die from it. Besides, they should give you a free one to replace it.'

Lily thought about it. No other shop sold this particular smoothie, but she was shy and the manager was terrifying, thinking all children shoplifters. 'They'll just say I put it there,' she said.

'No they won't. I know Mrs Bashett. She goes to the same Slimming World group as me. I'll take it back.'

Grandma did not know it was too late and that Lily had already poured all of the contaminated drink down the drain. When Lily told Grandma about this she initially expressed irritation but then said, 'OK. You didn't drink from it at least, thank goodness! But you paid for it. Aren't you upset? And, as I say, what if there's things in other drinks in the shop? We really should tell them.'

Lily produced the receipt from her pocket. 'I'll write,' she said.

'Write?'

'I'll send a letter to the company in America.'

'OK,' said Grandma, bemused.

When Lily turned to go upstairs to retreat to her room, Grandma said, 'Why don't you have a word with Travis about it?'

Lily span round on one foot: 'What!?'

'Being an American company, he might have some ideas.'

'What? How do you know about Travis?'

'You told me.'

'No I never. So who told you? Let me guess... Brian.' Grandma's face indicated this was correct. 'That little shit,' said Lily. 'When did he tell you?'

'About two months ago. And mind your language.'

'No. That's exactly what he is. Why didn't you tell me you knew?'

'I wanted to see when you'd decide to tell me, like you're supposed to. That was the agreement: you tell me what you're doing online.'

'Can't be that bothered if you've known two months. Anyway, it's not practical. If I'm on Facebook, what am I supposed to do—tell you about everyone I'm talking to? All parents say things like that, but it never happens.'

'Yes it does.'

'Who then?'

'Brian, for a start.'

'Oh yes, Brian. The little sneak. I can't believe it. No wonder you always have him round for tea. What does he do—pass you little notes or something?'

'Listen to me. If you're telling people you've got an online boyfriend, I have a right to know.'

'No you don't.'

'I'd know if it was a real boyfriend.'

'He *is* a real boyfriend.'

'Well, a boy round here then. I thought Brian was your boyfriend.'

'No chance of that now. Not after this.'

'Don't be hard on him. He meant it for the best.'

'No he didn't. He's jealous. He would like nothing more than to see me and Travis split up. Well he can go and—'

'Lily!'

'He can go and do one. It's the last time I invite him round here. What's the worry about the internet anyway?'

'It's full of people who lie and scam and pretend to be someone they're not.' She wanted to add 'predators' but at that moment did not like to think of the twelve-year-old knowing what such people were capable of, nor have to explain to her if she didn't.

Lily paused and then said, 'Bit like round here then.'

'And what's that supposed to mean?'

'You lie. You lied just now. You said I told you about Travis when I didn't.'

'That was just a mistake.'

'I see. And what about Auntie Gwynne? You always lie to her. Not that I care. Did you talk to her today? You usually do on a Wednesday.'

'Yes.'

'What lie did you tell her then?'

'I put her off coming here this Sunday.'

'So what did you say?'

'I told her we'd gone vegetarian after she said how much she liked the local meat we get.'

'That was a double lie then. I asked about us going vegan, and you said you'd think about it—' Lily stared hard into her eyes. Grandma looked away. '— and you haven't, have you? No. You told her I got an A-star in maths once, and you know I never got A-star in anything. And what about Fred?'

'What about Fred?'

'You told me he lost his phone off the side of a boat in Venice. When I asked Nancy "How was Venice?" she said they never went.'

'It's what he told me.'

'And Mauritius, and Barcelona. You know he never goes further than this house because of his back. Or is that a lie too? We were there one Saturday, and I went to the toilet and the postman came, so I picked up the letters, and I noticed they were all different names: Fred this, Fred that, everything but Fred Peacemaker. It's like this pea business. I wish I'd kept it to myself. They'll be saying they caught cholera or something next. So don't lecture me about lying and scamming and people pretending to be someone else.'

With that she went upstairs to her room.

3

Once in her room, Lily changed into casual clothes and lay on her back on the bed next to a couple of her cuddly toys—a black cat with bright yellow eyes and a white teddy bear—to centre herself and perform her daily ritual, a favourite part of the average day. In her ritual, she would use the edge of an open paper clip or the point of a pair of scissors and drag it carefully along her arm or press it into her palm and concentrate on the physical sensation.

None of her actions would leave a mark, nor must they. Pressing into the palm merely left it a little sore and itchy afterwards, which was not itself unpleasurable. Because she did not cut herself she did not consider it self harm, even though she knew most others did. She felt she obtained from this activity what a cutter found: a rush of freedom which to her meant freedom from the nagging desire to be dead and the guilt at being alive. When everyone posting on forums began with 'Don't do it, seek help,' they didn't understand what it meant to her and how she controlled it.

She had not always felt this way. Her primary school years had been happy with the house full of friends on her ninth and tenth birthdays. This year's would be just her and Grandma. Those friends of years ago had moved away physically or psychologically, and as she approached her teenage years she found she hardly had any friends at all.

Yet things in her life did not stay the same for long, and now a new person had appeared on the scene: a girl known as Mack who was in her year—very outgoing and perhaps, in her way, as eccentric as her. She'd encountered her a couple of times, and Mack had started up a conversation out of nothing, conveying the impression she wanted to know her better. She'd also seen Mack a few times in town, reminding her of a little wizard, always in black flowing clothes with her straggly red hair and flashing eyes, and always carrying the same book of French poetry in translation, which some might have thought pretentious, but what if they did? Mack hadn't been at the school long, the family having recently moved back to the area from Sussex. What inhibited Lily was that Mack was gay (her Facebook profile made this clear), whereas even though Lily was not gay, the bullies liked to claim she was. Being seen around with Mack would surely make this worse. Ironically, as far as Lily could tell, Mack did not care about such things. Or care much about anything. Every time Lily saw her she was smiling or laughing, and if there was one thing Lily wanted at this point in her life, it was laughter.

She checked her arms. One had a faint red line that would disappear within an hour or so. That was OK. Feeling subdued but content, she picked herself up from the bed, took her seat at the desk, and opened her laptop.

She was keen to see whether Travis in New York had written again. His computer had a problem and she missed hearing from him. His last message via Facebook had said he was worried it might be a virus and so he would not send anything more until it was checked out. She wondered why he hadn't given her his phone number, but then she'd never asked him for it. He'd said she should watch for anything strange, including messages from people she didn't know, and if in doubt, have her laptop examined for viruses. She should not write to him in case that also triggered a problem with malware. She did not completely understand but did not want to take any risk, or upset him by not complying, so had not responded. He had promised to contact her again when the problem was resolved. He was so considerate to her, but the waiting was awful.

Since Travis' warning, she was wary whenever she switched her computer on, and was always relieved to see the desktop picture of the Galapagos tortoise beside a cactus tree appear. She found no new emails or Facebook messages from anyone she did not recognise. There was no message from Travis, and he had not posted on Facebook. There was, however, a post from someone who wasn't a Facebook friend of hers, but whose post had been shared by another person who was.

The Facebook friend wrote: 'I don't even know who this woman is or her husband, and I've never contacted him, but I'm going to be even more careful about who I add as a friend from now on. Take care!'

Below this the shared post read: *You have been writing to Travis Tuo or Travis Trikoner or Travis TJ or TJ Trace or various other names, all aliases of the man who's been my husband for the last 30 years. I recently learned that over the last five years he has started relationships online with over 200 desperate lonely females. What began as an innocent if misguided attempt to provide pastoral care to those in need became a dangerous obsession and was exploited by people of evil intent requesting and later demanding money, all such demands being met and which are now the subject of police investigation...*

Lily pondered: she had met her Travis in an Instagram chat room for survivors of bullying—was that pastoral care?

She read on: *He even borrowed money against the house to pay these people and the house is being foreclosed...*

Lily was unsure what 'foreclosed' meant—did it mean they had to move? How terrible for them!

...He is seriously ill and does not wish to hear from predatory whores like you anymore...

'Predatory whores'!?

...and if you dare write to him again...

'Predatory whores like you'!? What did that even mean? She imagined herself asking, 'Grandma, what's a predatory whore?' She knew enough to know that wasn't wise.

...there will be serious consequences—these include exposure to partner and family, exposure to media, police involvement, and legal action for damages. You have been warned. For a full list of his aliases go to my website below.

Lily was tempted to press on the link but resisted. It might be a scam and she'd end up with the malware Travis warned about. Under the link she noticed in very small letters:

The next 100 visitors to the site will receive the offer to purchase an exclusive designer Jesus bobble hat at half price—an ideal gift for Easter!

What!? She read the woman's message once more in amazement. Again she was tempted to press on the link but did not do so.

She slammed her laptop shut, closed her eyes, and remained seated with her elbows on the desk and hands over her ears. She was breathing fast. After a couple of minutes, she opened her eyes and stood up; feeling giddy she sat straight down again, took a couple of deep breaths, and then slowly rose to her feet. No, it was a different Travis. It could not be the same one. The woman hadn't even written to her. None of these names were his. She was tempted to look at it again. She was tempted to look up the Facebook profile of this woman who was the wife of this other Travis. How had her post even come to her friend? It was obviously a scam. She must not press on the link, happy to forego ever seeing the famous designer Jesus bobble hat. That was the problem with the internet. There were so many scammers like this so-called wife of this other Travis.

Lily dawdled down the stairs. As she emerged into the lounge her grandmother, who was watching TV, said to her, 'You look pale - are you alright?'

'I'm fine. I just came down for a drink and a sandwich.'

'I bought some of that bread you like.'

In the kitchen she couldn't help thinking about Grandma's instructions about her use of the internet, stressing that it was a dangerous place and she should not engage with anyone over eighteen and could only have online friends that were her own age. At fifteen would she consider Travis her own age? She was beginning to regret not telling her about him from the outset. But she missed him so much. He always knew the right thing to say. He raised her spirits, made her feel life was worth living.

She took an ice cube from the freezer and pressed it to her palm, but only for a few seconds. She ran it under the cold tap and dropped it into a glass, then went to the fridge and took out a banana smoothie. Banana was good, but it was not blueberry flip. The lid was hard to remove. She realised that, by contrast, the lid of the smoothie with the foreign object, the 'pea' in it, had been easy to remove. She opened the bag of fresh tiger bread—her favourite—made a peanut butter sandwich, and ate it straight away.

When Lily returned to the lounge with her drink Grandma said, 'Come sit with me, sweetheart,' and she patted the spot next to her on the sofa. Lily was reluctant but acquiesced. Grandma put her arm round her and gently hugged her. 'Is it something online that's upset you?' Lily did not reply, but Grandma detected a slight shudder in her. She could afford to be magnanimous now. 'It's alright, you don't have to tell me what it is. I'm not going to interrogate you.'

'I might have a shower later, if that's OK,' Lily said.

'Of course,' Grandma said. She knew she didn't need to ask anything else.

'I'm sorry, Grandma.'

'It's alright, dear. I just get worried at what you might stumble upon and be hurt by. There are evil people on the internet would love to manipulate a girl like you.'

'I know, but it's not that. I'm sorry I threw the evidence away. You know, the smoothie.'

'Oh, it's alright. I didn't want to claim anyway.'

'No, not that either. The thing is, when I took the lid off this one it was difficult for me. And I remembered the lid of the blueberry flip came off more easily than usual, but then you came in the kitchen, took the pea to show Nancy and Fred, and I forgot. So now I wonder, you know.'

'That perhaps it was tampered with. And by dear, child-hating Mr Bashett. Hmm. Tomorrow let me open your drink.'

'So maybe it wasn't a pea after all, maybe it was one of Fred's Amazon things. But I got rid of all the evidence, so I'm sorry.'

'We won't tell Fred and Nancy or we'll never hear the end of it,' Grandma said. She added portentously, 'I've decided I will stop buying meat. Once we've cleared up what's in the freezer, and cans, and so on, we'll both be vegetarian. OK?'

Lily brightened. 'Yes, and then maybe progress to vegan?'

'Maybe,' said Grandma, rather less taken with that idea.

Lily gently squeezed her grandmother's arm as the two of them sat watching TV. It felt like old times to both of them, enjoying the soaps. The only difference was that now Lily had no idea who the many characters were, but Grandma, who like her sister Gwynne was an aficionado, gave her a helpful brief introduction to each scene. During the interval of *Coronation Street* Lily said, 'Can I use the old Olivetti, please?'

'Sure,' said Grandma who was so pleased to be spending time with her granddaughter she would have agreed to almost any request. 'Olivetti? That's a bit...'

'Old school, yes,' said Lily.

'What do you want it for?'

'To write to the smoothie company, of course. Maybe they'll investigate Bashetts.'

Grandma had temporarily forgotten about Lily wanting to write, what with her being upset over something on the internet, and the pleasure of watching TV together. She didn't see the point of writing, but she did not want to disrupt the mood so didn't challenge Lily over it, knowing it would be futile to argue anyway. 'I'm surprised you don't send them an email,' she said. 'Or write it on your laptop. I put a new cartridge in the printer just the other day.'

'No, I don't want to,' said Lily. 'Too easy.'

The Olivetti Lettera, which Grandma had meant to put on eBay years ago, was deep in the cupboard under the stairs, and extracting it could only be achieved with such effort and clatter that Grandma was forced to pause *Coronation Street*, so keen was she to ensure the spell remained unbroken. She couldn't escape the wish that Lily, who now dragged the typewriter in its case out herself and carried it to the dining table, could find the same sense of purpose for her homework. She told Lily she would help her with the letter once the soap was over, so why didn't she find a scrap of paper and write a rough draft of what she intended to write? Lily thought this a good idea, so after finding pen and paper she sat down at the table. She likewise was enjoying this time together, bearing in mind that overall their relationship had lately become fractious. However, whilst half-watching *Coro'* and drafting her letter, she could not stop thinking about Travis and his 'wife'. If the message had really been meant for her, why had it not been sent direct? She still felt a pang of guilt, not that she had done anything wrong to his wife or anyone else, but about her naivety which was a betrayal of herself. At least she would not be alone; the other 'females' would all be feeling stupid or puzzled or simply found out. Although, being called a 'whore', even in ignorance and one step removed, hurt. Imagine her bullies finding out about that! No, it could not be her Travis. He was not an old man. It was obvious, wasn't it?

Grandma put the TV on mute but said nothing. Lily, expecting some admonishment, said, 'Grandma, can we bake a cake tomorrow?'

'No. Listen. I've been thinking: I know you're unhappy at school, but I can't afford to take you out.

And what point would there be in it? Are you suddenly going to work? Because it's obvious to me you're not doing your homework and don't care about your lessons at all.' Grandma waited a moment for a reaction. Lily did not speak. 'From now on, I think you should do your homework in here. You're bright, now show it. And if—and it's a very big if—you engage with your work, I will consider withdrawing you—'

'But you said—'

'I will find the money. I will borrow the money. I'll go back to work if I have to.'

'But what about—'

'If the TV distracts you, I'll switch it off. But even distracted you'll do better than you do now when you're already distracted by other things anyway.'

'OK,' said Lily, baffled but impressed at Grandma's decisiveness. It made her wonder what CDs she'd been listening to. This was not George Harrison's *All Things Must Pass*, this was more Jay-Z, and what was the blue cover on top of the CD player? Oh yes, *Do It* by the Pink Fairies. She doubted any of it would happen. It wasn't that Grandma lied—that was harsh—it was that she meant it but couldn't follow through.

'OK,' said Lily. 'Whatever you say.' Then she added, 'I love you, Grandma.'

She went to the kitchen to retrieve the blueberry flip smoothie bottle for the company's address. Grandma found some suitable paper and set the typewriter up for her. Lily liked the Olivetti. It brought back memories of the distant past: typing up poems for

competitions she never heard back on. It brought
with it some of the happiness she felt in those days
when she could deal with bullies in her life. After
copying out the address in the States and adding her
own address, the date, and 'Dear Sirs', she hesitated.
She looked at the handwritten draft but didn't like it.
It didn't sound like her. She thought of a better idea,
began typing, then changed her mind, scrapped the
paper and tried again. For a moment, she wished
she had sent an email. She talked it through with
Grandma. After several attempts she was satisfied
and completed the letter. She wrote:

Dear Sirs,

*I love your blueberry flip smoothies. I buy them
from Bashetts (a.k.a. Retingham Essential
Supplies), in Retingham, Nottinghamshire,
England, UK. Your smoothies are the best. Today
I had one with a pea in it. I couldn't drink it and
this made me sad* [Grandma had suggested,
'This demonstrated a disappointing and
uncharacteristic lapse in standards,' but
Lily was not persuaded.] *I would like it if you
would please write back to say you're sorry, in
view of our longstanding relationship.* [This
latter phrase, which Lily found peculiar, was
Grandma's surreptitious attempt to extract
something more tangible than an apology.]
*Note: If your smoothies become available at a
major supermarket in Retingham please let me
know as they may be cheaper there.* [This sentence
was another subtle attempt by Grandma to
encourage a generous response.]

Yours faithfully and sincerely, [They couldn't agree which, Lily insisting: 'faithful to what?']

Lily Upshire (Miss)

4

Lily had to encounter Brian next day which was when he was supposed to come for tea. When they met at lunchtime he found her cool towards him and realised, without any discussion, that tea was off. She made her own way home after school without waiting for him. She had forgiven him for what she saw as a betrayal of confidence but could not countenance sitting at the tea table with Grandma and Brian at the same time, sharing either secret messages or mockery at her adverse mood whilst immune from any blame for it. After this day, relations would gradually thaw again. She had too few friends to jettison even one.

On the Friday, soon after arriving home, Lily asked Grandma, who she noticed looked harassed and pre-occupied, 'By the way, did you post my letter yet?'

'Yes. I went to the post office today specially for you,' she said in a grudging tone, 'and when I got home I found I had a letter too.'

'That's nice.'

'No it isn't. It was from school. About you. Serious. It's a warning letter. They could exclude you.'

'Does that mean, expel me? That would be cool.'

'No it wouldn't. Don't be facetious. They won't expel you anyway.'

'Shame. What's the letter about?'

'As if you didn't know.' Grandma snatched it from the table and thrust it into her hands. Lily skimmed over it: bullying, swearing at a teacher, not doing homework.

'What's this about bullying?' Grandma said. 'Are you a bully?'

'No.'

'So what is this then?'

Lily recounted the two incidents where the Runt had ended up slammed into the wall. Of the second incident she said, 'Everyone agreed it was an accident at the time, even the Runt, but maybe they changed their stupid minds since then.'

'Lily, you can't be doing things like that. I'm really disappointed about this letter. And it says you swore at a teacher—what was that about?' There being no reply, she pressed, 'What did you say to her?'

'I said a rude thing.'

'Like what?'

'You don't want to know.'

'I do. Do you think I haven't heard it all before?'

'Alright. I called her an ef-ing c-word.'

'What did you say?' At first she did not understand. 'Oh my God! You said the actual words to her!?' Grandma sighed heavily. 'Why on earth did you do that?'

'I didn't mean to say it. It just came out. She made some remark about my work, and I was having a bad day and just lost my temper.'

'Well, if you did your homework like you should... So what happened next?'

'I had to go to see Mrs Postle, Head of Department, and she told me I'll have to do detention... and apologise... and you would get a letter. And next time I'd have to be on my own for a day...'

'Isolation.'

'Yes.'

'Which, knowing you, you'd probably like. And have you apologised?'

'No.'

'Then you will—in writing.'

'She hates me.'

'No she doesn't. But even if she does, you still say you're sorry. It's the way the world works. You want people to write to you saying sorry, so you can damned well write to her. And I never want to hear such filthy language in this house.'

'Except on TV, then it's OK?'

'No! You're just trying to rile me now—as if this letter weren't bad enough. This is so... I can hardly believe it. I've brought you up as best I can and what have I got? A foul-mouthed child, who beats up other kids, and never does her homework. A little thug, that's what I've brought up.' But rather than harangue her, she put her arm round her and hugged her. As she ran her fingers through Lily's hair she found her own eyes were tearing up. She worried her sister Gwynne had been right all along: her laissez-faire approach had ruined the child. She was as upset with herself as with her granddaughter. She released Lily from the hug and picked up the letter again. 'At least they haven't said they'll suspend you, but that'll be the next thing.'

'Then withdraw me now. You know I hate it—and they hate me. Apart from Ms Hass, every teacher thinks I'm useless.'

'Well, if I was your teacher, I'd think the same as them. Everything your Auntie Gwynne said is proving true, which terrifies me. But...' Her tone softened again, '...I haven't got the heart to be strict with you. And it wouldn't work. It's too late. I've let it happen. It's my fault. And, no, I'm not going to withdraw you. There's a parents' evening next week. I almost may as well not go. What good can come of it?'

'You can tell them about the bullying I get.'

'What bullying? Who?'

'Mainly the Bizzell twins. And not just me.'

'What do they do?'

'Punch, kick, they spit in my hair, put gum in it, call me names and someone—probably them—writes things on the toilet walls.'

'What things?'

'Like...' She hesitated.

'Go on.'

'Like: "Lily Upshire Is A Fat Lesbian Slag."'

Grandma sat down as though her chair were a refuge from what she was hearing. She reached out her arms and Lily went to her to be hugged again. Grandma squeezed her tight and then released her almost immediately to hold her face close in front of hers. 'Look at me. We must address all this. We must write it down. Or have you already?'

'No. I don't like to think about it.'

'I know, but you must. Every time it happens. It's very important. You can bet your life they do. If you don't write it, it's like it never happened. Have you talked to anyone about it at school?'

'No. I don't trust them. The Bizzell family run the school.'

'No, they don't. That's ridiculous. I'm going to write back to that school when I've decided what to say.'

Lily reached out her hands to her. 'Don't worry. You'll be so proud of me one day.'

'You're such a one-off that it wouldn't surprise me.' She pressed Lily's hands gently. 'And, you know, whilst I'm desperately disappointed with your attitude to work and what's in this letter, if they lay it on thick at the parents' evening I could lash out.' For a moment she felt like the teenage rebel she herself had once been. 'It's not your fault you're bullied, but you must speak up. And Heaven help them if they haven't followed their procedures.'

It was at that moment they heard the doorbell. It was Nancy Peacemaker. She came in holding two smoothies which she said were from Bashetts where Lily bought hers. Nancy was full of herself as usual and did not notice anything with her hosts that might give her pause: 'We've got a fridge full of these. We don't even drink them... not very often... *occasionally*... but we thought, if there's a batch of dodgy ones it's our moral duty to find them. Poor Fred's so ill.'

'Oh dear, is it his back?' asked Grandma.

'No. He's lost his appetite, feels very weak. I think it's probably a form of food poisoning. It's since he had that... smoothie from Bashetts.'

'Did he really?'

'Oh yes. Before Lily had hers. Of course, we didn't put two and two together at the time, but when Lily found that—' she cast a disdainful look Lily's way '—I suppose we'll never know for sure what it was—well, it brought it all back.'

'Oh dear,' said Grandma, hoping the smirk she felt hadn't reached her lips.

'But, believe me, the company's going to hear about it.'

'But what happened with the residue on Fred's shoe? There was some, wasn't there, when you left here?'

'I'm afraid that damned husky at number 23 put paid to that. Left its doings at the end of our drive—a right parcel—and need I tell you who put their big foot right in it? Disgusting!' Both Grandma and Lily looked away immediately. 'Anyway, these are un-opened. Would you like them?'

'Are you sure you won't need them?'

'Oh no. Not with Fred in his current state. The only thing I ask is, if there is anything wrong with them please include us in the claim, seeing as how it was us that bought them.'

'Of course. What do I owe you for them?' said Grandma, missing the point.

'Nothing,' said Nancy firmly.

Grandma accepted them with thanks and wished Fred well as Nancy left. Once she'd gone, Lily and Grandma burst into brief laughter, but Lily had a dreadful thought: 'Auntie Gwynne's not coming this Sunday, is she?'

'No. I couldn't cope with her gloating... Besides, she wants to get *American Monster* off her planner.'

Lily had no idea what this meant, but it sounded hilarious. Grandma then sighed, 'Oh Lily, what are we going to do with you!?'

'We could bake a cake.'

'What!?'

'This weekend. Make a nice dessert or cake. Auntie Gwynne's always going on about my weight, so let's go completely against what she thinks. Be like old times. Normal rules, yes?'

Grandma thought it hardly appropriate, but she was feeling worn down by it all. 'And what will you do for me, or rather, for yourself? I never want a letter like this again. Ever. So what will you do?'

'Not use bad words...'

'And you'll write to Miss Cotton to apologise. What else? Don't pout. What else?'

'Erm... Try harder at school...'

'*Much* harder. And?'

'Write down when I'm bullied.'

'And learn to control your temper and keep out of trouble.'

'Yep. So can I make a list?'

Lily was to choose seven recipes off the internet based purely on what they sounded like. They'd discuss practicality, Grandma would choose one, working out a smaller version where necessary, obtain the ingredients, and Lily would then make as much of it as she could unaided. Over the next half hour Lily chose:

southern double crusted cinnamon sugar peach cobbler, [Lily put a star against this one]

ding dong cake, [Lily put two stars against this one]

swirled blueberry lemon thyme cake,

butter pecan turtle bars, [What was pecan like, she wondered?]

peach dump cake, [Not sure about the 'dump' aspect, she mused]

no-bake grasshopper pie, ['Not sure about that one, Grandma, but it says it's minty.']

key lime pie with Graham cracker crust. [Who was this Graham?]

She put links to all these into one email for Grandma, although before sending it she cheated by adding an eighth: chocolate fudge peanut butter ice cream pretzel cake, owing to the length of the name. Making the cake was how they'd spend Saturday afternoon. It was something to look forward to while doing the English essay for Ms Hass that morning.

Despite the school letter and its effect on Grandma, which she regretted, she went to bed happy that night for she felt she'd learnt something important. It didn't matter what happened so much as who witnessed it and how they recorded it—wrote it, filmed it, made it evidence. Evidence was what counted in life, even if you made it up like Nancy and Fred did. The Bizzell family knew that. They were masters of evidence and also they knew all the right people.

That was the other thing. With those two essentials combined you could get away with anything.

5

For swearing at the teacher Lily had to do detention after school. When she arrived at the designated room she found another girl there: Mack, the eccentric with her wild red hair, pretty freckles, and barely noticeable Scottish burr. The teacher who was supervising their detention was late so they chatted. 'What are you here for?' said Mack.

'Swearing at a teacher—Miss Cotton.'

'Really? Same thing as me, except it was Mrs Postle.'

'What did you say then?'

'Mongrel bitch.'

'Nice one.'

'I was quoting Shakespeare in English class.'

'Yeah sure,' said Lily, grinning. 'What play's it in then?'

'Lear.'

'If I was in her class, I'd be in here every week.'

'Your ma get a letter?'

'Grandma. She wanted to know what I said. I told her she really didn't want to know, but she insisted.'

'So what did you say?'

'I told her I'd called her "an ef-ing c-word." She was shocked.'

'Said it like that? Lily, you're so funny.'

'Bitch is pretty bad, though. B-word.'

'So is that how you talk at home: f-word, c-word, b-word?'

Suddenly serious, Lily said, 'Grandma's just very sensitive about swearing.'

'I mean, do you have normal conversations in your house, or is it all like that?'

'Like what?'

'Saying a-word, b-word, c-word all the time?' Lily merely smiled so Mack changed the subject: 'Tell me, so what do you do at weekends?'

'Not much. Instagram. Maybe bake cakes.'

'Cakes? Yum. Another c-word.'

'What do you do?'

'All sorts. We go to football, speedway, swimming, the beach, see a film. Fun things.'

'And your name's MacWhat?'

'MacKnokaird.'

'Yeah? Like I should worry.'

'Do you like your name?'

'Upshire? No.'

'Why not?'

'When you say it fast it sounds like "Shuddup, shuddup, shuddup."'

Mack started repeating "Upshire" and then laughed. 'I guess it does.'

'And it makes a noise like one of them crappy old steam engines.'

'So who do you usually hang out with?'

'No-one. Brian, maybe. You know Brian in...?'

'Panker?' Mack was giggling. 'The walking limerick.'

'He's alright—for a boy. No, actually he let me down, so I don't care. Say what you like about the dirty dog.'

'What did he do?'

'He's such a sneak. He told Grandma about my online boyfriend. I've forgiven him but not completely. I wouldn't trust him with any secrets. Not sure about the boyfriend either.'

'Fake?'

'Maybe. Still want to believe he's for real.'

'You say Grandma—what about your ma 'n da?'

'Ma 'n da?' Lily blushed. 'No.' She shook her head. 'Nor bro, nor sis. You?'

'Brother, yeah. Older. No sis. You'd make a good sis.'

Lily did not reply. She could sense Mack wanting to come over and give her a hug, which she would not have flinched from. 'Lily, you're so sweet, why do you get bullied so much?'

'Lots of reasons. They think I'm a useless, annoying c-word who deserves a kicking.'

'But you're not. Oh, you're lovely.'

'They always tell me to kill myself.'

'No!'

'So do they bully you, the Bizzells?'

'Having a big brother helps a lot. I try to laugh with them. I say, "OK girls, what you got for me today?" like a court jester. So the twins and that little twit sister of theirs don't touch me.'

'They could beat you up.'

'They couldn't. I know how to fight. And I sprint and work out. They're slow as fuck...'

'The Runt's quick.'

'...and if they did anything, my mum would be straight round theirs and the cops before they'd even sat down to take a shit. Trouble is, they're the prettiest girls in their year. That's how they get away with it.'

'And Mrs.'

'Mrs Bizzell? Oh, she's gorgeous. No wonder she runs the school.'

'She does, doesn't she? Grandma won't have it.'

'Of course she does.'

'You've only been here five minutes, how come you know all this?'

'Because I learn fast, and my brother tells me stuff. You need someone like him. Maybe someone in your class to hang around with. It would help put off the bullies.'

'How come you know what I need?' Lily was beginning to enjoy the conversation less.

'You said it yourself...' Mack felt like a deer that had inadvertently run into a swamp.

'Tell me,' Lily demanded.

Mack knew it would upset her, but maybe that was what she wanted.

'Please,' said Lily.

'OK. When you're a little different...'

'Like you are.'

'Alright. An individual. Your family can be your support network. See, we're like an Italian family.'

'Always squabbling.'

'No, we look out for each other. My brother loves me and helps me. He's sixteen. We talk about everything. And my mum. If you were in our family, you'd feel protected.'

'In your family? How could I...'

'No, I didn't mean literally...' Mack was frustrated by her own clumsiness and Lily's growing hostility, so changed tack: 'Why don't you come out with us one weekend? It would be fun.'

'Well, that sounds nice, but I have my own life.' Lily paused to take a breath. 'You might think it shitty boring compared to yours, but it's mine. And you can laugh at stuff I say and what I do, but it's the way I am, different or not, is that OK?'

'Of course. I didn't mean...' She could hear footsteps in the corridor. But it wasn't for this room. 'I didn't mean it like that.'

Lily's brain was like the frantic editor at a TV station when the star presenter goes off on an unscripted rant. This sweet, generous-hearted girl was seeking her friendship, but as usual Lily's tongue had its own ideas: 'Yeah you did. You are as bad as they are. You think my life's not worth living coz it's different to yours, because you've got a nice normal family and I haven't, well—'

'Lily—'

'—you can fuck off with your patronising talk. Fuck right off, I'm not interested.'

Mack was shocked. She said nothing for a moment. It was as though Lily had fired a needle straight through the heart of a swift and it was now twitching on the ground. Both girls were moved to apologise, but neither did. Lily's editor was back in charge, chiding the presenter, 'Well, that went well, idiot.'

Finally, Mack said, 'Forget I said anything. Forget I even said hello. You don't deserve friends, the way you go on. Forget it.'

To Lily the pain inflicted by these words was as exquisite as the point of the scissors she liked to press into her palm. To be told off so eloquently! 'You're right,' she said. 'I don't deserve anything.'

Later, Mack would wonder whether Lily had seen through her delusions. Ask any member of her family about their weekends, and they would have said the same as her. Families peddled their own lies, and whilst the picture Mack described was almost true three years earlier, now a typical weekend was her in solitude painting, studying books on alchemy, or reading her beloved Petrarch, with her brother out as much as possible, and her parents shouting at each other all over the house about each other's affairs. It was Mack the Bizzells called the Weirdo, but she amused them like an eccentric pet, whereas the insolent Lily they hated and, not that they'd admit it, feared.

Fortunately, the teacher, Mr Gapp, arrived at this moment as both girls were restless and bored enough to reignite the row. He was a shambly little man who shuffled around like a badger, with the air of being slightly displeased with wherever he happened to be. It was made easier for him by the fact that the two participants looked subdued rather than pleased with themselves.

'Would you like some liquorice,' said Mack, proffering the packet to him once he'd sat down.

'No thank you. But thank you.'

'I bought it specially. Good for you. Soft is best.' She grinned.

'OK then.' He accepted a piece, suppressing a smile.

'Want some, Lily?' Mack looked appealingly at her. Lily looked away, feeling Mack was taunting her. She didn't want the liquorice, but since she couldn't row with Mack, the next best was to redeem the situation, so she took a piece.

The girls had lines to write: 'I must not swear at teacher or in class' a hundred times, and then do schoolwork. Lily found it cruel. She loved writing, and this debased it. To make it less bad and quicker she wrote 'I' on each line all the way down a page before writing 'must' all the way down and so on. Now and then she would stop this work and stare at Mr Gapp as though to extract some concession from him. From time to time she would venture a conciliatory look over at Mack, and often their eyes would meet and one or both would struggle to suppress a snigger. Any sound from them would prompt Mr Gapp to look up, and on one occasion to cough, an action that prompted more laughter to suppress. Lily stopped looking. After completing their lines, both of them added their own variations. Mack loved playing with words and wrote a mixture of misremembered French poetry and her own spontaneous writing: 'The angel of night is a regretful waiter' and 'The armchair victim walks on salted air'. When she wrote 'The lovesick forester devoured by sorrowful briars' she changed the last 'r' to read '...sorrowful brians' and then broke into a giggle which even got Mr Gapp, who was known to hate both detention and writing lines as punishments, chuckling. 'Come on, MacKnokaird, share the joke,' he said. Mack did not reveal. She caught Lily's eye, and Lily was amused. Mr Gapp then allowed the pair to laugh themselves out before raising his hand, and they obediently stopped. Lily's variations were more mundane, such as: 'I must not call teacher an ef-ing c-word' even if they totally is one,' but she crossed them out in favour of 'Mr Gapp is a sweetie'.

When they were through with detention and were standing in the corridor, Mack, nervous this unpredictable girl might seek to renew hostilities, offered her a lift home with her mum. Lily said thanks but she'd already arranged to walk back with Brian. Mack said, 'That's OK. Some other time. How could I compete with a Panker? Can I have a hug?' Lily ignored her. 'Please,' said Mack. Lily went to her and Mack wrapped her arms round her. Lily found her warm and she smelt of liquorice. When Lily realised Mack was crying she let herself cry too, silently. As they parted Lily gave her a look that both pleaded for forgiveness and gave it. Mack, older than Lily by a few months but by years in experience, understood. She thought it possible friendship could grow from such an unpromising start but was not eager to find out.

Lily had to wait to meet up with Brian who was at choir practice. She wished she'd gone with Mack. Despite her own embarrassing outburst the conversation had been good for her.

When Brian eventually arrived they merely acknowledged one other. Lily was tired but couldn't wait to get home. She made sure they walked quickly. She was still annoyed enough with him to be stilted in conversation. As they approached the canal bridge, walking from the opposite direction were the Bizzell twins, Blue and Green, plus their sister, the Runt. Usually Lily crossed the road to avoid them, but on this occasion she felt more relaxed after laughing with Mack and being accompanied by Brian who was quite tall for his age. As they approached, the twins halted. They were bigger than Lily, heavier and more muscular, and they were all too aware of both their physical power and their ability to inspire fear. Lily began to feel the usual insecurity and they sensed it.

'Look who it isn't: our favourite gay,' said the one they called Green.

Lily said nothing. Then the Runt said, 'So did you pee your pants today, Upshire?' Lily did not reply and her tormentor added, 'Because you will before you get home tonight.' The Runt then leapt forward and made as if to swing a punch at Lily's face, but Lily moved her head in time and grabbed the Runt's coat and pitched her against the bridge wall. This triggered the twins into action. In a practised routine they cornered Lily, one of them kicked her legs while the other punched her hard to the body. Between them they forced her to the ground. Blue grabbed her bag and emptied the contents all over the pavement and into the road, while the Runt hit her in the face. She grabbed Lily by the hair and slammed her head on the ground and would have done this repeatedly had not one of her sisters intervened to stop it. It was not the twins' style to seriously injure their victims but to humiliate them as much as possible. Before they left they all smacked her hard on the bottom. They sauntered away laughing, and the Runt was proved correct for Lily had lost control of her bladder.

She lay on the ground not moving, just aware of her nose bleeding. She heard Brian say, 'Are you alright?' weakly. This triggered her into a fury that forced her to her feet. She hastily fixed her clothes. Blood dripped to the ground and both into and onto her bag as she retrieved her possessions. Brian helped her pick up the various items.'Where were you?' she complained. Humbled, he did not answer.

Determined, once she'd put everything back in her bag, she ran home. Brian tried to keep up and he called out to her, but she turned and shouted back at him: 'What use are you!? Where were you?' He protested that he'd been trying to restrain the Runt, but she shouted out, 'You weren't there for me when I needed you! You can go to hell, you useless twat!'

Grandma was distressed to see her: 'Who would do this to you?' She cleaned her up and helped her change her clothes. She said she would take her to A&E. Lily protested. She did not want the Bizzell family to have the pleasure of finding out they'd made her need a hospital visit. Driving there Grandma said, 'What is going on? I can't believe it. We can't have this. Horrible family. They're all like it. Even the parents. Oh, they get themselves wherever they can—on the council, on the board of governors—like a virus. Poisoning the place. Criminals. And with the police in their pockets.'

Fortunately, after several hours at the hospital, including scans and tests, there were no serious injuries found, and a stay overnight was not required. But Grandma was so furious about what had happened, she drove straight to the police station. She found the Bizzells had already been there. The police made their position clear that blame was equal. 'How typical!' she fumed. She phoned the school next day, but they weren't interested as it was not on the school premises.

Grandma kept her off school for the rest of the week. Lily already had one of the worst attendance records in the school, so this was no big surprise for them. It gave the Bizzell family time to impose their version of events, which was that Lily, a known bully, had provoked an attack on the youngest family member, and the twins had intervened to protect her; Lily had tried to fight them and been taught a sharp lesson. Neutrals accepted all this and agreed she'd got what she deserved. The campaign started the night after the incident with a Facebook post by the Runt's friend Mitch: 'Heard you got a good beating tonight—that'll teach you!'

6

Early one evening, the doorbell rang. It was one of the neighbours, a burly Yorkshireman in his fifties who did much of the local residents' plumbing, usually with disastrous results. He'd brought a large envelope that appeared to have been wrongly addressed, but it was unclear as the addressee was a 'Mr Upshaw'. Grandma said, 'It's American and it's business by the look of it, so it's probably meant for my granddaughter.'

'Is she a budding businesswoman?' the neighbour asked.

'I've no idea what goes through her head,' Grandma sighed, not looking forward to the next quarter of an hour or so.

Grandma called up to Lily who came down straight away. As she handed over the envelope Grandma said, 'It's for a Mr Upshaw. They can't even get your name right, but at least they could be bothered to write.' Lily opened it eagerly and found inside a letter from something called Global Universal Federated Finance. It read:

Dear Mr Upshaw,

We in the Consumer Champions Resource Team are in receipt of your letter dated March 9th. We are thrilled to hear from such a valued customer as yourself and much appreciate your taking the time to write us. Please be assured, satisfying our customers' needs is front and center of everything we do and we are committed to excellence in all things. The quality of our products is the very cornerstone of our existence.

We have fully investigated this matter and accordingly your claim is denied in entirety.

Nevertheless, purely as a goodwill gesture, we enclose two free vouchers for your favorite drink. For the avoidance of doubt, nothing contained in this letter or its enclosures shall in any way constitute an admission of liability on the part of the company or any entity associated directly or indirectly therewith. Nor shall it be construed that there is an acceptance of any assertions by you or your agents either in writing or orally or in any other way. This settlement is made on a full and final basis with all rights in law and equity expressly reserved in all respects. The company's position is self-explanatory, but in the event you have any question regarding it, you may contact Melody Roller, Head of Corporate Legal, at the above address within 15 days of the date of this communication. It goes without saying that in the absence of same, you will be deemed to have accepted the company's position as stated herein.

Entirely without prejudice,
RS
Service Ambassador
Forever focused on your every need

The envelope also contained two rectangular purple vouchers Lily found pretty. She did not understand much of the letter and found the language rather strange. She did not recognise anything that looked like an apology, however.

'It's something nice at least,' said Grandma, trying to cheer her up. 'Many people wouldn't have bothered to write back.'

'It's not what I asked for, though.'

'Oh, Lily, you're going to leave it alone now, aren't you? You've got these lovely vouchers.'

'And I can imagine them in Mr Bashett's fat fist when he scrunches them up. He's going to say they're a scam, or out-of-date, or he doesn't have to accept them. I'm one of the company's loyalest customers. Even with my new diet regime, I will still have my smoothies. They should listen to me, but they haven't even read my letter properly.'

'Alright. Send them back an email, sweetheart.'

But Lily was having none of it. She was determined to deal with it her way. Accordingly, out came the Olivetti again, and she began a rough draft of a new letter to RS, Service Ambassador in the Consumer Champions Resource Team, which she assumed was associated with helping customers with their complaints and enquiries. It all sounded very grand, though disappointing.

'Why are you bothering with all this?' said Grandma.

Lily did not respond, going over the letter carefully:

Please be assured, this was as soothing as warm milk: 'Please be assured, Ms Hass, that I will do my English homework;'

fully investigated, did that mean they'd actually spoken to Mr Bashett? That couldn't have been an easy conversation, especially the way he shouted all the time in great long diatribes;

For the avoidance of doubt, this was cool. She would use that in her response and elsewhere: 'For the avoidance of doubt, Miss Cotton, you are a big-arsed old bag;'

Entirely without prejudice, why would there be prejudice? Was it because she wasn't American? Were they trying to reassure her that, although she was not American she was being treated the same as if she were?

Nor shall it be construed, this was sublime...

'What does "construed" mean, Grandma?'

'Give me the sentence.'

Lily read it out.

'Well,' said Grandma, 'it means they don't necessarily believe you.'

'What, even as a valued customer with — what was the phrase we used in our letter? — oh yes, our longstanding relationship? Another thing, Grandma, I'm confused: it says to write to this Melody Roller...'

'Melody? What a lovely name.'

'...but the person who wrote the letter is called RS.'

'I don't know. You should do what they ask,' Grandma said. 'It's only polite.'

'But I think I should write to the person who wrote to me.'

'Whatever you like,' sighed Grandma, not wanting to have to pause *Come Dine With Me* and growing weary of Lily's ongoing 'smoothie saga'. But then there was an ad break. 'Where's it got to go to?' she said.

'It says: Irvine, California.'

'California? How nice.' Grandma thought anywhere in America sounded nice. Fear of flying precluded her ever visiting to find out.

'And it has to be there in fifteen days from when they wrote it. That leaves, erm, five days.'

'Oh,' said Grandma, taken aback. 'That does seem quick. They're obviously very busy. More important things to do than saying sorry to twelve-year-olds.'

'But I am a valued customer, so it said. Maybe the ambassador will deal with it.' When Grandma gave her a quizzical look, Lily added, 'The service ambassador.' She herself was puzzled. She thought ambassadors were big shots who were summoned by the government or appeared on TV whenever the UK was unhappy with the ambassador's country; or supermodels or film stars doing selfless work in some impoverished country. She said, 'It seems a lot of fuss to have an ambassador and the head of Corporate Legal involved.'

'Exactly,' said Grandma. 'You're wasting their valuable time. What do you want them to say sorry for anyway? Who cares?'

'I bet if I ask on Facebook who cares, there'll be plenty say so. Incidentally, what does "It goes without saying" mean?'

'Er, well, it means... I suppose it means it's true even if you don't say it.'

'Then why do they say it then? After that it says—'

'Lily, I don't know what it means. And I don't care. I've had enough—what with the school, the bullying, your attitude to work, having to keep you at home—I'm absolutely dreading the parents evening. I can't cope with it all. You spent a pound on a drink and now you've got vouchers worth two pounds. Normal people would think that a good deal, but you want to carry on with it. Let's move on, please, and let Nancy and Fred do their thing, and we'll keep out of it.' Seeing Lily about to say something else, she said, more stridently, 'No, on second thoughts, I'll tell you *exactly* what it means. It means, if I hear one more thing about smoothies or vouchers or companies not doing what you or some random person on Facebook thinks they should after today, I'll wring someone's neck—someone in this house!'

After much consideration in judicious silence, Lily decided to write to Melody with a copy to RS:

Dear Melody,

Thanks for the company's kind offer of vouchers for my 'claim'. In view of our longstanding relationship please could your reply include "we are sorry" or "we apologise"? It should not be construed that I have stopped buying your smoothies or have had further problems with them. The one I had with the pea in it cost me £1 but I am not seeking a refund at this time. All rights in law and equity expressly reserved... [She had no idea what this meant, but it was obviously something to use in business letters.]

For the avoidance of doubt, my name is Lily Upshire, not Mr Upshaw. You can call me Lily in your reply.

For the avoidance of doubt again, please be assured I am also without prejudices.

Yours sincerely,
Lily Upshire

She addressed the envelope to Melody Roller and put both letters inside with the two purple vouchers and, during the next ad break, asked Grandma if she could go to the post office next day in view of the urgency. Grandma stiffened. 'Since you're off school you can deal with it yourself, my dear.'

'OK,' said Lily, subdued.

'On second thoughts, I'll come with you.' She did not say that the reason for her change of heart was Lily's lacerations from being beaten up. If anyone asked about them, Grandma wanted to state clear and loud that members of the Bizzell family were responsible.

Later, Lily put up a comment on Facebook: 'Why do some companies hate saying sorry? I think people should say sorry for doing wrong, including companies.'

She received many positive comments in response. People gave examples of companies not saying sorry to them. Most gave examples of the biggest companies not apologising, suggesting they were the worst. 'Big companies don't care,' someone said. Another said they'd recently had a problem with a smoothie they bought.

'Me too,' said Lily.

'And me,' said another.

Someone suggested they should work together. Lawyers were always looking for new types of claim to make a name for themselves—and make money. There was a discussion on this subject, but Lily was not interested in participating.

Before going to bed, Lily looked at herself in her mirror, which depressed her because of the cuts and bruises. She said, 'For the avoidance of doubt, Upshire, you not only look a mess, but you are a mess. Please be assured, nothing in your whole life can be construed a success. We have fully investigated the matter and your claim to be a valued customer of life is denied in entirety. It goes without saying that you are a useless twat. You have fifteen days to respond without prejudices. Please accept these two unusable vouchers to a second-rate existence, and then shut the fuck up forever.'

7

It was Lily's thirteenth birthday, and Grandma was keen for it to pass without conflict. She'd asked her if she wanted to invite friends, but Lily had said no. She had no-one she would have invited anyway, especially after excluding Brian from her life. 'Just you and me would be great,' she said.

In the post office, Grandma said, 'What if they don't give you what you want this time?'

'I'll write back again, of course.' Observing Grandma's frown she said, 'I'm going to have my own business one day, so this is practice.'

'You running your own business?' Grandma was amused. 'I have to wonder what that would be. Well, to run a business you'll need priorities. You've got some work to do there. You couldn't be spending all your time writing to people for apologies.'

At Lily's request they went to charity shops to look for games. They found mahjong and backgammon (both of which Grandma had once known how to play) and a couple of packs of playing cards. Lily was keen to learn new things. She even asked Grandma if they could listen to her Indian music, a request a puzzled Grandma was happy to grant. 'This is surely your oddest birthday ever,' she said.

'I'll enjoy it. Different.'

'Next year, you'll have friends round.'

'Just one friend is all I want. I have found one—at least, I think so. They don't know it yet. I want someone I can have fun with, and argue, and play fight, and know all the time we love each other to bits.'

'It sounds like having a sister. But don't get carried away. Look who I ended up with: your Auntie Gwynne.'

Grandma had always wanted to learn to play bezique which required two packs, and they worked out a version of the rules between them. Lily was totally engaged in the game, but suddenly she fell quiet, a sign Grandma recognised; some random thought had triggered this, and if not allowed expression, it would build into a flare up. 'What's the matter?' she said. 'It may be your birthday, but the blue devils can still show up. Don't fight them, dear.'

'Blue devils?'

'Blues. So what's the matter?'

'It's the rain starting. I feel I should have gone to see my mother today, to her graveside, but it is raining now, and I am so enjoying this, and I feel guilty. I need peace with her.'

'Peace?'

'Yes.'

'Why?'

Lily was reluctant but finally said, 'I have a feeling often lately that I was cursed at birth. I feel she never wanted me, no-one wanted me. I feel I was meant to be aborted, but it was too late. That's what it feels like.'

Grandma was used to such somber talk and to coaxing her out of it: 'But it's not all the time, is it?'

She pointed at the cards. 'Your trick there, by the way.'

'No, of course not. Just a few moments every day, but it's enough.'

'It's not true anyway. Your mum did love you.'

'OK, but maybe she never *wanted* me in the first place. And when the bullies talk about my mum and dad, that's what it taps into. Do you understand that? You told me I was turning into a thug. I could become one without wanting to unless I can stop being so upset by what people say. But they don't stop. And please don't go to the parents' evening. You'll come home upset, and we'll have a row. I never want to go back there anyway.'

Grandma had no interest in arguing and said nothing further on the subject. Instead, after another hand of bezique she introduced Lily to a simplified version of mahjong.

But then came the questions. Where did the name backgammon come from? Was bezique related to the word 'berserk'? And the music: Lily was fascinated by George Harrison's *Wonderwall*. Had Grandma seen the Beatles live? Was George her favourite? Why was he so interested in Indian music? Was he still alive? She asked one question after another rapidly without, it seemed, expectation of answers. But then the personal ones:

'Was Jane Upshire really my mother?'

'Yes of course. Why even ask?'

'Some people say it was really Julia Bizzell.'

'Where do they get that crazy idea from?'

'They say as a teenager she looked just like me.'

'When I was young I was told I was the spit of Princess Grace of Monaco. I can assure you she was not my mum.'

'Did Princess Grace of Monaco live in Retingham.'

'No.'

'Not relevant, then. It'd explain why her girls hate me so much.'

'No it wouldn't.'

Although Lily did not say it, it would also explain her near infatuation with the woman. On the occasions she'd seen her, she'd been entranced by her. 'I wish Julia Bizzell was my mum,' she said.

'Why?'

'Because she protects her kids. They can be as bad as they like and get away with it.'

'They won't always.'

'Why is there only one picture of Jane, the one where it is me she is supposedly holding?'

'It is you she's holding.' Lily let this partial non-answer go. She was used to it.

'Is Brian's dad, Ted, my dad too?'

'Nnn-o.' Lily stared at her: why had she hesitated?

'Why did I overhear Auntie Gwynne say to you last time she was here, "I don't know why you even bother—it's not like she's even yours?"'

'Did she? She merely meant I'm not your mum.'

'Hmm.'

'Let it go, Lily. Look forward, sweetheart. Lighten up.'

'You don't get it, do you? I'll always be blighted, but if I can understand what's true, maybe I can deal with it.' It was frustrating: seasoned visitors to police interview rooms were not less forthcoming than her grandmother, but for now Lily did not pursue it.

She received cards from Nancy and Fred, also their daughter Sally. There was a card from Auntie Gwynne, addressed starkly to "Upshire" and blank inside bar a small squiggle of biro. The picture was of flowers looking sadder than any in nature, sadder even than dying flowers, sadder-looking than those on last year's card which had borne exactly the same picture. Brian dropped an envelope through the letterbox, but Lily tore it up as soon as she realised who it was from. With hindsight, Lily wondered whether she could have invited Mack round, but she was still largely an unknown, and Lily was a little wary of what she might say, imagining her blurting to Grandma, 'This is fucking brilliant!' or 'You're not like the old witch Lily warned me about.'

Grandma had asked Lily what she wanted as a present, but Lily had said the only gift she could give her was to withdraw her from school. So Grandma got her what she called 'boring practical things' like USB sticks and a new cover and charger for her phone.

Asked if she'd like a special meal—anything she fancied—Lily said she'd be content with a Chinese takeaway ('Vegetarian dishes please') and a cake from Asda.

At the restaurant, owing to the rain Lily waited in the car while Grandma went inside. When she returned Grandma said, 'That was interesting. Mrs Bashett was in there. She said her husband is going mad because people are going in his shop, buying half a dozen smoothies, then returning next day saying there's something wrong with them. See what you started?'

'Me?'

'Yes. You don't know the consequences your actions cause.'

'It's not my fault.'

'No, but you just never know. It doesn't mean you shouldn't do things, sweetheart. Poor Mrs Bashett, I do feel for her. She says she gets a takeaway from here every Thursday.'

'Not Tuesdays, straight after the Slimming World weigh-in? Isn't that how it works?'

'Yes, except she goes to the chippy then.'

On the drive home Lily was babbling away happily about Chinese food while Grandma fretted about the future. She could see Gwynne being proved right: delinquency, drugs, debt, prostitution, more drugs, criminality, death. It had already happened to a girl in their street. She'd been doing well at school but fell in with a bad crowd. And what other sort of crowd could Lily, who struggled socially, hope to fall in with? But on reflection, it was no comparison: any crowd Lily stumbled into would likely push her back out; and moreover, it was the other girl's dizzy popularity that led to her downfall, making her socially overconfident and reckless. Grandma was determined to protect her charge, who she accepted was winning the argument that the school was wrong for her, and she now had to weigh up whether to move her to a different one or explore equity release to pay for tutors. Whatever it took, she would do. She would write all this in her journal after Lily had gone to bed, a book she kept strictly private, although every word was written in anticipation, and indeed hope, that her granddaughter would one day read it.

Instead of buying a cake, Grandma had made one from Lily's list, in fact the one she'd chosen for its long name: chocolate fudge peanut butter ice cream pretzel cake. Watching Grandma carefully cut her a slice of the dark brown creation with the little pretzels on top, Lily felt supremely happy. Safe and loved, she wasn't tempted by her rituals, although out of habit while waiting for the kettle to boil for her grandmother's tea, she pressed her fingertips on the frost at the top of the freezer for thirty seconds.

In her room she was tempted to send Mack a Facebook friend request but resisted, not wanting to risk spoiling the day. She'd been wary of Facebook since the shameful evening Travis' so-called wife had warned his apparently many girlfriends not to contact him again, or risk 'consequences', claiming he was a man in his fifties.

As she settled down for bed she heard Grandma's mobile ring, and then, after a few moments of quiet, she heard her talking surprisingly loudly. She opened her door and listened: 'You know I've always encouraged... but after this... And he did nothing. He just stood there...' Lily guessed it was Ted Grandma was talking to about Brian. Grandma lowered her voice, so Lily crept down the stairs. '...Is that what he told you? Confessed. That would be right... He's not his father's son, that's for sure. I can't imagine a thirteen-year-old Ted Panker standing watching while his supposed best friend gets beaten up... Ashamed of himself? Good. So he should be. No I don't think... She wouldn't want to see him and I can't blame... Like I say, I've always encouraged... I saw him as a calming influence, but when it comes to it, those girls could have killed her. What use is he just standing there? What use is a friend like that? One of them was bashing her head on the ground for Heaven's sake. And the kicking and the smacking. The hours in A&E. And the psychological. It's a disgrace. Whatever she's said or done she doesn't deserve that. And quite honestly, I don't need it. Not at my age. Anyway, I'm going to see Julia Bizzell and tell her what I think.... The police? Not interested. School, not interested.... No, we had a good day, thanks. She had a good day, I think. And thanks for the... I'll put it towards something for her. Every year you do it. Just a shame I can't say.... A lot of men wouldn't bother... I know it's the historical but even so... Much appreciated. I'll say thank you now on her behalf.'

Lily stole back upstairs and gently closed the door. So Brian's dad, Ted, who Grandma had said was not her real dad (although she'd hesitated), was giving Grandma money to spend on her. 'The historical' she called it. Weird. But she would love Ted to be her dad. He'd called round a few times (and why?) and always made a fuss of her. Kind and strong—a perfect man? Except unfaithful to his wife, everyone knew that, so not perfect. But the wife, Maisie, could be mean, so understandable. Who wanted perfect anyway? Kind and strong, that was enough.

8

Next morning, Lily checked Facebook to see if there were any birthday messages for her. She was surprised to find one from Travis. He explained the woman claiming to be his 'wife' was his jealous ex-girlfriend who was also fifteen, a whizz on social media, and 'evil'. He apologised for her actions, asked how Lily was, and said he would always be there for her, no matter what. She began to cry because the message brought to mind over a hundred previous ones that had always made her feel better. Travis was skilled at knowing the right words to reassure, console, coax, intrigue, even excite her. She saw it as harmless and did not see how perhaps these messages, sometimes as many as twenty in a night, had made her dependent on him and the dream he'd created for her, and made her vulnerable since, now more than ever, she was unhappy at school. Because Travis' latest talked about his ex claiming to be his wife, it meant he was the Travis the woman meant rather than some other 'Travis'. It was now therefore a question of which of them she could believe and whether he was a boy of fifteen or a man in his fifties. The tears came quickly—tears for her more naive, more innocent self before the so-called wife's intervention. If Travis really was who the woman claimed, it undermined every word of reassurance he'd ever sent her.

She also received a strange direct message from a new source on Facebook: 'Hey, brat, leave my dad alone. You're making him ill. Making him ill messes with me. Stop.' It was someone called Cindy in South Carolina.

'Who are you? Is your dad Travis?'

'Travis? Stop your campaign, maggot.'

'I have no campaign. I'm an individual. Leave me alone. Who are you?'

'The Angel of Death—your death.'

'Really? I've been waiting for you all my life.'

'Ha! Ha! Don't tempt me, worm. Just be a good maggot, and go away.'

'I know you—you're a cyberbully.'

'You're the bully for the longest time—first me, now my dad.'

Lily decided against sending a reply. It was so obviously fake. 'For the longest time' was something Americans said, and it was the kind of thing an English fraud would use to pretend to be American.

Lily never considered herself a bully, but she had been a fighter at primary school. Other kids liked to chant at her, 'Your mum's a ho! Your dad don't know!' which was crueler than the words because her mum was dead. They did it because they knew she'd react and in a violent way. Seven girls and four boys had felt her fists during her primary school career, and not one of them got the better of her. She was known as Lily Vicious but was popular, not least because less pugilistic kids looked to her as a kind of protector. When she started at Retingham High, Grandma hoped it would all be different, but within a week Lily got into a fight. A stern letter from the school followed, with a screed about the school's 'policy', and Grandma made her commit to only respond physically if hit first.

Despite the school's avowal of 'zero tolerance' of violence, in a matter of days there was a stabbing outside the school gates and a mass brawl at lunchtime a month later. Regardless, her Vicious persona was no more, put away like an obsolete theatre prop, and she became morose and insular, gaining weight but no friends, and losing confidence.

At breakfast, Lily said to Grandma, 'I need your advice. I've done something very silly. There's a girl at school wanted to be my friend, but I said something really bad to her. What can I do? I feel I should say sorry to her, feel I should make an effort.'

'Your mad mouth again?'

'If you say so.'

Grandma suggested getting a card.

'But I don't know her address, and I don't want to ask her on Facebook. Her name's Alison MacKnokaird.'

'You'll have to write it down for me. I'll ask Mrs Bashett. If they have their papers delivered, it's maybe through them. If not, I can probably find out through someone I know at the school.'

'If I give her a card, will she laugh at me or think me pathetic?'

'Why should she? Not if she's a nice girl like you say she is.'

Grandma helped her choose a card—a safe choice: Van Gogh's *Sunflowers*—and inside Lily wrote, 'Hey B-word, sorry it got messed up—my fault, C-word.'

Grandma said, 'Let me see what you wrote... What's this B-word and C-word? Is it what I think?'

'Don't know what you think. It's pet names. She's Bear and I'm Cat.'

Grandma peered at her. 'I see,' she said, unable to resist a smile. 'I've always wanted to meet a bear.'

Late in the afternoon, having obtained the address from her friend at the school, Grandma drove Lily to Mack's place, a journey lasting the three and a half minutes it took her and (with less gusto) Marc Bolan, to sing *Spaceball Ricochet*. Grandma stayed in the car parked on the street, and Lily walked up the long gravel drive to the imposing house with its white stone pillars, and tall heavy-looking front door, and large windows, and rooms with high ceilings, that all seemed to say: this is the home of people of substance. She hoped no-one would be in, certainly not Mack. She pressed the doorbell so lightly it struggled to make a sound. A stocky woman with straight, short, red hair answered the door, and a large fluffy dog bounded out nearly knocking Lily over. 'Are you here for Alison? Get down, Jimball!'

'Yes. Just to leave this.' Lily showed her the envelope.

'Oh, how sweet! She has a friend here. Do you want to come in?'

'Thank you, no. My grandma is waiting for me in the car. I should go. Perhaps you could give it to her?' Lily passed her the envelope.

'That's lovely. She'll only be a moment, though. And who shall...'

'Lily... Upshire.'

Lily decided to wait. She heard laughter and felt small and stupid. She was tempted to sneak away. Then she heard Mack shout, 'Upshire!' before she even appeared at the door. Then she was there: energetic and enthusiastic with a broad grin on her face, and in a long, dark blue dress with small, bright yellow moons on it, and barefoot. She was holding the envelope and now opened it. 'Oh it's beautiful. Thank you!' And she beamed with joy and chuckled on reading what Lily had written. 'Is that your grandma?' She indicated the car.

'Yeah.'

Mack waved extravagantly in that direction. 'Candy's here,' she said. 'We're playing video games. You know her?'

'Ford? Yes.'

'Like to join us?'

Lily sensed this suggestion was more from politeness than sincerity. 'Thank you, but my grandma's taking me shopping in a minute.'

'That's nice. Some other time then.'

'Are we friends?'

Mack was taken aback by the question, suddenly serious. 'I seem to remember you rejected me,' she said.

'I didn't mean it.'

'Listen, Upshire, this card is lovely, but no-one, except maybe my brother, has ever told me to "fuck off" in my life, and you said it twice. That hurt me from someone I felt I wanted to get to know. So I thought after that: I'll steer clear of her!'

'I'm sorry.'

'You said I was patronising. Maybe I was—'

'You were.'

'—and I'm sorry for that, but, for God's sake, it is possible to be patronising and nice at the same time.'

'I know.'

For Mack it was payback time: 'I mean, I can throw a strop same as anyone, but you're off the frigging chart, girl.'

'I'm sorry.'

'I'd be wondering all the time if I'd said the wrong thing and you were going to have a go at me again.'

'Give us a chance.' Lily felt pathetic.

'I can't deal with all that right now. I've got things going on in my life, and I need calm. I'm sorry.'

'OK,' said Lily, disappointed. 'You've made yourself clear. I shouldn't have come, should I? I wish I hadn't.' She turned to leave.

'Hey, C-word, don't just walk away!'

Lily did not respond. She quickened her step.

'Don't be rude, Upshire.'

Still no reaction.

'Lily, come back here!'

Only when she heard Mack's naked feet on the gravel hastening behind her did Lily turn round. 'What do you want?' she said. 'Another row? I'm not in the mood for one. I don't need your shit in my life either.' In Lily's head the editor was saying, 'That's it, mess it up again.'

'My shit?' Mack was annoyed. She thought: how rude! She was on the edge of telling this ignorant girl what she thought about it, but the pointlessness of it stopped her. She felt she was dealing with two people: the gentle, caring one with the card who made her laugh, and the sweary, truculent one with the crazy tongue. 'Come here,' she said, stretching her long arms towards her. Lily stood still, forcing Mack to take the further steps towards her. Lily felt shame at her own meanness. Mack put her arms round her stiff shoulders. 'Look, why wouldn't I want to be your friend when you're so sweet and adorable—that is, when you want to be?'

'Are you taking the piss?' said Lily. 'Coz if you are, don't.'

'I don't take the piss. And I can see through the nonsense. I can put up with your hangups, but you're work, Upshire. You're really work. Just right now I've got so much stuff...'

'What stuff?'

'My parents are divorcing, so I learned this week. My brother's moving out to live with his girlfriend who's twenty-one. It's all falling apart.' She fell silent. These revelations had been made to her after Sunday's family lunch and had taken all of seven minutes. The only one not making a speech had been her. Instead, she'd rushed to her room and wept. Later, she'd lain on her bed messaging friends and skimming through her favourite poetry books, desperate for words of consolation.

'I knew there was something,' said Lily. 'I knew it wasn't the way you painted it.' She raised her fingers to touch Mack's hair; it was shorter than last time, now merely to her shoulders, and neater. She could sense Mack was about to burst into tears and for once spotted a chance to show kindness. 'You know, we're both wary of each other. A little aggressive. Maybe what we need is to arrange a fight.'

'Fight? Are you serious?'

'Yeah. I don't mean to hurt each other. You couldn't hurt me anyway.' Lily sniggered.

'Excuse me—you want to fight *me*?' She looked at Lily—compared to Mack she was slow, unfit, and overweight—and she roared with laughter. A laugh that seemed to sweep through every part of her, a great wave of all the emotional energy that had built up ready to break into tears a moment earlier. But when she noticed Lily grinning, the thought occurred to her that Upshire was the tricky, sneaky sort who could steal a win through cheating in, say, a wrestle, and her laughter dropped as the thought flourished, so sudden the change in her expression that it triggered a chuckle in Lily, and Mack caught it and she was off again, feeling alive as lightning, and she held Lily tight and said, 'Oh Lily, you are the funniest, sweetest thing ever! Just like a... a sweet... I don't know, a very sweet pepper is what you are...'

'A chili, I'd rather.'

'No, pickle.'

'Gherkin? Thanks.'

'Onion. That's it: a sweet pickled onion.'

'Cheers.' She decided Mack, at least in conversation, was quite the maddest person she'd ever met, but she liked her all the more for that.

'But seriously,' said Mack, 'we are both in a pickle, aren't we? Especially me, I think.'

'I can help you through it. I want to.'

'This from the person who told me they weren't interested in anything I had to say. Do you know how hurtful that was? You know, for someone so quiet and shy, in your funny little way you've got some front. And how do you imagine you could possibly help me?'

'Because I'm a human being, not some unfeeling monster.'

'I know you're not.'

'I can listen. I've got so much to give and no one to give it to—not my own age anyway. I know I have anger issues. I don't know where these rages come from. I'm sorry. But I'll be worth the work as you call it.'

'And you won't just say you're not interested and don't want my shit in your life, another hurtful thing you just said?'

'No.'

Mack gently stroked Lily's cheek with her forefinger. 'Such a beautiful face. Those eyes, that cute nose. They're jealous of you. That's part of the reason they do it. And although I thought after our last conversation: "Sod that for a game of soldiers", when I heard what happened I wanted to get in touch, but I wasn't sure how you'd react. So I'm glad you called round. I'd like to say we could fix the Bizzell family, but I can't see it. It will just carry on because they see you as different. They'll get bored with it one day, though. Is it them that gets you so riled up?'

'I guess. Them and everything else.'

'You'll need more than your rages, Upshire. To fight bullies you need skill and power and speed.'

'You got them, then?'

'Sure—because I train. I learned to fight to protect myself. And it stops me getting depressed now with things falling apart I can't control. But we don't want to be fighting anyone, right? Merely defending ourselves if we have to.'

'Yeah.'

Mack kissed Lily on the forehead, and then, with the gentlest touch of her lips, upon her cheek. 'There, does that feel the tiniest bit better? You look so stunned, like no girl ever kissed you on the cheek before. I feel better anyway.'

Lily nodded. She was desperate to say, 'Would you be my sister?' but failing to say what she meant was typical, as was the regret that followed, and then the feeling that it was a daft idea anyway.

'Oh well, my little... chipotle, that's what you are, I'd better get back. Candy will be wondering where I've got to. She'll be jealous. We'll get together soon, right?'

'Sure we will.' Their palms touched, and Mack hurried off, while Lily lingered a little as she wanted to think. She heard Mack shout behind her, 'Bake a cake, yeah?'

Lily turned and caught Mack's eye. 'Yeah we will.'

Mack was clever. The word 'jealous' was like a burr that stuck to you. It was on Lily now. She felt jealous of Candy. Candy who was as sweet as her name. And she hated feeling jealous. And it was unnecessary. She and Mack had something between them. Something important. She felt she'd won a small victory. As for her anger, it might be her best friend of all, a caution to those who meant her harm.

It was a shame that it had also put off someone like Mack who'd only wanted to befriend her.

In the car Grandma was reading in the newspaper about a financial scandal. 'You look pleased with yourself,' she said. 'She's a nice girl, I can tell. Don't you go being mean to her again.'

Later that day, people on Facebook asked if she'd had any 'joy' in pursuing an apology from the company, so she told them about the letter she received and her response. They found it hilarious. 'You're our poster child,' said one.

'But I don't want to be a poster child. That would be awful.'

'We'll be your champions,' said another.

'Champions?'

'Yes, we'll be the Champions of Lily Upshire.'

'No! Oh no, the bullying would be impossible!'

'Friends, then,' said another.

'Friends of Lily Upshire? No, definitely not! Please no. I'd rather die than that.'

Later, she found a Facebook friend request from Mack. This was another victory. Of course she would not accept it yet but put it aside to enjoy later like a new bar of chocolate.

9

Grandma decided to go to the parents' evening. She was pessimistic and went ready for an argument. She made sure Lily had the Peacemakers' phone number in case she had any concerns during the two or three hours she was out. Lily herself was apprehensive. Either Grandma would tell her off afterwards for not working, or she would have ripped into the teachers for not helping her, which would have its own consequences, especially with Miss Cotton.

Ten minutes after Grandma's old Ford left, Lily, to calm her thoughts, went into the kitchen and took an ice cube from the freezer. She held it against the palm of her hand over the sink until it began to melt. It cleared her mind. It was then she heard the doorbell.

The ring made her jump. She wanted to ignore it. She took slow steps, hoping the person would give up and go away. The bell rang again. She heard 'It's only me—Sally!' and ran to the door. Nancy's daughter was smiling and relaxed as ever, but she sensed a nervousness in Lily.

Sally, who'd recently visited to cut Grandma's hair, had since then changed her own and was sporting a short blonde bob Lily found attractive. There was always something a little conspiratorial in her manner, and Lily saw her as a mate. 'Are you OK?' Sally said as Lily let her in.

'Sure.'

Sally was unconvinced, finding her flustered although also pleased to see her as always. Lily made tea for her.

'What's the matter, Lily, love?' said Sally on the young host's return to the lounge.

'Nothing.'

'Are you sure?' Lily did not reply and Sally said, 'You're not OK are you?'

'Yeah I am.'

Sally decided not to pursue the issue. Instead, she invited her to meet the following Saturday at Martha's Coffee Bar in the town centre's pedestrian area. She gave Lily her phone number: 'Ring me any time. Really, I mean it—any time.' They watched TV for a while, not saying much, and then Sally left.

Grandma arrived home in a predictably bad mood. The evening had been much worse than she'd anticipated. The school had decided that Lily needed help but that such help would be a wasted effort because she wasn't interested. All the teachers said she was a bright child who was unable or unwilling to apply herself. Apart from English, that is: 'Ms Hass speaks highly of you. So there's hope there at least.'

'I love her,' said Lily. 'If you withdraw me, can she be my private tutor?'

'Well that won't be happening any time soon. By the way, I apologised to Miss Cotton myself since you didn't, like you were supposed to.'

'Why? That old crow hates me.'

'Damn you, will you listen to me for once!?' They were both shocked at Grandma's sudden flare of temper. 'Please. I am trying to do my best for you. I have always done my best. It has been a very stressful evening. Most of the teachers, I could tell, didn't even want to see me.' Grandma then said that she'd talked to Miss Cotton about the bullying. 'She wants you to have counselling.'

'No.'

'What do you mean "No"?'

'Because of the woman who does it.'

'What's wrong with her?'

'Everyone knows she's up Julia Bizzell's arse.'

'Lily!'

'And so's Miss Cotton.'

'Stop it!'

'And the head.'

'I've heard enough. Go to your room!'

'Go to yours!'

At this Grandma lost her cool. 'Insolent little bitch!' she shouted and she slapped Lily hard across the face. Lily was too shocked to say anything. But it was Grandma who felt it most; it was she and not Lily who went to her room to weep. She was enraged. The girl was impossible.

Lily could hear her grandmother crying, and she felt guilty. She made her a cup of tea in an attempt at conciliation. As she proffered it to her, she said, 'I'm sorry,' and she meant it.

Grandma did not even look at her. 'Take it away,' she said. 'I don't want it... I don't want you.'

This last comment stunned Lily. Silent, she walked away with the cup. She would contact Mack. Maybe she could stay there overnight.

'Lily!'

She did not answer at first but finally said, 'What?'

'Come here please... Please.'

She went to her grandmother. She wanted to tip the tea over the old woman's head, but instead she gently handed her the cup. Grandma put it on the bedside table. Lily noticed her face was all red, especially around the eyes.

'I'm sorry I hit you,' said Grandma, 'but quite honestly, you deserved it. You just won't listen. Are you prepared to listen now?'

Lily wanted to tell her to go to hell but instead she said, 'OK' quietly.

'The word the teachers use to describe you is "distracted". And I find you that way too. You need to pay more attention.'

'To what?'

'To your schoolwork. That's if you want to make something of yourself.'

'Something of myself? I have no idea what that means.'

'What do you do of an evening? You certainly don't do your homework.'

'Nothing special. Nothing you would understand.'

'Try me.'

'Alright. I've been working on Instagram. I have my own account now. There—any the wiser? No.' With that she turned to leave the room. Grandma called her back, but she went to her bedroom. Once inside, she took the scissors from the drawer of her bedside table and without thought jabbed it into her palm. The sudden pang alarmed her—not the pain itself but the fact she'd done it.

It was true that Lily had an Instagram account, but in reality she did little with it. In the main, she looked at other people's accounts to see what they were doing. She liked to follow others, especially people in the fashion and lifestyle fields. She was fascinated by models, exotic locations, luxurious dresses, dancers. She dreamed of being someone five or six years older and as beautiful as these young women. But even if she was not as beautiful or glamorous as them, by then she would have found ways to make money from social media. This was what she wanted to learn about, not stupid maths and physics.

10

When Lily returned to school she was quiet and subdued. Everyone knew what had happened. She'd been properly beaten up. She was a loser. Victims were losers. She had bullied the Runt, and the twins had paid her back. What had she expected? She was shunned. Whenever the opportunity arose, unnoticed she stuck her fingernails into her palm.

She saw Mack at the end of the first day back, but found her guarded as though their recent heart-to-heart had not happened, as though Mack felt she'd opened herself up too much and now wanted to be aloof. Their conversation was stilted. Mack was waiting for another girl, tall and skinny, whom Lily did not recognise. It was obvious they were close. She felt jealous, and it bothered her that she wanted to hurt this skinny girl she didn't even know, most likely a gentle unassuming person like Candy. Where did these awful feelings come from? Was she perhaps the bully people accused her of being? When Mack said goodbye as she and the girl left, Lily felt a sense of loss.

That day, Lily received another envelope from the US. It contained more smoothie vouchers. This time, a whole sheet of vouchers came.When Grandma saw this she said, 'Now that really must be it. But well done, Lily, you've done very well.'

The letter, which was from BS, another service ambassador, said,

> *Dear Lily Upshaw,*
>
> *We're always delighted to hear from such a valued customer as yourself. At the personal behest of Chief Executive Officer, Frank Salesman, I have great pleasure in enclosing a month's supply of vouchers for your favorite product ex gratia.*

This was followed by a similar screed to the last letter beginning *For the avoidance of doubt...*, but this time there was no invitation to write to Melody or

Frank or anyone else. Instead, it said starkly, *No further correspondence will be entered into.*

Lily was unmoved: 'I don't want vouchers. I want an apology like I asked for.'

Exasperated, Grandma was happy to see the Peacemakers call round at that moment. When they came in, Nancy said Fred was 'really too ill' to be there but was making 'a special effort'. She added that a number of people were complaining about being ill from smoothies. 'See what you've started,' she teased.

'But I'm not ill,' said Lily.

'Not yet maybe, but food poisoning can take months to manifest,' Nancy said happily. She said they were calling round to inform them they were having the roof done and were apologising in advance for any disruption, but they soon returned to the subject of Lily's 'claim'.

Lily left the room to go to the toilet and on her return Nancy said, 'So your grandma tells us you got another letter from the company.'

'Yes.'

'And what have they offered you this time?'

'A month's supply of vouchers.'

'So, say, thirty then?' Nancy pressed.

'I suppose,' Lily answered vacantly.

'Very generous in the circumstances,' said Grandma.

Nancy scoffed, 'It's nothing to them. Think of the vast profits they make. No, it's nothing. It could have been awful. You could have been killed.'

'Could I?' said Lily.

Nancy was now in full stride as if giving a crucial presentation to the council: 'It could have been something poisonous in it. A toxic chemical. It could have been tampered with along the way. Maybe Bashett, you never know.' Lily and Grandma exchanged glances. 'There are terrible people will do such things. And you could have taken a sip and dropped dead.'

'That's a bit dramatic,' Fred interjected, as if suddenly shaken from sleep, his teeth enjoying a good shift.

'No, she could have,' Nancy insisted. 'It's pure luck she didn't. Then there's the anguish of it all.' Lily looked decidedly puzzled as Nancy added, 'Your poor grandmother was worried sick. She went pale, she wasn't eating.'

Embarrassed, Grandma intervened, 'But the fact is, we haven't got any evidence so Lily will accept the kind offer of the vouchers.'

'Did they actually send them?'

'Oh yes,' Grandma replied.

'There you are then,' Nancy said in triumph. The others looked at her expectantly. 'There you are, they're worried. They know they could have to pay out thousands. Think about it. Anyway, my dears...,' she stood up mid-sentence '...we didn't come here to talk about that. We've told you about the roof and now we'd better get back as Fred is very tired, poor lamb. But we'll leave you with this: if you decide to do something about the poisoning case, Fred knows someone can help. And I expect *your* roof will need fixing soon, so you might fancy the cash. Smoothie vouchers indeed! You can't patch up the roof with them, you know.' Before they left, Nancy asked Lily, 'How are you doing at school these days?', expecting the usual flat answer.

But Lily replied sharply, 'What has that got to do with it?'

Nancy was a little stung: 'Perhaps you might do better if you hadn't had that contaminated drink. I mean, can you concentrate fully?'

Grandma said, 'She does have a problem with concentration, don't you, Lily?'

'I guess.'

'Well, a lack of concentration or some other mental effect usually has a physical origin. It could be that you're not doing as well as you'd like at school because of some chemical in the smoothies. You drink more of them than anyone else, after all. Anyone I know, at least. Anyway, some of us will be making a claim. You and your grandmother might wish to join.'

'I don't think so,' said Grandma.

'I just want an apology,' said Lily.

That evening, Lily decided to write a third letter. She was becoming almost as frustrated as Grandma with it all. When she realised what Lily was planning to do, Grandma had the idea of surreptitiously keeping the vouchers. A month's vouchers was worth thirty pounds. But she dismissed the notion: it would have been a breach of trust that was unacceptable to her, let alone Lily.

Lily decided to write to Mr Salesman direct. The service ambassadors and legal people did not understand, so perhaps he would. She imagined Mr Salesman as a kind of idealised head teacher figure with great wisdom, and patience, and a controlled temper for when need arose. She felt she'd provide a little more background in the hope he would be better informed. This time she would not use the Olivetti, however, as it would be a longer but quicker letter. She brought her laptop downstairs and sat at the lounge table. She did a brief Google search looking at sample business letters while Grandma sat on the sofa knitting and listening to a play on Radio 4 Extra. Lily was annoyed, both with the company and her own compulsion about it, and she wrote fast:

Dear Frank Salesman,

Thank you for your personal behest. It is kind of you to offer this valued customer a month's supply of vouchers, but I only asked for an apology. Even if I could accept the offer, I could not use the vouchers. This is because Mr Bashett no longer sells the smoothies I like best in his shop. In fact, he has stopped selling your smoothies altogether. This is because people kept returning them, saying there was something wrong with them. For the avoidance of doubt, I did not return mine. Instead, I threw it away. But now it turns out my interests have been prejudiced. [This sentence she'd found on the internet under 'How to write a business complaint letter'].

The shopkeeper, Mr Bashett, is a most intemperate man as Mrs Bashett can attest. [This was based on a line she heard in Grandma's play.]

My grandmother goes to the same Slimming World as Mrs Bashett and the worry is that Mr Bashett may have to close his shop because 'this smoothie business' as he calls it has damaged his reputation so much. If his shop closes, it will be a shock to the town because it has been there since before my grandmother's grandmother was born. Over a hundred years. Incidentally, I may have to start going to Slimming World myself soon. My weight is going up and my love of your smoothies, as well as chocolate, is well known and so people connect the two, especially the bullies. Is it true that all your drinks have twice as much sugar as other brands? It is what people claim, but I say it makes them taste better. However, with my weight going up I have to listen to what they say.

Now Mr Bashett is no longer selling your smoothies perhaps you could start selling them somewhere else. We have good supermarkets here: Aldi, Asda, Morrisons, Iceland etc. They already sell other smoothies but someone on Facebook said that all these different brands are actually owned by your company – and it is a fake competition to keep prices up. I find that hard to believe but others, more cleverer than me, do believe it.

I appreciate you are very busy but I am as well, what with school and Facebook and Instagram and now my grandmother has given me chores for me to do. But I have been careful to get your name right. I have not called you Frank Salesmat or Salesmutt. I did not call Melody Roller, Melanie Baller. My name is Upshire, not Upshaw. It may be unusual but so's Salesman and Roller, and it is what I was born with. It disappoints me as a valued customer that your company cannot get this right. What would it have called an unvalued customer, I wonder? When I run my own business I will make sure we get people's names right. And we will say sorry if we get something wrong, which is something your company seems unable to do. You can say strange things like 'ex gratia' and 'personal behest' but you cannot say 'sorry'.

Incidentally, I have no involvement with the Friends of Lily Upshire, or the Champions of..., or whatever they are calling it. Although I wish them no harm, I wish they did not use my name. There do seem to be more of them every day. Anyway, as Mr Bashett no longer sells your smoothies and the vouchers are of no use to me, our longstanding relationship is now at an end. No further correspondence will be entered into.

Without prejudices,
I remain
Lily Upshire

['I remain' was another phrase she found on the internet. She thought it marvellous although it was usually followed by 'your obedient servant' which was nonsensical, especially for a valued customer. There was a strength to it, however. A defiance. I am unchanged. I remain. She could say to the Bizzell family, 'Regardless of what you do to me, I remain. And I will always remain.']

Before she went to bed she reported back to the 'Friends'. They were a nuisance, but she liked the attention. One commented, 'It shows that if you push you get. Keep pushing, Lily.' She did not think it showed any such thing but did not want to engage in further discussion about it.

More people were complaining about foreign objects in sugary drinks, and chocolate bars, and biscuits all made by companies owned by GUFF. 'They know we're on to them,' said one person in Luton. But Pharaoh from somewhere in Texas wrote, 'You're digging your own grave, Upshire. Time to call it off, maggot.'

Again, reference to her as a 'maggot'. Was it because she was pale?

She wrote back, 'Go fuck yourself! You're fake. Stop pretending. I'm real, you're just some trash. Go back down your hole.'

'Go back, you say?'

'Go back.'

'It's what you always say.'

'I never said it before.'

'Yes you did.'

Lily thought this person mentally unstable so did not respond further.

11

Lily met Sally as arranged. Sally had chosen a venue, Martha's Coffee Bar, that would be quiet with plenty of distance between the tables. Lily had been there several times with Grandma, usually sitting in the torn leather armchairs in the corner farthest from the door, but these were taken so they sat at a small wooden table in the window. She noticed there were the usual landscape paintings for sale on the walls and a bicycle (also for sale) suspended from the ceiling. The Italian proprietor, female but not called Martha, made a point of coming over to greet them and ask after Lily's grandmother.

Sally ordered an Americano with a piece of poppyseed cake. Lily had a strawberry milkshake.

Even in conversation with her friend, Lily's attention wandered. She felt nervous and self-conscious, and Sally sensed this. Sally had something to say to her she thought might upset her but did not want to spoil the moment.

Lily glanced out of the window frequently, and on one occasion was captivated by the sight of a small charcoal-black dog led by a waif-like girl of about ten. She wished she could be that child. 'Look at that beautiful dog!' she exclaimed. 'What sort is it?'

Sally peered out. 'It's either an Italian greyhound or a young whippet. I'd say, whippet.'

'Do they make good pets?'

'They do. My brother-in-law has two. Always lolloping about. They're correctly named—always whipping things. They can be pretty funny. Don't like cats, though.'

'We have a cat.'

'So does my brother-in-law. They get used to one in the same house. It shouldn't be a problem. See, it's because they were bred to catch small animals like rats and rabbits. They don't yap, hardly ever bark, and don't moult.'

'Are they sweet-natured?'

'As you are.'

Lily blushed and then grinned. 'I'll need something to entertain me if I get chucked out of school,' she said.

Sally looked pained. 'Why on earth would that happen?' Lily told her about the letter her grandmother had received accusing her of bullying. 'What's the matter, Lily? Sweetheart, what's happening? Bullying? That's not you.'

'I hit a girl in the school corridor. I just snapped. She and her sisters bully me all the time, and one day the Runt, as we call her, was there with her evil friend and they started pushing me around, and I lashed out and hit her. Her head hit the wall and she wailed like a baby. And of course a teacher saw it and the Runt told her I bullied her all the time, which was a total lie, and I got interviewed by the headteacher, and that didn't go well so they stuck it in the letter. Then there was a second time, but everyone agreed that was an accident.'

'Was it?'

'I don't know. She ran at me and tripped—I thought she was going to nut me, you know...'

'Ooh!'

'So she tripped and hit the wall, and I remember slamming her face into the wall and her nose was bleeding.'

'Broke it?'

'No. But I talked to my friend Brian—friend at the time, not now...'

'Ted Panker's son? Why's he not your friend now?'

'He's a coward. He was with me when I was beaten up. Three of them: the Runt and the twins. He was nowhere to be seen. I had to go to hospital. The Runt had my head and was banging it on the ground. She wanted to kill me, but the twins stopped her. They're clever. They know when to stop. And he just stood there. I hate him. They call me lesbian, and gay, and dyke. I'm not but don't really like boys either. Brian seemed different... sensitive, but actually he's just useless.'

'What did he have to do with the other time, the time you slammed that girl's face into the wall, or thought you did?'

'He wasn't there, but he told me it couldn't have happened the way I described it, the way I remembered it. He even asked his sister about it. Paramedic. She said it had to be an accident. So I believe that, even though I wanted to hurt the Runt. And if the chance came...' She noticed Sally's expectant look. '... Yeah, if the chance came, I would do it again. They make my life hell.'

'It sounds like he cares about you, though.'

'He probably does, but what use is someone who cares but is a coward, lets you down when it matters?' Lily now accepted the piece of Sally's cake offered her. Then she drank the shake right down.

Sally decided not to ask about the swearing incident. She was worried for her young friend. 'So what's it really all about?' she said.

'You mean... like, big picture?'

'Yes.'

'I don't know. I don't make friends easily—that doesn't help.'

Sally was becoming concerned she might not have the chance to say what she intended, so she simply came out with it, 'Did you know, your grandmother thinks... now don't get mad with me... you're self-harming?'

'What!?' Lily stared at her.

'She's worried about you. Is she right to be?'

Lily was upset. She did not like this subject coming up. 'Private,' she said. 'Is this the reason for this? To ask me about it?' Sally blushed. Lily said, 'She has no right to say anything about it. And nor do you.'

'She's worried.' Lily stood up. Sally said. 'I'm sorry. I didn't mean—'

'Well you did.' Lily put on her coat and walked out without further word, catching a glance at the black whippet as she did so. When she reached the main road on the way home she was tempted to throw herself into the path of an approaching car, but she looked at the face of the driver, a young woman, and she thought about how the woman would feel, and Sally whom she loved, and Emily Hass, and Mack whom she hadn't even got to know properly yet.

When she arrived home she could see Grandma out in the garden talking to Nancy over the fence. She was tempted to go outside and have a row with her out there, but instead she went upstairs to her room. She spent the rest of the morning on social media, looking at Instagram posts. What she really wanted to do was talk to Travis. She wrote to him: 'Please contact me. I need to hear from you. I need to know you're genuine. Can we talk on Skype? Or on phone? Send me number.'

She avoided her grandmother until lunchtime when she challenged her, 'What are you trying to do to me?'

'What do you mean, my dear?'

'You've turned one of my few friends into your spy.' Lily stretched out the undersides of her arms towards her. 'You think I'm self-harming. OK then, here you are, for your inspection. Have a good look.'

'Don't be ridiculous.'

'Leave me alone.'

Later that afternoon, she phoned Sally to apologise. She said, 'I lost it. I didn't mean to walk out on you. I just seem to lose it all the time right now. Your friendship means so much to me. Please forgive me.'

Sally was understanding about it, reassured her it didn't matter, and said they'd meet up again soon.

Later, Lily wrote again to Travis, 'I'm not sure I can believe in you. Prove you real. If you real, meet me on Skype.'

There was no response from Travis. Instead from Blakey in Des Moines came: 'Hey, maggot, you got what you wanted. Now leave it alone.'

'What? You've got the wrong person.'

'No, Upshire, you got the wrong person.'

'I know who you are. You're just an online bully.'

'You bullied me, so it's you deserves to suffer. Now leave my dad alone and go away.'

Again 'maggot', again the reference to bullying and the father. These people sending messages must be all the same, mustn't they? The alternative—that they were part of a coordinated campaign—was too disturbing to contemplate.

12

On another Saturday morning, when Lily was to meet Sally again she was feeling groggy. This was because she had slept badly after receiving a message from the woman claiming to be Travis' wife. The message had come direct this time: 'I warned you to stay away from my husband. You ignored me. If you don't stop trying to contact him, you will face serious trouble.'

'He said you fake. You jealous ex.'

'Ignore me at your peril, slut.'

'I'm not slut. I'm 13, Travis 15.'

'And 16, 18, 23, 27, 32, 35, and probably every age between, depending on which desperate loser got their hooks into him.'

'Please be nice. I never asked for or got money. I'm girl at school. Like my Facebook pic. Travis is kind to me.'

'And two hundred others. The pic on Facebook he contacted you from is his nephew's. He has a different pic for each fool. Look, I'll accept who you say you are if you stop all contact.'

'But I don't know who you are.'

'Do you want photo?'

Lily had an idea she'd seen on TV: 'Can you send pic of you holding paper saying "Lily U" in next 5 mins?'

There was a pause. The 'wife' was checking how to do this. 'OK,' she said at last. 'Then you must leave him alone. He's very ill.'

A few minutes later, a picture did arrive: it was of a kind-faced woman, who could be as old as Nancy Peacemaker, holding in one hand a photograph of her with an even older-looking bald man, and also a sheet of paper reading 'Lily U' in large letters. She then received a link to a Facebook page showing the photograph she'd come to love of 'Travis' but bearing the name Jack Wozner. Jack was 17 not 15, and not in New York but Austin, Texas, and was in a relationship with Mary Slipper. She flicked through his list of friends. There were several Wozners including the woman and the bald man whose Christian name she saw really was... Travis.

Lily felt cold in her stomach. Her relationship had been an illusion. It was all a mess. She wrote back, 'OK. Sorry. I never meant harm. Didn't know.' She'd been cheated out of the dream she'd clung to for months. She felt a mixture of sadness and anger, and she turned these feelings upon herself. How foolish she'd been! How naive and stupid she was!

When Lily met Sally in Martha's Coffee Bar they sat by the window at the same table as last time. The dark-haired Italian proprietor came over to greet them, even more jovial than usual perhaps because her nearest rival was closing, although the town talk was that a chain would replace it. Lily noticed on the main wall the paintings for sale had a new hopeful addition, a delightfully happy beach scene, while the disconcerting bicycle suspended from the ceiling was still there. Sally, whose blonde bob had new pink tints in it, noted that Lily, contrite at her outburst last time, was particularly subdued. Sally said, 'Have you seen that little black dog since last time? You were a little bit in love with it.'

'No, I haven't,' said Lily who ordered a Diet Coke with toast and honey. 'It was lovely.' She glanced outside to see if it was out there. It wasn't. They talked a little about Lily's 'smoothie' letters and how Sally's dad Fred was, Sally's expression indicating she regarded his perennial health issues with a mixture of scepticism and resignation.

Lily's increasingly fractious relationship with the world around her had made her want to find out more about her mother in the hope of obtaining some inner stability. Grandma was rarely forthcoming, and Lily thought she would ask Sally what, if anything, she could remember about her. The Peacemakers had moved next door to Grandma when Sally was just starting school and Jane would have been about sixteen, and Lily reckoned the two would have been neighbours for about three years. 'Tell me something different about her, something I maybe never heard before. I'm sure she was an interesting person, but I know so little about her.'

'OK.' Sally took a sip of her Americano. 'You want to know something wild about her?'

'Yes, very much.'

'Well...' Sally hesitated, unsure what response she might provoke. '...your mother claimed to have certain powers. Whether she did or not, no-one ever knew. Did you ever hear about that?'

'No. What sort of powers?'

'She claimed she could make things happen. Things that happened to other people. Bad things. Accidents.'

'Like what?' Lily found the idea of 'powers' exciting.

'Someone would cross her, she would curse them, and then sometime later—say six months—they would have an accident.'

'Six months?'

Sally cracked a smile. 'I know what you're thinking.'

'Would it kill them?'

'Fatal? Could be. But it would be a pure coincidence of course.'

'Why "of course"?' Sally shrugged and Lily then said, 'Is it like a hex? It sounds cool. But she believed it, right?'

'Yes.'

Lily was fascinated. If her mother really did have powers, perhaps she herself had them. Six months was a long time, though. 'My grandma never said anything about it.'

'Maybe she didn't think anything good could come of it. How's things between you and her?'

'I had a nice birthday with her, but apart from that it's not been good. I know she loves me, but we just argue.'

'Your grandmother loves you deeply. That's something to hold dear. Many people haven't got that. She's probably worried about you at school. She probably thinks you could go off the rails.'

'Why?'

'Is school going well now then?'

'No. People have low expectations of me, and I never disappoint.'

Sally's expression was a cross between a smile and a grimace. 'I haven't low expectations of you, Lily, but it doesn't matter what I think.'

'It matters to me,' said Lily.

'Do you want to talk about this? Because if you do, I don't want you getting upset and walking out on me again.'

'I won't,' said Lily. 'I said sorry about last time.' She took a bite of toast and honey.

'I suspect she feels you should be doing better for someone as intelligent as you.' Lily gave an embarrassed smile. 'If you don't work, you will fail your exams. Go ahead and fail if you want. And there are jobs you could get if you're lucky, but they won't pay much, and your options will be limited. That's at best.'

Lily replied, 'What would be the worst, then? It seems such a long way off. Why do I even need to think about the job I'll get one day?'

'Look around you. I don't mean in here.' Lily looked outside for a moment and then at Sally, noticing her fingers playing with an empty sugar packet, rolling it up and twisting it. 'I mean, out in the wider world. Or even out in the street. Just under the surface, look for the signs. What do you think is out there that your grandmother might be worried about?'

'Drugs? I don't know... drink maybe.'

'And self-harming...'

'Oh don't. Not that again. It sounds like Grandma's obsessed with it. At least I don't need to worry about anorexia. What else is there?'

Sally was taken aback by Lily's rather casual air and raised her voice suddenly, sufficient to startle her young friend, '...and you can add violence, sexual abuse, every kind of exploitation. That's what I think she's worried about. Depressing isn't it?'

'All together it's quite a list.'

'It is. And she doesn't know how to protect you from everything—all the dangers—and it worries her. Don't be hard on her.' She grabbed Lily's hand and squeezed.

On the walk home she looked in vain for the mysterious little girl with the black dog she'd seen last time. Out of habit, she called in at Bashetts' shop. Mrs Bashett was at the counter, and she was as delightful as her husband was obnoxious. Lily bought a can of Rio for herself and a Bounty bar for Grandma. In

Saviour Park a group of small boys were playing football with an empty lager can. How she would love to join in! The highlight of the walk was a dazed-looking young man leaning against a metal lamppost by a zebra crossing. She watched fascinated as he opened his eyes and with great difficulty slowly nudged his way up the post to almost a standing position, then his eyes closed and he slid right back down again. He did all this three times while Lily watched. She was worried he'd step out into the road. She thought about going back to the shop to tell Mrs Bashett, but other adults came by, glanced at him and walked on. And he was smiling, not in obvious distress, merely somewhere else in his mind, so she left.

When Lily arrived home Grandma was watching an episode of *Millionaire Matchmaker*. She paused it to ask her about her meet-up with Sally. Lily said, 'It was nice. We talked about all sorts. She's not convinced about Fred.'

'Who is?'

'We talked a bit about my mum. I wanted to know more about her. Tell me something...' She flipped open her can of Rio '...did she really have some sort of powers?'

'Eh?' Grandma laughed nervously.

'You know, powers to make things happen.'

'Was that what Sally said?'

'Yes.'

'OK. Your mother thought she did.'

'Then do *you* have such powers?'

'No. I'm afraid not.'

'How do you know? You might have, surely. It could be in your blood.'

'It could have come from her dad's side.'

'I suppose. It seems odd you wouldn't know where it—'

'Lily, you're going to keep picking at this, aren't you?' She drew breath. She had something to reveal she'd kept for years, waiting for the right time whilst half-hoping it would never come. But the right time had arrived, and she would not flinch from it: 'OK then, I know because I'm not your maternal grand-mother. I was your mother's step-mother.'

'What!?'

'Your mum's mother died before you were born.' There—she was free of it now.

Lily sat completely still for a moment, trying to come to terms with the fact she had never known this. She felt deceived, betrayed. 'I have to go up-stairs,' she said. 'I have to make sense of everything.' Leaving her drink she ran upstairs to her room. She lay on her bed, her mind whirling with what Sally had said, and the intoxicated man, and above all Grandma revealing after so many years she wasn't her real grandmother. She cried into her pillow for a few moments. Then, to centre herself, she performed her ritual, this time pressing her nails hard into her palm. She was tempted to rip the skin on her arm as she stroked it with an open safety pin, but she was able to resist it. She took several deep breaths and closed her eyes in the hope of sleep, but this did not come.

When back in the lounge with Grandma, Lily said, 'I just wish you'd told me before now. You ask me questions all the time about what I'm doing, and yet you couldn't be bothered to tell me that.'

'I'm sorry. I was waiting for the right time.'

'You had a go at me about Travis, but this is far more important.'

'I said I'm sorry. And I am. But think about it. To all intents and purposes, it should really make no difference. I am your legal guardian after all, and I have always loved you. I have loved you more than if you were my flesh and blood.'

Lily pondered for a moment. She felt too stunned to be angry. 'I accept that,' she said at last. 'I know you love me very much, even though we don't always get on.' But the possibility of powers mattered more to her: 'So, um, do you think my mother really had some sort of psychic...'

'You can't let it go can you? She was a dreamer, a bit like...'

'Like me?'

'Yes. And I knew you'd want to know all about it, confusing yourself with the notion that you yourself might have such powers, real or imaginary. The power of coincidence, more like. And no good ever came of it, only harm. It was irresponsible of Sally to raise the subject, but being persistent as you are you'd have found out one day.'

Lily said nothing further about it and returned to her room. She felt a deep sadness. It might be self-pity, which was supposed to be so bad for you, but she had looked to Grandma, her movements, her words, interests, passions, for clues as to who that mysterious person she would never know, her mother, had been and thereby find clues to who she herself was. Knowing that was impossible gave her a feeling of irretrievable loss she'd never known before. Now all she had was one photograph, but a photograph of a life mattered less to her than the stories from that life. She took the point of the scissors to her palm for a moment and then tossed them across the room in disgust.

13

A few days later, Nancy called round and informed Grandma that 'poor Fred' was now too ill to even go to the doctor's. This raised Grandma's suspicions because Nancy also revealed he'd been well enough to have a long call with his friend about making a claim against the big bad company in the States, the shop, the irascible Mr Bashett personally (which would be the most interesting bit), and anyone else the claims company thought appropriate. Nancy wanted Lily to join in because she had complained in writing and that should help their prospects, but she accepted the contrary child probably wouldn't and so suggested Grandma herself make the claim. After all, had she not suffered all the mental anguish on behalf of Lily? And perhaps she had tried another of their drinks that didn't taste right, and couldn't she have claimed for that? So what was the harm in saying she'd tried the blueberry flip smoothie and then realised it contained a snail?'

'A snail?' Grandma said.

'Of course. It might have looked like a pea but it was much more likely a small toxic snail. And isn't even thinking about it making you ill at this very moment?' Grandma confirmed she was feeling a little queasy and Nancy said, 'There you are then,' confidently.

Still Grandma was sceptical. She reiterated that she could not in all conscience be associated with 'poor Fred's claim.

Nancy, veteran of many council meetings, was well-prepared. She pointed out that the wooden fence between their properties needed replacing—it could not wait—and it was 'unarguably' Grandma's responsibility, but poor Fred had 'out of the kindness of his generous heart' offered to pay half the cost, which would not be insubstantial. Of course, however, when he realised Grandma was not joining the claim, which could fatally impact his own, he might decide he could not afford such generosity, and so she needed to 'think on that'.

Thus, when Lily came home, Grandma recounted her conversation with Nancy, but in a rambling, over-excited fashion that left Lily initially bewildered, and to which Lily responded, 'Is this actually a joke?'

'No, my dear. Not at all. The fence needs replacing, and if you or I don't join in Fred's claim, he won't pay half the cost.'

Lily stared at her grandmother in disbelief. 'Grandma, I love you dearly, but this is pure silliness.' Furious, she ran out into the garden, heard Nancy mooching about on the other side of the fence and walked along the fence herself, saw a couple of panels beginning to fray at the bottom, including the spot where cats came through, but little damage otherwise. She went to the kitchen doorway and shouted as loud as she possibly could—certainly the Peacemakers and a host of other neighbours would have heard it, possibly even the old man in the lawnmower repair shop on the corner would have been woken up—'NO! The FENCE does NOT need REPLACING!!' She then ran indoors and upstairs, changed her clothes, did her ritual, and opened up Instagram to begin a post called 'My favourite animals' which would include a photograph of their cat, a black whippet, and a small marmoset.

She noticed she'd received a message from Travis: 'I miss you. You mean everything to me. I've had difficult times. My ex-girlfriend's crazy, but mom got a restraining order, and she's blocked from my Facebook. I think about you every day, wishing I was there to fight the bullies for you.'

Such words no longer had any impact on her. They left her cold, and she did not respond to them.

14

Lily went to the cemetery to visit her mother's grave. It was in a secluded corner hard to locate. Every time she'd visited the cemetery in the past, she'd been confused as to where it was. It was a simple headstone with the name Jane Upshire and dates. Lily always went through the calculation of how old she was when Jane died—one year 173 days.

She kneeled down beside the grave with its untidy grass and buttercups. She placed against the base of the headstone the small bunch of flowers she'd picked in Grandma's garden. She looked around to see if anyone was within earshot and then began talking to her mother. She apologised for not visiting recently, and for not doing well at school, and for having been a disappointment to her grandmother. Her own disappointment at discovering she was not her real grandma was tempered by the fact she was not too strict. She said, 'I understand, dear mum, that you had certain powers you found useful to you in your life. Powers that made things happen. I am wondering if I have inherited these powers from you. My life is not very happy at the moment. In fact it's quite miserable. I am bullied a lot and have very few friends. I am hoping things will get better but am wondering if the powers you had could help me. Perhaps this is selfish of me, but I need help. So I wonder if you could send me a sign somehow. Maybe a lightning strike or something. Whatever you think best. I hope to make you proud of me one day. I am so sad I never really knew you. I promise I will come to visit you more often, especially if you come through with the special powers... I mean, regardless of the powers.'

With that she left, although she did glance back at the grave once for reasons she did not understand.

An hour later, Lily was on Facebook. She found that an American teenager called Brandi wanted to be her friend. She had short red hair, liked dogs and painting, and lived in Coral Gables, Florida. Lily was wary after her recent Travis experience and the crazy who kept calling her 'maggot', but this girl, from her Facebook profile and photographs at least, appeared genuine. They had no mutual friends, but Lily decided to accept the friend request. After Travis, Brandi would be a fresh face in her online life, new and exciting and fourteen years old.

That evening she found online:

Retingham Newsbeat

A thirteen-year-old girl successfully fought off two thugs who attacked her last night at approximately 8pm. Alison MacKnokaird was waiting for a lift outside the Retingham Gym Centre after boxing training when she was set upon by two youths. Trained also in kung fu and Thai kickboxing, Alison was able to fight off the pair, sustaining only mild bruising herself. Alison, or Mack as she prefers to be known, approached *Retingham Newsbeat* accompanied by her mother to highlight the problem of violence young teenagers face in the town. An eyewitness said, 'It was like watching Bruce Lee!' Police later confirmed the arrest of two seventeen-year-old males. The *Retingham Post* has long campaigned about the Gym Centre carpark, which is notorious for drug dealing and petty crime.

Read the full story in this week's *Retingham Post* out on Thursday.

Lily sent Mack a Facebook message about it: 'You didn't tell me.'

'Why would I?'

'I guess I have to bow down to you now.'

'No just accept my friend request, twat. Do you want to be my friend or not?'

Feeling ashamed, Lily did now accept the request. 'I meant to. I'm sorry,' she wrote. 'I consider myself told off.'

'You forgot because you don't care. Fuck you not caring.'

She sent Mack her phone number, but there was no response. In Lily's head a room full of editors were shaking their heads at her error. She said to her mirror reflection: 'You messed up again, Upshire. Big time. Complacency or bloody-mindedness? How could you? You really are a twat. You said you'd be there for her, and where have you been?'

15

Frustrated at her latest lapse, Lily sent Mack a bunch of flowers. They were expensive, and she had to borrow against her pocket money. In her mind she was like the stupid smoothie company: forever hitting the wrong note, clumsy in relations with others who wanted to be friends but became exasperated.

Mack responded graciously, apologising for being harsh and oversensitive. She added, 'I'll get used to you. I do love you, Lily, even though you drive me a bit mad. But I was mean.'

Lily wrote back, 'And I love you, even though I mess everything up.'

Nancy called round one morning. Grandma noticed that her neighbour looked rather preoccupied as she came in. She was concerned, fearing she was about to be given an ultimatum about the fence.

She made tea. Nancy had brought some cakes apparently as some sort of peace offering, and Grandma put them on a plate. She tried one, but they were not to her taste, so she took another little bite and then made the excuse that she had just eaten.

The purpose of Nancy's visit, however, was to warn Grandma that 'people' had been making enquiries about Lily.

'What people? What sort of enquiries?' said Grandma.

'Oh, about who she is. You see, the company is worried. Lily hasn't accepted their offers, and they don't like it. It worries them. Lily isn't following the script.'

'I'll admit she's a one-off,' said Grandma. 'That's why we love her so much.'

'She really is one of a kind,' Nancy said.

'So how do you know they're making enquiries? Who've they approached? Have they asked you?'

'No. But they approached Mrs Laveson at the end of the street. And a couple of others, so she said. She knows everyone in the town. Everyone worth knowing anyway. You know her, don't you?'

'Not really. I met her once. All she talked about was her ailments.'

'Anyway, she said they've been asking round the shops. It's a young man and woman. They don't think Lily's for real. They think she's some sort of fraud.'

'What a cheek!' said Grandma.

'I know. As if anyone we know could be such a thing!'

Grandma detected no irony in Nancy's tone. She was tempted to ask after Fred at that moment but thought better of it. Instead, she asked about the latest with Mrs Laveson's ailments, but that was the dullest of subjects so she switched as soon as expediency allowed. 'And how's Fred?' she asked.

'Between you and me...' said Nancy in a hushed voice which was absurd because the chances of anyone overhearing were nil, 'Between you and me, I think he's worse. The doctor came out to see him and prescribed some pills. He says he feels the same and spends all day in bed.'

'Why do you think he's worse if he feels the same?'

'It's his mind, you see. He's lost his enthusiasm for everything.'

'Depression?'

'Depression, anxiety, insomnia. Schizophrenia, I shouldn't wonder.'

'Really?'

'Oh yes. He's not the same man at all. His personality's changed completely. All since this smoothie business. They'll have a lot to answer for, I can assure you of that.'

'Has he had any more contact with his friend about it?'

'The person he knows? I wouldn't call him a friend. Well, you see, poor Fred can't muster the strength to do the paperwork. I said I'd do it for him, but he said, "I'd have to talk you through it, so I might as well do it myself," which is true. Even talking on the phone is too much for him now.'

Grandma was bemused. What Nancy said about him from one time to the next made little sense. 'Poor Fred. Does he eat?'

'He might as well be fasting. That's how little he eats. I'm sure if he put his clothes on, they'd fall straight off him again. Your average anorexic eats more than him. Anyway, my dear, I should be going. I just wanted to warn you.'

A couple of nights later, Lily put up a post on Facebook saying 'Such a lousy day!' Amongst the responses was one from her new friend Brandi: 'Why so bad?'

Lily described a fairly typical day made worse by Miss Cotton taking her to task over her homework. There were multiple messages back and forth. Brandi said she had reached out to kids her age in other countries because she was bullied at school and self-harmed: 'So they bully you much, Lily?'

'Yes.'

'Is it bad?'

'Yes.'

'What do they do?'

Lily hesitated but then replied, 'Call me names and stuff, hit me, write things about me, do anything to make me miserable.'

'Just like me. I get very depressed. I cut myself.'

'On your arms?'

'Yes. And legs. It's hard to love yourself when people tell you how terrible you are.'

'So true.'

'It's my secret. What's yours?'

Lily paused. 'I haven't any.'

'You must have. Do you have friends?'

'One or two.'

'I prefer girls, do you?'

'No, but you're nice.'

'I wish you were here with me.'

Lily wrote 'Me too' but then deleted it. She left the conversation there.

16

One afternoon, Lily arrived home from school to find there was a new member of the family. Asleep on a blanket in a basket was a small black dog. It was a whippet just like the one she'd seen with Sally. Lily was overjoyed. 'Oh, thank you!' she said in tears, running to Grandma to hug her. 'I'm... I don't know what to say!'

'It was Sally's suggestion. I asked her for ideas. She didn't know at first, but then she thought of the dog.'

'I didn't expect it. I know I don't deserve it. Why have you done this for me?'

'It's partly a belated birthday present but also a plea to you to work at your studies, to show what you can do. I know you're not happy at school. I don't expect you to be, but you're capable, and I expect you to show that. I want you to focus. The world is full of chaos, full of people who will do you down. I want you to rise above it, not for my sake, not to make me happy, but for yourself.'

Lily smiled, for a moment wondering what programme Grandma had seen on TV to inspire this speech. 'I get the message. I promise to try.'

Grandma then said, 'I've worked out a plan for you. I've spent a lot of time thinking about this so please hear me out. I worry for your personal safety, so first of all you are not to walk to or from school under any circumstances. I will drive you or make arrangements for you when I can't.'

'OK.'

'Second, you are to take up some form of martial art. This is purely for self-defence. If you ever use it in any other way, I will cease funding it.'

'OK. Wow!' She imagined herself doing kung fu moves outside the school gates and the twins fleeing from her.

'You keep saying you want me to withdraw you from school. That is not practical at the moment. However, I am going to explore the possibility of at some point hiring a tutor for maths and science, your very worst subjects. It is up to you to show that you can work well with a tutor. If you don't, there is no point me withdrawing you. I refuse to withdraw you just because you are bullied. Bullies are a factor in every aspect of life, not just at school. Better that you learn to live with it now and develop some resilience. The martial art will help you gain confidence in this regard. One other thing: your tutor for maths, if this proves a success, may later teach you business studies. I can't stress highly enough how important it is that you commit to study now if you are to achieve your dreams, whatever they may be. Do I make myself clear?'

'Yes.'

'So what do you make of what I've said?'

'It sounds brilliant. Can I ask, who will the tutor be?'

'A Mr Pitcairn. He has a daughter a little older than you. He comes highly recommended by people I trust, but of course he is much in demand.'

'And when?'

'Unfortunately, he's fully booked up just now, and it may be quite a while, but it'll be as soon as I can arrange it and, so we're clear, it will continue through holidays whenever he's free. You will work during the holidays. If you want to run your own business one day, I assure you you won't be taking much holiday then.'

They decided to call the dog Molly. Lily played with her while thinking about what Grandma had said. She stayed downstairs, not bothering with her rituals and not needing to escape onto the internet. Only when Molly was asleep again in the cage Grandma had borrowed for her 'settling in period', did Lily go upstairs to check her laptop.

There was nothing new from Brandi. Instead, there was a message from Travis: 'Lily my darling I've missed you so much, but we can continue now.'

She did not reply.

17

Days later, Lily came home from school, courtesy of a lift from a classmate's mum, with her head heavy and feeling depressed at persistent taunts about being fat despite losing weight. Her reaction to such bullying was to retreat into her imagination, and in her bedroom she would explore Instagram and You-Tube where her heroes lived. She couldn't wait to play with Molly and then go upstairs to find out what the influencers she followed were up to and maybe find and follow more. The world of influencers was a wide ocean, and she was keen to explore it.

But this time when she arrived home she found a second car on the drive, a BMW. Indoors, Grandma was in the lounge talking to a young man—medium height, all smiles, smartly dressed in a light grey suit. Grandma looked happy.

'Ah Lily, this gentleman is from the smoothie company. He has brought something special for you. A very generous offer.'

'I see,' said Lily coolly.

The stranger presented his card. He was all syrup.

'You're not from America then,' Lily observed.

'Sorry to disappoint you,' he said. 'But I can pretend if you want.' He made a rather weak attempt at an American accent which did not endear him to her. He then went through a script, assuring her once more what a 'valued customer' she was and insisting the company held 'the customer's best interests' above everything, and took 'suggestions where we can perform even better' with great seriousness, and was grateful to Lily for drawing the company's attention to the situation, and...'

'Do you mean the pea in the smoothie?' Lily interrupted—rather rudely, Grandma thought.

'Yes.' He looked chastened.

'So have you come to say sorry on the company's behalf?'

'I've come to give you something special, like your grandma said, so you can have your favourite products free of charge for a very long time.'

'But no apology then?'

'Hear the gentleman out, Lily,' Grandma said as sternly as she could.

Lily said nothing further and allowed the visitor to continue without interruption. He proceeded with his rather elaborate patter, making Lily wonder if this was what was meant by a 'dog and pony show', being something she'd seen mentioned on a Facebook post. His little speech ended with the statement that 'purely as a goodwill gesture' the company was giving Lily vouchers to the value of a hundred pounds.

'I would like to have what I politely asked for,' said Lily.

'I just need your grandmother to sign this document,' said the man, bringing out a thick wad of papers.

'Shall I sign it, Lily? Think of all the stuff you can have.'

'A hundred pounds worth. I heard the man. But I wanted—and still want—the company to say sorry.'

'Why be churlish?' said Grandma. 'Why be difficult? This man's come all the way from—'

'Sheffield,' said Lily. 'All of twenty miles.'

There was an embarrassing silence, at the end of which the visitor said, 'I can see this is a very difficult decision for you both but—'

'Not for me,' said Lily, earning a scowl from her grandmother for interrupting again.

He coughed. 'So I tell you what I will say: not a hundred but one hundred and fifty pounds worth of vouchers—for any of the company's products.' Before Lily could say anything, he stood up and said, 'Say nothing now. Have a think about it. Have a chat amongst yourselves. I will come back in—' he looked at his watch '—say an hour and a half? You can tell me then what you've decided. Of course, if you don't take the offer, which I think you will find very generous...'

'Indeed,' said Grandma, prompting a scowl from Lily. The visitor did not complete his sentence and left as quickly as possible—although not as quickly as he'd liked as Molly had stolen his cap, which was now on the back lawn accompanied by a hairbrush and a bag of bread rolls.

The gentleman duly returned ninety minutes later, by which time Lily had set Grandma straight: she did not want vouchers but an apology. When the visitor came in, Lily remained in her room and Grandma told him what Lily had said. She observed the man's expression change from sickly sweet to plain sickly.

Although Lily could not hear the conversation downstairs clearly, the fact it was going on at all meant she could not concentrate, so she ran downstairs and, barely able to muster a terse 'Hello again', pulled out the Olivetti from the cupboard under the stairs. While the others engaged in embarrassed, time-filling chat, she quickly wrote a two-line letter thanking him, as the company's representative, for the offer but repeating her request for an apology. She thrust it into the man's hand: 'Here. Just write

"Sincerely sorry" across this in big letters and I'll accept it. All done.'

The man visibly wilted and, with an irony apparently lost on himself, apologised that he did not have authority to do this and, weary with it all, made a weak offer to 'see what I can do to get the company to stump up another fifty,' which would make it two hundred pounds worth of vouchers. But Grandma, feeling she should support Lily even though she disagreed with her, gave this idea short shrift. He put the letter in his briefcase, said he 'fully understood' the position, even though he did not at all, and left.

Grandma could not help feeling proud of Lily in what she saw as her wilful eccentricity. 'You're a tough customer and no mistake,' she said. 'Good for you, my dear.'

Next day, while Lily was at school Grandma went to see Nancy. She wanted to let her know she saw no chance whatever of Lily joining in the claim, in which case she would not either.

'I'm not surprised,' said Nancy. 'She's a firebrand, that one. And she made herself clear about the fence.'

'I think she's right,' said Grandma. 'About the fence, that is.'

'But it doesn't matter. By the way, please don't say—' she mouthed the word 'smoothie' '—only it sets him off.'

'Smoothie?' said Grandma, puzzled, and the next thing she heard was a loud groan from upstairs. 'Oh sorry,' she said, no longer puzzled.

'No, the reason I say it doesn't matter is because there's so many other people who've had problems with you-know-what.'

'What sort of problems?' said Grandma.

'Illnesses of various kinds.'

'So how is poor Fred?'

'I'd like to say he's better. He never gets out of bed now except to go to the bathroom. Poor man, I tried aversion therapy. I bought some new sm— you-know-what and took two bottles to him—different ones—and said, "Which one would you like?" She now assumed the pained air of someone in high office uncomfortable at what their role requires them to say next: 'He couldn't look at them, he shook his head and hid under the covers. I then emptied the contents of the bottles into two large glasses and tried to coax him out.'

'So even the sight of the bottles sets him off? Oh dear, what a state he must be in! So what happened next?'

'After about five minutes he came out of hiding with his eyes shut. I tried to get him to open them, but he couldn't, and then...' she looked away '...he drank the whole lot straight down.'

'What, both glasses?'

'One after the other. Every last drop. He was thirsty as anything, poor mite. He just couldn't bear to look at them, that was the thing.'

'How very odd! So who else has been ill?'

'Mrs Brazenose at number 17. Then there's Mr Peck on Kings Road. There's already some kind of online campaign group. I expect others to join. A claims company lined up. All they were waiting for was Lily to be its poster girl.'

Grandma raised an eyebrow. 'Well, as I say, that'll be an impossibly long wait.'

18

Before going to bed one night, Lily wrote to her new online friend Brandi, merely saying: 'How you?'

Brandi wrote back, 'Better now I hear from you. Mom been on my case. You?'

Lily told her about the dog, and Brandi was pleased for her and envious but seemed only interested in writing about bullying: 'Do they really get to you?'

'I try not to let it, but yes. I feel worthless. I believe what they say & want to die.'

'Me too. But you don't. And I don't. We fight on to spite them.'

'Yeah.'

Next morning, Lily found a message from Brandi sent overnight: 'In a bad way. Big fight with parents, left me really down. Feel no one cares, no one understands, except maybe you. I'm OK. I won't do anything silly. I'm quite strong in my way. I'll be back.'

Lily replied: 'Remember I'm always there for you. Let's Skype soon.'

Brandi did not respond.

Lily ran into Mack at school. She felt Mack had been avoiding her, as though she'd concluded the pair would never have a worthwhile relationship despite the fact both wanted it. Perhaps she could not accommodate the 'work' she thought Lily presented.

When they spoke, Lily again apologised about ignoring the friend request Mack had sent. 'Don't you use Facebook much?' was Mack's response.

'Yeah I do, but I have this online friend called Brandi who writes to me all the time. She writes about bullying and stuff so I try to help her and I guess she helps me.'

'Is she cute?'

'She's nice. That's all.'

When they parted Lily felt bad as though she were letting her down, and she suddenly had an idea. She called out, 'Hey Mack, I got this cute little dog for my birthday. Would you like to see her? You could come for tea tomorrow.'

'Sure. That would be cool.'

Later she wrote to Brandi: 'You OK?'

'Very depressed.'

'Why?'

'Everyone on my case. Parents, teachers.'

'I'm sorry.'

'Your parents mean too?'

'I live with grandmother.'

'Not mother?'

'No.'

'Why?'

'She died.'

'Oh I'm sorry. Dad?'

'No.'

'Must be tough. Do you cut yourself?'

'No.'

'I find it helps.'

'I do other things.'

'What things?'

'Ice cube in palm. Stick things in skin without drawing blood. Pain but no marks.'

'So haters don't know.'

'Right.'

'Do you hate your teachers?'

'Most of them, yes.'

'What school you go to?'

'Retingham High.'

An hour later, Brandi wrote: 'You OK?'

'Yeah. You?'

'Very depressed—self-image.'

'Sorry to hear that.'

'My sister says I'm fat.'

'I'm sure you not.'

'You don't know. I send pic just for you so you see.'

'No.'

'Why not? Make me feel better.'

'OK.'

'So you want me to send?'

'OK if you like.' She didn't want a picture, except to make Brandi feel better.

The picture came through, but Lily did not look at it.

'You get it? You like?'

'Yes. Beautiful.' Still she did not look at it.

'Now you send pic just for me.'

'I can't.'

'You must. Or how can I trust you? You don't get pic if you don't send one—that's how it works. You have camera. You said: Let's do Skype!'

Lily wondered how to respond.

'You must send me pic like I sent you.'

'No. Can we talk on Skype?'

'I got too much going on for that. I send you new pic if you like.'

'No.'

Lily decided Brandi could be what was known as a catfish.

A little later:

Brandi: 'Sorry my mom has seen your messages. I showed her. She thinks you not who you say. She said if you real you would send pic. She will write to your school. She don't think you are girl in UK. She thinks you are man in Florida who preys on kids. Mom will report you to police.'

'No I not fake.'

'I know you not. I know you real, but she don't believe it, so send pic, and then I can prove it to her.'

Lily did not reply.

19

Mack came round next day after school. The girls played in the garden with Molly. It was fun. It was overdue. Both of them had been disappointed their friendship had not taken off. Lily blamed herself over it.

Grandma fussed over Mack but without being embarrassing. For tea they had Welsh rarebit and a hummingbird cake (a spiced banana-pineapple creation) Grandma had made specially.

When they were in Lily's room Mack said, 'Your grandma's lovely.' Lily encouraged her to open up about her family situation, but Mack wanted to talk about Brandi. She called her 'your girlfriend'.

'She's not my girlfriend,' said Lily.

'Isn't she?' Lily noted the jealousy in Mack's tone.

'She was never. And it's all over now anyway.'

'Why?'

'Because she's probably a catfish, if you know—'

'Of course I know. I think you should stick to online friends.'

'Why?'

'Because it's easier than real friends. You can be who you like online. And I wonder if you're capable of real friendships.'

This angered her host. 'That's not a nice thing to say,' said Lily. She sighed, sensing another row approaching.

'You don't get it, do you?' said Mack.

'What do you mean?'

'We might as well be talking different languages. It breaks my heart. When I wrote in my message that I loved you I don't think you understood. I wish now I hadn't written it.'

'I know what love means.'

Mack was almost in tears. 'I don't believe you do. When I say I love you, I don't mean like an auntie or sister, I mean you are the world to me. OK I know I'm vulnerable right now, desperate for some kind of stability in my life, but foolishly I thought you were the person who could provide it. How on earth could I think that? I didn't realise you were so... immature. Well, you really caught me there, didn't you?'

'Please,' said Lily. 'I'm capable of more than you think. Please don't give up on me.'

Mack gave her a sad smile. 'Whatever you say, Lily. I get you. I'm sorry I'm so emotional. So do you want me to look at this Brandi? And then can we do some fun stuff?'

'That would be great.'

Although Mack was disappointed with Lily, she was not about to give up on her. She knew she'd travelled way too fast, but in this version of the fable there was no race to lose. All the hare had to do was wait if she could.

Lily first showed her Brandi's Facebook page. Then she offered to show her the latest messages, but her friend demurred. 'How do you even know her?'

'She showed up as a friend request.'

'Oh, one that you actually responded to? But how else do you know her?'

'Well, I know her now. I still want to think she's genuine.'

Lily felt nervous at what felt like an invasion of her privacy, albeit one she'd invited. All her secrets including her rituals exposed. She dug her nails hard into her palm. Mack for her part was alive to Lily's sensitivity and backed away from the laptop. Lily said, 'I know you'll say she's fake.'

'Only if I believe it.' Mack was irritated at the suggestion of bad faith. 'I don't want to upset you, but I guess I already have. Maybe I should go now. It was a nice idea, this. I thought you wanted us to get to know each other better. But, being as sensitive as you are, I'm always going to be upsetting you, aren't I?'

'Don't go,' said Lily, standing in the doorway. She felt helpless. She was tempted to wrap her arms around Mack and squeeze her tight, begging her forgiveness for everything. 'Please,' she said, 'I need to know if Brandi's fake. And you understand this stuff better than I do.'

Mack relented. She instinctively knew Brandi was suspect, based on what she'd learned of her brother's experience of scammers, but could not decide whether she was a complete fake or merely using someone else's picture but otherwise real.

Even a quick review raised serious doubts. She found the profile picture was that of someone in Estonia and determined the account was linked to various others, all ostensibly friends of each other but with almost no friends outside that circle. Mack pointed this out, explaining this was a telltale sign. She suspected all the others' profiles were fake.

'How do you know all this?' said Lily.

'My big brother is up on it. He taught me. He could even be Brandi.' Seeing Lily's shocked expression she said, 'Just kidding.'

'She wants me to send a pic.'

'Don't.'

'I haven't, but why not?'

Mack made a face. 'I wish I was as nice and innocent as you. So trusting. No, you absolutely must not send a pic. Believe me, you do not want your picture sent all over the internet.'

Lily then showed her all the correspondence.

'She's seriously bad news,' said Mack.

'Are you a hundred percent sure? What if it's someone genuinely wants my help...'

Mack sighed, tempted to reply 'Try someone real instead,' but merely said, 'Well, something odd's going on.'

'It could be Travis' wife,' said Lily.

'Who's that?'

Lily blushed and then told her about the saga with her online boyfriend and the so-called wife claiming he was a man in his fifties, even mentioning the Jesus bobble hat (at which Mack shook her head in disbelief). When the tale was told Mack said, 'Lily, you do get involved with some weird stuff!'

20

The following evening, Mack rang Lily and told her she'd discovered Brandi was a Facebook friend of someone linked to the Bizzell twins and the Runt, possibly a cousin. This was beyond Lily's worst fears. Mack had done a reverse phone search on the number she found on Facebook and discovered it was from a phone app that generated numbers with fake area codes and could have been activated from anywhere. Although Brandi's profile picture was from the page of a teenage girl in Estonia, that was also a false identity, and the true source of the pictures was a fake Instagram account of a model, probably established by an angry ex-boyfriend of hers. Lily scratched her head on hearing all this. Mack said the real person behind 'Brandi' was maybe seeking to obtain secrets and pictures from her that could be passed back to the Bizzells for their bullying campaign. She speculated that the twins themselves were probably experts in this kind of chicanery.

First Travis and now this. After ending the call she wanted to go out in the garden and scream her head off, but then she thought of something Brian once told her his dad, Ted, liked to say: 'If you get knocked down, feel sorry for yourself for a moment, and then get straight up and return stronger.' She missed Brian because of his calming influence, but as Grandma had said on the phone to Ted, what use was a friend who let you down as badly as he had?

She resolved not to contact Brandi again. She could not reveal what Mack had discovered about her. At some point the Bizzells would use what she'd told Brandi against her. She felt she could not simply do nothing, so she cursed Brandi with all her might in the hope that whatever befell the person behind the fake would stop them doing it to someone else. Even if something happened to Brandi, no-one, including Lily, would ever know whether it was the curse that was responsible.

21

The next thing Grandma knew was that the newspapers were sniffing round. Or more particularly, the local press. They were keen for any story because they had so few. They had caught something in the air. Something about contaminated drinks. It was like marijuana smoke from a neighbour's garden on a breezy day—one moment you smelt it, the next it was gone. But they had a young new reporter called Rayzor who wanted fame. He saw his job on the local paper as the first step along the way. He read the star columnists in the *Times* and *Guardian* and decided he would be one too. Then he would work for the *New Yorker* and write books that would win prizes and big-budget films would be made of them. But that was for the future, maybe next week. This week, he had to make his name on the local rag. He comforted himself with the thought that even *New Yorker* writers probably started with stories about stolen lawnmowers and sheds on fire. He saw the drinks story as worth exploring. It was only a story, but that was its strength. Stories had power even if they weren't true. He didn't know yet whether the drinks story was true, but that was irrelevant; it was a story with its own life.

The first task was to locate the shop. It could be any one of many. But most of the rumours were from one part of town, so that was where the shop must be. A big shop would make a dramatic show of denying it. It had to be a store that lacked the power of denial of a supermarket chain. A small shop. Having decided on one, he went to see the shopkeeper who said there could have been the odd recent complaint about smoothies, but he could provide no details and said with noteworthy pride that anyway he would have chased any such complainants off the premises with a baseball bat. Having settled on this shop, Rayzor had to find a street to be the focus of his investigation. He went walking. He made enquiries. He called on people like an annoying market researcher, seeking to learn anything he could on the subject. Eventually he found the right street, being the street where Lily, her grandmother, and the Peacemakers lived. Others had said they'd had problems with smoothies, but he wasn't convinced by them. With some people you only need to ask if they'd been ill, and they'd immediately buckle as though seriously afflicted.

Rayzor had heard about the Peacemakers and was interested to visit them, although on doing so he soon concluded they were not the real story. Initially the meeting went fine. Nancy invited the stranger in for tea and biscuits and made such a performance of having expected a journalist to call that Rayzor was inspired, captivated even. But then, like a garish, overacted film, it suddenly ceased to be compelling. Whilst he talked to Nancy, who struggled to convince him that she had herself suffered health problems from contaminated drinks, he could hear loud groans from upstairs. It sounded like the husband was dying, but she was more interested in talking to a journalist than attending to her spouse, which he found odd. Nancy even ventured that a single sip of a smoothie from 'the brand in question' could kill the average person 'stone dead', whilst her husband, being a man of great fortitude, was fighting the effects bravely. Rayzor asked to see this medical hero, but when he did he found that, despite an impressive display of tics, shakes, shudders, and enough gargoyle faces for a hundred cathedrals, Fred was nothing more than a malingerer. This conclusion took him half a minute, whereas even the most cautious of doctors had taken three. None had found anything wrong with him. Even the dubious doctor his friend at the claims company suggested could only advise complete rest, a prescription Fred had embraced with gratitude and, indeed, enthusiasm. Rayzor could see that all Fred suffered from was delusion. He wanted a story but not one so fantastical it would make him a laughing stock. He wouldn't get away with it at the *New Yorker* or *Rolling Stone,* so he wasn't going to try it with the Retingham rag.

When finally able to get back downstairs, thoroughly disappointed with Fred, he asked Nancy, 'Didn't all this start with a young girl. An eleven-or-twelve-year-old?'

'But you've seen my husband with your own eyes. He's the real story. A story of great heroism.'

'Yes, but where did it start?'

'I'm telling you, it really started with him. He was the first to be declared... to fall ill from it.' However, the more Nancy persisted the more even she began to realise that, outrageous as it might be, Mr Rayzor was not interested. 'I suggest you talk to the lady next door,' she said brusquely, pointing in the direction of Grandma's house. 'It's her granddaughter that caused the fuss. Why don't you talk to them? Then you can come back and learn more about my Fred, about his struggles, his battles won, and now this, his biggest and perhaps—I hate to contemplate it—his *last* battle of all.' In her youth Nancy had done amateur dramatics. It had been a short career, but she now managed to use what she'd once learned to its fullest effect, such that for a moment, although only that, Rayzor thought there might be something in it after all.

When the journalist called on Grandma he found her in a deflated mood. The latest school reports on Lily's progress had shown no improvement. It was the same story: Lily was a bright child who didn't apply herself, with the exception of English, although even there the teacher felt she was not realising her full potential. Grandma received few visits, even less now Nancy was resigned to her inability or unwillingness to persuade Lily to support what was now 'Fred's cause'. Grandma invited the stranger in. He declined a drink, made a fuss about the 'beautiful ornaments' in her lounge—in reality thinking them all cheap junk—and the 'wonderful garden'—a scrappy lawn with a few flowers, mainly worn-out roses, in the borders—and asked her to tell him the 'fascinating story' of her granddaughter's 'adventure' over the adulterated drink.

The stranger's interest raised her mood tremendously. She told the journalist everything she could think of, which was relatively little. Lily had bought a smoothie, found a pea in it, and thrown it away. She told him about the letters Lily had sent and the responses. Rayzor asked to see them. Lily kept copies of her correspondence with the company in a file in her room. Grandma went upstairs and Rayzor, uninvited, followed her. In Lily's disordered room there were several files on the desk called variously: *Yummy Things To Eat*, *Cute Animals in Danger*, *Hair Products*, *Animal Testing*, *Clothes,* but this was crossed through and replaced by *Meat Substitutes*, and finally *Smoothie Letters*. Grandma took the file, combed through the documents inside, and then handed it to Rayzor. He was tempted to ask if he could borrow it, but Grandma suspected this and gave him such a steep frown of disapproval he decided not to risk it. He read the documents, not especially carefully, and then asked, 'And how does

Lily feel about all this? I bet she's disappointed, isn't she?'

'Oh, but they've been quite generous really.'

'But have they? A big company—not merely American but global—and they can't say sorry to an eleven-year-old?'

'She's thirteen now. She didn't even taste it.'

'But that's not the real story is it?'

'They sent someone round. He offered her two hundred pounds' worth of vouchers for the company's products, and she said no. It was all a bit cynical, though. Now other people are saying they've had problems with drinks.'

'Sometimes sorry is the hardest thing. Take it from me, Mrs Upshire...'

'Deacon. My name is Deacon.'

'But Lily is...'

'Upshire, yes. I'm on her mother's side. The family's another story, but not for today, if you don't mind.'

'Of course, Mrs Deacon. Now is that a picture of Lily on the mantelpiece?'

'Yes. I have it on my phone. I can send it to you.'

'Oh, please do. Such a beautiful child.'

'She is, but she's filled out a bit. Too many smoothies and cakes.'

'Too many temptations these days,' he said.

'Indeed. All the ones we had in my day and a load more besides.' After that their conversation tailed off into niceties as Rayzor focused on trying to decide what headline he would use for the story. What would suit, say, the *Sunday Times*? When he left he made sure to walk in the opposite direction to the Peacemakers' house.

22

Lily received certain messages via Facebook from one of the so-called Friends group, asking her for the latest on the smoothie company. In response to her reply about the company rep visiting, she received a link to an anti-corporate activist, targeting, in particular, Global Universal Federated Finance, ultimate owner of the smoothie brand. The activist's name was Mervin Patch, an Australian relocated to Texas. He had a personal campaign against the company after breaking a tooth on a stone in a wholemeal loaf and receiving short shrift over his complaint twenty years ago. Lily learned this from Mr Patch's website, and it made her hope no resentments she felt would ever fester that long.

In Patch's latest blog entry he mocked CEO Frank Salesman's denial of flaws in the company's quality control. This had come to a head over failures with the company's new 'luxury gourmet' soup range which it had hyped so much. Mice and other creatures had been falling into the soup vats, something Patch found hilarious, especially given the company's play for the vegan market. He said the company had at least 543 current product recalls in everything from lamb chops with metal in, to exploding light-bulbs, to suppositories (he did not elaborate about them). He said the company's complex web of subsidiaries, affiliates, and joint ventures owning the various brands, meant the average shopper in, say, Boring, Oregon did not realise they were all owned by GUFF and if the company's investors knew of all the product recalls the share price would fall 'flat as a shit carter's hat'.

Patch had received leaked company correspondence in which Frank asked colleagues whether the company would be better off simply denying everything when it came to 'future Upshire-type situations' rather than 'fooling around with vouchers'. In response, Chip Stonecold from Consumer Relations said no-one believed denials anymore.

Patch agreed: 'If you could believe company denials over the years, movies would still use asbestos for snow like in *Wizard of Oz,* and you could put it on your Christmas tree. If you could believe them, you could smoke two hundred cigarettes a day and live to 105. You'd still be driving around in a Ford Model T while knocking back triple whiskies every ten minutes to calm your nerves. You'd have arsenic in your wallpaper and DDT on your greens, add sugar by the ladle, and pop opioids like breath mints. Spas would give you radium water for your health, and you'd believe no chemical or pharmaceutical ever caused harm to anyone, and you could put any waste products you liked into the air, ground or water, without causing harm to even the most sensitive species, except for pests which would all helpfully die.'

Frank had responded to Stonecold, 'If someone dares to make an allegation about our very highest quality products we should always strenuously deny it, but that's just for the lawyers. In our bones we believe in constantly and urgently improving—and we will continue to succeed in this, time and time again.'

Patch posed the question: 'So when is being positive merely a denial of reality?'

23

Lily received another letter from the company. It arrived by recorded delivery, and Grandma signed for it. Lily was apprehensive. She thought it meant trouble. She had upset the company and they'd sent the Angel of Death. She wondered if the envelope might contain poison. She'd had a rough day and almost felt the arrival of the Angel of Death might not be such a bad thing. She opened the envelope, read the letter, then read it again. She gave it to Grandma.

'Oh, my word!' Grandma exclaimed. 'They're inviting you to the States, Lily! This is wonderful.'

'Is it for real?'

Grandma thought for a moment. 'No, it can't be, can it?'

'You'd come with me, wouldn't you? It says two tickets.'

'Why would the company do this? I couldn't go anyway because I can't fly. But it's not about me. It's about you. You deserve it. We could ask someone else...'

'Like who?'

'Auntie Gwynne's always wanted to go.'

'That's not even funny. If you can't go, I don't want to go either.'

'Oh, but you should. What about Sally?'

'Yes, but Sally would want to go with her boyfriend. I don't want to visit the company. I just want to drink their smoothies—I'm still hoping Mr Bashett will stock them again—not see how they make them. It might make me sick. And there'd be all the corporate stuff to put up with. Can you imagine!?' It didn't help that she'd recently seen the Slurm factory episode of *Futurama* in which the characters discover the popular addictive drink they love so much comes out of a giant worm's anus. 'It seems an awful lot just to avoid saying sorry for the one with the pea in it,' she said.

'Even so, Lily, you'll be famous. It's just a shame it's too late for the paper.'

'Paper? I don't want to be in the stupid paper. How embarrassing would that be? No-one reads it, but people would still find out.'

'Don't you want to be famous, dear?' Grandma became concerned; she'd said nothing to her about the reporter calling round, not really thinking anything would come of it and believing if it did, it would be a lovely surprise for her.

'No, I just want their apology. Besides, look at the small print.' She handed the letter back.

'I can't read it,' said Grandma.

'The last date for reply is three days time. It doesn't sound very sincere, does it? And the trip has to be completed within four weeks of the date of the letter. And it doesn't cover transport to and from the airport or the hotel stay in Newark, New Jersey. They just want me to be flattered at being asked without actually being able to go.'

Nancy called round next day. She said, 'Any news from the paper?'

Grandma said, 'No. Should there be?'

'I heard the journalist's been ill. But the story should be in this week's.'

'How's Fred?'

'Barely well enough to read his will, so he says.'

'Why does he need to do that?'

'I don't know either. He's taken out some new life insurances, I know that. I suppose he felt he should in view of his physical condition.' Grandma privately wondered whether one of Fred's many aliases was due for an early demise. But faking the death of a fictitious person was of a different order to losing a Rolex watch off a boat in the Seychelles, even if you'd never been there. She became so taken with this idea that Nancy had to say 'Anything from the company?' twice before she received a response.

'Eh? Oh, yes, they've invited Lily to the States now.'

'How ridiculous! It just shows how desperate they are. Will she go?'

'She doesn't seem very interested.'

'She's such a one-off, that one. I'm sure most kids...'

'Lily couldn't go because of school anyway. The trip has to be completed within four weeks of the date of the letter. But maybe they could be persuaded to be flexible.'

Grandma then suggested that Sally be offered it instead. Nancy sniffed and, after pretending to deliberate, said, 'I'm afraid I wouldn't be able to accompany her. I hardly need to explain why: Fred needs my care.'

'We were wondering perhaps whether Sally's boyfriend could go with her.'

Nancy shook her head. 'Not appropriate at all,' she said.

'Lily would like it,' said Grandma.

'You're missing the point as usual, Grace. If the company can afford to take two people to the States, think how much they'd pay out in cash if they were pushed. Everything they do digs their hole deeper. And if anyone should go, it should be Fred, but he's too ill.' She then added hurriedly, 'Anyone apart from you or Lily of course. Anyway, more importantly, the claims company's putting some ads in the media. We've got together a big group already. It doesn't matter that Lily won't join because you could still join on her behalf. And on your own behalf. We're on the cusp of something big, believe me. That journalist should have come back to us. He's missed the big story. He could get the sack over it. But it's too big for the local paper. This will be a national story. An international story. I only hope poor Fred is alive to see it. But if he isn't, the rest of us will fight on in his memory.'

24

After Rayzor's article *Faceless Firm Breaks Child's Heart* appeared in the *Retingham Post*, Grandma's place was inundated by visitors. Most of them hadn't even read the article but had heard about it and brought their own stories of dodgy drinks from Bashetts and indeed elsewhere. Nancy popped round daily now. Although miffed at having been ignored by the journalist, with neither Fred (as brave invalid) nor her (as loving carer) even mentioned, Nancy could always tell which way the wind was blowing. She insisted that all they wanted was 'just compensation', and their actions in this regard would proceed more effectively outside of the public gaze.

Grandma was delighted with all the publicity, but Lily hated it. She knew what it meant: more bullying at school. Once again, she felt betrayed by her grandmother and spent as much time as possible in her room.

She wondered if she'd hear from the Angel of Death again, there having been a long period of silence. Sure enough, from Melinda in Boise, Idaho: 'Saw you were in the paper. My dad was upset.'

'I never asked to be in the paper. Leave me alone.'

'Your fault, though, maggot.'

'I'm not maggot, I'm Lily.'

'I know who you are only too well.'

'Are you the Angel of Death?'

'No. Angel of Life. Stay safe, maggot.'

Lily did not reply. She wanted to know who this strange person was but was afraid to find out.

Next morning, a Sunday, she was looking out of the window when she exclaimed, 'Look, Grandma, there's a chicken in the garden! I've always wanted a chicken. Can we keep it?'

Grandma explained that the chicken was being missed by someone and would have to be returned. 'It probably came in from number 12. I'll go and ask them.'

'It's escaped,' said Lily. 'It wants to be with us. It's because we're going vegetarian.'

While Lily went outside to keep an eye on the chicken, taking care not to cause it stress, Grandma went round to number 12. They had five chickens and said they hadn't lost any, but could take it in if its home wasn't found.

Grandma thanked them and then paid a visit to a couple of other neighbours who kept chickens. No joy there either.

Grandma told Lily it wasn't practical to keep it. She wanted to take it to the RSPCA and was worried it would be eaten by a fox or possibly attacked by Molly. Lily was insistent and Grandma acquiesced, meaning that she'd think about it. She decided to return to number 12 to ask them to take it until she'd bought a hutch. When she got back home she said, 'They'll come and collect it in a minute, and then I'm afraid it's staying there until the owner's found.' When Lily protested, Grandma, greatly relieved at not having to catch the creature herself, said, 'I had a chat with them. Lovely couple. They explained it's cruel to keep one on its own as they are social animals. Do you want to be happy at the chicken's expense? Of course you don't. You're a caring person.'

'I try to be.'

She put a picture of the chicken on Instagram with a note explaining what happened. This generated many followers for her. Vegan influencers particularly became interested. She was set on becoming vegan, but she and Grandma were still clearing up all the meat in the freezer and in cans, and she wasn't convinced Grandma would even go vegetarian. At some point, however, Lily was going to force the issue. She felt good about herself, but to her dismay what followed was a furore online about whether they should have given the chicken over or not. Some said they should have allowed it to wander wherever it wanted and let it be eaten by a fox because that was 'Nature's way'. The chicken did not belong to anyone, and they had no right to 'entrap' it. There was an argument about who was entitled to eat the chicken's eggs, or whether they should be given away, or the chickens encouraged to eat them. The arguing became quite nasty, bewildering her.

'All this stuff I have to worry about?' said Lily to herself in front of the mirror. 'See what you cause, Upshire? You can scarcely say anything, do anything, or think anything without causing problems.'

She phoned Mack in exasperation and told her about it. 'Tell me I'm a worthwhile person,' she said. 'All I think about is the trouble I create. I try to do a good thing and it ends up with people at each others' throats.'

'Stop feeling sorry for yourself. You didn't need to tell the world. Why couldn't you keep your "good thing" to yourself? No, instead you have to tell the world: "Look what a good girl I've been, doing this." You don't need all that. That's for losers.'

'So how've you been?' said Lily. 'Tell me. Take me out of myself. Let me into your world and out of mine.'

Mack held the phone closer. 'If we could only be together, one day no-one could touch us,' she said.

25

Rayzor's article became syndicated and went round the world. Over the years, the big bad company had tried to buy up press agencies and media outlets to support its own interests through propaganda, and the negotiations had been so hostile these entities exploited any opportunity to attack it. The company roughing up a young girl who just asked for an apology was platinum. Then there was social media: Twitter and Facebook blew up.

Grandma could not believe how much coverage there was. Reporters were forever coming round. And money was forthcoming. The tabloids were intrusive, however. They wanted to know about Lily's parents, a subject so sore it was taboo. In the articles they called her 'poor Lily' and 'the troubled teenager'. The photographers liked to catch her looking down with a sad expression.

For her part, after another change of heart, Nancy came round as often as possible in the hope that a reporter would want to interview her and be coaxed into visiting 'poor Fred'. She even bought new clothes for the photographers, but while her husband remained unvisited in bed but content as he dreamt up new accident claim scenarios, Nancy began to think that it was her and not her husband who was the real story, and she told the bemused journalists everything about her own many 'struggles' and 'triumphs', some of which might even have been true. Grandma was delighted with all the attention. Lily endured it all, saying as little as possible to anyone. She knew the bullies would love it.

She was right. 'Poor Lily!' they called after her. 'Poor Lily with no mother, are you still troubled?' When they saw her approach they'd shout, 'Here she comes: Little Miss Up-Herself.' They mocked her posts on Instagram about things she liked. They were relentless, the Runt's friend Mitch in particular: 'How's your heart, is it mended yet? Poor Lily, how do you cope? Poor broken-hearted Lily. At least it wasn't a boy. But it would never be a boy, would it? No boy wants an ugly, fat lump like you, eating crisps and drinking smoothies all the time, sitting on your arse writing letters. Such a loser. No-one cares about you. No-one wants to be your friend.'

She thought about Mack all the time. She rarely saw her at school to speak to, realising this was not aloofness on Mack's part but a desire to protect her, although Lily would rather have been more open about their friendship.

One day, there was a mix-up over her lift home, and she had to walk through town on her own. When she reached the bridge over the canal she encountered the twins. 'Here she is, the thick troubled swot,' said Green. They wrenched her school bag off her back and threw it in the canal. Then they ripped off her jacket, stamped on it, and threw that in the canal. Then they ran off laughing.

This incident led to Grandma complaining to the police and the school, again with no action taken by either. Lily added it to her own record of the bullying.

She retreated ever further into her own world on Instagram. She thought about creating a new persona: Cabreravegan. No matter that she had no connection with the name Cabrera, and she wasn't a vegan except in intention. The person she would be on Instagram was more real to her than the self she presented to the physical world.

When she told Mack about it her friend told her not to do it. 'Why?' said Lily.

'You're setting yourself up. You're not even a vegan.'

'So what? I will be.'

Mack, who with her mother had moved out to cheaper accommodation, had sent her a message on Facebook. She asked if Lily still wanted to spend time with her, or was she too busy becoming a celebrity? 'Of course I do,' Lily replied. 'Why do you even say that?'

'Be tough,' said Mack, 'but not so tough you decide you don't need me.'

'Don't worry,' Lily replied. Although determined to toughen up, she would never shut out Mack.

26

The press coverage led to the formal creation of the Friends of Lily Upshire group. It had been mooted before but was now official. The group soon had over a thousand members. These were all people who believed they had a claim against the big bad company. They approached Lily for her endorsement via Facebook, but she declined. She did not want publicity and did not intend to claim.

In their latest emailed newsletter the group said Frank Salesman was growing increasingly angry with the press. 'What lies are they telling today?' he'd complained in one of his tweets. Also included in the newsletter was a link to an interview he did for a business magazine's podcast. Lily listened in.

Frank ranted: 'The press is unbelievable. Such ingratitude. I can't believe these people are so mean.'

'You sound very bitter, Frank.'

'Bitter? It's just that I see how it works and how everything we do supports their prejudice—the evil, nasty, big company ripping everyone off. And American too, which to feeble minds is everything bad in itself, even though really we belong to the whole world. We're always only interested in doing the right thing. *Faceless Firm Breaks Child's Heart* indeed. That's beyond cruel. The biggest libel on good intentions since Little Red Riding Hood. Why it's the darnedest cruellest thing anyone's said since that douche canoe claimed our new cough mixture—disclaimers for ninety-three medical conditions—made him think his family were iguanas.'

'Why are you so upset, Frank?'

'Because this ridiculous non-story besmirching our great company's reputation has appeared all over the international press: the *Times of London... Times of India... Washington Post...* even our old friend the *Wall Street Journal*. Even the *Boulder Daily Camera* I bet, even the *Tombstone Epitaph* probably. Some drudge churning out copy for fun. Some chucklehead in shorts on the internet in a greasy spoon. But I bet it's one of our competitors behind all this.'

Lily thought: was Mr Salesman always like this? He must be exhausting. Odd language, though. It would be nice to include "chucklehead" in an essay for Emily Hass. Maybe not "douche canoe", whatever that meant.

'There's no evidence of it.'

'Oh yes. We've gone toe to toe with a few of them lately. We've played fair most of the time, certainly never sunk to this.'

'What about—'

'Hold your "What about?" right there. OK, when we find out who's behind it we'll respond in our preferred way—buy them out. For now we have to do the boring stuff and go hire some dozy libel lawyers—yawn—and they'll charge a chunk of change we could have used to buy up a struggling corner shop. So next time you see your favourite family store boarded up, just think we could have saved it but for this newspaper nonsense. Terribly disappointing. Human nature is not what it used to be, I guess.'

'Will you put a statement out?'

'No. We won't pay them the compliment of arguing. Malicious and erroneous, that's the press for you. They're Minnesota nice when they want a story, then they stab you in the neck. Last week, we saved a defunct shopping mall for a dollar—why don't they put that in their papers? I mean, as a true human interest story. One pea in a smoothie never hurt anyone, not even emotionally. Nor did our generous offer of vouchers to the Upshire girl. All so much about nothing. Whereas last week, we threw in a new school with our environmentally sensitive supermarket development. That's a *real* story. Give us the credit we're due is all I ask of those boozehounds.'

Lily thought: So I'm 'the Upshire girl'. Could I also be 'Minnesota nice'?

'If it comes to litigation, Frank, it could take years.'

'Don't get me started on that circus. Maybe instead we could get the local sheriff to put the squeeze on the paper, get them to say the story was a big misunderstanding and make us the good guys we are and tell them we're learning lessons from it all. That's what all these clown companies say when they land in the doo-doo: that it happened on the previous crew's watch, and they were all idiots and incompetents asleep at the switch, but now the brand new team is sparkling, and caring, and learning lessons from it, and they won't make the same mistakes, or indeed any mistakes.'

'So cynical, Frank.'

'You know it's exactly what they say even when the new team's the same dumbasses who messed up the first time.'

'By the way, there's no sheriff there to help you.'

'Sure there is. Retingham. Nottingham. Sheriff of Nottingham. I know history. OK, that was olden times before the stagecoach or electric shavers, but they still have sheriffs in America, and so must they.'

'Yes, but theirs don't do things like that.'

'So what do they spend their precious paid-for time doing?'

'Enforcing court judgements. That kind of thing.'

'Then we'll have to get that changed. Remember what we say: working with governments, working *in* governments. Just kidding—well, maybe.'

'But this is England, Frank, not some tinpot banana republic.'

'You forget, everyone in their Parliament will be shareholders of ours. Even the lefties have pensions. And we sponsor a bunch of ethical awards, so we've got that covered. So who does have the power in this stinking backwater? I mean, thriving community. Is there a mayor?'

'Yes, but they don't go round telling the press what to write.'

'I bet they do. OK, when we take the paper over we can say what we want in it. And if we have to, we'll go all the way up the food chain until we reach the big beast at the top, who'll be some weedy weakling compared to us, and we'll snaffle them up. Newspapers are a thing of the past anyway—we'll switch all that online. Environmentally friendly too, which is one of our core values. OK, can we wrap this up now? Time's a-wasting. Today we have to buy up a chain of Italian restaurants in the Philippines and a Belgian waffle maker. That'll give the share price a bounce, which is always handy.'

'Before you go, can we ask about the fire in your flagship steak restaurant?'

'All our restaurants are flagships. Besides, losing the odd restaurant makes people nostalgic. It works for the brand.'

'The story on the street is that it was arson.'

'Not on our street, it's not. The place was serving meals at the time, so what are you suggesting? That some old crosspatch in the kitchen left a pan of fries on too long accidentally on purpose? Not our sacred employee folks.'

Lily wrote down 'crosspatch' as a word to look up afterwards.

'The place was totalled. Diners fleeing down the street.'

'So they left without paying? How discourteous! OK, one flagship restaurant in New York's gone, so we have a new one in London. It's the way of all things: here today, over there tomorrow.'

Lily stopped listening at this point. She was famous everywhere, it seemed. Her name was mentioned by Frank Salesman in an interview. She didn't want it. It was embarrassing. But it was all about her name. That was more important than she was.

27

Lily talked to Mack on the phone about going to see Julia Bizzell. 'I need to know,' she said. 'I need to know if she's my mother.' Mack was not convinced it was a good idea. Lily said, 'It's alright for you, you haven't got this problem.'

'I just don't want you to get hurt.'

'I know.'

'Do you want me to come with you?'

'No, I don't want you involved. You have enough to cope with. And I don't want you targeted by them.'

She did not tell Grandma about it. Grandma would have tried to prevent it.

The Bizzells' place was surprisingly small. She'd expected a mansion, but it was more like a country cottage. Now part of a cul-de-sac, it was an old farmhouse with low oak beams from the time Retingham had been a rural village.

When Julia answered the door she was on the phone and she was smiling and gracious until she saw who it was had arrived. 'Oh! You've come to the wrong house,' she said, making as if to close the door.

'No,' said Lily.

'What do you want here, you little rat?'

'I wanted to ask you something.'

'I see. Well, since I don't want people seeing me arguing out here with you, you'd better come in.'

The lounge Lily was ushered into was unkempt, low-ceilinged, and dark with a rather random collection of sofas and armchairs with floral covers. The air was stale. Amongst the many pictures on the walls were recent-looking photographs of the three girls who caused her such torment. Seeing them made her wish she hadn't come.

Julia demanded, 'So what do you want exactly? I tell you, it's a good job the girls aren't here or they'd rip you to pieces.'

'I'm not scared of them.'

'Feisty little thing, aren't you?' Julia bared her teeth involuntarily. 'Being in the paper gone to your head? I'm going out in a minute, so get straight to the point, please.'

'OK.' Lily took a breath. 'I wanted to ask if you can tell me... I mean, if you know whether we, erm, could be related.' She paused in anticipation of a response, but Julia merely looked blank, waiting for her to continue. 'Well, some people think that... perhaps...'

'Yes?' Julia rolled her eyes.

'That you, and not Jane, well... are my real mother.'

'You what!?'

'Erm...' Lily was flustered. 'There are rumours because I look like you did at my age. So people say. Erm, of course they're... maybe wrong.'

'Is that so!?' Julia leaned forward from her chair and stared hard into Lily's face. Lily, composed again, did not flinch or look away. To her, up close Julia no longer resembled the confident school governor everyone admired, but rather an anguished woman in need of sleep and possibly on the verge of a breakdown. 'Listen to me,' Julia said sternly. 'If I'd been your mother, I'd have strangled you at birth, and since you're still around, you can safely assume I'm not. So now you know.' She backed away, took a cigarette from the packet on the coffee table beside her, lit it, and took a deep draw. She might have escorted Lily to the front door at this point, but she was annoyed and wanted Lily to know it and feel it: 'You've got some neck coming round here to ask me that. It's about the biggest insult you could give me, other than saying I murdered someone.'

Lily was unfazed. She looked past her reluctant host at a ceramic pinto horse, white and chestnut, on the mantel, focusing on it to give her strength. She said defiantly, 'You obviously hate me as much as your daughters do. Why? What harm have I ever done you?'

'Just by being alive, if you must know.'

'I must.'

Julia was unnerved by Lily's assertiveness. She'd anticipated a nervous, brittle creature she could punish by frightening her. She blurted, 'Your evil mother had you after seducing my dad.'

Lily was too amazed to react. Finally, she said in a conciliatory manner, 'So we're half-sisters.'

Julia was infuriated, not only at Lily's words but her tone: 'Don't you ever say that again. Never use "half-sister" and my name in the same sentence. Your mum seduced men of worth, and one of those she got her claws into was my dear dad. He was the manager at the bank she used... And you're the little brat that resulted.' Julia became tearful and Lily found herself almost feeling sorry for her. 'It broke up my parents' marriage. He ended up taking an overdose.' Julia paused to take another draw on her cigarette and then stubbed it out. 'And you're the reason. That's why I hate you—because I blame you. You should have been aborted, and I told your mother so. I felt the reason she didn't do it was to spite me and my mother. Every time I see you I am reminded of it. How do you think that feels?'

Lily swallowed. 'Pretty bad.'

'Pretty bad, she says. "Pretty bad" doesn't cover it. I've tried not to despise you, but it hasn't worked.' Julia looked away momentarily. 'Still, the way you're going, you'll probably be dead before you're twenty.'

'Do you have no feelings for me at all?'

'None. I won't rest easy until I never have to see your face again. My hope is that you just move away.'

'What was your maiden name?'

'Oh no you don't.' Julia shook her head. 'You can look for it yourself if you must. He was my dad, not yours. I know you'll be looking him up on the internet, trying to find out about him like the little sneak you are. And don't you dare tell the press!'

Lily was hurt. Julia noticed this and was glad, but Lily was not done: 'Your mum was not more important than mine. You say my mum seduced your dad, but what was he doing, allowing himself to be seduced? Your parents' relationship can't have been so great for it to happen.' She then stood up, glanced once more at the pinto horse as if to thank it, and turned to leave without looking at Julia, who said nothing and remained seated. Lily saw herself out, aware that Julia was crying. So be it, she thought. She hadn't called round to row with her. But on the walk home she thought perhaps she'd done wrong in going to see her. But at least she now had the clarity she'd sought. And yet what made no sense was that Julia's children did not know, because if they did, surely they would not taunt her about who her father was.

She talked with Mack about it that evening on the phone, careful to ensure Grandma couldn't hear her. Mack said, 'Why can't she be at peace with it after all this time?'

'I tell you one thing,' said Lily, 'I'll never call her nice or gorgeous again. That's all an act.'

Next day, she heard one of the twins, Green, begin calling her names in the playground. Lily ignored her. Determined to get a reaction, Green pushed her. Lily finally snapped and swung a huge haymaker with all her might into the girl's face. It hit her hard on the nose and it began bleeding. Lily ran off and went straight to the head and told her. Grandma was phoned to request Lily be collected. At home Lily wrote it all up. She later heard that Green's nose was broken. Lily was suspended once more.

A couple of days later, the news on Facebook was that Green had almost been killed when a car she was in blew a tyre at speed and went out of control. Mack phoned Lily to ask if she'd put a curse on anyone. Lily said she hadn't, but if she did in future she'd obviously have to try harder.

After the call she looked in her mirror and said, 'Upshire, if you don't do something you really will end up selling drugs or your body.' Inspired by Mack, she thought about taking up boxing to improve her confidence, but decided she wasn't yet ready for it.

She stopped drinking supermarket smoothies and eating chocolate for three weeks—and then started again.

28

One Saturday, Mack came round and the girls took Molly out for a walk in the summer sunshine. They sat on a bench in the park. They spent a fun time together, with a swearing contest and talking about puberty, and periods, and sex, and flashers, and makeup and 'Do you prefer my hair like this? Or up...like this?', and teachers they liked and disliked, and (a favourite of Mack's) ridiculous accidents, and general nonsense. Lily's favourite topic was the many boys she could never want to go out with, and why. She said, 'I like boys but the trouble with them is, well—'

'They're just boys?' Mack said.

'Yes.'

Mack learned from her brother stuff about sex and crazy stories of all sorts, and she liked to relay these to Lily who, being naive, was often shocked, which was part of the pleasure in telling her. Mack said, 'Sometimes I wish I really was your sister. Then I could warn you about the evils of the world. I would protect you. In school there's a couple of older girls, lesbians, who go around together, and they've helped me. Now I help out other girls.'

'They've helped me too,' said Lily.

A favourite topic of both of them was unusual names. Lily said, 'With all this publicity I've wondered about changing my name. Ever thought of changing yours, MacKnockers?'

'MacKno*kaird*. No, I'm happy with it. In the same clan it could have been MacFuktur. Or even Fuktour or Fuckater.'

'They would be cool. I wouldn't mind Fuckater.'

'Of course you wouldn't.'

'Mine's pretty lame. When you say "Upshire" loud, people think they're going to get covered in wet snot. They jump out of the way.'

'Lily's alright, though. You know, there are people in the States with names like Walkingstick. Imagine if you were a model called Lily Walkingstick.'

'That would be great. I like Walkingstick. It does suggest thinness.'

'Better than Paloma Pisswhisker.'

'Or Flossie Fartbuckle.'

'Pitbull Parmenter, there's a name.'

'Not for a girl, though.'

They sauntered through the park and Mack would offer her hand and Lily would take it but only for a moment, and then they would touch fingertips. Mack was so quick, if she saw a small plane in the sky, it could prompt her into raising something random she'd read about, say, Lawnchair Larry, who 'really did fly' at 15,000 feet on only a patio chair with helium balloons, and in the next minute she'd be softly stroking Lily's blonde hair while dreamily quoting phrases from Petrarch in both English and Italian. Lily felt lightheaded and was sure she'd never been so happy, so much so she didn't notice Molly was rolling on her back on the ground. 'Oh no!' Mack exclaimed. 'Fox poo! That's the worst!' The spell had been broken. Molly was in disgrace. 'It's alright,' said Mack. 'We can bathe her. Bathing a dog is fun. They freak out afterwards when you put the towel on them.'

'Molly freaks out anyway. Grandma says it's a whippet thing. They laze about all day, and then once in a while they go bonkers—tearing up and down stairs, racing from one end of the house to the other and to the end of the garden. Here we are, looking at all this beauty, while she, who's so adorable, just wants to find the most disgusting thing she can and roll in it.'

They walked home briskly and immediately took Molly upstairs to the bathroom.

After the entertainment of washing and drying the dog, at Lily's suggestion the pair moved her bed aside and they play wrestled on the floor. Mack was stronger but also ticklish, so Lily cheated and claimed victory, while Mack sensing her friend's determination let her win.

This afternoon, with no trace of the earlier discord between them, was typical of many they would spend together in the months to follow.

29

Lily continued to receive strange messages from America calling her maggot but now without hostility. One day, she received a message from someone in Elizabeth, New Jersey: 'I take it all back—you're not the bully I thought. I got you wrong. I apologize.'

Lily didn't know whether to respond. She told Mack about it on the phone. Mack said, 'Oh no. Not another of your weird correspondents! How do you get yourself in such a mess?'

'I just attract online weirdos, I guess. Maybe because I'm one myself. I want to write to them to accept their apology.'

'You don't even know what it's for. Or who it is. It could be a trap. A scam. They want you to respond, so don't.'

'Maybe you could help me find out who it is at least, couldn't you? I think it's the same person who always calls me Maggot.'

'Maggot? Maybe I should call you that.' She sighed. 'OK, I'll come over.'

Mack's mother brought her. Grandma made hot buttered crumpets for the girls. Mack was happy. She loved doing this kind of 'online rescue' work for Lily.

Mack's analysis showed that behind the various fake Facebook profiles was a sixteen-year-old called Gloria living in California. 'Is there a surname?' asked Lily.

'Yes, Salesman.'

'Gloria Salesman? Oh my God!'

'What's up?'

'The boss of the smoothie company's called Salesman. This person was always saying I bullied her dad. How weird. How could I bully her dad?'

After accompanying Grandma to take Mack home, Lily wondered about contacting Gloria. What harm would accepting the apology do? If you asked for one like she'd done with the company, should you not accept it when you received one?

She wrote back, 'I accept your apology.' Nothing further was necessary.

Next day, there was a reply: 'Thank you. I feel I should explain myself.'

Lily replied, 'I would be interested, but only if you want to.'

Gloria wrote back: 'I can't tell you how stupid I feel writing this. Stupid and ashamed. I will attempt to explain. When I was very young, an older girl who looked exactly like you shouted at me in the street, "Go back to Mexico, you dirty spic!" It was the first of many such situations, but it stayed with me because of the downright viciousness of the girl. When my father, Frank Salesman, started receiving correspondence you'd sent, I looked you up, and there I saw what looked like the face of the girl who was so nasty to me, and immediately I hated you. It was irrational and wrong, and I am so sorry for the pain I caused you. I must stress my father knew nothing of this. My mother suffers from depression, but maybe it is my own mental health I should worry about!

There is no reason you should want anything to do with me, but if you do, I would love to hear from you. I realize this is quite forward on my part. However, having got to know you a little I have come to admire you.

Gloria'

30

Lily was increasingly interested in the broadcasts by the Friends group. She saw a film made of Frank Salesman talking to some protesters who'd gathered outside the head office building in Irvine, California.

As he emerged into the sunlight Frank, a tall, lean man in dark glasses, said cheerfully, 'This feels a bit like being the President in the White House Rose Garden.' In mockery the filmmaker played a short extract from *The Star Spangled Banner*. Then there was a recording from a microphone on an activist who'd inveigled himself amongst company technical staff just to pick up the CEO's impromptu comments. Frank obliged: 'Look at them all: the tree huggers, the birdbrains, the dirt-slingers, the dreamy-eyed back-to-landers, the mountain men, the schlumpy misfits. All of the sanctimonious, holier-than-thou whackadoo busybodies.' Then he muttered, 'If I'd known they were coming, I'd have baked a cake. Except if I did that, some of them'd complain I was wasting power and resources, and adding to the obesity crisis, and throw in some cultural issues if they could immediately think of 'em, which is impossible because most of 'em are slow as molasses.'

Lily was fascinated—some words she was unfamiliar with, but she got the gist.

[The narrator, Mervin Patch, then said, 'When Frank and the other company officers were all gathered outside, security staff frisked some of the "environmentalist folks" as Frank likes to call them.']

The press secretary, Pipou Flake, read a statement on the company's behalf that was brief and bland. Frank then said, 'I'll take questions.'

[The narrator said, 'The reason he looks so nervous is because the former environmental director left the company only hours earlier and is amongst the activists, with heavy-looking security men on either side prepared to whisk him away if he becomes problematic.']

A young woman in a blue scarf asked the first question: 'Why aren't you on social media more to put your environmental message across?'

'We are,' said Frank. 'We're constantly tweeting and whatnot about how much we care for the earth: growing green industries, saving critters from extinction.'

[The narrator said, 'Look at old Frankie's expression. He's scanning the faces and thinking: "None of these creeps could ever hold down a job."']

Lily thought, how does he know what Mr Salesman's thinking? People were always ascribing thoughts to other people, and they were often mistaken.

Frank said, 'Remember: this company by its sustainable nature is an environmental activist company. Pick up one of our *Change The Climate* T-shirts before you leave. Free today.' He held one up. It showed a group of monkeys up a tree holding umbrellas bearing the company logo. 'Our poverty amelioration work centres made this specially.'

'That's sweatshops to you and me,' shouted a cynic, earning much laughter.

'What is your environmental policy in a few words?' said an old man in a red cap.

'Good business nurtures the environment, bad business causes harm. We have a great story. We get our activism ambassadors...'

More ambassadors, thought Lily. Was everyone who worked at the company an ambassador?

'...empowering people with our products. We don't stand on the sidelines.'

'Why aren't your coffee cups recyclable?' This from a studious-looking person of uncertain gender with large spectacles.

'They are, indeed, entirely recyclable and—'

'But they're not recycled.'

'Only because the recycling plants can't handle them.'

'Excellent!' shouted the cynic. 'Blame everyone else for stuff not happening. It makes you look ahead of the game.'

Frank was annoyed: 'We are ahead. And I tell you, son, we're lighter on our feet than anyone when it comes to this stuff.'

'And lighter on ideas,' came the reply, gaining applause.

'Well,' said Frank, undeterred and looking like he was ready for a scrap, 'You can sneer all you want, but I'll say this: others can't touch us. The big lumbering industries can't keep up. It's not our fault others are behind the times. We beg them to keep up. If necessary, we'll build our own recycling plants.' Then he added, 'In a matter of weeks,' causing laughter throughout the crowd.

A young man asked, 'In your restaurants and supermarkets is all your food from sustainable sources?'

'Absolutely,' said Frank, 'Sustainable everything is the essence of what we do.'

'What about local food producers you put out of business?'

'But we *are* them because we buy them up—sustainably.'

The cynic was savouring this: 'Of course you love "sustainable". It means "scarce", therefore higher prices. Perfect.'

'Exactly. Everyone wins...' Frank smiled, then frowned heavily: '...That is, higher prices are unavoidable and regrettable.' More laughter followed. If Frank had caught his colleague Pipou's agonised expression, it didn't stop him talking: 'And we're going to do all this other stuff visionaries can only think about. Making clothes from plastic bottles and glasses from waste oil. Growing moss walls. Building floating islands of solar power. Creating new crops for outer space. And to save on precious natural resources we'll use more manmade materials: nylon, polyester, and especially plastic.' The crowd noise grew louder with every sentence.

'You're reading the wrong speech, you schmuck!' It was the old environmental director. More mirth amongst the activists.

Frank looked ragged. 'Eh? You're awake, then. Of course it's the wrong speech. I was testing you. It was a speech from your days. Our company scientists are at the forefront twenty-four seven to find exciting new ways of using *less* nylon, polyester, and especially plastic. In fact, to use none at all. We've already removed the toys from things like cereal packets to cut out plastic and so little kids don't swallow 'em—'

'Just swallow your gunk by the bucketload,' shouted the cynic. 'And you save money in the process.'

'Not that saving money's the reason,' said another member of the crowd.

'Absolutely not,' said Frank. 'That would be far too clever, er, cynical. But I maintain, saving money goes hand-in-hand with greenwashing—saving the environ—'

At that moment there was a sudden, heavy shower. Pipou Flake was seen to mouth 'Thank you, God,' and they rushed off the scene. Frank was shown watching the activists run for their cars, all except the former environmental director and the cynic who were being beaten up by security men. The noise of the rain and car engines starting up smothered their cries.

Lily was fascinated, though perturbed. Was this what being a boss in business meant? Being laughed at on camera? And all the trouble? And people getting beaten up?

31

For her fourteenth birthday present, Lily asked Grandma if she could take up boxing. Grandma was pleased. Taking up a martial art had been part of the plan she'd outlined for her. When she'd thought of a martial art she hadn't meant boxing, but she was sure Brian's dad, Ted, who had his own gym in his double garage, would look after her. Perhaps also it would rekindle Lily's relationship with Brian, which

Grandma would be glad to see, although Lily no longer considered him a friend since the time she was beaten up.

Ted hadn't realised his potential as a fighter—too prone to cuts around his eyes—but he was renowned as a trainer. All the kids whom he'd worked with spoke highly of him. His inspirational quotes, which were scribbled on boards around the gym, were legendary and remembered by his students with warmth: 'Take nothing', 'Expect nothing', 'Wake up!' and, above all, the enigmatic 'Dreams are for sleepers'. Ted and his wife Maisie lived with Brian in a ramshackle cottage a few streets away from Grandma's and towards the outskirts of town. Lily had never been there before. The couple had three grown-up daughters who still lived in the area.

Grandma and Lily walked round to Ted's place. He was a big man, warm and welcoming. He led Lily into the lounge, disturbing an Old English sheepdog sprawled on the leather sofa, while Grandma went to see Maisie who was in the kitchen.

Ted offered Lily a drink and when he'd brought in her orange squash, he said, 'So why do you want to take up boxing, my lovely?' Ted's familiar tone was embarrassing but she liked it. She recalled Grandma's conversation with him, which she'd overheard, suggesting he was her secret benefactor.

She replied, 'Because I feel like a loser and don't want to feel that way.' She hadn't intended to say this but was unprepared for the question—the words just tumbled from her mouth. Her head down, she did not look at him.

Ted was kind but uncompromising: 'Lily, whether you learn to box or not, you will need to improve your basic fitness.'

'OK. I'm not as slow and unfit as I look.'

'I'm sure. But you're a pretty girl, so why would you want to get bashed about in a boxing ring?'

'I get bashed anyway by the bullies. Pretty? I'd rather have an eyepatch and a scar on my cheek.' She grinned. 'Not really.' Gaining confidence, she began venturing glances towards him.

'OK. Well, if it makes you feel better, I've got four other girls at the gym who are already in competitions. They weren't especially fit when they joined.'

'I don't want to be in competitions. I just want to protect myself. I want other kids to think: I don't want to mess with her—she has a big punch. And if other kids are getting beaten up, I want to help them out.'

'Cleaning up the mean streets of Retingham, eh, Lily?' He was trying to be lighthearted, but she merely frowned. 'OK,' he said. 'But just remember now, when you can look after yourself, and you know you have the power to hurt someone else with your fists, there's always the temptation to use them—and that can get you in trouble. Big trouble. I'm not training you to beat up other kids.'

'I understand,' she said. In truth, she didn't care about what he'd just said, but she had to humour him. Every time she imagined one of her tormentors, they had a black eye and blood streaming from the nose.

'I'm not sure you do understand,' he said. 'Sometimes the bullied child becomes the bully. That's not going to happen with you. Not while you're with me anyway.'

'OK,' she replied. Then she said she'd spend all her money, and as much as Grandma could afford, on getting fit and paying for boxing lessons.

He cheered up. 'That's my girl—determined. But you don't need my lessons for now. Get yourself a punchbag and a skipping rope. Get to a regular gym. Oh, and by the way, a fast flurry of small punches is your best hope. Just imagine a hailstorm.'

'How do you mean?' She looked up at him.

'You ever been caught in a hailstorm? Not very pleasant at all. Be like that. Besides, I had a big punch, but I could never land it.' Ted became pensive, 'Trying to land a big punch and not being able to, and not being able to understand why. That's what finished my career. I'd get cut around the eyes and then it'd be punch after punch, and I wouldn't know where I was. With one punch I could have knocked the guy out, but I had no chance to land it. Not a bad metaphor for life, Lily—swift persistence over lumbering power. The boxer who looks the part but can't land his punch. I'm sorry, Lily, I talk too much. But you're such a good listener.'

'But what if my opponent has a big punch?' she said.

'You've got to put your guard up. Defence. That and dancing out of the way. So get training. To give you an idea, I tell my kids to watch Manny Pacquiao.' He stood up and found a pencil and small notebook. Then he called out to Maisie to bring her iPad in. She did so, not acknowledging Lily. He stared hard at the screen then wrote down for her: *Manny Pac-*

quiao insane SPEED. 'YouTube,' he said. 'It can be a wonderful thing.' He showed it to her, all thirty-one seconds of it. She couldn't believe it. 'Is this for real?'

'Of course.'

It wasn't just the speed of the hands, it was the way he moved his feet back and forth and to the sides. 'Panny...'

He laughed. 'No, Manny... Pacquiao.'

'What age did he start then?'

'Fourteen. Maybe months older than you. See, you have a head start on him. Mind you, he worked extremely hard. You don't have to take up boxing, Lily, but whatever you do, work hard at it.'

32

A few days later, Grandma and Lily called round to see Fred and Nancy. Fred was upstairs in bed as usual, while Nancy seemed distracted. As her visitors sat on the prim red couch in the lounge she paced back and forth, complaining about all the work the council had to do. She stopped suddenly. 'Did you ever hear any more about that trip to the States in the end?'

Grandma replied, 'That was ages ago now. No, I wrote to them to say thank you, but it wasn't possible for Lily because of school. It only covered the flights and the drive from the hotel to the factory.

And with it having to be taken within a few weeks of the letter it was all a bit cynical and impractical. We never heard after that.'

'Mad,' said Nancy. 'Just like their plans for the town.'

'Really?' said Grandma.

'They want to invest—and in a big way. This smoothie business has drawn attention to the town and the CEO, Frank Salesman, has made it his personal project. I can't give any details because I haven't seen them myself yet. But if what I've heard is correct, it's going to be a real headache.'

'All talk, I expect,' said Grandma.

'Oh no,' said Nancy. 'They're definitely doing something. They're buying property all over. That derelict warehouse site on Eastville Road, and Rutsall Farm that's been on the market for years, and offers on other sites. All different buyers, but all roads lead back to the company. They've got ideas, alright. Or rather, the CEO has. Crazy ideas, I reckon, but the town needs investment. It's going to be smothering the town with love, but some on the council are very sceptical. Some wouldn't approve anything. To them the love's more like smoke that's going to choke everyone to death. Julia Bizzell's in favour...'

'Of course she is. Kickbacks.'

Nancy was genuinely affronted: 'Julia? I don't think so! How could you think that?'

'Very easily, as it happens.'

'Anyway, my poor head's fairly scrambled with it all.'

Grandma asked how Fred (she was tempted to say 'that lazy oaf') was. Nancy said he was slowly beginning to recover but was still incapable of doing anything productive.

Grandma expressed her sympathy at having to do so much on the council while having to look after Fred. Lily then spoke up, saying young people might like some changes if they made the place more interesting and fun.

Nancy gave her a look of 'And did anyone ask you?' and turned to Grandma, 'I wish I could be an advocate for them, but I fear they'll drive me mad.'

33

In the GUFF boardroom, Frank Salesman was being filmed in an interview for an environmental magazine, not realising it was fake. It was a stunt by activist Mervin Patch and a link to it appeared in the Friends' newsletter. Lily watched, intrigued.

Frank was fired up: 'We are relentless in all this environment-saving stuff. The world has changed. Long gone are the days when to be earth-friendly all you needed was a back-to-nature fashion range and a TV wildlife show. Nowadays, it's a bigger deal. There's so much to know, like hyperloops and super wave technology, whatever they are. It's not just the future of rare plants and animals, it's all our futures, and we are in the vanguard to meet such important challenges: growing wheat in disused coalfields, building houses from old coffee. We will make cars out of fish gut.'

'Really?'

'So Product Development tell me. Fish gut is the glamorous, exciting, new material apparently. What else? We will rewild the world. We will bring back the Dodo and other critters from extinction.'

'How will you do that?'

'By accepting it's possible, for a start. We don't know the exact mechanics yet, but it's just a matter of time for us. Our new environmental director is intelligent, down-to-earth, and keen to learn. She can deal with all the climate change preachers trying to jawbone me day and night. Her predecessor, who resigned to join the tree huggers, was too in love with the New Age "woo woo" so popular nowadays. The reality is, everything we do is devoted to protecting species. Even the ugly little critters no-one cares about, like parasitic worms, and grubs, and fire ants. I care for them. If some little critter could go extinct because of where our sustainable industrial chemicals park is to be, we'll move it.'

'The plant?'

'The critter! Moving the park would cost too much. No, we'd build a new synthetic habitat for them. Fish gut or something sympathetic like that. If we don't build the plant, someone else will, and they won't have our enlightened values and standards. If necessary, we'll buy up the planet to protect it.'

'The whole planet? That's a tough ask.'

'Entirely doable. This is like the conversations I have with the board. Remember, we don't have hopes, we have intentions: climate neutral by today, climate positive tomorrow.'

'Ambitious.'

'Everything is never enough. Not for environmentalists, not for us. We will move rivers, green the deserts, create new seas. We'll do everything from sustainable caviar farming to building habitats in space.'

'And how about next week?'

'Next week? How about the next ten minutes? How about we clean up the world? Use our size and power. Always remember: big business means big solutions to pesky problems. We are the friend of the planet. Redefining quality, enhancing value, creating synergies. It's what we do.'

'Eh?'

'I was being tongue in cheek. Does anyone even know what it means? Be tough on it. All the corporate guff can be summed up as "Be Kind". That's all we need. Save a few forests too—be kind to them.'

It was at this point that the formal interview stopped, but Frank was inspired. Still being filmed, he spoke into his dictaphone: 'Note to Advertising: when in doubt stick, "Stop polluting the oceans" in your next campaign and include a koala. That will shift a few hundred thousand units, which makes everyone happy.' He paused for a moment and then began again: 'Note for autobiography, suggested title: *Change Is My Blood*. Need to check if used before. Section on important thoughts: Privately I worry about climate change. To make profit for the good of the world a company must grow, and to grow it must make more stuff, and more people have to buy it. More resources are consumed and more waste created. Therefore it's said we have to make less stuff. But I say: who will get less? The poor folks, of course. The rich will still get and do whatever they want; if anyone attacks them over their carbon footprint, they grow more trees on their vast estates and ranches and claim they're carbon neutral. In other words, inequality increases. It gets my nanny goat because I'm for the little guy. I want him/her/them to be able to do and have what the rich guy has.'

Lily thought: no wonder Nancy was worried. It seemed nothing was beyond the bounds of Frank's imagination—but at least the coming times would not be dull.

34

Grandma bought the punch bag and skipping rope and paid for some gym lessons as Ted had recommended. Lily enjoyed the gym work but couldn't wait to start boxing training proper. Ted invited her to come and meet some of the other kids at a barbecue he was hosting in his garden. She was worried in case any of the bullies would be there and was tempted to demur but in the end went along. She found she was not the youngest. This relaxed her. The others were welcoming towards her, and in their conversations she noted they all cited bullying as a reason for taking up the sport. They all seemed fit and full of energy. It made her feel fat and dumpy and, worst of all, self-conscious. She asked one of them what 'Dreams are for sleepers' meant. They said Ted was very down-to-earth and he really had a single, simple message: pay attention or you'll get hit—no woolgathering, no daydreaming.

Brian saw Lily at the barbecue and tried to talk to her, but she was not interested. Later, he wrote to her on Facebook suggesting 'hanging out like we used to'. She was tempted not to reply, to leave him to marinate in his own misery (assuming he was actually experiencing any), but it played on her mind. So a few days later, a time period she imagined perfect for causing him the most pain, she wrote back, intending to crush his hopeful heart: 'Brian, apart from with my new best friend Mack, the only hanging out I do is over the top of my jeans. I have zero interest in seeing you. At the time I needed your help you were nowhere. What use is that to me? I had to go to A&E that time, and I felt destroyed by the whole thing. I still feel it.'

35

The Friends of Lily Upshire had a mole set up a covert filming operation. Lily watched the resulting film featuring Frank in animated conversation with his team.

He was responding to the news that numerous claims had come in from England, particularly the Retingham, Notts area, for foreign objects in smoothies and other drinks. He said, 'And no doubt every crook and swindler in the region will take a generous cut. You watch: they'll have planned their luxury holidays already. Or maybe they'll be setting up in business. Hick businesses. But most likely one of them runs one of those claims companies our lawyer warned us about. Maybe that old fool was right. The next thing will be a story that the girl Lily Whatsername consumed the pea, which will become a mouldy pea, then not a pea at all but something more dangerous like a decomposed insect, then she'd been made ill by it, got some life-changing condition needing a doctor in Geneva to fix, costing some ludicrous sum in compensation and a ton of medicals. Then there's all the mental anguish and emotional distress on top. And not just her but the old witch as well...'

Lily thought: Old witch!! Poor Grandma—old witch indeed!

'...And punitive damages so high the wicked company never dare do it again. And no doubt, after all the relatives and greedy neighbours have taken their cut and bought their new houses and flashy cars, and set up their risky businesses, there'll be next to nothing left for poor Lily. That's how it works all over. The world's rotten, even a place like Retingham. By the way, I understand it's a such a weird little time warp place it even has an open air market three days a week to emphasise its quaintness. The dozy investigator our lawyer sent over from the States said he went expecting a place full of people writing letters with quill pens, and wearing smocks, and talking in Shakespearean language. Where do people get such crazy ideas from? Do they think the shires of England stopped in 1600? OK, let's be realistic: it's just a regular little market town out in the boonies. No shopping malls, so clearly ripe for beneficial development. I'm thinking new industry, like a smoothie plant. I was also thinking maybe a Robin Hood theme park.This company is after all a corporate Robin Hood, bringing the good life to those who otherwise can't afford it. That's unlike our competitors who are just hoods. I thought maybe people in period costumes could live there like in Plimoth Plantation. Is Publicity here?'

'Yes! I've been here the whole time listening.' [The narrator said this man's name was Todd Giff.]

'OK. I'm thinking that out of generosity, we could throw in a hospital for their old fashioned diseases like rickets and other stuff we don't have here anymore.'

'Rickets? Er, we still have it,' said Giff.

Frank peered at the speaker, a little upstart. 'Seriously? Are you a doctor?'

'No, but I know that much.' *

'OK then, good old scurvy. I bet...'

'Yeah we do.'

'I'm sorry? OK then: bubonic plague. That's stumped ya!'

'No, sorry, we do.'

[The narrator said Frank looked as though he could crush Giff like a flea if he could catch him.]

'OK then,' Frank sighed. 'I'm sure obesity's a big problem. Remember old Friar Tuck—see, I know history. Let's get Innovation to check out the viability of all this. Send one of our ambassadors in to meet the mayor. Maybe we could build a brewery to make their strange local beers.'

'We can try anything you want, but I should draw your attention to the cost. You're talking about building a smoothie factory, brewery, hospital, and theme park. And for what purpose? Some of these are purely cost, and the others probably won't generate a profit for years, if ever.'

'That's such negative thinking. It's because you're new.'

'No, it's reality.'

'That's not how we work. Here we know that reality's fluid, negotiable. If reality's negative we change it. We must always be positive. All we're doing is what we've always done: turn minor adversity into major success—face it, you can't get much more minor than a garden pea.' He stared hard at the smart alec, Giff: 'Though, no doubt, some clever person will point out there's many things smaller than a pea.'

He turned to the rest of the team, 'Our approach has served us well, but it takes investment. When Serendipity calls, you have to be ready to jump. Lily Upshire is like the apple on Newton's head. Or the pea, if you must. These old-timey places, without shopping malls or stores the size of small towns to make them happy, are our big shining future. So I don't want to hear any more yammering about cost. It's like any other investment—pay in big now, collect bigger later. For starters, I thought we could sponsor a nice cover for their quaint outdoor market and make it indoors instead. Better than standing in the English rain, as the Beatles' song goes.'

'They won't want a building in the middle of the market square.'

'What you're saying is: they always complain about the rain but want to stand out in it anyway. How typically British! There's no helping some people.'

'It will have to go through the planning committee,' said a man identified by the narrator as Armitage Ozog from Development.

'Why so slow? This is not the way we work. We do something, we build somewhere, then we argue about whether we should have done it afterwards. So we should buy up the city centre, build what we want, then fight any ignorant critics afterwards. Any holdouts we buy up if other measures don't work.'

'We won't be able to buy the city centre.'

'Then we'll build a shopping mall on the outskirts. All their shops are closing down anyway. There must be plenty of people wanting to sell their land. We've already bought out a few deadbeat farmers.'

'So many obstacles.'

'Like what?'

'Ancient woodlands, meadows.'

'Move them. Make them part of the theme park.'

'Expensive homes.'

'Owned by people who want to keep the poorer people down. I'm sure there's ways to make them want to sell cheap.'

At this point, the narrator of the film said: 'One thing they've thought of doing is to pose as travellers: Occupy a nice green space, send in a few caravans, and buy up as much land as possible. Then create a kind of "theme park" with a couple of small shops. Then more shops spring up. Before you know it you've got a shopping mall of a hundred units. Eighty would be their own shops with another twenty for little bijou businesses they'll buy up when they struggle—which they will, because as landlords the company will triple the rent every quarter until their tenants squeak.'

36

Lily went to see Nancy and Fred. To her surprise she found Fred on his own, sitting in his dressing-gown in the kitchen, eating a boiled egg. When Lily arrived he brightened. She commented that he looked well.

He blanched. 'Really? Are you sure?' Worried, he crumpled down into his chair and was suddenly unable to finish his egg. He motioned to the kettle for her to help herself to tea. 'Where's Nancy?' she said.

'Oh, Sally's had to take her to hospital. Poor Nancy's had a bad turn.'

'Oh dear. Not to do with the contamination, though.'

'Oh, could be. Food poisoning effects can take a long time to show up.'

'But it's been over a year now.'

'It could be a new batch. New batch but same old problem. Just hoping we get the claims moving soon. We can't get the company to bite, but the lawyers seem confident. The company won't want anything going to court.'

They heard a car enter the driveway. It was Sally. Fred got to his feet but then, remembering himself, sat back down again. They could see Sally was alone. Lily sensed that if she wasn't there with him, Fred would have scampered off to bed and would have started groaning the moment Sally entered. He was an old rogue, a fraud, but she found him compelling and harmless. He wouldn't scam an individual, wouldn't dream of it, but a big faceless organisation was easy prey. If he'd had the wherewithal and the energy, he'd have been what Grandma had read about in the paper called a 'salami slicer', skimming off a few dollars now and then from thousands of corporate accounts in a big bank. Fred saw Lily as a kindred spirit, someone who would cheat a little if they had to, in order to win.

Sally came in and flung her arms around Lily, so happy to see her. 'Poor mum has had to stay in hospital,' she said. She explained that her mother had fallen over after an attack of vertigo. 'How awful! Has she had it before?' asked Lily.

'No. But, you know, it's since she became involved with the planning committee that she started getting headaches. The council can't cope with it all. It's the smoothie company with all their wild schemes. The way they're going, they'll soon want to turn the whole of Retingham into a model village, so Mum said. The company's mad keen on doing something big. They've got millions to invest in the town, which would be wonderful, but they keep coming up with more and more crackpot ideas. It's the chief executive, Frank Salesman; he comes up with one of these notions and expects it to all be done by the following week.'

'And the town needs the money, doesn't it?' said Fred. 'Desperately. It's getting more run down by the week. All these shops closing. Or so it says on Facebook. Of course, I haven't seen it myself.'

'But what would a model village even be like?' asked Lily.

'The whole town would effectively be run by the company,' said Fred. 'It would provide everything—schools, hospital, library, everything—and everyone would work for it.'

'I remember it from school,' said Sally. 'No drinking allowed, as I recall.'

'They'd have to allow it or there'd be riots.' said Fred. 'Besides, the company has a drinks division.

In fact, it has a division for everything, so in theory it could do it.'

'Dad, it's never going to happen. Can you imagine?' They all laughed.

'So how long will she be in hospital?' said Lily.

'Several days at least.'

Lily stood up, thinking she ought to get back. 'OK, I'll tell Grandma. She'll want to go and see her.'

Lily thought: the town's dead or dying and maybe some of the ideas would be good. At least it'd make people think.

37

Gloria sent Lily a recording of her father talking about the model village idea after Lily asked her if she'd heard anything about it.

Frank had been discussing various ideas with Osh Frightener, head of what Frank called Workers' Stuff, when Osh said, 'Perhaps what you want is a model village.'

'You mean, a model village with bowling greens and theatres and galleries?'

'Yes, although I was joking.'

'But I'm not. I can see it now: sprinklered lawns and chocolate fountains with model workers all polite, and joyful, and walking around in a happy daze.

Yes, I'm warming to it. It's a great idea. And maybe there'll be a school and hospital, and spa, and all healthy food, and a life expectancy of a hundred and fifty. Or two hundred. And how much would all that cost? Oh, but it would be worth it. We wouldn't need to pay them anything.'

'Nothing?'

'That's right. All their needs provided.'

'But what about their freedom?'

'Freedom? They wouldn't want freedom. Freedom to do what? They'll be so happy, they won't even want holidays.'

'That's maybe a tad unrealistic. Everyone wants their freedom.'

'I can't see why. Freedom to make trouble, I suppose. Don't tell me we're stuck with ungrateful stumblebums in the workforce, or that the culture we have is too soft and all we attract is deadbeats. Some people think we should toughen things up—cut pay and holidays and increase their hours—but, no, I'm too benevolent for that. It's always been my failing. But think about this model village idea. How about if we turned little old Retingham into one and dressed everyone in smocks? That would get the Friends of Lily Upshire where they live—quite literally.'

'It's a little too late for all that, I'm afraid,' said Osh.

'Late? What do you mean, late? We don't believe in late. Things are either done or they're not done, there is no late. Things that haven't happened yet can always be made to happen.'

'It might have worked a hundred and fifty years ago, but I can't see it being well received nowadays.

Unless it was a cult or something. Besides, those model villages had quite a reliance on temperance. It's certainly too late for that.'

'"Can't do", "too late". Give me something positive.'

'Unionisation is what the workers would rather have.'

'Unions? Don't need them. Never have, never will. Too old-fashioned. No, we need a direct approach. Get people on social media saying what a great company we are to work for. Failing that, we'll make everyone a contractor. There's the freedom they want. They can be independent and autonomous. They can work for whoever they want. Brilliant.'

'We may struggle to get them working for us in that scenario.'

'I can't see why. And what if we do struggle? Struggle is good if you win in the end. But, OK, if all else fails we'll invest in artificial intelligence. We can be at the vanguard of the leisure future using robots for everything. Ending slavish work, ending all work. Robots will be the future, saving the poor workers groaning under the weight of oppressive management. We won't need management. And we won't need to pay anyone.'

'This is all rather hard to take in. It's giving me a headache.'

'Headache? What's the matter—can't keep up? So let's hear your latest ideas. Remember, our workers' wellbeing is at the forefront of all our concerns. That and... whatever it was.'

'Because we're so focused on our workers' wellbeing, we've introduced monitoring to help them. We give them special necklaces which can monitor their heart rate, blood pressure and breathing quality—'

'All good. A healthy worker is a happy worker.'

'And purely as an incidental by-product, it monitors their performance.'

'And then what?'

'Obviously if the service ambassadors are struggling to meet their entirely reasonable productivity standards, they can be given assistance by our productivity champions.'

'How do they do that, assuming I understand any of what you just said?'

'They give the service ambassadors messages of hope not failure.'

'Service ambassadors? Didn't we used to call them workers, by the way?'

Lily paused the recording. She thought: thank you, Frank—so many ambassadors!

Osh said, 'Yes. Of course. We protect our service ambassadors by monitoring them twenty-four hours a day.'

'Sounds boring as old hell. And creepy. Can we go back to calling them workers again? Only, it's quicker.'

Lily shouted, 'Hooray!'

'OK. It may sound dull but in fact our workers are never bored.'

'Never bored? But we like boredom here—it encourages new imaginative thinking. If people didn't get bored there'd be no need for the wonderful world that automation provides.' There was a pause. 'OK, Osh, I guess it's time for you to get on home. And, on reflection, maybe a model village wasn't your best idea, since all this monitoring would probably be part of it.'

38

Lily began her training with Ted, the early lessons being at Grandma's. The old lady felt a sense of pride at watching her. Until now, she'd mainly been doing resistance training, gym work, and skipping rope. From the start, Lily enjoyed the lessons with Ted and his inspirational talk. She reminded him of his eldest daughter who'd been so enthusiastic when she started. He said, 'If your spirit was electricity, you could light up the whole town with it.'

'How about the whole of England?' she replied.

He said, 'I could make you into a champ if that's what you wanted. But I know you don't.'

Lily saw Mack often these days. Mack was still doing her boxing at the town's gym centre. She was glad she wasn't going to Ted's because she did not want to spar with Lily. 'Besides,' she said once when they were in Grandma's lounge playing mahjong, 'if I fought you I would always win.' This was the prompt for Lily to initiate a wrestle with her on the floor. It always felt good. Mack was stronger, but Lily was more committed. In other words, she cheated through pinching and tickling until she won—or

Mack let her win. After their wrestle, they liked to lie on the lounge carpet side by side holding hands before returning to their game. They loved being together. Once, Grandma arrived home and found them lying on the floor holding hands. Mack tried to release her hand, but Lily would not let go, keen to prompt a reaction in Grandma. But there was none. Grandma was just pleased to see her so happy.

39

One day, Lily and Grandma were visited by a representative of the Friends of Lily Upshire. It was a woman Lily had never seen before. Lily found her appearance: expensive-looking trouser suit, scarlet lipstick and nails, as well as her green cloche hat, a little absurd. The woman had called round to ask her to join the campaign. Lily was annoyed because she had told the group from the start not to use her name, although she was beginning to see it as a potential opportunity. The training was improving her confidence and giving her a sharp edge. She told the woman she did not want to join but felt entitled to a share of whatever the Friends got since they had the cheek to use her name without her permission. She'd read the Friends were planning a worldwide boycott, and she told the woman she thought it nonsensical and did not want to be associated with it.

To them she was just an unusual name they thought they could exploit for their own ends, whatever they were, although making money was clearly the main one. She informed the woman she would even consider suing them if she found a suitable lawyer.

The group's representative was taken aback but amused in a condescending way by her feisty attitude. Grandma was embarrassed by the whole episode.

The claimants' group now included even the families of Lily's bullies. The fact she hadn't joined became another cause for their verbal attacks. They called her 'stuck up', too snooty to join their group. They said, 'You haven't got real friends, so they created some for you, but you won't even join.'

They were wrong: she had Mack, and Mack was all she felt she needed.

40

One morning, two police officers arrived at school with a couple of black labradors. It turned out to be a drugs raid and everyone was excited. At the end of her maths lesson Lily was told to go to the headteacher's office. When she arrived she found the officers there—one male, one female—with Miss Cotton present too, as well as the pastoral care / counsellor woman. Lily wondered whether they were going to give her a special undercover assignment like she'd seen on TV.

The headteacher said that a packet of cocaine had been found in her gym bag. What was her explanation?

'I don't know,' she said, shrugging, bewildered. 'I don't know anything about it.'

The policewoman produced the packet.

'I've never seen that before,' she said. 'It's a mistake.'

'Isn't it your bag? It has your name on the tag,' said the male police officer. Lily looked at it. It clearly was her bag—a smart new black one Grandma bought for her when she started boxing training.

'I don't understand,' she said. 'This is a set-up. I want my grandma here.' She refused to say anything else. She thought: will I wake up from this in a minute?

In a daze Lily was taken to the police station. Grandma was already there. Lily reiterated that she had no knowledge of how the drugs came to be in her gym bag. 'They've been planted in there,' she insisted.

'Planted on the day of a surprise visit—is it a regular occurrence or just today?' It was the male officer who'd been at the school.

'Never happened to me before,' she said.

Grandma then said that it was inconceivable that Lily could have put the drugs there. Or known of it. She had no contact with drug dealers and no interest in drugs.

'Possession is a very serious crime,' the officer said. 'You could be put away for this, Lily. You could get a reduced sentence if you confess now, especially being a minor. Now, once again, I'll ask you: How did the drugs come to be in your bag? Who were they for?'

'I don't know.'

'Who asked you to put them in your bag?'

'No-one.'

'Are you dealing?'

'Eh?'

'Are you selling?'

'No!'

'What's your role in this? Are you storing for someone? Are you transporting? Are you recruiting?'

'No! No! No!'

'If you think someone planted them, presumably you have some idea as to who it was.'

'I have a pretty good idea actually' she said. This prompted Grandma to look over at her expectantly. 'Go on,' said Grandma.

'Go on,' said the policeman.

'One of the Bizzell girls. They hate me and they bully me.'

'Everyone knows the Bizzell family is heavily involved in drugs,' said Grandma firmly. She noticed the officer becoming twitchy. 'Why don't you do something about that instead of arresting my granddaughter? It's obvious this is just another part of the bullying that's been going on.'

So strong was Grandma in her protestations that the police stopped short of formally charging Lily at this stage. But they said when they had more evidence they might charge her, and if it happened again they would certainly do so.

Grandma drove her home. 'I believe you, Lily. It's not something you would do. No doubt, the school will exclude you, so you'll have that to contend with, but it'll be a respite from the Bizzells.'

Sure enough, that afternoon Grandma received a call from the school to say that 'in the circumstances' they had no alternative but to exclude Lily. Grandma said to her, 'I know it's not your fault, but it's all becoming too much for Grandma to cope with.'

Lily began to realise what a burden to her grandmother she was. For a moment she felt she would like to do away with herself, to cease to be that burden, but perhaps prior to today the burden had been worth Grandma bearing. She wished Grandma had real grandchildren; Lily would feel jealous of them, but they would give Grandma a joy that she believed she couldn't give her.

41

Depressed, Lily sat in her room staring in the mirror. She said, 'You're still pretty. It may be the only thing going for you, Upshire, but you still have that.' Yet the more she looked, the more she saw blemishes and imperfections in her skin, her teeth, her nose, her brows. And she'd lost the confidence she'd recently acquired. She was sure it was the bleakest situation she'd ever known. She tried not to think of school, but it was impossible to avoid it. 'I hope the place burns down,' she said. 'I hope it kills everyone except Mack and Ms Hass.' But she didn't really hope for deaths. Apart from the Bizzells and a few teachers, there was no-one she hated, and even with them she'd rather have them corralled away so they couldn't harm her anymore.

Instead, she wanted to take her hurt out on herself. She wanted to cut. She did her rituals but in an angry, careless way. She rang Mack. Mack had been off sick and hadn't heard about what happened at school. She couldn't believe it at first but then said, 'I'll come over.'

'Are you OK to?'

'Yeah. I made myself ill. I couldn't face going in today. Homework not done. That's your influence.'

Before Mack arrived Lily felt worse. She had a sudden impulse to contact Brandi. It was irrational. She'd had no contact with her for over a year since Mack established she was fake. She wrote, 'Please contact. Want to start again. I'll send you pic, whatever you want.'

The response was quick and harsh: 'Go away, you catfish. This is Brandi's mom. I am reporting you to your school and the police for requesting pornographic images to put on the dark web. A picture she sent you privately is now all over the internet. She had to set up a new account. You will be blocked. I hope you are arrested.'

This rebuke cut her like a blade. The hurt was delicious, better than physical harm because it destroyed her reputation. Except she knew it was merely pretence: it was not a real person's mom, and no-one would contact the school.

Lily dug her nails hard into the fleshy part of her hand. She then went to the kitchen, and took an ice cube from the freezer, and held it tight in her palm. On her return to her room she sent a text to Mack: 'Please get here quick. Desperate. Want to die.'

Mack arrived within half an hour. She held Lily in her arms and squeezed. She kissed her on the forehead and then softly on the lips. Then she noticed on Lily's arms there were scratches. Lily had been less careful with the safety pin. 'What do these marks mean?' she said. 'How did it happen?' Lily explained the latest incident at school had completely unhinged her.

Mack was tough with her out of kindness: 'Do you want to show the world your pain?' she said.

'I don't care anymore.'

'Yes you do. You should care. I care.' She held Lily tight and told her she would always love her.

It had been agreed that Mack would spend the night. She would go to school from there. Her mother would pick her up next morning.

Mack had brought a sleeping bag, but she persuaded Lily that they should climb into bed together. It was only half past eight. Lily was so depressed she would have let Mack do whatever she wanted with her, including slit her throat, although, on reflection, that would be unacceptable, as it would not only upset Grandma but also leave her with the mess to clear up, as well as the embarrassment of court proceedings, and Mack being put away for a long time. And of course Molly might wonder where she was, although she had already decided Grandma was the leader of this particular all-female pack. It was the desire not to cause upset or inconvenience to Grandma and other loved ones that had kept Lily from killing herself before. She told Mack she felt she had nothing inside her. It was as though she could see inside her soul and found it empty. What Lily did not say, because she could not perceive it, was that when a bully called her a dirty slag who deserved a good kicking, she not only believed it but unconsciously accepted it as reality.

Prior to getting into bed, the girls talked about make-up and different perfumes they liked. They each put a favourite fragrance on. Under the covers the scents were so intoxicating, they immediately threw back the covers and burst out laughing. Mack said, 'Don't worry, I won't touch you. Pretend I'm your sister.' They lay side by side in their pyjamas holding hands, happily jabbering until Mack said, 'The problem with you is that you don't want anything. Not really. You're a dreamer but you have no dream.'

'Yeah I do.'

'So what do you want to do with your life?'

'Be rich.'

'Why do you want to be rich? You can't just want to be rich. You have to get rich by doing something.'

'I think if I get to be rich, then maybe I can help someone I love who's fallen on hard times. Maybe you if you're still my friend.'

'Why wouldn't I still be?' said Mack, affronted. This hint of neediness in her friend eased Lily's feeling of desolation a little, and made her warm to her even more.

Mack said, 'So if you were rich, you would rescue me from poverty? Like a saviour?'

'Yeah.'

'That would be romantic, although I'd rather not need a saviour. The trouble is, I don't want to have to be poor first. I'd rather we both of us weren't rich but just doing OK. Maybe when we're older we could be flatmates.'

'Yeah, maybe.'

'Lily, when we're old enough, will you marry me?' She pressed her fingers into Lily's palm.

'No.'

'Really?' Mack withdrew her hand, 'That's harsh. OK, can I ask you in a year's time?'

'If you want to. But you'll forget about it by then.' Lily didn't take it seriously. She could only imagine marrying a man. She said, 'I wouldn't want to get married for a long time. Especially if I were rich. I wouldn't trust anyone. I'd think any charming young man just wanted my riches.'

The word 'riches' set Mack off giggling. 'I'd steal your riches first,' she said. 'Truthfully, you know what your trouble is?'

'Tell me. Go on. Don't hold back.'

'Your trouble is that, when it comes to it, well, you're still a bit of a useless c-word. You need to be more of a mean b-word.'

'I'm mean to myself instead. Desolation.'

'I know you are. Do you think I haven't felt that same... desolation? Do you think I haven't wanted to die? But instead of killing ourselves, let's kill someone else in our minds. Let me guess...'

'I don't want the twins dead, just in gaol.'

'No, they need death. Although what they need most of all is ridicule. They inspire fear, but what if they inspired ridicule? I'd take out Blue. She's the worst of the two.'

'I'd take out the Runt,' said Lily.

'She's younger than you.'

'Let's wish for all of them. Can you stay all week while we work on it?'

'I'll try to. But how would we do it? What would be coolest would be a ridiculous death like, say, a banana that exploded as soon as they put it in their gobs.'

'I never heard of such a thing.'

'I think food is the way to go, though. Something that would make them fart so bad they blew up their house. Killed the lot of them.'

'Actually I read that if you mix chemicals for cleaning the toilet, that can cause an explosion, so it's not so crazy.'

'You told me you've got powers. You could be a warrior prophet wiping out bullies.'

'That would be cool.'

'Although they make you dangerous to know.'

'Why so?'

'Because you could put a hex on someone you hate and it rebound on someone you like.'

'I'm afraid of the powers and whether I'll hit the right person with them. But then, every time I see the twins coming I still want to wet myself. Even now with the boxing. I have to deal with it. I can't go on like this.'

'You have to use the powers then. Maybe you should think hard about all of them. And when it happens they'll just think they're victims of coincidence. I'll concentrate hard on Blue even though I haven't got powers. Let's do it now.'

Next day, Mack called her from school and told her Green got beaten up by a gang of girls.

'Bloody hell!' Lily exclaimed.

'She nearly died.'

'I wouldn't wish that. Not really.'

'I would. You've got to learn to hate, Lily.'

Lily thought about the implications of it all. They were strange powers. You could only wish for bad outcomes and never got what you actually asked for. It was like wishing up the kidnap of A and ending up with the murder of B.

42

Lily watched the latest from the Friends of Lily Upshire group. It was another interview, this time with a major newspaper. The interviewer asked Frank to comment on the upcoming boycott of the company's products which had been announced that very day. 'So these so-called Friends of Lily Upshire have started a boycott?'

'It's worldwide.'

'Plotters, hucksters, people of cunning, troublemakers. It has to be a joke. It's no problem, though, because they'll be swept aside in the rush for our new products...'

'Even if they're the same old ones repackaged to look like something different?'

'Of course. I suppose it was that caper out in the Mojave that started it.'

'Yes. The music festival where they've decided not to sell your products anymore.'

'I'd liked to see that. The place would literally fall apart. Everything would collapse. Boycott our products and all there'd be left is cola with no cups and burgers with no buns. Well, so be it. We'll have our own music festival where only our products are sold. We can easily do that: everything from the tent they sleep in, to the highly nutritious artificial foods they eat, to the sustainable stages the bands play on. Everything. In fact, we'll have all our own music acts playing there. We'll buy up some of the big bands, like the Stones and U2. They're bigger than most companies anyway. If they won't bite, we'll set up our own groups, like the Monkees.'

'Who?'

'This great company's creator knew of them. But our groups would be better, singing songs about revolution and how good our products are. A big company needs a cultural face. We'll set up art galleries and music venues. We'll sponsor our own artists, too. We'll sponsor a new Warhol with our products instead of Campbell's soup tins. I hope you're getting all this.'

'I was more focused on the boycott.'

'A boycott can never work because we are constantly spinning off to create new companies. They could never track all of it down. This company changes every day. It's the Shapeshifter, the Trickster, the sprite. It cannot be contained. It can be small, vulnerable, and meek one minute, and strong and all-powerful the next. Trying to catch it is like trying to catch electricity, or mercury, or water in a mountain stream. They can never win.'

43

Lily threw herself into the boxing training but found it hard. Sit-ups were particularly difficult, as was an exercise they did as a group in which they would shadow box going from their haunches to their feet up and down. She was easily winded. And there was Ted's constant patter: 'Don't look down. Stop feeling sorry for yourself. Take it easy. Relax. Keep your feet alive. Loosen up. Keep your balance. Be comfortable. Body shots. Body shots.'

After training one day, Lily was walking home when she encountered the number one bully, Blue, on the bridge over the canal. She had a dog with her. A small but vicious dog. Lily wasn't afraid of it, but she was wary. She slowed her steps. The dog growled and Blue mocked her discomfort. 'Afraid of a little dog, Upshite? What a coward!' She then released it from its lead and told it to attack. It merely stood there yapping, and growling every time Lily made as if to move. Then it leapt forward. She bent down to knock it away with her fist, but it was quick and bit her on the hand. She was shocked and the bully laughed out loud. Upset, Lily made a quick lunge towards the dog and grabbed it; it tried to squirm out of her grasp, but she was determined. She ignored its further attempts to bite, and lifted it up high in the air, and, as Blue stared in horror, hurled the beast over the bridge wall. There was a splash. Blue was stunned. 'You can't do that!' she wailed.

'Yes I can—I just did it,' said Lily, 'and I don't care. It attacked me. You shouldn't have a dog if you can't control it.'

In tears Blue ran down to the towpath and called out the dog's name, 'Minty! Minty! It's alright, darling!' Lily walked on without looking at the canal and did not see the dog drifting under the bridge as its little legs struggled to keep it above the surface. And nor did she see a barge that had just appeared round the bend seventy yards away.

Lily continued along the road home. She knew she would be in trouble over it. It was ironic because she loved animals, but she knew some animals were not loved by their owners and became terrible, just like them. She looked at her hand where the dog had bitten her. Grandma would phone the doctor for her.

44

A few days later, Lily arrived home from school feeling better than usual. It would have been typically miserable but for football, in which, after being kicked all over the pitch by the Runt's friend Mitch the Bitch and another girl known as The Ship, Lily blatantly dived in the penalty area. Her grateful team then won from the resulting spot kick.

Grandma told her, 'Julia Bizzell has been round. She was not happy. She said the family dog, poor little Minty, nearly drowned in the canal, and it was you who was responsible. You never told me that. You just said a dog bit you. What have you got to say for yourself?'

Lily said nothing, and Grandma said, 'She said you threw Minty in the canal! I thought you loved animals.'

'I do, but that thing is horrible. Just like her and her daughters. Why do you side with them? Their dog attacked me! I picked it up after it bit me. You had to take me to the bloody doctor's! Because it's the Bizzells you go all soppy. Just like Nancy does. No wonder they get away with everything. I bet they never got busted over those drugs they put in my bag.'

Grandma was temporarily lost for words. She waved her arms about, but all that came out of her mouth was an impotent shriek. Finally, she was able to say, 'Mind your language. The fact the dog was off the lead does not mean you have the right to pick it up and throw it. Julia said to me, "You do realise, any other family would have told the police about it." What have you to say about that?'

'So what? She should keep her dog off the street—and her stupid daughters, for that matter.'

'She's giving you the opportunity to apologise. You should do so. Go round there now. You know it's the right thing to do. You should always do the right thing.'

'I'm not sorry, so why should I apologise? If one of the biggest companies in the world won't apologise, why should I?'

They argued but Lily was unmoved. She said the Bizzell family should apologise to her but never would. After a quick snack instead of tea, she went to her room. For a moment she wondered whether Julia wanted to talk to her about her father, but after last time's unpleasant experience Lily had no desire for that.

A while later, Grandma came to see her. She ran her fingers through Lily's hair and said, 'You're right, Lily. I'm sorry. But what's the matter? Why are you still so restless?'

'You know why: at school Mack and Emily Hass are the only ones who care if I live or die.'

'That's not true.'

'Yes. And the Bizzells just do whatever they like and get away with it.'

'I don't like you thinking this way, but let's not argue anymore.'

The following Saturday, there was a visit from the police. It was a man and a woman, both young, or at least much younger than any of the police Lily ever saw around town. She was worried they were there about the drugs in her gym bag, but it was the dog-in-the-canal incident instead. Lily denied all involvement. She told them she was doing boxing training at the time. Then they asked her about two other matters: the burning down of the Bizzells' shed and the latest beating up of the Runt outside the school gates. Lily denied them too, which was easy because she knew nothing about them. The police told Lily about the need to tell the truth and made some oblique reference to youth detention. Grandma, who was alarmed by Lily's denial of the dog-in-the-canal incident but managed to hide it, told the officers Ted could vouch for Lily. She gave them his address. What she didn't say was that Ted would also remind them about the bullying—with any luck that would be the end of the matter.

As soon as the police left, Grandma phoned Ted and then admonished Lily about lying so brazenly. Lily replied that it seemed to be the only way to get on in the world, and that, as regards the incident itself, she remained unrepentant. The Bizzells' dog was used as a weapon. It wasn't the dog's fault, but it wasn't hers either.

45

Weeks later, Grandma fretted as she listened to the latest diatribe from Lily about how awful school was until she sighed at last, 'You used to be such a nice, happy girl, Lily, before this pea-in-the-smoothie business happened.' She was deceiving herself: Lily had never been both and often neither.

Lily said, 'But I don't want to be nice. Or happy. All that matters in this world, it seems, is money and how you get it. And I'm determined to get some. I'm not going to be poor like my mum.'

Frustrated, Lily decided she would fake illness. She never wanted to go back to school ever again. Even another week of it would be a terrible compromise. Frustration soon turned to resolve. She decided to go and see Fred who was an Olympic champion at feigning illness.

Lily saw Nancy initially and asked her about Fred's symptoms. Nancy was sceptical about her sudden curiosity because she felt Lily had never taken his illness seriously before. Moreover, her lack of interest in joining the entirely reasonable claim against the company, her rejection of the Friends, and even complaining about them using her name, had all been noted, and this obduracy on her part could not be so easily forgotten.

But Nancy was at heart a spiritual woman, and she had the capacity for forgiveness, or at least the capacity for believing she had it. Thus, she indulged Lily. More particularly, she saw an opportunity. If Lily was interested in Fred today, perhaps tomorrow the press would be interested too, and after all this time the forgotten man would have his moment.

After a brief chat, during which she told Nancy, without hesitation or irony, that she would soon be top of the class, Lily went upstairs to see Fred. She was mainly interested to know about the early symptoms he'd had so she could recognise them (and acquire them if necessary). But her more intense interest was in how he'd been able to con everyone that he was ill, or con enough people to get away with it, or at least pacify sceptics sufficient for them to remain quiet. Fred was delighted with the attention and put on a fine show of being ill for her. Lily was impressed, although more with his acting ability than any evidence of real ailments he might have.

Lily read online about something called school phobia and was satisfied that was what she had. She pretended to have an upset tummy and be off her food. She claimed to have no energy (although she still went to training) and to have trouble with simple tasks, especially when it came to doing chores. Grandma was unmoved: she could see Lily was merely pretending and not very successfully. 'Please stop this charade,' she said. 'I know you're not ill. You wouldn't fool anyone. I know you only went to see Nancy and Fred to get ideas about feigning illness. Do you think they don't realise it?'

'I get on well with Fred,' Lily countered. 'We talk about boxing and stuff. He likes to spar—a little.'

'Oh yes. It would have to be "a little", otherwise he might have to make an effort, maybe then do something useful. That would never do. And don't you go the same way because it leads nowhere good.'

Afraid about what the bullies might do next, or teachers might say, or the police, and worried about what else she might be accused of, Lily began to feel ill. Or at least she convinced herself she did. She was determined she was never going back to school.

46

At the start of the Easter holidays, soon after Lily's fifteenth birthday, Mack called round looking crestfallen. For once it was Lily who would be the strong emotionally supportive one. 'What's up?' she asked her dearest friend, who merely shook her head. Grandma welcomed her and offered her tea, but it was clear Mack wanted to go straight to Lily's room. Once there, Mack threw her arms around Lily and started crying. She then revealed she was having to move home. And quickly. Her mother could no longer afford the rent and had obtained a job in Scotland where her family's roots were, and Mack was going with her. She said, 'I confess I never cried so much since my grandma died. Even more than being told of the divorce. Now I must adore you from afar, helpless as you end up finding someone rich.'

'I don't think you need worry about that.'

'I know. You'll be rich by your own means.'

They lay on the bed in each others' arms for a while and then took Molly for a walk for possibly the final time together. It brought back memories of so many other times, talking about all their favourite subjects and playing with names and words. Lily offered her hand and Mack took it. They talked about the future, both sad whilst trying to be positive. When they were back at the house they baked a German bee sting cake with Grandma's help.

Later, when Mack said goodbye and went home, Lily felt maudlin, as though part of her was gone forever.

Lily told Grandma it was time to withdraw her from school, otherwise she was sure she would be expelled. In fact, she would *try* to be expelled. Grandma told her she was concerned about her unhappiness but would not respond to threats. She said, 'I told you I would pay for it, but it won't be easy. One more term and after that it's another year with new teachers.'

'How can you afford not to? I will be rich one day, and what it costs now will seem like nothing. I'll pay it all back.'

'You're living in a dream world, Lily. Where are you getting these ideas?'

'The dream as you call it is my reality. Don't believe me if you don't want to. It's not a dream that

I would rather be dead than go to this school for another day. And my favourite teacher—the only teacher who likes me, Emily Hass—is leaving as well as my best friend. I'm not lazy. I want to start now.'

'In the holidays?'

'Yes!'

Grandma said she would contact Mr Pitcairn again. 'Not that I'm responding to threats,' she insisted gamely.

Lily reached out to Gloria on Facebook: 'Hey, how are you?'

'Lovely surprise! I'm cool. Just got two for the Anteaters.'

'What?'

'Two goals. My college team. Soccer. Football to you.'

'Wow!'

'We tied 3-3. My friend, Analisa Garcia, scored the other. We break from deep so fast we catch them out. Our defense is leaky as hell though. So what's with you, Maggot? Sorry not been in touch but busy. Trying to keep out of dad's corporate stuff.'

'I'm feeling down. My best friend's leaving for good. She's been a great inspiration.'

'Sorry to hear that. I will try to cheer you up. You're *my* inspiration. By the way, expect things to kick off soon with the Friends and the company. I don't like asking Dad. He gets so mad about them.'

47

Lily watched a filmed interview with Frank Sales-man, courtesy of Gloria. Lily wondered why Gloria sent it because surely the Friends would like to see it, but perhaps it was a test of trust.

Frank was in a jovial, combative mood with the head of Operations, Abel Stench: 'How's your chakras today, Abe?'

'Pretty good. No complaints from me.'

'Good. So what are these activist folks moaning about now? Let me guess: too much sugar in our milkshakes?'

'Right.'

'OK, being at the forefront of scientific research to improve our customers' health in every way possible since the first millisecond of our existence, our de-velopment team working day and night has created a new and totally natural and wholesome sweetener. So what is it?'

'Sugar.'

'Exactly. A new type of sugar. Asked and an-swered, as lawyers love to say in court. The new sug-ar is just sweeter.'

'Then there's farmers complaining about the pric-es you pay them.'

'Farmers complaining? Is that news? It's in their DNA. You ever seen a farmer rolling on his back with joy? No, of course not. We should have our own farms so we don't have to rely on them. Anything else? This is not a very deep barrel, by the way.'

'Another consumer complaint says our products don't list all the flavourings and preservatives on the containers.'

'Big deal. We tell them what's in their interests to know. What whacko came up with this complaint? If we listed all the ingredients in our products, the writing would be so small no-one would be able to read it even with a magnifying glass. Then they'd complain our labels gave them eye strain. Besides, every ingredient is clinically tested to the highest possible standards. We know that because we invented the standards.'

'They also say wine from grapes supposedly from a highly celebrated and prestigious vineyard are actually from a nondescript local cooperative.'

'Are you serious? Does this even pass the "So what?" test?'

'Maybe not.'

'Then you'd think wrong! Of course it does. There is no "So what?" test for us. Every detail is as important as every other detail. Of course it matters where the grapes come from. The point is, the grapes from the local cooperative are better, that's why we use them—and why we celebrate them. OK, we'll soon be releasing a whole load of new products. Brand new recipes. Here's a working list off the top of my head: egg-free cake, soy latte, iced doughnut, key lime pie, cherry dump cake, sweet buttermilk pie... I hope you're getting all these... pineapple cream cheese pie, chocolate pecan pie, fudge brownie pie, chocolate banana galette, fluke crudo (whatever that is or did I just make it up? No, I didn't: something fishy, best with Meyer lemon), innovative seaweed products (let's get that new underwater farm running!), and that's just the first minute. Then we could do a switcheroo between entrée and dessert, so that the people that follow all these ridiculous trends end up with cheesecake with their peas and carrots, and beef with their ice cream. Yum or yuk, I'm not sure which. We'll blitz the joy list anyway.'

'And what's our latest response to the ongoing boycott?'

'Easy. It's a dog and pony show without the pony. Or the dog. OK, in response, which I'm sure will be instantly all over the media, we give the customary heartfelt spiel on behalf of the company: express disappointment, remind them it's a huge misunderstanding, stress our dedication with every fibre of our being to meaningless, er meaning*ful* change and constant improvement, and reaffirm we are humbled by the support of all our genuine customers.'

Abel Stench became excited: 'And we could remind them our main competitors are not so hot either. Last month, one of them produced a bunch of fancy sweeteners for fizzy drinks that were pure poison.'

'Give me more.'

'Another one put out their so-called top-of-the-range caviar that was so low-grade even starving dogs wouldn't touch it.'

'That's it!'

'And one bunch of jokers let a fraudster hack into their slipshod system and claim to be their buying department...'

'I love it.'

'They ordered a bunch of stuff, sold it off, pocketed the dough, and disappeared before the company even woke up.'

'We admire the inventiveness of crooks, Abe. They are amongst the most creative people in the world, but they'd never trick us down that rabbit hole.'

48

Despite being unable to understand Lily's attitude, Grandma found in her heart an admiration for the teenager's growing mental strength. Lily's independent thinking had triggered a memory of when she herself had been a teenager. She'd had that same rebellious streak, although in her case she'd always been respectful at the same time, just the good side of surly, and she wasn't sure Lily had learnt that art yet, or would even want to learn it. She decided she should actively pursue home-schooling. Accordingly, she wrote to the head teacher formally requesting Lily's name be removed from the register.

In the following days, tutors were hired, though sadly without Emily Hass who had by now moved away. At the introductory meeting, Lily found Mr Pitcairn, who was to be her principal tutor, a 'funny little man'. He smiled a lot and had a neat moustache, small round glasses and a full head of grey hair. He was, he proudly declared, a member of the Friends of Lily Upshire. Lily was famous now, or more precisely her name was, and the tutor was delighted to associate with her for that reason. This did not initially endear him to her, but she was wise enough to know not to object to him.

Mr Pitcairn was always dapperly dressed when he came to the house for tutorials, wearing a tie and smart suit that looked brand new. The lessons were to be held in the lounge, and therefore Grandma bought a portable TV to watch in the small back room. Mr Pitcairn's main subject was maths, but he taught science as well. Lily remembered Grandma saying he could teach her business also. It transpired that he had run a profitable business once but sold it to look after a terminally ill friend. When the friend passed away he'd decided to spend his time teaching maths to children who needed help. When he told her this, Lily said, 'So you chose to work with thick kids like me with behavioural issues.'

Pitcairn was embarrassed. 'It's not the way I see it,' he said. 'Your grandmother is paying me to help you with your studies, and I will do that to the best of my abilities.' Then he asked, 'What do you want to be when you grow up?' It was the same old question.

'Rich.'

'And how do you intend to achieve that?'

'Business. Can you teach me the basics?'

Lily informed Grandma she had already talked to
Mr Pitcairn about including business in her studies. Grandma did not object. Lily told her it was her
route to riches, and Grandma would not argue.

49

Talk about claims the company was receiving fired
up Frank for a call with the head of Operations, Abel
Stench. Gloria forwarded a recording to Lily:

'So you want my comments on this latest flapdoo-
dle, Abe? I understand it's the work of these appall-
ing Friends of Lily Upshire people.'

'Yes.'

'Sick-making. I bet they don't even know who poor
Lily is. They take her name in vain. I would never
do that. I would name a subsidiary—something vital
like, say, a dog toy supplier—after her. So what's the
latest clamour about?'

'As you know, a number of claims have been received.'

'Help me here. One is a number. A billion is a
number.'

'Thousands.'

'OK, we're getting closer. I'll take it as 2,000 rather than 999,999. The sad fact is that there's always
the odd moocher hanging around with a handful of
gimme and mouthful of much obliged, as the old

song goes. That's where our lawyer has always come in.'

'This is bigger.'

'These are claims about what?

'Contaminated ice cream, accidents in the stores, salmonella in melons, mouldy bread...'

'Mouldy bread? Enough already. We've had this before. OK, so it's a bunch of hick carpetbaggers. Mouldy bread indeed! Believe it or not, folks, if you don't eat bread, it goes mouldy. This is so ridiculous it could not be a more obvious scam. I bet every creep and panhandler this side of the Rio Grande is on to it. Tell them we're more than used to it. We know they see us as a Find-the-Lady mark. So what have the Friends of Lily got to do with this latest?'

'Their lawyer is coordinating all the claimants.'

'Of course he is. I bet there's ads all over the internet seeking new suckers. And who do you think responds? The dregs, that's who. They think we fell off the turnip truck, but I'm more than confident we can resist an onslaught of such swindlers.'

'Will you instruct counsel?'

'No. We're big enough to deal with it ourselves. Our usual lawyer's getting on in years, and it'll soon be time to put him out in the sweet grass. There's no need to bust our tail over this flimflam, but we'll do it differently. We used to respond with ornate things like: "Surprised to hear...", "We regret...", "Entirely without prejudice", etcetera...'

Hearing these phrases reminded Lily of the letters she received from the company years ago.

'...You know the lingo as well as me. It's the easiest thing in the world to make up, but now we sum it up very easily: "Have at it, my friends. Have at it. Whatever your claims—whether it's fake butter, jelly bean sugar, or a director's negligent handshake, have at it." And let's put paid to this bunch of palookas!'

50

As part of her business education, and at her specific request, Mr Pitcairn explained to Lily how shares worked. He described how companies started off little, owned by one person or maybe two or three, then as the company got bigger people brought in more money called capital, and then when the company got big enough it changed from a private company to a public one by selling shares.

'Like on the stock exchange?' she asked.

'Yes. And then the shares are traded whenever the stock exchange is open.'

'So did the Blueberry Flip company start off little?'

'Yes it was a weeny artisan bakery when it started in small-town America. It had a rival bakery across the street from it.'

'Competition is good, isn't it?'

'Yes, but sometimes there can be too much. Two fancy bakeries in the same street can get along, but what if there's six? No-one makes money then.'

'So eventually some drop out? Is that what happened with Blueberry Flip's rival?'

'That's the subject of legend. The bakery you call Blueberry Flip struggled to get market share. There just weren't enough people wanted fancy, expensive bread...'

'People would rather go to the supermarket, right?'

'Yes. It looked like curtains for old Blueberry Flip, but it got a lucky break.'

'Their rival moved out?'

'More exactly, the mice moved in.'

'Yuk!'

'That's right. That's what customers thought too. But it wasn't mice they found but mice poo. Even more yuk! Just before the health people came in. Very inconvenient.'

'So that was lucky for Blueberry Flip.'

Mr Pitcairn gave his odd crooked smile that Lily already found endearing. 'People say you create your own luck.'

'So they cheated! People accuse me of cheating, but I would never do anything as bad as that!' She wondered about this statement. It was true she would never do anything like that directly, but she would use her mother's power to put a hex on someone if she had to. 'So is Blueberry Flip a good bet, Mr Pitcairn?'

'I can't advise you on that. I would not be allowed to. But let's see...' He showed her where to look online for GUFF as the company was now called. 'The price has been going down lately. It's at 637. I would say that's a big drop today, so I expect it to bounce a bit and then maybe drop again. So it may be a good time to buy but not to hold. The thing is, every time you trade you have to pay.'

Later, Lily followed the smoothie company online, watching the share price, reading incomprehensible company statements including what the CEO Frank Salesman had to say, also new product launches and company acquisitions. She watched the share price continue dropping over the next few days to 572, then she persuaded a reluctant Grandma to buy as many shares in the company as she could afford.

51

Months passed. With Mack now gone and only responding to Lily's approaches with occasional brief Facebook messages and phone texts, she found a new friend online. Her name was Petra. She lived in London and, like Lily, was a boxer. She was a blonde with long hair and blue eyes. She looked at her picture all the time. To Lily, she was a dream girl. She was perfect.

Petra was more and more keen in her requests to meet. Lily was thrilled. She wanted Petra to visit and told her she believed it was a good time. Petra agreed and seemed excited at the prospect. She would come to Retingham on the train.

Part of Lily feared she would turn out to be another catfish. Petra was more straightforward, however. She talked about her and Lily one day becoming friends for life, and Lily believed her because she wanted to.

Petra asked whether she could visit the boxing gym where Lily trained and suggested perhaps they could have a 'playful spar' together. Lily thought this a great idea. Not only would it give them something to do, but it would be a way to bond. It reminded her of the times she and Mack would play wrestle, and Mack would accuse her of cheating, and how she would protest her innocence even while privately acknowledging it was true.

She talked to Ted about Petra's suggestion. He was not keen, saying his gym was intended only for people he trained himself, not outsiders. He insisted that Petra would have to produce evidence of being professionally trained, and for how long, and a medical. Lily didn't understand, but Ted said that if Petra got injured, there could be a problem with insurance. In any event, Ted was adamant, and so Lily had to request the evidence from Petra which she found embarrassing, although Petra did not seem to mind.

But Petra was suddenly indifferent about visiting, and Lily sensed there was something the matter. Was she another impostor like Brandi, possibly even connected to one of the Bizzell sisters? Lily was tempted to do a Facebook search which was what Mack had used to expose Brandi, but she lacked Mack's expertise. Lily could not afford to isolate herself, and she wanted friends; therefore, she did not conduct any research on Petra.

52

The Friends of Lily Upshire filed a lawsuit in the UK courts against the company. It prompted an angry statement from Frank Salesman: 'This is the most ridiculous lawsuit in the history of litigation. It all began with an entirely spurious allegation about a pea—a small harmless garden pea—that some low-life in a hick town in England claimed they found in a smoothie, which was impossible because of our quality standards—the highest such standards in the world. Nevertheless, being entirely reasonable in all our dealings we attempted to satisfy the claimant, but they were too greedy, others piled in, and now we have this goat rodeo to contend with. Defeat it we will.'

Spurious claim? Lowlife? Goat rodeo? When Lily heard about the CEO's statement from Mr Pitcairn, she was so upset she put a hex on Frank. Next morning, the company finance director, Milton Pinch, was kidnapped from his superyacht. Coincidence?

She received a message from Gloria apologising for what her father had said: 'He was rude. He'd run out of his new medication, I think. He hates the Friends, but he has private admiration for you.'

'You said things would kick off, and now they have.'

'Don't worry, Maggot, it all works to the good. This lawsuit is just the beginning.'

53

Petra sent her a message: 'When can we meet? I can't wait to see my girlfriend in the flesh.' This made Lily giddy: she was also keen to meet. Lily could not stop looking at Petra's picture. A freckle-faced blonde with blue eyes, not much different in looks from herself. Lily asked her for more pictures, and Petra complied. Lily sent pictures too, although these were out of date within a few days, because the next time Sally called round she asked her for what she called 'a hot skinhead look'. As part of her plan to toughen up she'd decided to have her hair cut extremely short, but she still wanted to look attractive. Grandma disapproved but kept quiet about it—Lily had worn her down so much she now just wanted her to be, if not happy, at least appeased.

Now she wasn't at school anymore, Lily liked to pop next door after her tutoring sessions were over and before she started on her homework. She went mainly to see Fred for whom these days she found an odd kinship as a fellow rebel. For his part, Fred was so delighted to see her that when he knew she'd arrived he'd almost leap out of bed, only at the last moment remembering his precarious health situation and taking it slowly.

Today as he arrived downstairs he greeted her with 'How's my Li'l Fighter? Are you winning?' and his teeth enjoyed a happy shift.

She smiled and said, 'I'm fine.' She asked him how he was. He replied that he was feeling much better, thank you, although still not quite well enough to actually do anything.

Seeing her appearance transported him back to his teenage years. He'd been a skinhead then, and he began to relive those days. He'd had so much energy then, and strength, so invigorated he could leap from his bed and sprint to the shops before breakfast, and work out for half an hour, but now of course even the thought of it was hazardous to his wellbeing. It also brought back memories for Nancy who, incongruous as it sounded to the teenager, had been a skinhead at the same time as Fred.

Fred told her how much he admired her for taking up boxing. Claiming to be a former fighter himself, he had a sparring session with her in the lounge until a twinge in his back and the sheer effort overwhelmed him, and he retired panting to an armchair. After this they sat in the dining room with Nancy until he dozed off. Nancy was full of stress. It was such a busy time for her on the council. The big bad company was buying up all the ailing businesses in the town centre and submitting impractical plans for future development that could not be dismissed lest the company take flight. This dilemma had made Nancy and the rest of the council seriously busy with many lengthy meetings, feasibility studies and reports to read. Thus far, not one proposal had been accepted.

54

Lily was approached about being involved with a new group, the Real Friends of Lily Upshire. This was in opposition to the Friends group, so the charming, well-dressed young man who called round explained. He was full of sweet talk, telling her how wonderful she was. This played well to her vanity, but she was wary.

They sat in the lounge drinking tea. Grandma fluttered around, clearly enchanted by the handsome visitor. He asked Lily what she thought about the Friends set up in her name. She replied she was bemused at how her name had become public property and wasn't particularly pleased about it, but if she could find a way to make money out of it, she would. She told him she wondered why he had come to see her: was it part of the campaign by the Blueberry Flip company everyone complained about? He

said his organisation was run entirely independently, but, naive though she was, she realised this was
a lie. The man asked if she knew the people behind
the Friends organisation. 'Not me or Grandma,' she
said. 'But most people in the area are in it.' He told
her the company was determined to beat the Friends
group, whatever it took. 'But always within the law,'
he stressed. 'We're looking for information about the
Friends.'

'What sort of information,' she asked.

'Are they good people?'

She thought about Fred, the notorious malingerer. 'Yes,' she said. Then she thought of the Bizzell
family. 'But not all,' she added.

He was rather too transparently interested, and
with a 'tell me more' look in his eyes.

'Information is expensive,' she said, thinking
about all the dirt on the Bizzells—how valuable that
would be to the company!

He seemed prepared: 'How expensive?'

'A million pounds,' said Lily without a moment's
thought.

He was not so well prepared for that. He was embarrassed. 'Why so much?'

'Personal expenses.'

'But that's an awful lot.' He couldn't decide whether she was joking or mad.

'I need to buy Grandma a new house. People are
not happy about us not joining so we need to move.'

'You could easily get a house for much less than
that.'

'Not with stables and a paddock, and vineyard...'

'You might need more than a million for that.' He was enjoying the joke.

'...and an orangery. OK then, say £1.5 million. And a swimming pool, and tennis courts. Put down £2 million. And a squash court.'

'I don't think the company will pay anything like that. Or anything at all. It might seem like a bribe.'

'Their loss,' she said smiling. 'But I am not one for groups. I prefer to work alone. Don't you think it will cost more than £2 million in the end? I predict it will.'

55

Frank Salesman was high on his new medication when the next recorded interview took place, forwarded to Lily by Gloria. Frank told interviewer, Picard Snook, he felt a deep antagonism towards the Friends group: 'All over the internet, there's friends of this or friends of that. Even serial killers have friends. Sometimes it seems the only one who hasn't got a group of friends is this sacred company. We're well used to it. For a company like us trouble's always in the mail. I bet the leader of this Friends of Lily group doesn't even know her...'

'Right.'

'...just some dozy klutz buffaloed into it by a bunch of attention-grabbing schmucks. A bunch of losers hollering "Your brand is toxic!" from the latest bandwagon...'

'Indeed.'

'...a bandwagon full of Animal Crackers. There's always some grasper out there sees us as an easy mark. I tell you, they sure know how to harsh my mellow.'

Lily felt sorry for Frank, but she often hardly understood a word he said.

'Just like that singer who claims we used her precious image in ads without her permission.'

'I remember her.'

Lily thought: used her image without permission? Hey, that's what I'm going to claim against the Friends!

'It was her biggest break, promoting that lousy shampoo and conditioner—never mind the only customers that liked it were llamas in the zoo—and we gave the world the highly reasonable impression that she endorsed it, like a million deadbeat wannabes would have jumped at the chance to do. So what that she'd never heard of it? It was more famous than her. Now, purely coincidentally, since she started this fight with us her career's on the slide. Right?'

'Yes. So she's included that in her complaint as well.'

'She thought she was too big for our shampoo. Too bad. I like her spirit, a real spitfire. But in her heart, she's just a loser, and she knows it but can't accept it.'

'There's plenty like her.'

'Ten a cent. Sore losers, the lot of them. Just like Lily's so-called Friends: it's a travesty for those beefheads to use her name the way they do...'

Lily brightened.

'...I hope she goes after them...'

She brightened even more.

'...If I could sow that idea in her mind, I would. I'm even wondering if we shouldn't set up our own group, the Real Friends of Lily Upshire. Just kidding.'

'It's already happened.'

'Really?'

Lily was puzzled. She wondered if he was simply out of touch with what others in the company were doing.

'Marvellous! Let them fight keyboard wars with each other day and night. These Friends people won't break us. Hell, they won't even touch us! They want to make us look like the corporate equivalent of a roach motel and make our precious workers feel hollow and tawdry; but we must always hold before us our core values: integrity, fundamental commitment to quality, and customer service, and, above all, ...whatever you like.'

56

Petra came to visit Lily, arriving from London by train. Lily went to meet her, looking for a girl with long blonde hair and blue eyes, a girl who looked just like her before she'd had her hair shorn, this being the reason she'd chosen her. But the girl she was expecting was not on the train. Lily waited inside the station in case she showed up. Finally, she noticed a tall, oval-faced, mixed-race girl with her hair in a braid, carrying an expensive-looking sports bag. The girl approached her. 'Lily?'

It was Petra. A totally different person to the one she thought she'd been writing to. Was no-one online who they said they were?

They shared pleasantries, but Lily was preoccupied with her thoughts about Petra's deception as they walked home. They said little. At home Grandma made a fuss of Petra, much to Lily's embarrassment, although it served to relax the tension between the girls. Grandma had made only a light lunch because they were going to Ted's place. After lunch, when briefly alone together, Lily felt compelled to say, 'I told you I'd been catfished before. Now you've deceived me. You're not the person you said you were.'

Petra, irritated, said in response, 'Nor are you.'

'What did you say?'

'You're not who you said you were either. You were supposed to have long hair. You're a skinhead. If I'd known you were a skinhead, I wouldn't have come.'

'No, I'm not. It's just a look.'

'I never intended to meet you anyway. You or anyone. It started as a joke for me, but you insisted.'

Lily was pensive but then brightened. 'It doesn't mean we can't be friends,' she said.

'You're right. It doesn't.' Petra hugged her. But they were both disillusioned.

After a quick play with Molly, the girls changed into their boxing gear and walked to Ted's gym. When they arrived, after the introductions, Petra stood surveying with a frown the small, makeshift set-up; there were a couple of boys in their late teens sparring at the back, oblivious to the new arrivals, and a trio of girls doing squats supervised by Ted's daughter, Maria, who was both a professional gym instructor and trained paramedic.

Ted sensed Petra's disapproval, no doubt comparing his gym unfavourably to the clubs she was used to; disapproval he was familiar with and, by his own admission, was oversensitive about. She requested a match: three rounds of three minutes. Lily bit her lip, unwilling to show weakness.

'Two minutes,' said Ted sternly as he reviewed the medical form she'd given him. He glanced at Lily who said nothing. 'OK then,' he sighed, trying to hide his feelings.

As Petra stood on the scales, Lily thought she looked so much bigger and stronger and in the mood to punish her. When Petra joined in the exercises, temporarily out of earshot, Ted said, 'Lily, you're going to get a beating if you're not careful.'

'I didn't even want a fight,' she said. 'Just light sparring, is what I told her, like you said.'

'She looks angry, doesn't she? My guess is, a skinhead beat her up once, and she wants payback.'

'But I'm not a skinhead.'

'I know. And you'd probably never meet her in the ring because she's in a different weight class. She's not much heavier than you though, which ought to surprise me, but she's at light flyweight and you're a pin. You might as well take a dive in the first. Get it over with. It doesn't matter. It doesn't mean anything.'

'It does to me.'

'Yeah, it doesn't mean much to me, only my license. Look, the upside is, she's going to be slow. Powerful, yes, but slow. The opposite of you. You have to do what we've talked about in training: you've got to back off her, quickly in, combination, boom boom, get out of her way. *Don't* close your eyes—that's a bad habit you've slipped into. Stay light on your feet. Always quick.' But he was worried. He knew from the training sessions and her weight that she hadn't been working out lately, hadn't been to the gym, hadn't been using the punch bag her grandma bought. 'How often have you skipped rope this week? Don't lie.'

'Once.'

'Once is not enough. If you trained like you should do—like you said you would, like you used to—this would be a doddle. But you don't, so you will struggle. What do we always say here?'

'Train hard, breathe easy.' It was one of his mantras like the ones on the gym wall: 'Wake Up!' and the weird, crushing 'Dreams are for sleepers'.

'Train hard, breathe easy. Don't dabble. As you know, all three of my daughters learned to box to a good standard, and it set them up for life. The mental discipline of it. And every time they got hit in a fight I felt it. And it's like that with you. You're like my fourth daughter. I've known you since you were a little kid. If you're hurt, I'll feel it too.'

Fourth daughter? She felt guilty. 'I'm sorry, Ted. You can call it off if you want to.'

'No. That would be worse. That would be more humiliating for you now than losing. If I think you're suffering, I'll stop it.'

Petra now approached. She had big muscles. Everything about her exuded power and strength. She said, 'What's the matter, Lily? You look scared. Are you a little bit of a coward? Afraid you'll get hurt? I'll try not to hurt you. Not too much anyway.'

Lily stared at Petra's big arms and shoulders, and she trembled inside. She didn't mind getting hit, but she was afraid of losing, lest her confidence evaporate, and she'd want to give up boxing altogether, the way she had given up so much in the past because she was a 'dabbler'. Petra wanted to dispense with helmets, but Ted was adamant. He felt she would have dispensed with gloves and hand wraps as well if she could. He would have loved her as one of his boxers for her physique and the fire he saw in her, and yet he couldn't avoid finding her intensely annoying. It was that arrogance of manner and imperious gaze that confirmed to him her dismissal of his gym as inferior purely because it wasn't in London. It was this, combined with his unease about the upcoming few minutes, that triggered for a moment the unwelcome memory of his last professional fight, when his young opponent from the East End of London had taunted him as 'thick northern scum', the shambolic defeat ending his career. In this moment of recall he felt irked with Lily for having created the current situation, irritated with Petra for her haughtiness, and disappointed with himself for letting it upset him.

After a warm-up with shadow boxing, when the three of them were in the ring Ted said, 'Take it easy on each other, girls. Remember that you're friends, and you'll still want to be friends afterwards.' The start of the fight was cautious, the exchanges tentative. Lily felt nervous and sluggish, and her punches were not connecting. As for Petra, she was a clumsy fighter, not really a boxer at all. But she had frightening power, and out of nowhere, towards the end of the first round, she produced a big punch that hit Lily so hard to the body it knocked her halfway across the ring. Winded, Lily rocked on her heels as Petra stalked her, and then hit her hard again. Lily fell to the floor. Ted began the count. The fight should have been over then, but the sight of Petra dancing with joy, and not even in her corner, angered Ted so much that perversely he slowed the count. Lily, now crouching, took some deep breaths and managed to leap up just in time, but she was so lightheaded she floundered like a shot bird as Petra bore down on her once more. Brian immediately rang the bell for the end of the round, a good twenty seconds early. Petra marched angrily back to her corner. Lily had escaped, thanks to the ref and Brian's dodgy time-keeping. Ted said to her, 'You OK?'

'She caught me off guard. I wasn't paying attention like I should. That's all. I'm fine.' She sent a smile Brian's way.

'If she hits you again like that, I'll have to call it off. Move your feet. Think of Muhammad Ali, think of your beloved Manny like we've talked about from day one. OK, she's got a big punch, but she has nothing else. You can outbox her.'

Despite the brave talk, Lily's confidence was still low, but when Brian rang for the start of the second round, for a few moments Lily was able to imagine she was her hero Manny Pacquiao, and she ran towards her opponent and caught her with a rush of early punches. Petra was taken by surprise and temporarily bewildered at the speed, allowing Lily to land a string of further scoring blows. But with her lack of fitness she quickly tired as Petra's strength returned, and she was only just able to dance out of the way of a huge punch that, had it landed, she feared would have rendered her unconscious. From this point, Lily clung on, clutching Petra's arms, but also landing low blows to distract her. She survived to the bell. The final round followed the same pattern, with another dazzling start by Lily, but at the end of the round, exhausted, she took a knock to the body that made her stumble backwards, although it looked more like a slip. She struggled up, then wobbled, Ted made as if to start a mandatory count of eight but changed his mind. Brian rang the final bell. A relieved Ted declared a draw, Petra made a face of resigned disgust, and Lily was bemused. She felt she'd lost, knowing she'd cheated with her clinging and low punches, and she felt very small. She opened her arms and almost fell into a hug with Petra, but the latter pushed her away, saying, 'You're not pretending to fight now, skinhead.'

Maria checked them over individually, taking her time, talking with each of them privately, and after thanking Ted they walked home, barely exchanging words. Lily was beset by the fear that Petra, frustrated at the result, would try to beat her up as they made their way through the empty side-streets and alleyways. But this worry was both irrational and unfair: Petra was merely contemptuous, thinking her just an idiot, too stupid to realise that 'skinhead' was not merely a fashion or 'a look', and too ignorant to recognise that Petra had suffered more bullying in her life than Lily had—no-one had ever attacked Lily over her skin colour—but unlike Lily, who paraded her bullying almost as a badge, Petra held hers within herself. Petra hated her, but she'd seen the ring as the place to express it.

When they arrived at the house they showered and changed clothes. In Lily's room Petra demanded, 'Admit that I won, skinhead.'

'It was a draw. I landed some good punches. I can box.'

'You know I beat you. You cheated. The ref was biased. And that grasshopper—'

'What?'

'That Brian—he's all bony arms and legs, like a giant locust or something.'

'Oh, he's OK.'

'You know, you and Brian would make a good pair. You're both nerdy—and needy.' Seeing Lily's expression of hurt, Petra said, 'I forgive you' and then startled her with a kiss on the mouth which became a long, deep kiss before Lily even realised it was happening. Its effect on her was every bit as strong as the biggest punch Petra had landed in the fight. 'There,' Petra said gently, smiling.

Grandma had made a special tea of sandwiches, crumpets, cakes, and trifle. The girls, starving after their exertions, scoffed the food down and it was a happy interlude, but afterwards Petra checked her phone and announced without explanation that she needed to catch an early train.

On the platform Lily asked Petra when she could visit her in London, but the latter was noncommittal. She said it was a busy time for her but didn't elaborate. As they parted Petra kissed her on the lips and said, 'Goodbye, my pretty little skinhead girl,' and hurried on to the train. She did not wave, and Lily suspected she would never see her again.

57

Lily received a message from Gloria: 'Hey, Maggot, here's something to make you laugh. My dad was talking to someone today re your Top 5 Things in the World. Was that something you posted?'

'Yes, but ages ago.'

'It made me laugh. The company's blueberry flip smoothie is second to a baby giraffe. Dad said, "Second to a giraffe—not exactly aspirational!"'

'What else did he say?'

'That you love things like boxing.'

'I do.'

'Can we speak on the phone?'

'Sure.' They exchanged numbers.

Gloria rang her. Lily immediately loved the re-laxed warmth of her voice. Gloria said, 'You've be-come what's known as an influencer. My dad said to me, "Influencer? Excellent. She's joined our club. That's what we've been doing all along. Influenc-ing governments and trends." He told me he never used to say sorry about anything. Now he says it fifty times before breakfast. He said you'd be good in the Inventions department or whatever it's called. He said they could do with a shake-up because they're not inventing much. He told me someone proposed hacking into your Instagram account. My dad said, "And what would be the point of that?" The person said it would trash your reputation, destroy your credibility...'

'My reputation? What reputation?'

'There's some dirty tricks they can do with an in-fluencer. They can fix an account to promote sketchy investment schemes and drinks that make kids sick so that real brands won't want to support them. The idea with you was to ruin your reputation like this so they could ruin the Friends group bearing your name. My dad said he admired the logic and ap-plauded the research, but he was not interested in hurting a genuine customer. He said the company only wants to be good. An exemplar to the world. He said they should spend their time instead on netting a few angel investors and shooting vulture funds out of the sky. So, Maggot, it means you're on the same side as my dad.'

'That's cool. Now I shall start calling you Glowie. Like a glowworm.'

'I like them.'

'I've never seen one.'

'I have, but they're rare. They're pink.'

Lily looked up pink glowworms in Southern California on Google, then checked out the latest interview Gloria had sent.

Frank was saying, 'I see a bunch of so-called influencers are claiming to be sponsored by our biggest rivals. So be it. How those people like to show off! And then there's those fading celebrities with all their ateliers, and beauty ambassadors, and whatnot. I can't abide such pretension.'

'And there's the scams they work up,' said Abel Stench of Operations.

'Scams? We like scams. That is, we admire inventiveness. Give me an example.'

'They put up a post promoting makeup they bought, and it looks like the company's sponsoring them—but it's not. Or they make it look like they've been paid to go to a restaurant or fashion house or something—but they haven't. Or they will claim to be paid for a trip to somewhere nice, say, in Spain, and they'll thank the hotel and restaurants, and put up images of themselves sitting in the lounge or enjoying a meal, and say they're being sponsored, but the hotel and restaurants know nothing about it.'

'This is almost interesting. Certainly weird. We never thought of that. But why do these influencer folks do this?'

'To get real sponsorship. What the influencer's saying is, "Look at me with all my millions of followers promoting a brand—it could be yours."'

'And in our case, it will be. I'll admit I don't under-stand why people choose to invest their money and time backing such fruit flies, but I guess we should want influencers. We want to attract all the young folks we can. We want to be part of their dreams. We could cultivate these so-called influencers and keep sending them free stuff—the more the better. We could sponsor a singer from Retingham. Get them on one of those TV singing shows where a bunch of losers with big dreams sing karaoke, except some-one is gracious enough to call one of them a winner, and they get a record deal, and tour, and stuff.'

'Not that easy. And what if the one we sponsor doesn't win?'

'We buy up the judges.'

'And what if they're incorruptible?'

'Always a "what if". Believe it or not, I was only kidding. But we could have our own TV show and broadcast it on our own channel which I just thought up. It'll be the Lily Upshire Show. We'll get Lily to give out the prizes. We're the real Friends of Lily Up-shire, and we'll carry on being them when her so-called Friends and their pathetic lawsuit have been flushed down the toilet and long forgotten about. But this is small potatoes—not much of a sugar rush. I think we need to adopt a new, much more aggres-sive acquisition strategy. We will focus on fast-grow-ing companies, the foals that will soon be thorough-breds. Unicorns—we will have stables full of them. Meanwhile, any little ship in need of a safe harbour from the storms can come to us.'

'Excuse me... are these little ships different to the unicorns in the stables?'

'Eh? Of course they are. A ship is not a unicorn. You're too darned literal, Abe. These are merely metaphors and here's another: we want to be the young dog sniffing the spring breeze for any new delight.'

'Cool.'

'And remember: to this day we've never had a flop. Not a single one.'

'I think we have.'

'Wrong thinking. It's just that some of our brands are more popular than others. And we will outlast everyone.'

'It's not what the business press says.'

'It's what *our* business press says and will continue to say, whatever poop the others spout.'

'Finished, they say.'

'Finish? Like the luxury finish on a new Ferrari.'

'No, "finished" in the sense of: reached the end.'

'I don't buy it. We're not ready to quit Camelot yet. Finished, indeed! It's like telling John Wayne in any of his films he's finished, or telling James Bond, or Captain America, or Superman. No, it's merely time to clean house. We'll bring in image management consultants and find a turnaround expert who agrees with everything we're doing.'

'And new investors?'

'Only investors with the imagination big enough for us. So let's get to it, let's paddle that platinum canoe. The new world is coming, and it won't wait!'

58

As an odd present to herself for her sixteenth birthday, Lily decided to hire the meanest lawyer she could find, which was a Mr Topp in America. She found him in *The World's Toughest Lawyers* online handbook which Gloria had recommended to her.

She talked to Mr Topp on Skype. He was an elderly, frail-looking gentleman in a cowboy hat, a former Texas Ranger.

'Are you really the world's meanest lawyer?' she asked.

'I don't like to think I am, but I've been called it.'

'Can you teach me how to be mean, Mr Topp? I try at it, but I have a lot to learn.'

'Why do you want to be mean, Lily?'

'I want to protect myself.'

'You got your own gang?'

'I'm on my own. How can I be a gang?'

'Sure you can—a gang of one. Say, the Lilywhite Gang.'

'How about the Lily*stone* Gang?'

'That's pretty cool. That sounds like a gang to be in. But I'm a lawyer—what can I do for you?'

Lily explained about the pea in the blueberry flip smoothie and the claims other people had made, and the so-called Friends of Lily Upshire which didn't even have anything to do with her, and how she'd been bullied at school and had taken up boxing training, and how she'd decided that if the Friends of Lily Upshire got any money out of it, then she wanted a share. So she wanted a mean lawyer to work for her.

'To protect your interests,' he said.

'If that's what it's called, yes.'

'Are you sure you want to do this, Lily? The world of litigation can be strange and surreal. It could take years for your case to be resolved.'

'I feel compelled to do it. Unless it will cost a ridiculous amount.'

'It *will* cost a ridiculous amount, but only if you win.' Mr Topp gave a little laugh. She decided she liked him and thought having him represent her could be fun. He explained that because Lily was a minor her grandmother as her guardian would have to formally instruct him. He would send her the documents for her grandmother to sign.

When the documents arrived, Lily explained to Grandma what she'd decided to do. Grandma had serious reservations about it. She wanted to talk to the lawyer before she signed anything, and she didn't understand what Lily hoped to achieve by it. Why didn't she simply join the Friends of Lily Upshire and let them do the work? Lily said she had no interest in them, and that what they were doing was a scam, and they had used her name without permission. Grandma said she couldn't see how hiring some lawyer in Texas was going to help her, and she argued hard, but in the end Lily declared, 'If the documents aren't signed by tomorrow, I'm going on hunger strike.'

Grandma said she'd think about it, although she knew from their previous disagreements that a determined Lily always got her way.

Grandma reluctantly agreed to sign the documents Mr Topp sent, and he was duly appointed to act for Lily, even though he wasn't yet sure what practical steps he could take, and nor was Lily.

59

The Friends were saying in their latest podcast that the company had been hit by both declining profit figures and a new ransom demand for Milton Pinch, the finance director. The very latest news was that Frank Salesman had set up a new department called Great Futures, which was really a front for an espionage operation into the company's enemies, be they competitors, activists, or extortionists. This was a development the Friends said needed careful monitoring.

Their podcast also included a leaked conversation between Frank and his team. Frank complained, 'In recognition of our current stratospheric success, this company is being called a sleeping giant. Such an insult! I'd rather the company were a dwarf with matchsticks in its eyes than a dozing, snoring giant with his toes being nibbled by a family of mice.

Meanwhile, the also-rans come huffing and puffing a good country mile behind us. But the real work goes on which includes my plan for Retingham. I'm thinking in terms of a big new blueberry flip smoothie plant. Maybe strawberry too. Maybe mango.'

'Planning permission may be difficult,' said Armitage Ozog from Development.

'Then we'll throw in a school. We'll put the mayor on the local company board.'

'He may not do it for us.'

'Then we'll get him out of office.'

'Not that easy.'

'Then we'll make it so. This company is about solutions—I don't like to hear "not that easy" and "won't do it" and all that negative talk. I'm sure the town doesn't want to stay in the past forever. Remember what that management guru used to parrot: "Things that don't change, stay the same." That's enough to terrify the residents of most towns and cities.'

'But some people prefer things to stay the same.'

'Yes, the privileged few. Of course they do. Change for them is a threat. We're not here for them, but for the little guy. The guy with aspirations. Aspirations that can never be met because that's what keeps him buying our stuff. So a struggling town like Retingham needs to move ahead fast, and we're here ready and waiting to do whatever we can to assist the folks there in their great adventure.'

60

When Ted heard Lily boasting about the fight with Petra, he said, 'It was nothing to brag about, Lily. Don't ever do that again or you and me will fall out.'

'What are you talking about?' she asked, even though she knew.

'You know you lost that fight. You blatantly cheated. I only let you get away with it because I didn't like the other girl's attitude. She wanted to beat you up and I wasn't having it—which doesn't excuse you. Do that in a real match and you'll be disqualified. No fighter of mine has ever had "DQ" in their record, and if they did, they'd be finished as far as I'm concerned.'

'I couldn't lose to her,' she said. 'She destroyed me. No-one's ever hit me that hard, but I was determined not to be beaten, whatever happened.'

'That's what your defence is for.' Seeing Lily was upset at having disappointed him, he softened, 'Look, you'd never meet her in the ring anyway. Take it easy. But get used to losing because it's going to happen sooner or later—in the ring and in life.'

'No,' she replied. 'It's not going to happen. Not in the ring, at least. And if I can't win fair in life, I'll cheat, and I'll do it so subtly no-one will know.'

Ted did not answer for a moment, merely shook his head, but then he started laughing. 'Alright,' he said at last. 'It's a good job I like you. Now get to it.'

Late one afternoon, Lily was walking home from town when she saw two boys beating up Brian in a side street. He was rarely a target because, although he was seen as odd and couldn't fight himself, everyone knew he was Ted's son. He was gentle, and after the Petra experience she craved that kind of sensitivity, which she found especially uncommon in a boy. She threw herself into the non-fight with such force and speed the bullies were taken off guard. Her ferocity shocked them. One of them was able to land a sharp blow to Lily's face that would turn into a bruise later, but her intervention worked because they ran off. Turning round, she discovered Brian had sneaked off down the street. She called after him, but he didn't stop, although he did raise his arm in recognition. She was disappointed. She thought he would be grateful and profess his love for her, which she would naturally reject, but instead he broke into a run, perhaps ashamed at having to be rescued, especially by a girl—so ashamed, as she later learned, he spent half the night in the treehouse in the family garden, refusing all meals.

61

Gloria phoned Lily to tell her what happened the day the big, new, international lawsuit came in: 'Dad was late into the office. Usually, he liked to be in by six, but that day an accident on the freeway jammed up the traffic for miles. He always said that being late was invariably followed by a problem at the office. In this instance, there was a bunch of his colleagues waiting for him.

'It immediately got him thinking some balloon had gone up. It was like Panic City, he said. Everyone with their hair on fire. Then Clem Horseneck of Corporate Legal told him they'd received a multi-billion dollar lawsuit in seventy jurisdictions around the world.'

'Sounds terrible,' said Lily. 'How did he react?'

'Coolly. He called it a "slightly more difficult day in the neighbourhood. Someone blowing a little smoke. Worth nothing more than a horse's laugh." That's the way Dad talks.'

'A horse's laugh?'

'I asked him if he was even bothered. He said, "Maybe when it's been through every court in the world, and we've lost in all of them, then I might be bothered for two nanoseconds." That's him alright. Never phased by anything. Always upbeat.'

'Is that good?'

'Very wearing.'

Gloria then sent a recording of a conference call Frank chaired about it: 'How predictable! I even dreamed it. What it means is that every loafer from every one-horse town in the world is lined up on the promise of a big-ticket day. A bunch of lazy hayseeds led by a topper who just wants to be the bringer of the biggest suit in world history. Oh, don't I know now how poor Gulliver felt! Tell the small-minded creeps to scamper back to Lilliput. I wonder how many of these so-called Friends of Lily Upshire there really are. You only need a handful of people standing round a hayrick shrieking and there's your claimants. I bet Lily's got more real-life friends than these fakers. It could even be a group of one with a parrot and a lawyer as a hired gun.'

'I think there's rather more than that,' said a woman with a brassy voice. Lily wondered if this was Melody Roller of Corporate Legal whom she wrote to once.

'It's a classic activist number they're pulling: make a big noise with a tiny physical presence. Everything online. Then other moochers pile in.'

'It's certainly a big noise at 1,593 pages,' said the woman.

'So much to say so little. I don't know why they don't just allege everything this company has ever done, or will do, or ever thought of doing, is bad and wrong, harmed everything and everyone, and there-fore must be punished in the most unimaginably harsh way to deter others and for the good of the universe, wiping out its very existence and history from both the physical world and the virtual. And by the way, 1,593 pages is a waste of precious resources, whereas I've no doubt they've laid on the sanctimo-ny with a gigantic syrup ladle about the environment they claim to care so much for. They just think we're saps because we're such a generous company.'

'The opposing lawyer says, "Corporate America's on trial"', said the woman.

'Then let Corporate America pay for it. This law-suit is a misdirected arrow. The rest of the corporate world is full of con artists, full service fraudsters, and people who don't deliver what they promise, but that's not us. No, Sir. Then again, you could say that we *are* Corporate America, indeed Corporate Everywhere, because that's where we are.' Frank could be heard banging the table with a mixture of enthusiasm and frustration. 'Those losers are just sticking pins in their treasure maps. Let them. We'll give 'em Hell, Harry before dinner time. We'll crush 'em. We'll make 'em say Uncle.' It then sounded like Frank pushed back his chair and rose to stand. 'When they see our team coming, they'll be running for the hills so fast they'll have nosebleeds! I never lose, so we'll get the very best lawyer—a Joe Rough-neck or a Daniel O'Bastard. Someone with a sign in his "war room" reading, "Stop Bitchin', Start A Rev-olution" or some such motivational stuff. Someone who can defeat bad magic. Someone who'll put their dukes up and make their lawyers eat crow before they're ten seconds older. OK, it's showtime. Circle the wagons, folks.'

Lily sent Gloria a simple message: 'Bloody hell!'

62

Lily had just finished talking to her lawyer Ernie Topp late one afternoon, a conversation in which he asked her whether she'd ever given any indication she was OK with the Friends using her name, and she'd said emphatically 'No!', when she was called downstairs by Grandma. 'There's someone at the door asking for you,' she said.

When Lily was in the lounge she asked her who it was. Grandma simply kept smiling in a knowing way which Lily interpreted as meaning that it was a boy. She was not in the mood to see one. She opened the door abruptly for dramatic effect. Standing there was Brian. He was shaking with a bunch of flowers in his hand. An expensive-looking bunch. Without looking into her eyes he thrust the flowers into her hand, tried to say something, thought better of it, and rushed away.

'Thanks, Brian!' she called after him. He did not look back.

Grandma said, 'He didn't even want to see you in person. He wanted me to take them for you. I told him, "Man up, Brian," and he just stood there trembling.'

'Poor Brian,' Lily remarked.

'So what is it with him?' said Grandma. 'Why is he so nervous these days? He never used to be like it. Not when he used to come to tea. I think he's in love. But he seems conflicted in some way. As though he feels he shouldn't be in love. You're the forbidden fruit, Lily.'

Lily did not know what to make of it.

A few days later, Lily met Brian in the park. He'd invited her. They sat on a bench together. He'd brought some doughnuts for them. She didn't like doughnuts, owing to her diet, but she accepted one. He said, 'I was wondering if we could hang out together?'

'Hang out together? Is that your way of asking: "Will you be my girlfriend?"'

'Well, we're hanging out together now.'

'Petra said if she had a boyfriend like you she'd tell him to toughen up.'

'That's what your grandma said. She said "man up" though.'

'I've never completely forgiven you for the time you left me to get beaten up. Then you ran off when I rescued you.'

'I'm sorry. I've been a coward. Is Petra your girlfriend?'

She thought of Petra's lips on hers. 'That was long ago. No,' she said, looking sad but keen for him not to notice.

'And do you have a boyfriend?'

'No.'

'So can we...'

'No.' This broke him up. She savoured it. 'I'm a little madam,' she said. 'That's what my Auntie Gwynne says, but I hate her anyway. I don't want to be a little madam. You deserve better than me.'

'No, that's not right.' She could tell he was in bits and she loved it.

Finally, she said, 'I will if you meet my conditions.'

He brightened, 'Alright. What are they then?'

'First, stop being a wimp.'

'Right.' He sighed.

'Second, take up boxing.'

'I'll do it.'

'Third...'

'Third? How many more are there?'

'Not many.'

He sighed again.

She said, 'It could be worse. Petra said to me that if she had a boyfriend like you, she'd torment him mercilessly. She'd get him to spend every penny he had on her, drain his bank account, then she'd dump him in the most humiliating way she could think of.'

'Why do you keep telling me what she said? I think you're still infatuated with her. Anyway, you're not Petra.'

'No. She's beautiful.'

'So are you. You're more...'

'Yeah I am.' She was tormenting him, just like Petra suggested. 'Not really. But I am too much in love with myself. And because I'm so in love with myself, I want you to buy yourself new clothes. Or I'll buy you some. When we're out I want people to say, "Look at that cute couple in their elegant clothes."'

'OK.'

'Fourth...'

'Fourth?'

'Fourth, don't stop being kind.'

'What?'

'You're a sweetheart. Stay that way. In my heart I know I'm an awful person. I threw the Bizzells' dog in the canal because they were using it to bully me. That was terrible.'

'It wasn't your fault, Lily. The horrible creature didn't even die, wasn't even hurt. I know what the dog was like. They used to literally throw it at people sometimes. The RSPCA should have been on to them.'

'You're kind to me, Brian. But how could you not be kind when you're Ted's son?'

He hugged her tight. It felt good to be held by him. And she loved his earthy smell. She knew he was hers for life if she wanted him. The only problem was, it was Petra she really wanted. She was tempted to kiss Brian, but she didn't want either of them to be destroyed the way Petra had destroyed her, so she held back.

63

The next news from Gloria was that her father was in a fighting mood. She phoned Lily, 'He said, "We're under siege as never before." He's going to do what he calls distraction techniques.'

'Like what?' said Lily.

'Oh, launch a new product. Or put an old one in a new package. Or announce some new deal—one they did last year, but they call it new because no-one will remember it. They'll tell the world profits are up.'

'Mr Pitcairn, my tutor, says they're down.'

'They'll say it anyway. And if the indexes are not good—'

'Indexes?'

'Share price indexes. So if they're not good they invent new ones that say something else. The company's always been creative. It's never lacked ideas. So it'll tell the world it's restructuring. Dad calls it "getting out of wounded animal talk". He can turn anything around. They told him the company's huge profits is one of the plaintiffs' attack points, and he laughed and said that big profits mean more taxes, and they pay for everything. Of course, the company hardly pays any because all its wealth is kept in tax havens. But the corporate structure is so complicated it can never be unravelled, and that's the company's best defence. He says the company's like smoke or mist. The lawsuit's just another little hurdle to glide over.'

'Why do you tell me all this stuff?'

'I love my dad, but I don't have to love his company. And I don't. And I love you, Maggot. And I trust you to keep things to yourself. It's our secret. Anyway, it turns out the lawyer he calls Daniel O'Bastard, is unavailable...'

'Is that his real name?'

'No, it's just what Dad calls him. So he instructed a new firm—marque label, so they claimed. They fell over themselves to get the instruction but then decided it would be ten times more expensive than they first thought. When he queried it, they squawked, "It's an expensive solution to an expensive problem."'

'Oh dear!'

'Don't worry, Dad expected it to be twenty times more and planned accordingly. Their team's led by a man called Big Red Rackham. Dad had never heard of him. You got the meanest one, Ernie Topp, so my dad says. But Ernie's best at attacking the fortress, not defending it, so he wouldn't have been right for dad this time.'

64

Lily began suffering from an annoying jealousy over Brian. She noticed there was a dark-haired girl called Hedi who hung around Ted's gym and was paying Brian a lot of attention, and Brian was clearly enjoying it. Lily had to contemplate that Brian might prefer Hedi to her.

She invited Brian out for a meal but, to her frustration, he told her he couldn't make it. Next day, she learned from Facebook he'd gone out with Hedi instead. She was furious. How could 'kindhearted' Brian do this to her?

She phoned him. She asked to meet him in the park again. He sounded reluctant but eventually acquiesced. This time, he did not bring doughnuts or any other 'treats'. Lily feared the worst. She got straight to the point: 'Are you dumping me, Brian? I deserve to know.'

'No, Lily, I would never do that.'

'Are you two-timing me then? It's obvious you and Hedi have something going on.'

'No, we are good friends. I like her, but she told me she likes girls best.'

'So you asked her then.'

'I've known Hedi for years. Longer than I've known you. It's just that now I've taken up boxing, because you insisted on it, she has decided to take it up as well. I've always liked you, Lily. I've always thought you were beautiful. Even when you had spots...'

'Spots?'

'Even when you put on weight...'

'Trust you to mention spots.'

'...and were being bullied. I wanted to comfort you then.'

'I never had spots bad, did I?'

'No, you didn't.'

'I'm sorry I set conditions,' she said. 'It was wrong. It was patronising. Now it's come back and punched me in the face because of my stupid jealousy. I'm sorry.'

Brian laughed and assured her there was no harm done. Lily relaxed, determined it would be the last time she ever made that same mistake regarding 'conditions'. Brian said, 'I'm afraid you're stuck with me now.'

65

In the latest interview filmed by a business magazine, Frank was asked about 'the share price continually falling'.

'You're always the dampener, I'll give you that.' Frank was unfazed.

'It's reality,' said the interviewer.

'But it's not true reality, is it? The critics like to say the share's been a dog for months, but we go from strength to strength.'

'I'm sure you'll agree, trading has been the tiniest bit subdued. And things like your luxury gourmet soup range were hit by changing tastes...'

Frank raised his hand. 'Others' excuses we never make. You see, we can run fast as a cheetah, but we like to give the pack something to chase, so we sit just a little ahead—even though to us it feels like the walk of a tranquillised lion. Others lack our bounce. They have the bounce of a pancake with no pan to catch it in.'

'Your biggest competitor is your noisiest critic.'

'Are you trying to put me to sleep? What are they squawking about?'

'That you need a big cash injection.'

'From them, no doubt. They think we're in the ketchup with the lawsuit and stuff so they want to be in on our action. But we see them coming with their puny strategies. In more normal times they couldn't even stand on the same street as us. We can't help their foolish ambitions. We can save the human race, but we can't save it from its own folly.'

'Defiant as ever.'

'Exactly. We've got some crackpot so-called saviour wants to devour us. An overoptimistic entrepreneur—that's the pleasant way of putting it. Stacked up on stupid money, they're acquiring companies like a drunken Santa Claus buying in stock. They'll make their reckless power grab while we hold the cash register key glued down: *No Sale*. We tell 'em,

"You'll fumble it so keep outta the way or we'll take *your* future, thank you."'

66

One night, Lily wrote to Petra on Facebook: 'I have to know: Do you still want me in your life? Are we still friends?'

'No.'

'Why?'

'Forget about me.'

'I can't. Tell me why.'

'You're not the person I fell in love with. You broke my heart. But it was all fake. You are fake.'

'Was it the fight?'

'Leave me alone.'

'I can't.'

There was no response. Lily took her new iPad, which Grandma had bought her as a reward for doing so well in her studies recently, downstairs at teatime. Grandma did not normally allow this, but Lily had explained she was waiting for an urgent message. Grandma brought out buttered crumpets, which was one of Lily's favourites despite, or perhaps because of, her diet. No message came. Not that mealtime. Not that evening. Not the next morning. Or afternoon. Or evening. It was not until the evening of the day after that she heard again from Petra, this time in an email:

Lily,

I didn't want to write to you but you insisted I do so. So here it is. I'm sorry but we were not right for each other. I thought I loved you, but it was based on an illusion. You are very beautiful and intelligent, and I miss you. But you're not real. You're a made up, messed up person. Maybe it's not your fault. The boxing match was trivial, but it showed what you are. And what you are is selfish, venal, and vain. You could not bear to lose. I knew after the first round the fight was rigged against me. I eased up so as not to punish you. With hindsight, I wish I'd thrashed you which I was more than capable of doing. You are no boxer. Don't kid yourself. You can't land a punch, and you certainly can't take one. You are a cheat. A disgusting cheat. There's a reason low punches are not allowed in boxing. But that oaf Ted let you get away with it. You can't bear to lose because your vanity won't allow it. You're a pathetic, immature little girl. You need to get used to losing because you're going to lose big. Is Ted even a proper trainer? He would make a better dance master, certainly based on the way you box. You wouldn't last five seconds in a club in London, although, if Ted was counting, it would be more like fifteen! It was not just the fight but everything else as well. You are eccentric, for sure, but that doesn't make you interesting. You are really quite boring, and that's because you are so self-absorbed. A boring little girl in a boring little town. The only person I liked in Retingham was your grandmother. She is kind and wise. So there's some hope for you, I suppose. Too bad that her granddaughter is so unworthy of her. Goodbye, Lily. Look after yourself. I do still care for you, even though I wish I didn't. It's a shame because it could have been so good, but you ruined it for both of us. Don't contact me again. I will not respond. You broke my heart, and I broke yours back. I have someone else now. Someone who loves me. Someone real and not fake like you. Find yourself someone else. Someone who will indulge your nonsense. Someone to save you when you self-harm. Don't self-harm.

Your erstwhile friend, Petra — by the way, Petra is not my real name, but then I doubt Upshire is really yours. I can't deny that my online profile is fake, but so is yours. Everything that truly matters with me is real — unlike with you.

Lily felt as though she'd been slammed to the floor. For a moment she could barely breathe. Total destruction. She felt lightheaded. At least she knew at last. Good riddance. But self-harm? Why had she even mentioned that? Lily had never self-harmed. Not really.

She found a safety pin, opened it, raised her left arm and slowly stroked the pin the length of her arm all the way to her wrist. She did not break the skin. Maybe being vain wasn't such a bad thing. She threw the safety pin onto the desk and lay back on the bed with her iPad and cuddly toys beside her. She lay there for half an hour, her mind flicking over the words, occasionally checking to see what Petra had exactly written, occasionally crying. Petra's words had knocked her flat.

Eventually she forced herself up. She looked hard in the mirror and said in a mocking voice, 'You're beautiful and intelligent... You're selfish and venal and vain.' Venal? She looked it up. Corrupt? It hurt, but she could live with it. All but one thing. The comment that she was unworthy of her grandmother was like the twist of a rusty serrated blade.

In the following days, Lily was very quiet and kept to herself. Naturally, this raised concerns with Grandma. After being evasive and returning partial answers, Lily gave way and showed her the email Petra sent. The old woman said, 'I'll say one thing: she is older than her years, that one. It's not true, though, what she's written. Incidentally, your name really is Upshire. I don't know where she got the idea that it wasn't. That was mean of her. She is clearly cruel and malicious. If she wasn't, she wouldn't have written some of these things. You're better off without her. Brian will be good for you. But is it true that you cheated in the boxing match?'

'I want to deny it, but I can't. I'm not proud of it. Ted was not happy about it. I just couldn't stand to lose to her. I didn't even want to fight, only to spar, but she insisted. She upset Ted—you know how easygoing he normally is. But in terms of boxing, I was better than her, and she was a different weight class, so I just evened it up a bit, which is fair.'

'I could tell something was a little off with her. Never mind, Lily. You'll get the odd pang of pain now and then, but you'll be over her sooner than you think. You've got other things to do with your life. More important things.'

67

Lily wanted to contact Petra, but pride stopped her. She thought about her all the time. Petra had already destroyed her twice before—once with a punch and once with a kiss—and now she'd done it a third time with her message. To put Petra out of her mind she devoted more time and attention to Brian. She now regretted her 'conditions'. She had meant well, but it was misguided. They hadn't succeeded anyway, not yet at least. His attempts to be 'tough-minded' seemed to make him more nervous than ever; she bought him clothes, but his choices were eccentric, and she did not want to be a nag so she put up with them. As for boxing, he gave it a go but was awkward, even slack-twisted, and he was terrified of hurting anyone either by intent or mistake. On one occasion in Ted's gym, for a joke, Lily pretended to be hurt by one of his punches, and she rocked backwards and lost her footing, ending up on the floor. Brian, being as soft as he was, was filled with panic that he'd hurt her and was so solicitous she felt it would have been cruel to laugh about it, so she kept up the pretence whilst stressing she was fine to continue.

Lily had thrown herself into her studies, so keen was she to please her tutors, and she was rewarded with an impressive set of GCSE results. She and Grandma were in the kitchen making a celebratory cake (a swirled blueberry lemon thyme cake), when Grandma asked her, 'Has Brian got a new girlfriend?'

'Ted's son?' Lily blushed.

'Yes. I thought he was interested in you.'

'Girlfriend?'

'I saw him with the Pinks' girl.'

'Hedi?'

'I think that's her name.'

'I don't know,' said Lily. 'I haven't seen him lately.' This was untrue. She saw Brian every week when she went to boxing training, even though he'd stopped participating. And Hedi was usually there too. In fact, she'd sparred with Hedi once or twice. She would make a point of hitting her harder in future. She felt a pang of jealousy and hated it but couldn't prevent it. She'd always believed that she and Brian ending up together was inevitable, and this latest seemed like a betrayal.

That evening, she looked up Hedi's Facebook page. On it was a photograph of her with Brian. How long had it been going on? On her profile it said 'In a relationship with Brian Panker'. Pinks and Panker—it sounded like a firm of interior decorators. She then checked Brian's Facebook. His profile did not say that he was in a relationship with Hedi so there was hope yet.

Lily invited Brian round. She knew Grandma was going to the doctor's late one afternoon and then she was going shopping. They'd have an hour and a half, maybe two hours if her appointment ran late or the supermarket was busy.

Lily had decided it was time she and Brian consummated their love. She wanted to be a woman, to say goodbye to her unwanted virginity. In her room for the first time, he understood implicitly what she wanted, but he felt she was using him. He would go along with it, though. She had done everything she could think to prepare herself for him, to be what she thought he wanted in a woman.

When she had encouraged him onto the bed she said, 'I want you to break me, Brian.'

Unbeknownst to her, although he was shy and nervous, he'd lately and somewhat incongruously become known as a bit of a local stud. He was seventeen now, and the girls who liked him were nineteen and twenty. He was well-endowed and eager to please, and though he considered the girls who wanted him sluts, he realised he liked them that way. He always carried condoms. But Lily he had always put on a pedestal, and it upset him to find this illusion disturbed. To find her so keen embarrassed him and put him off. He felt he might fail to do what she wanted so much.

'What's the matter, Brian?' She felt frantic.

'I can't do it.'

'What is it—don't you want me?'

'I love you. I always have. I love you too much. It doesn't feel right. It's like you're my sister.'

'What!? I'm not your sister—I'm just some girl you picked up at a club for sex. Some little tart.'

They tried several times, both of them increasingly frustrated. Finally, she felt a change in him. She gazed deep into his eyes. She had seduced him, now any moment she would win him.

But it didn't happen. There was a loud clatter downstairs, and before she knew it Brian had stood up, pale in the face, and was scrambling for his clothes. He was in a panic. She tried to reassure him, but it was hopeless. He left without a word, rushing downstairs. She stayed there naked, helpless on the bed. If her grandmother came in and asked what had been going on, she would tell her straight. She didn't care anymore. She was wet between her legs. She had failed to break his heart, but at least she was no longer a virgin, and that was what mattered to her then.

68

Gloria told Lily that in the litigation the Friends' lawyers were seeking the former finance director, Milton Pinch, to ask him tough questions. This was a concern to Frank because when Pinch was kidnapped, it was discovered he'd been embezzling company funds. A ransom had been paid and Pinch fired, but he'd disappeared before the police could arrest him.

He'd put messages on social media badmouthing the company but couldn't be traced until now.

'Do they know where he is then?' asked Lily.

'On his personal superyacht off the Seychelles apparently. Just waiting to be picked up. Dad wonders if Pinch could have an accident. It has been known for people to have unfortunate mishaps in luxury locations.'

'Like what?'

'Hypothetically, his superyacht could explode. Or mysteriously catch fire while he's in a deep sleep after a strong sedative. Or he could have a fatal accident shooting wild animals.'

'Or drown while fishing for marlin or something. You need my friend Mack. She knows all the weird and wonderful ways of death.'

'Yeah. My dad says the Grim Reaper has limitless imagination when it comes to snaffling up the frail and fragile. He says the company will live on, long after all the bosses are tucked up in their final beds. He thinks Pinch was in cahoots with the kidnappers and is now in cahoots with the Friends. He told me, he's as crooked as a Virginia fence, which was why the company employed him in the first place. Dad's frustrated. What upsets him, he says, is that the company spends millions on research and development—the most inventive, creative people in the world, he says—and they can't fix what he calls "this dirt hole". He's fed up with the cost, says the litigation makes him feel hollow, while the Friends' tactics are to dance around the boxing ring until both sides are exhausted and out of moves, barely enough strength for an embrace—and then they'll pick the company's pockets.'

'How much do you think they'll get?'

'My dad would pay a million to get rid of it, but they want billions. It'll cost over a million in fees. He wants to pay up and bounce back bigger and stronger than ever. It makes him mad. He sees the company as this great benefactor to the world with its work put at risk by what he calls "a bunch of lazy losers, who never did anything useful in their lives, never did anything at all except holler and whine all day and night, but think they have the right to take everything over." He calls it grand larceny. Aren't you glad he's not your dad? He used to be such fun, but now he's obsessed.'

69

Lily was tempted to contact Mack. She missed her and wanted her back in her life. She thought about changing her appearance to what Mack would like, which would mean growing her hair again. This she had no desire to do. She had chosen her close-cut look as a way of saying 'Mess with me and I'll fight like the devil to defend myself and hurt you.' It had made her more confident, although even now when she walked around town she was instinctively alert for any signs of her old enemies looking for the opportunity to strike.

But she had Brian now with her in Retingham, whereas Mack was far away and not communicating, almost a fantasy now. Her hope was that Mack would become jealous, and she would end up in the delicious position of being wanted by both of them.

'Come back into my world, Mack,' she said as she looked out of the window at the night sky.

That same night, her rival for Brian's affections, Hedi, posted on Lily's Facebook page: 'This evil slut tried to steal my boyfriend. She failed. She deserves to suffer.'

Lily tried to see Brian, but he was elusive. She called at the house, but he was not there. She tried phoning him, but that fared no better. Was he blocking her? She left messages for him. Maybe it was the fact Hedi's attack was all over Facebook that had put him off. How did Hedi even know? Lily was desperate. Nerdy and needy, was what Petra had said.

Eventually he did phone her. Persistence had worked. She was so surprised that she fumbled her words: 'When... can I see you again?'

'It's not easy.'

'Why, because of Hedi?'

'No.'

'Then why? What is it, Brian? Are you angry with me?'

'No.'

'Don't lie.' There was another long pause. 'I'm sorry, Brian. You don't want me, do you?'

'It's not that.'

'I must know: What is it you see in her?'

'I don't know. She's fun, I guess. Fun to be with. She likes things like going to gigs.'

'What? I can like gigs.'

'She likes parties and football.'

'I can like football too. So I'm no fun, is that it?'

'She wants me, and she gets what she wants.'

'So what? And why did you tell her?'

'I didn't. She worked it out.'

'I can't believe you're such a fool.' Another long pause. 'Look, I already lost Petra...'

'By the sound of it, you never had her.'

'I lost Mack...'

'That was in the past. Why do you cling to it?'

'Now it feels like I'm losing you.'

'You haven't lost me. But what if you did? You could find someone else easily enough. You're a pretty girl.'

'Stop it. I'm not giving you up so easily.'

'You used me, Lily.'

'OK, but only because I love you, Brian.'

'I put you on a pedestal, but all you wanted was your first shag. "I know: I'll ask Brian. He'll shag anything."'

'No. Not true. And I won't give you up. So let Hedi learn that!'

70

After boxing training and showering one day, Lily went to see Nancy and Fred. Fred was sitting in the lounge, which was a surprise. He said that he was recovering slowly and had 'thought about' trying a little light gardening. At this stage of his improvement, however, thinking about it was itself exhausting, and so he had not ventured outside. He asked Lily about boxing. 'Are you winning, Lily?' he said. She told him she'd had a match against a girl from London who was much bigger than her, but she'd defeated her. 'It's that speed!' Fred enthused, giving his teeth a joyful shift.

'That's right,' she said happily. 'Ted called it a draw to save the girl's feelings, which was fine with me, but she couldn't wait for the fight to end.' Fred was purring at this and said he'd love to have a spar with her, but 'not today' as the effort would be too great.

Nancy came in with tea and lemon cake. She apologised that the cake was bought, but she'd been so busy with council work she hadn't had time for baking. So busy, indeed, that 'poor Fred' had been forced to prepare his own lunch on one occasion, a ready meal from Asda that had taken three minutes to cook in the microwave, an experience that left him so weary he barely had the energy to eat it, so she said.

Nancy asked the inevitable question about her exams. Lily was positive, and this was genuine because without the bullying to contend with, and thanks to the efforts of the tutors, she'd made phenomenal progress, especially in maths. She revealed to the Peacemakers how Mr Pitcairn had been teaching her about business, which she would do at A-level, and about the stock market. She said her grandmother had bought shares in the Blueberry Flip company, as they liked to call it. She said she was confident Grandma would make money on the shares. This intrigued Nancy. She turned to Fred. 'That might be something you could do,' she said, 'while you're still recuperating.' He did not reply. The couple merely looked at each other. 'Maybe not,' she said. 'I will look into it myself.' She sighed, 'I tell you one thing: if this company's profits were based on its ideas, your grandma would make a mint. They never stop with their crazy plans for Retingham. And it all creates so much work for the council. The most bonkers thing is, now they want to build a new football stadium. That'll get the protesters out. They already call GUFF public enemy number one.'

'A stadium sounds cool,' said Lily, grinning.

'Yes, but they want to get Manchester United to play there. They want to buy the club and call it Retingham United.'

'That's even cooler. Maybe Grandma should buy more shares in them.'

'Just don't encourage them. Everything they do creates more work for us.'

71

Lily asked Gloria about the football stadium idea. Gloria said she had talked to her father about it, and he'd been in a restless mood: 'He told me, "After all the bitter pill stuff lately—yuk—what I need is candy. And that means spending money. I need retail therapy just like the average folks who buy our junk..."'

'Did he really say junk?'

'Then he corrected himself "our highest quality products—want something to ease their cravings, enrich their lives." And he said he felt the company needed a boost. Thus, after thinking about it for two nanoseconds, which probably seemed like an eternity, he said it should invest in football. So I said "American or soccer?" He said, maybe both. You see, since you showed up he's become obsessed with Retingham. His little dynamo, he calls it.'

'So he wants to buy Manchester United and move it to Retingham?'

'Yes. He sees it as a franchise and can't see why it can't be moved the way American football teams move around sometimes. I told him it was unimaginable. He said, "To others, maybe. Everything is possible to the creative, the successful, the enterprising."'

'Well, I guess that's true.'

'So my dad got on the phone to the Acquisitions Manager, Dean Pasture, and said, "Here's the deal.

We build a stadium that's capable of hosting inter-national football, say the size of Wembley. Or bigger. We'll buy up Manchester United, but if they won't come we'll buy up another team called United." He said there are a few other big ones around.'

'That's true,' said Lily.

'So Dean said, "But the entire population of Ret-ingham wouldn't fill more than a quarter of it." Dad then pointed out there's a bunch of major cities round about...'

'Yeah. Sheffield, Doncaster, Nottingham.'

'He said there's an airport and rail links...'

'That's right.'

He said, "We could throw in a few NFL games a year. Every time the stadium's mentioned it will be an advert for us." He asked for a viability study in five days.' So Dean says, "I can tell you in five sec-onds. And three words: It Won't Happen. And for the longer version: Manchester United will not move to Retingham, and a ninety-thousand-seat-or-bigger stadium will not be built next to the hundred-unit shopping mall that doesn't even exist and probably never will exist in our lifetimes."'

'Bloody hell!' Lily exclaimed.

'Oh, Dad was furious. He said it was a good job Dean wasn't around when the first moon landing was envisaged because he'd have sworn it was impossi-ble. Then he said, "I can employ a hundred thousand acquisition managers to tell me things can't be done. But I am looking for the the one diamond in the tur-key poop that will tell me it can..."'

'Turkey poop!'

'He said, "We have to snaffle up these ideas like truffles or others will. Remember: we already do what others are merely beginning to dream. And speaking of the moon, this next idea's a little more difficult..." Then he said he liked to imagine a world in which a little child, an innocent little child, looks out of their window at night in wonder and sees the beautiful mystical moon, and across it in red is the company's sacred brand logo.'

'Oh God!'

'Exactly! Poor Dean couldn't get off the phone fast enough. I asked Dad if he was serious about the moon idea. He said, "Not really...", then he winked and said, "but then again..."'

72

Lily was approaching Ted's house for her latest session of boxing training and sparring, when she heard a female voice: 'Look who it isn't, the whore who tried to steal my boyfriend.' It was Hedi. Lily did not respond but merely glanced at her: prettier than her with longer legs and bigger breasts—no wonder Brian was interested. She was with a couple of other girls who were friends of Lily's too, being associated with the gym. How could she possibly spar with her or even be there at the same time? Hedi was not done: 'You dirty slag!' Still Lily said nothing. Finally,

Hedi shouted, 'Like mother, like daughter!'

Lily could no longer restrain herself. She was suddenly so angry she leapt straight at her. She went for Hedi's face with her nails, and then began punching her. She would not be stopped. She bloodied Hedi's nose, broke her glasses, and even one of her teeth. Hedi could put up no defence and it took three others to stop Lily. The police and ambulance were called. The others tried to hold her until the police arrived, and someone went to find Ted, but before he arrived Lily had managed to break free. She ran all the way home.

Lily was charged with common assault. The court case followed weeks later in the magistrate's court, there being no youth court available. Lily, who was in a surly mood on the day, pleaded guilty but claimed extreme provocation. The magistrate said that the assault had been serious, but in view of the evidence regarding provocation and the historic bullying she'd suffered, she would impose a light sentence. Two hundred pounds plus costs and compensation, plus a restraining order forbidding her from going within two hundred metres of Hedi. Unfortunately, Lily caught sight of Hedi smirking at the judgement and, enraged, swore in her direction. The magistrate told her off, and then Lily made a rude sign at her which upset the magistrate so much she called her 'the vilest of the vile who has shown not the tiniest shred of remorse or regret,' and doubled the amount of the fine. She told Lily that if she ever appeared in her court again, she would impose the harshest penalty allowed, custodial if possible.

During the car journey home, Grandma expressed her impatience with Lily. She had given her everything, and what good had it done? She complained, 'I've spent all this money on tutors and boxing lessons, and where have you ended up? The magistrate's court, and a criminal record, and fines to pay, and in the press.'

'I won't be named in it, though.'

'No, but everyone knows about it. And you've earned a reputation as a harlot. I'll be broke soon, the way you carry on.'

'I'm sorry.'

'You need to pay your way. You need to pay me back.'

'I will.'

'When? I can't afford you anymore.'

'I said I'll pay it. If you want cash, sell the shares. And then I'll get out of your life that I'm such a plague on.'

Grandma tried to cool the argument, but Lily acknowledged no further comment from her. She resolved to leave home as soon as she could afford to.

73

Lily tried to arrange to see Brian again, but he was never free. It was obvious that he was seeing someone else, presumably Hedi. She felt jealous. Sitting alone in her room she felt sorry for herself. She went online and onto Facebook. Brian's page gave no clues. Hedi's, however, still declared she was in a relationship with him.

Lily looked at Petra's profile picture. Petra hadn't bothered to change it. Maybe it was still all a joke to her. A cruel joke. Lily was better off without her, and yet she still felt the same pang of loss and couldn't help wondering whether the Saturday they spent together could have turned out differently. She sat at the exact spot at the end of the bed where Petra had kissed her. She brought that moment to mind as vividly as possible. If she herself could learn to kiss like that, it would win any heart. Maybe she could win Brian's heart if she could kiss like that. Brian didn't deserve it—but he had a heart at least, whereas Petra didn't seem to.

Lily examined herself in the mirror. She liked what she saw. If I was a boy, she thought, any boy, I would want to go out with this girl. But Brian was the only boy she liked. Yet in her heart she realised that the person she wanted most in her life, above all others, was her old friend Mack, but she was now so distant. She looked at her picture and said, 'Oh Mack, I'm nothing without you. Come back to me.'

One afternoon, Auntie Gwynne broke off from watching her "Serial killer special" to phone Grandma: 'What's all this I hear about the child? As soon as I read it I thought it must be her, and my other contacts in Retingham confirmed it. She's proved herself again—beating up other girls. Grace, my dear, face facts. It's too late to save her now, get rid of her.'

'Rid?'

'Yes. Let her be the runaway, whore, drug addict she's going to be. Her mother was trash, and she's trash as well.'

'No.'

'It's reality, Grace. You deserve better in your old age. Get rid.'

Lily wrote to Mack to tell her what had happened to her, but found her unsympathetic: 'I was keeping my love for you. More fool me. I can't believe you lost your cherry to that old goat. He's like his father—he was a serial shagger in his youth. He even tried to get with an aunt of mine, but she rejected him. Brian will be back with flowers, wanting a blowjob when Hedi's not putting out, and you'll let him in because you're a dog, and then he'll be gone, and you'll feel like crap, and you'll deserve it.'

Lily picked up the scissors from her desk and stuck the point into her palm. Later, she wrote: 'Mack, please don't be angry with me. When can we visit each other? Or even talk?'

'I'm sorry, but I'm not interested. I've got a girl-friend who's a biker. We have fun. Even if she wasn't around, and it was just about sex, there's girls here who'd finger me if I wanted it. What do you even aspire to be in life—Brian's little doll? Slutshire, you've destroyed everything. Such a shame!'

Lily got drunk on Baileys she'd found in Grandma's drinks cabinet when she was out and sent Mack a Facebook message: 'Go to hell, you Scottish twat! I hate you.'

Next day, Lily wrote again, 'Mack, I didn't mean it. Please forgive me. Please don't desert me.'

Mack did not reply. Nor did she reply to the nightly, drunken, pleading messages from her erstwhile friend that followed. She was gone, intending never to return.

74

Lily messaged Gloria in the hope her American friend could help ease her depression: 'Anything new with you? Any more goals?'

'Three assists. Analisa got a hat-trick. We crushed it 5-2. Got a new boyfriend on campus: Tommy.'

'Sounds great.'

'Hope so. Not much on the company front. Dad seems more worried about the future but tries to hide it. So what's new with you?'

Lily wrote that she was feeling very down, and Gloria then phoned her. Lily told her about how her personal life had gone spinning out of control, and Gloria suggested she go to the States to visit her. Lily was touched by the offer but felt she should decline. The truth was, she had no money, and her confidence was so low she felt sure she would mess it up and lose another friend. 'Some other time,' said Gloria.

'Yes, definitely.'

Gloria wanted to send her a video: 'But you absolutely must not show it to anyone else.'

'I keep everything to myself. I mess up all the time, but I'm good at keeping secrets.'

'I know you are,' Gloria said in a reassuring tone. 'The video may be a set-up for all I know, but I treat it as real. A young man, the son of a "friend", is studying business and starting a company of his own and wants tips from my dad. Dad couldn't recall the "friend", but this was no great surprise as he knows so many people, and people like to call him their friend even if he hardly knows them.'

'A bit like me, except my so-called Friends are nothing to do with me, and I have hardly any real friends.'

'You have me at least. Anyway, the young man wanted the meeting videoed so Dad agreed. You might find it interesting, especially as it mentions you.' She then sent it.

In the video, the young man was saying, 'Your company was a little start-up once—anything I can learn from you?'

'Yes, avoid the Lily Upshires of this world, but especially anyone claiming to be friends of them. Avoid English market towns. Say sorry—it's cheaper in the long run. Lawyers are fine, but ultimately you have to know when to ignore their advice. They can always be paid to give you whatever advice you want anyway. They are, in that sense if no other, attentive to their clients' needs.'

'Any advice on angel investors?'

'Yes, find me a bunch. I wish they'd throw me a lifeline, never mind wasting their money on start-ups that'll be out of business in three weeks.'

'You don't mean my start-up do you, Frank?'

'Oh no. I didn't mean... I'll give yours six weeks. Just kidding. I get so bitter about everything.'

'Why are you so bitter, Frank?'

'Well, it's the people who've abandoned us, and whose absence shouts so incredibly loud. Some say the lawsuit's the blow we can't get up from, but I refuse to believe it—even though our famous flagship stores are now charity thrift shops.'

'You never stop fighting.'

'Absolutely. When we're back and winning, and those that abandoned us want to schmooze back in, we won't let them bask in our glory. No, we always remember those who helped us and those who refused. That's the best advice I ever got: pay back according to how they treated you on the way up.'

'So what's been the problem? Where's it gone wrong?'

'"Problem" and "gone wrong" are not part of our lexicon. Alright, I'll be the first to admit, some people in the company thought we expanded a tiny tad too quickly. Maybe it was a little too ambitious for such timid souls, but the fact is, if you don't go ever higher through the stratosphere, then what?'

'You fall from the sky.'

'Exactly. We flew too close to the sun for some, but at least we got close. Some of the others never got off the ground. If I was sorry for myself, I'd say I was born under an unlucky star, but I don't make excuses. Anyway, have you had enough laughs for one day?'

'Yes, I mean, no—most enlightening.'

'And if this great company bites the dust (which it won't, I assure you), you can make a business study out of it. In fact, when it roars back to the top, which could happen the very next minute, it will be an even better study!'

'So it will. Thank you.'

Lily found the video fascinating. It showed Frank was a bit concerned about the litigation, so maybe there was still chance of a payout to her from the Friends.

75

Mack was correct. Lily became what others like Auntie Gwynne thought and what Mack said of her. She began to believe she was worthless. She hated herself. She suddenly hated her body. Her breasts were too small, her legs too short, and her face was no longer pretty—her nose was wonky, her smile crooked. She was a skank. Unlovable. But her body, imperfect as it was, was a commodity to sell. People would buy it and discard it when they'd done with it.

There was a break from study and without tutors to keep her busy she lost her compass. She stayed in her bedroom with the door barricaded and went online, sitting in front of her webcam, flirting with strangers. When they asked to see her body she was tempted but declined. She loved the attention and found it fun to tease but knew it was a bad idea. When she couldn't flirt she harmed herself, usually with a safety pin, or she would bite herself hard, or jab the scissors into her palm, which she preferred most. She was able to resist the temptation to leave marks. A different way she found to hurt herself was to set up fake Facebook profiles from which to send abusive posts onto her own page, claiming she was a serial destroyer of relationships. Alcohol gave her crazy and dangerous ideas, such as moving to London to be an escort and seeking out men to have sex with so she could gain experience.

It was madness, but she was too addled to see it because she would spend all evening drinking either red wine or gin which she took from Grandma's drinks cabinet when she was out. She would go out in revealing clothes and sit in Saviour Park in the hope of being picked up. If a man who looked under the age of thirty walked by, she would make eyes at him. She made it obvious she was available. Her mother had been a whore, so people said, and she was following the family tradition. And she hated it and hated herself for doing it.

The problem she had was that her availability put men off. The local men were wary of someone so trashy-looking. But on one occasion a teenage boy about her own age who she'd seen before walking in the park stopped to ask if she was OK. Without the merest pretence at coquettishness she said that she was unhappy at home and had no friends except on-line. He asked her if she wanted to go to his place to watch TV. She knew this was an invitation to have sex, and she wanted it to be. He was nice-looking and seemed kind-natured, so she said yes. He said he would ring his mother to check if this was OK. He walked a few yards away to make the call. When he returned he said it was fine. So maybe no sex would be involved and that was good, too. She would make a new friend. The boy led her through town to a quiet rundown street. As they came to his house, which looked as sorry for itself as she felt, he stopped and said he'd better let his mother know they'd arrived. He phoned. The mother didn't answer, so he sat down on the wall facing the road and motioned Lily to sit beside him. It was pleasant catching the afternoon sun. They chatted nervously. A moment later, she looked up and there were three other men standing round the couple. 'These are my brothers,' he said. 'They're going out.' The three brothers, who were older and didn't look like brothers, entered a nearby car. 'They're going to a bar,' her new friend said. 'We could go with them if you like.' He didn't give her chance to answer but grabbed her hand firmly and walked her to the car. She knew what it meant: sex with four strangers. The whore victim in her didn't care, but the rest of her was wiser. 'No,' she said.

'Get in.' He was insistent. This is what it meant. She wanted love and she would get rape.

'No,' she said. 'Please.'

One of the men inside the car shouted, 'Get her in here! Come on, let's go. I got the stuff. What's the problem?'

She understood: drugging her would be part of the proceedings. She wrenched herself free of the boy. He tried to grab her, but she kneed him in the groin. He was weak and hadn't expected her to fight. One of the others was getting out of the car, but before he reached her she'd snatched her handbag from the ground and made a run for it. She heard shouting behind her, but she ran fast. Despite weeks of drink and ruining herself, she was still fit from all her past training. She wanted help but could see no-one ahead. She ran, and the boys did not give chase. She heard the car start up.

She took the first turn into another street that ran to the edge of town where the last houses were, and then there would be fields. If she could reach that far, she could escape into the countryside. It was another hundred-and-fifty yards. She then heard a car approach and slow down beside her. Without looking round, she picked up speed. The car approached again. Its window was down, and a male voice called out, 'Get in.' It sounded familiar, but she ran on. The voice called out, 'Lily, get in!' She recognised it now: it was Ted. What did he want? Had he come to gloat, or leer, or tell her off? She ran on. He called to her again. She did not know what to think about him since Hedi and the court case. She stopped and, breathing hard, got in the car.

'What's it all about, Lily?' She did not reply. He turned the car round and drove a few streets, during which she forced herself to look at the faces in other vehicles in case she saw the four wannabe rapists. Then she said, 'Drop me off here, thanks.'

'I need to talk to you,' he said.

She'd recovered one gram of self-respect from the previous incident, and now he wanted to take it away again. 'Well, I don't need to talk to you.'

Maybe he'd keep her locked in the car to listen to his lecture. She was so confused she didn't like to think what would happen next. 'OK,' he said, and he unlocked the door. She got out but then lingered. She looked at him. He seemed sad. Ted had done so much for her in the past. If he hadn't pushed her training as much as he had, she wouldn't have been able to escape from the rapists. 'What exactly do you want?'

'Honestly?'

'Yes.'

'I want the Lily I used to know. I want you back at training.'

She got back into the car. 'Take me for a drink,' she said. 'Let me get drunk.'

He took her to a bar by the canal where they could sit outside. She asked him to get her a gin and tonic. Double. He refused. She had a Diet Coke. He had a low-strength beer. When they had sat down he said, 'I want you back.'

'How would that even be possible... assuming I wanted to?'

'I'm not going to force you. Not that I could. But if you want to come back, I'll make it happen.'

'Why? I beat up your son's girlfriend.'

He grimaced. 'Do you think I need reminding? Lily, you've lost it. You've completely lost it. And if you'd got in that car, you'd have been lost for good, most likely.'

'I feel terrible about what happened. You believed in me and I let you down. I've lost any decent reputation I had. I really messed up. Do you honestly think I deserve another chance?'

'Some would say not. I don't care about them. The fact is...' Ted suddenly looked up, as if for inspiration for his next words. It wasn't for effect, it was genuine. '... you and I... There's something special between us.' She merely looked at him expectantly. 'Yes, there is,' he said. 'You obviously don't know. Perhaps I should explain.'

'Please do.' She was reminded of the phone conversation she'd heard between him and her grandmother on her thirteenth birthday.

'It's about your mum.'

'I assumed so, but I know very little so...'

'When she was tragically killed in the car crash...'

'Yes?'

'Well, I was the one waiting for her to come home.'

'You, Ted?'

'Yes. I was living with her at the time. We were very happy together. But of course, it was all too brief.'

'Tell me more, Ted.'

'I was married to Maisie with her daughters from another relationship. She wanted me to give up boxing. I couldn't and I walked out in the end. Your mum and I had been together before Maisie, and I met up with her and it all started again. I was too wild to be the typical husband, what with the boxing and all, and your mum was so understanding.'

'I didn't know all this. About you, I mean.'

'Your grandmother never told you? She has her own good reasons.'

'I've heard two disturbing things about my dear mother that I don't understand.'

'Go on.'

'The first, that she had some kind of powers. Is that so?'

He laughed.

'Not you as well,' she sighed. 'Well, did she?'

'She certainly believed she did.'

'That's what Grandma said. She was clearly sceptical about it. She talked to me about coincidences being dressed up by my mum to be things she caused to happen. Is that right?'

'Yes, although I wouldn't say "dressed up". That would be unfair. She did like to put a curse on people who were against her, of which, I'm sorry to say, there were a few.'

'Who? Julia Bizzell, I suppose?'

'We all have people against us.'

'Even you?' She looked at his face expectantly.

'Yes. Anyway, sometimes it would happen and sometimes it wouldn't. And sometimes it would happen to someone unintended. She could be a dangerous person to know! She was interested in fortune-telling, but I don't think she did it much.'

'Did people think she was weird?'

'She didn't talk about it much. It was just like a hobby. In other ways she was pretty ordinary, I suppose. She was a good mum. Before that, she'd held down a job in a shop. She was popular. She didn't dress strange or anything. What was the other thing?'

'Your son's girlfriend more or less said my mum was a prostitute. When I was little, kids called out: "Your mum's a ho."'

'That's awful.'

'And when I told my grandma she more or less agreed.'

'She wasn't. She just went through a period of time, not very long, a few months maybe, when she cultivated older men who had money. They lavished gifts on her. She enjoyed their wealth. She was unfaithful to all of them, and they were all married anyway. Does that answer you?'

'Yes. It doesn't make her sound very nice.'

'It's easy to judge. She was very kind, always helping the old lady who lived next door to her, and she loved you, be assured of that.'

She asked him about her grandparents, but Ted said he never knew them. He'd only known Grandma. Nor did he know the surname of Julia's father but said it was irrelevant. Lily was shocked because Julia had been adamant. He explained that people liked to think Julia's father was hers too 'out of mischief'. No-one knew for sure. He said, 'It's convenient for Julia to claim he was your father so she can blame you for his suicide. Even if you both took tests, it wouldn't prove it. Anyway, I am not your father—I can at least assure you of that.'

'What you're saying in a roundabout way, is that I could be the daughter of any of several men. You're just glossing it over. She was a slut, and now everyone thinks I am. Like mother, like daughter. Even I think it.'

'Because Hedi said it?' This comment brought a tear to Lily's eye. He shook his head. 'I know what she said hurt you almost as much as your fists hurt her.'

'That whole business left me feeling worthless. I am so easily destroyed by words. I thought I would develop resilience, but I haven't. I'm just as brittle as ever.'

Ted got to his feet to hug her. It was a clumsy hug. She then stood up and held him tight. 'I love you so much, Ted,' she said in a breathless voice.

He drove her home. She said, 'I miss Brian. I didn't know he already had a girlfriend.' Although Ted thought this was probably a lie, he didn't care. Lily's lying was part of her appeal. 'Ted, he was my soulmate for years and I want him back.'

'Shall I tell him you want to see him?'

She brightened. If he could have looked over at her, he would have detected the hint of a salacious grin. 'Yeah. Tell him I've got something for him.'

When he pulled up outside her place, he said, 'So we can expect you next week, can we?'

'Yes.'

'The others will be delighted to see you. And me most of all. Don't worry, Hedi won't be there.'

76

Soon after Lily turned seventeen, Gloria told her about a possible takeover of the company. As usual, Frank had not missed the opportunity to talk. When asked in-house about press chatter concerning a bid, he replied in a recording Gloria sent: 'Pure speculation. And what has brought it on?'

'The share price going down. It makes us vulnerable.'

'And of course, the press love it. This company deserves better. They should be paying us for what we've given the world. But no, life isn't fair. It's always the big guy picks up the tab. Making us smaller so others get bigger, that's how petty minds see it. But this company was always meant to be big.'

'Others don't see it.'

Frank was heard to sigh heavily before continuing, 'It's just like big and small in the animal world because of predators. Without predators, little darting fish become fat and slow and start ailing. Knowing they're at risk of being gobbled up any moment keeps them fit and healthy, as well as tasty. So I welcome the excitement a predator brings. Of course we're bigger than any predator, and he knows we'll eat him up instead. He'll be a victim of his own bravado—the hunter becomes the hunted. They're the ones we like the best, the ones with big ambitions, because they're the crunchiest and tastiest. So who is this so-called predator?'

'It's the company we bought the smoothie operation from years ago.'

'But we saved them.' Frank banged his fist on the desk in frustration. 'We kept them afloat!'

'And meanwhile shareholders are bailing out.'

'Typical! Everyone knows that what makes a big company vulnerable is the share price going down, so bad people make mischief with it. Shareholders are the most fickle, lily-livered caste of humanity. The average investor has as much resilience as a carpet moth in a wind tunnel. When they see profits on the slide, never mind the company's just drawing breath for a big push, their Chicken Little hearts go a-flutter, their brains turn to mush, their little legs itch like mad, and they just have to fly—fly away from us. And then the no-friends-to-us media are all over it.'

'Will we put out a press release for shareholders?'

'Yes. But it makes me mad. We can assure them and give them entirely realistic and unbiased assessments but no, they prefer to listen to the rabid press, as if it were ever reliable. It's the usual buzzkill. Out come the dumb stories—so predictable a machine could write them, and probably does. A very unsophisticated machine at that. Something like an old-fashioned computer—big as a house, breaking down all the time, and producing everything on little cards. A relic. I tell you, keep us free of that rat circus!'

77

Lily studied the share price of the big bad company every day. She noticed it kept going down. She talked about it with Mr Pitcairn, whom Grandma had retained for both maths and business studies for her A-levels. She asked him how to tell when was a good time to buy. He reminded her he couldn't give any advice as he wasn't qualified or authorised, and anyone who was would charge a fee.

'But I can't afford any fees,' she said. 'And I can't ask Grandma. Who can I turn to?' Pitcairn suggested she talk to Mr Topp, her lawyer, about it.

When she called Ernie Topp he had just come in from shooting armadillos and wild hogs. She was tempted to ask him why it was necessary to do that but said nothing, lest it upset him, especially as she was so happy to bathe in the enthusiasm for her very existence that he expressed every time they spoke. 'Lily? So you've come to make my day again. What is it I can do for you today?'

'Is the share price of my favourite company going down today?'

'Oh yeah, it's in bad shape. A takeover bid failed and it's tanked since then.'

'Is that good for us?'

'Not if it goes bust, but if they get desperate to put the share price up again, they might settle with the Friends, and then we can settle. But here's the deal:

there's going to be some bad stuff about the company coming out in the next hour or so that will send the share price way down, then a bit later today the company machine will send out a press release denying it all, and that will put the price up again, even though no-one will believe a word of it. The thing is, the big boss, Frank Salesman, has to sign off such press releases, and he'll still be tied up in a legal deposition in the Friends case. By the way, are you familiar with the term "deposition"?'

'Is it when they get one of the company guys in a room and give them the third degree and the company guy tries to say nothing?'

'Yes, that's pretty much it. So because of the deposition they won't be able to send the press release out straight away. See how it works?'

'Yes. So the price will continue dropping for a while...'

'That's right. So it's not a bad bet. How much would you want to put up?'

She hadn't thought about that but didn't want to waste his time. 'Say, five hundred?' she said, wondering where on Earth she would get this amount of cash. Neither she nor Grandma had any money available for it.

'Five hundred thousand dollars?'

She now wished she hadn't raised the subject of these stupid shares. How could she extract herself from this embarrassment? Poor Mr Topp, stuck with an idiot for a client. 'No, I meant five hundred pounds. I'm sorry. I didn't realise. I didn't know how it works. I can't help being ignorant.'

She heard what sounded like a chuckle being suppressed.' Lily, my dear, five hundred pounds isn't going to get you very far.'

'I know.'

'Don't you want to make some real money?'

'But I'm broke, and I can't ask Grandma for more than that. Even that much will be very difficult.'

'I know. Don't worry, my average client doesn't have half a million to spare either. OK, I'll tell you what we'll do. My brother's a day trader. He's going to be buying a few millions' worth of shares and selling them later today after the press release puts it back up. How about if we put up a million for you, and we'll take what you make off your legal fees? That'd be the best way to deal with it.'

She didn't understand it. It sounded too absurdly good to be true; there must be a catch. What if it all went wrong, and the shares crashed, and she lost her case as well? It couldn't happen, could it? Well, if it did, she would turn round and sue him. No doubt the Texas bar association would have something to say about it, especially with her just turning seventeen. She said at last, 'Would it even be ethical?'

'I'm sorry, Lily, I'm having trouble hearing you.'

'Ethical. Would it be ethical?'

'Sorry, it's a bad line all of a sudden. Did you say ethical?'

'Yes.'

'I never think about it. I'm an old-fashioned lawyer just focusing on the law, you know. I have others keep me honest on all that stuff. If you're worried, don't do it. My brother will be doing it anyway. I'll make sure you don't lose at the end of the day. And I guarantee this: Frank Salesman and his lawyers will string out the deposition because they'll be putting some of their millions on the bet themselves. You want me to ask them about their ethics?' He laughed.

She sniggered. 'No. I just want the money.'

'That's my girl!'

A few minutes later, Ernie Topp's brother scooped as many shares as he could afford, having made a decent profit on his last raid on the company.

Later, the shares were sold. But Lily didn't find out what profit she'd made because she'd told Ernie that it didn't seem like real money; she'd wait until the day of reckoning when she got her settlement in the legal case, if she ever did. Until then, she didn't want to know and would like to forget about it.

78

Lily went to visit her mother's grave. She said, 'I'm sorry I haven't been to see you lately. I let everything go so wrong, but I'm getting sorted now. I did wrong beating up Brian's girlfriend, but she was bullying me and had it coming to her. I wanted to die, but Ted came through for me. He told me about you and him. I am gradually finding out more about you. Grandma told me nothing, not even that she was your step-mother. I wonder sometimes what else I don't know. I just came to say, I want to do the right thing by you. I also miss my old friend Mack. I upset her, but she had no reason to reject me. I hope she will come back, but whether she does or not, I want her to be safe.'

She stayed there in silence for a few minutes, watching the breeze amongst the leaves of nearby trees, and then left.

Lily did not hear from Brian. When she rang him he was evasive. She began to realise she meant nothing to him. She imagined him telling her: 'You're just a shag now. I have other girls who are better shags.'

Eventually he came to see her. He apologised.

'I know how it works, Brian. You've just come round for a shag. Don't worry yourself, I won't deny you.'

They barely talked. She did not interest him these days. Emotionally he gave her as little as he could get away with. She knew it. She said nothing about it. She was there to be shagged. Later, she would be angry with herself. She knew she deserved better and was frustrated that in her heart she still did not believe it.

Grandma knew what was going on, 'You've become your mother,' she said. It was as much as Lily could do to stop herself hitting her.

Lily decided material wealth would be her substitute for love. In the interim, she would work hard on her A-levels with her two favourite tutors, Mr Pitcairn and Emily Hass, who'd returned to the area and was fulfilling a promise made when Lily was twelve.

79

Gloria sent Lily a recording of her dad from when he was working at home.

Frank's assistant Dora Dongle rang him, 'Our new finance director is on the line.'

'Where is he phoning from?'

'He works from home.'

'And where is his home?'

'A private island in the Caribbean.'

'Good day, Sir,' Frank said.

'Good morning. As requested, I have prepared a four point plan to rescue the company.'

Gloria told Lily her dad said afterwards he could not recall such a request but was desperate for ideas.

'Excellent. I prefer a one point plan but let's hear it anyway.'

'The first point is to incentivise the board. That means giving directors more in salary and bonuses.'

'I hear you, but remember: money's in short supply these days.'

'If you want to keep the top people, you've got to pay top dollar.'

'I agree a good board director is worth their weight in gold.'

'Oh no, that wouldn't be enough at all. A kilo's worth of gold is less than fifty thousand in value. Someone of just over a hundred kilos would only pick up five million, hardly worth a real high flyer getting out of bed for.'

'I see your point. And I've no doubt they would see it too. So what did you have in mind?'

'I think an average director could command north of fifty million.'

'So more like a tonne of gold then.'

'Right. In fact, if it could be paid in gold to their personal bank vault, that would be an added incentive, say with twenty million a year for day-to-day expenses. The second proposal is to increase workers' productivity.'

'And how can we achieve that?'

'By reducing workers' weekly hours—four days instead of five; thus, a twenty per cent decrease.'

'Marvellous.'

'Everyone knows you get more done with less time because people are more energised. So people produce as much in less time, and automatically your productivity issue is solved.'

'Excellent. And for the same money too?'

'Oh no. That's point three: we need to cut wages by twenty-five percent to save on costs.'

'I see. I think the more numerate might catch the discrepancy there—a twenty-five percent wage cut for twenty percent less hours.'

'Only a few troublemakers would care. The rest would be grateful. People need to realise that if they want a job, they have to accept less money. If they believe in the company, they'll be happy. That brings me to point four: we need to give the workers less paid holiday time. That will push up output.'

'But it won't be popular.'

'Then a further possibility would be to pay workers not in money but vouchers instead.'

'Workers being everyone below board level?'

'Yes. Instead of money they'd receive vouchers to buy things in our shops.'

'On a discounted basis?'

'Of course not. That would be like giving them a pay rise which we can't afford.'

'So it's back to the old company store then. And what about giving them loans for the stuff in our shops they can't afford?'

'That was my next suggestion.'

'I meant it ironically. And when the worker dies the debt passes to their heirs?'

'Indeed. Entirely fair since the family benefited directly from the purchases their loved ones made.'

'I think that's called debt bondage. I don't think it will fly. Not in this day and age, and not when we call workers our valued service ambassadors or something like that.'

'Mere words. We can call it something else—and them.'

'But wouldn't that be in breach of our fancy new four-hundred page Human Resources manual?'

'No, we scrapped that. We replaced all those things with the mantra "Be kind" exactly as you wanted apparently.'

'But it's not being kind to the workers.'

'I would say it is. And it's certainly being kind to shareholders which is our number one... er, one of our priorities.'

'I see. And if we gave each worker one share out of their wages, they'd all be shareholders as well, so logically it'd be kind to them too.'

'Exactly!'

'No, I think you can just dream up something else altogether. It's all a bit too grim-sounding for me.'

'Grim-sounding? But we have to face reality. Desperate times need desperate measures.'

'I can't disagree with that. I'll say this, though: we won't need to worry about whistleblowers—there'll be a whole fanfare of trumpets all across the world's media every single day. But when you thought this up, taking your early morning dip in the surf, or sitting on your private sandy beach meditating or watching turtles, or whatever you do, did it occur to you the workers might see an irony in all this?'

'Irony?'

'You on your private island advocating gold for the board and pay cuts and vouchers for everyone else.'

'That would be typical of the cynicism that's held this company back all this time, and a gross mischaracterisation of what I'm suggesting. I'd remind them that this is a very hazardous environment I work in.'

'In your multimillion dollar mansion on your private island?'

'Yes. Hurricanes are a constant threat for seven months of the year. Living on a private island in the Caribbean is no beach picnic, I assure you. It's very stressful.'

'Really?'

'Yes. I've just been off sick for a month with anxiety.'

'You don't say.'

'Easing my way back. Twenty minutes a day.'

'Take it easy. A whole month off, you say? No-one no— I mean, no won*der* you came up with such groundbreaking ideas.'

'I thought them up in ten seconds over my breakfast this morning: freshly caught marlin with avocado and lobster in vanilla butter with 1996 Dom Perignon champagne.'

'Was it good?'

'I prefer lobster slightly chilled but otherwise acceptable.'

'OK, all this will certainly give the Employee Outreach resources something to do, trying to persuade the workforce why being paid in vouchers is so great.'

'Well, I'd better sign off. Got to prepare for cocktails with a few movers and shakers.'

'Is that part of your twenty minutes?'

'I hadn't thought of that, but you're right: I'd better relax first. Don't worry, I won't overdo it.'

'Constantly on the go as you are, you need to get proper rest.'

'Thank you. It's not corporate business, by the way. It's a Support for Billionaires event. Billionaires save the world, and yet they're the most persecuted sector of society.'

And with that he was gone 'like a chili through a rat's colon'.

Gloria said Frank paced back and forth in his office. '"Ideas," I heard him say to himself. "We need ideas. Ideas so hot to hold they burn the brains of lesser folk to a crisp. The only new ideas I'm hearing are too awful to consider. I want ours to be a good company. How can we be good if we have the finance director talking about bonded labour and paying wages in company vouchers? I want our workers to be paid more, not less. That way they'll buy more which is what we all want.'"

80

Many months passed. Lily worked hard on her A-level studies while the litigation wore on. One afternoon in November, Nancy came to see Grandma. She was excited after hearing from the lawyers of the Friends, the firm of Twatten Baumgardner, via an email sent to all members of the group in the lawsuit. The email said settlement discussions would soon commence with lawyers for the big bad company, who, it was asserted with confidence, had 'no desire to go to court'.

Nancy gushed, 'The lawyers are going for millions. Of course, there's thousands of us so we won't get a million each, but Fred should get more than anyone for all he's been through, poor mite. It's just a shame you'll miss out, Grace.' The lack of sincerity in this last comment was not lost on Grandma, but she didn't care because she felt no envy for them. 'So you think it could be life-changing, then?' she asked.

'Oh, I don't know. I don't like to think about it. We rarely get what we deserve in life, do we? The crooks and the ne'er-do-wells get all the gravy, and people like Fred, who are so deserving, get the stale biscuit crumbs. So I say that if people think I have a sense of entitlement, I make no apology for the way I've lived, and for all I've achieved, and for any modest rewards that come my way...'

Grandma felt her neighbour had slipped into her role as member of the planning committee making, a stirring if theatrical speech in the council chamber, and she deflected her: 'How's your health been lately? No recurrence of the vertigo?'

'Fine, thank you. My head was fairly spinning that time. Lack of sleep, most likely. All these crazy ideas from the company demanding so much attention just to go through them. They're all ludicrous, but you have to analyse them carefully all the same, especially as the company wants to put so much money into the town. So we have to try to find something we can agree, such as the Olde England theme park they want. And to think all this started from something in Fred's smoothie. It's remarkable really.'

Lily had been in and out of the lounge while Nancy was there and picked up the point about an upcoming settlement. When Nancy had left, she phoned Ernie Topp about it.

He said, 'Well, they need to take it easy. The company can settle with the Friends, but then they have to settle with you. To date, I've done the minimum to pursue your case, almost hiding, but when they settle and their clients are clamouring for the cash, that's when I'll be in their faces and won't go away. And Lily, I don't speculate. I won't say to you when you'll get anything, or even whether you will, and certainly not how much. It could be millions, a few thousands, or zero. And for some clients they'd be better off without millions for all the trouble it causes them. I can say you made on those shares, though. Don't worry, they were all sold. Right now, the Friends are deposing the former finance director, Milton Pinch, again, and he won't stop talking. And the company won't settle until they've put on the record stuff contradicting him. Then there's other former directors who're unhappy with the company too. Old Frank says the bad stuff was all Pinch's doing and he's cleaned up the stables now, and the former directors blame each other, and blame Frank, and all that squabbling plays into the hands of the Friends' lawyers.'

'Is that Bumburger?' Lily was glad Mack wasn't there or the two of them would have collapsed into laughter.

'Twatten Baumgardner. But they won't want to settle all the time Pinch is gushing like a tipsy goose. Now the other thing is, there's thousands and thousands of claimants—your neighbours and all the rest—so none of them will get very much, whereas you're alone. The only person you have to share with is me. So don't listen to your neighbours, don't tell them anything, and forget about what you might ever get.'

'Could I be deposed?'

'They did get close to asking, but I told them it won't happen. Theirs is not a case about what you did or said, and your case is about the Friends using your name. If they tried to depose you, I'd depose every one of them. We're really piggy-backing on them. Don't worry: you chose me, and I'm honoured, and I won't let you down.'

81

Once all the depositions were done, which took several more months, the case settled. It was strictly confidential, but in five minutes the news was all over the internet that it was $350 million, of which $150 million was recoverable from insurance. Lily learned this in a call from Gloria: 'Dad said, "Pah! We sneeze that much every morning. It'll send the share price zooming." But it didn't. Investors had already predicted it.' Gloria said smart investors were always one step ahead, but her dad was disappointed the insurers didn't pay more. 'He said, "They've fought us all the way. So much for the safety net the friendly broker promised."'

Gloria forwarded an interview her dad had done in which he sounded under siege. Frank said, 'We'll sell off a few prime locations if we have to. Nothing's sacred, but we didn't come this far to punk out. We're on the rebound, and the next bounce will reach beyond the stars. We'll get rid of the so-called advisers, those self-serving crows who hold us back. Our managers will become superheroes of excellence. We'll build new shopping malls with all aspirational lifestyle brands. As a company we will always be Serendipity on strong steroids. So tell the media's so-called experts that.'

The interviewer said, 'They say the company's on the slide and the whole business is a distressed asset.'

'Such an insult!'

'What about suppliers wanting payment up front?'

'We'll never agree to that. We'll fight 'em. We'll buy 'em out if necessary. And we'll make landlords cut rent to us. If they won't, we'll buy them out too, like we've always done. We'll clean up.'

'Wield the axe on brands?'

'Look with fresh eyes,' said Frank. 'Authenticity is key. We've always been real. As rock-solid real as Betty Crocker.'

'She's not real.'

'Sure she is. Her picture's on the box.'

'Yes, the picture of a made-up person.'

'Made-up?'

'Imaginary.'

'Well, maybe, but the brand is real. And we've got real people out there promoting our stuff.'

After the clip, Gloria commented sadly, 'As dad told me afterwards, the trouble is, all these "promoters" are a liability. Either their politics are extreme, or they're in court, or even gaol. They had to pay an actor to stop wearing the company's sportswear brand, after images of him wearing it appeared on TV during his court case. When all else fails, they'll put cute animals in their ads. They always sell stuff.'

Lily said, 'Why was the settlement so much?'

'Well there were over two hundred thousand claimants, and so the average was under two grand. Be glad you don't have the job of sorting out who gets what!'

82

Ernie Topp wrote to Lily about the settlement between the company and the Friends, confirming that it would take months more to finalise. He was negotiating with the Friends' lawyers to get the best possible deal for her, and until that was resolved the Peacemakers and the rest wouldn't get their money.

Lily, now turned eighteen, started tentative discussions with a company in Retingham with a view to buying a share in them. It was a pretentious little boutique something-of-nothing. She wasn't quite sure what they did and didn't care overmuch. She just wanted something local that wasn't a dead loss. Something that needed temporary help and could one day become a moneymaker. She talked to the owners but sensed they were merely humouring her.

She was also interested in a bank loan to establish the business she was planning. The first bank she went to laughed at her. The person she saw, a fierce-looking woman, Janet Topless, said, 'And what business is that?'

'Buying and selling companies and shares.'

Ms Topless, grateful for the amusement, then called in an associate, Ray Shakes, a seedy uncle type who was having a dismal afternoon with his horse selections and had grease marks on his tie. He was no less sceptical. It was like a private joke between them. They did not believe she even had a business plan. They saw her as a teenage fantasist, which she was—and proudly so: her venture into business was a triumph of the imagination. Instead of seeing whether they could help her, the bank tried to sell her insurance products and even a mobile phone contract. Lily became frustrated and eventually walked out, saying, 'I'll be bigger than this bank one day, you'll see.' As she left she could hear them laughing, believing they were out of her hearing. They weren't. She walked back in and gave them what she understood was a hex sign.

Lily visited two more banks. She got a similar response but without the mockery. Finally, the fourth bank agreed.

As for the bank that had laughed at her, that night she cursed it with all her might. A few weeks later, the branch closed. But so too did a branch in Lincoln and another in Sheffield. Was it a coincidence, or did the power sometimes strike more than once? Maybe the power had hit one of the other branches and Retingham's had been a coincidence. It was all too complicated to unravel.

83

Lily received a call from Gloria: 'My dad's apoplectic. He can't believe it: the company's been fined by the American Government. He went: "America the golden? America the beautiful? America that nurtured this fledgling company that's now a gigantic eagle, the very embodiment of American values?"'

'How much was the fine?' said Lily.

'Three-hundred-and-eighty-nine million dollars. It's about money laundering. The authorities said the company's standards weren't adequate, and drug cartels and dodgy billionaires were pumping their money through subsidiaries that conducted no legitimate business.'

'How could that happen?'

'The trouble is, the company has so many subsidiaries no-one knows all of them. It looks like the old finance director...'

'The one sacked for embezzlement—Milton Pinch?'

'Yes. He set up these subsidiaries without telling anyone and did all these sweetheart deals with crooks.'

'Ouch!'

'Ouch indeed. Dad hopes they can negotiate it down, say to a hundred million, but coming on top of the settlement it's a bit of a shock. And it's bad for the company's reputation. Your Grandma sold those shares, didn't she?'

'Yep. During the depositions. I learned about all that from Ernie Topp.'

'When do you get your payout from the settlement?'

'He's still negotiating.'

'By the way, I should warn you: Dad said that whatever they pay in fines will seem like loose change, once they've changed Retingham into a major profit centre, an all-purpose beacon to the world and advert for the great company, so bright it can be seen from outer space.'

'I can't wait,' said Lily.

84

As the weeks raced by, in an attempt to broaden her interests Lily decided to step up her social media profile. To date she'd only played at being an influencer. She'd seen what other influencers did and found it pretty uninspiring as to content. Her own content did not inspire her either. It seemed rather childish now. She was named in a magazine as one of the latest crop of 'exciting young influencers', but found this a little embarrassing since she'd achieved so little. Once again, it was her name that caught their interest, not her. She talked about it with Mr

Pitcairn, who was now almost as much business adviser as tutor. He queried whether the work involved was really worth it, bearing in mind it seemed out of proportion to the reward, but added that his own daughter, Cerise, was also an influencer, and she too had been wondering whether it was worth it. He said that she also went to boxing training at Ted's, and perhaps they could get together to share ideas.

Cerise was older than Lily but had been at Ted's for a shorter time than her. Lily had a brief chat with her there, and they arranged to meet in town for coffee one day. Lily already had a niche in the vegetarian/vegan sector of the influencing world with thousands of followers. She also promoted boxing and fitness for teenagers, whereas Cerise was more interested in fashion and beauty. Cerise was pretty with short dark brown hair, self-possessed, and without discernible ego. When they talked, it became clear to both of them that if they worked together, they could make something worthwhile. Cerise & Lily became their new enterprise.

Lily saw Brian every now and then. It was always the same. He would go through the ritual of making love to her, telling her she meant the world to him while (she suspected) thinking about Hedi or someone else. It was rarely satisfying for her and eventually she dropped him. She went on dates with other boys and had fun, but none of the dates developed into anything serious.

85

Gloria reported that Frank was in an exasperated mood. The business was collapsing. He'd told her it was one thing to be the butt of a joke, but now he had to believe the joke was true, even though it wasn't funny. It was into the heart of Hell the company was going. There was nothing he could do about it; all the good water was under the bridge and past successes would soon be forgotten. Maybe the company could become a public benefit trust that people would think well of—employee-owned, doing work for the poorest.

'So what will he do?' said Lily.

'When in doubt, he always gets busy. The company will get the apologies out while it can: sorry to the employees, the suppliers, the customers, the shareholders, the art galleries they used to sponsor, the charities, everyone else they can think of. Sorry for all the things the company couldn't control like global recession, climate change, pandemics. He was in his office, and he stopped speaking on hearing a rumbling noise. When he asked what it was, he was told it was all the desperately fat cats running away.'

'How could they run if they were desperately fat?' said Lily.

'Good point. Waddling, then. He shouted, "Tell them the company's not dead yet. It's not even on the gurney," but I thought maybe that's on the way.

The business magazines are mocking up their covers all ready for the company's final demise, but Dad says they'll be caught out. He said, "Don't worry, the suckers will be back before they know it. There's always someone out there pushing a handcart of dreams, looking out for help. We still look the part and a great future awaits. Be confident of that.'"

86

It was the day after Lily received her A-level results (A-stars in Maths, English and Business Studies), when she heard from Mr Topp that he had secured an award for her from the Friends of Lily Upshire settlement fund. Authorised to sign on her behalf, he said the final figure, net of contingency fees and costs, was still being calculated, but the paperwork would be sent via email shortly, with the proceeds to follow in a few days. He said he hoped the amount would be 'a nice surprise' for her. For many eighteen-year-olds it would have gone straight to their heads, but acquiring resilience had brought coolness. She told no-one about it except Grandma who asked about publicity. Lily was adamant that, no, the money was all they needed, and anyway the settlement was confidential and, 'We must keep it so. Besides, if I had publicity, I could be Young Business Person of the Year, but that would be pure vanity.' Grandma told her not to get ahead of herself, at which Lily, suddenly playful, stuck out her tongue, but then apologised.

Grandma said, 'I am so proud of you but will not tell anyone what you've achieved.'

Ernie Topp was so clever he made the paperwork reflect that the money came from the company and not the Friends. It merely referred to the money going to a trust described as number ZA365. That way it did not draw the attention of the Friends, including Nancy and Fred, to the fact she'd benefited personally.

When Nancy called round the following day, Lily made sure she didn't see her. She listened on the stairs like she always used to. Nancy revealed that the couple received twenty-three thousand pounds out of the Friends' settlement, and Grandma later told Lily that Nancy seemed content, perhaps accepting in her heart that their claim had been false. Fred's condition had improved to such an extent he could now do gardening, although this was short-lived: on his first visit in many years to a restaurant to celebrate, he slipped on a pickled gherkin, resulting in an arm injury and a claim against the venue.

After deductions and including the profit Ernie Topp's brother made for her from trading the company's shares, she cleared £5.2 million. A giddy sum for an eighteen-year-old. She wasn't super-rich, but she was the richest person she knew, except for Ernie Topp and maybe Gloria and her dad. She had achieved what she wanted, but with so little effort on her part she almost felt she didn't deserve it. It was strange, not something to shout about but to hold in silence. Everything she'd wanted and it would transform her life, yet it felt no more real to her than something in a TV cartoon.

A few coins in your pocket were like sweet almonds, but a whole treasure chest could be pure cyanide to your thoughts: £5.2 million? Why not 5.5? Or 6 or 7 or 10 million? £5.2 million was more than she'd dreamed of, but after she'd given some to Grandma and maybe Sally and Ted and her favourite charities, would there be enough to properly develop her business? And why was it not more? How much did Mr Topp take? What were the deductions for? Why this? Why that? A shouting cavalcade of thoughts came charging in. But she stood outside her thoughts and shut the clamour down: No. No. No!

She discussed with Grandma about what to do with her money. She said she would treat her to a new house as and when she wanted it. Apart from a few gifts to others, she would invest the bulk of the money in companies, employing Mr Pitcairn as her adviser if he would agree. Years of tuition on business had built a strong relationship based on mutual trust between them.

87

Something happened in the States that was to severely test Lily's friendship with Gloria and her belief in her. Gloria told her of a strange incident involving her father, who'd been rushed to hospital after an extreme reaction to his new medication.

When Frank awoke in his hospital bed, he found a mysterious shape standing beside him. He grumbled, 'Do you know, I've just dreamt some kid called Lily Upshire in a little no-horse town called Retingham in England found a pea in a blueberry flip smoothie, and it triggered a remarkable chain of events that resulted in our great company, with a huge presence in every country in the world, and even owns the government in a few of them, descending almost into oblivion. It's incredible!'

'Indeed,' said the shape as it turned into a smart-suited, middle-aged gentleman with a serious expression. 'Except the dream is reality.'

'Excuse me, Sir, who are you? Are you interested in us buying your little enterprise? It's what we do. What is your line of business?'

'I'm afraid those days of rampant acquisition are long gone, Frank. It's now a matter of selling the company, or at least those few bits anyone might want to buy. That's assuming there's anything viable left. I've reviewed the company's history...'

'So you've come to buy some tiny bit you might be able to afford, is that it?' Frank laughed. 'I think you'll find most of it beyond even the most ambitious budget. Want to buy a burger stand or something? Our burgers are entirely sustainable and environmentally friendly.'

'It's time to stop the high-hat talk, Frank. Your company now consists of two Winnebagos in a trailer park. Most of the staff are volunteers from a hippie commune next door.'

'I see I'm still in that awful dream. I was sure I'd woken up. I would remind you, it's the biggest, strongest company in the world.'

'In your world, maybe. In the real world, little of it remains.'

'I bet the Napa Valley vineyards are still there...'

'They are, but its business withered away, and the wine turned to vinegar.'

'And my beloved champagne company in France?'

'Popped its cork, I'm afraid. And the fancy water company dried up.'

'The scotch distillery—on the rocks, I take it?'

'Yes. And the Italian ice cream parlour melted, and the pancake division flattened. And the bakery went stale. And the wheat company got shredded. And the biscuit maker crumbled.'

'And did the much loved yogurt maker sour?'

'Yes.'

'And what about the medicinal cannabis company? We had high hopes.'

'Up in smoke.'

'What about other divisions—are you saying the carmaker ran out of road?'

'Yes.'

'The boutique airline?'

'Crashed.'

'Container ship?'

'Ran aground.'

'The cruise liner?'

'Had a good launch. Plain sailing for a while but ran into heavy weather—'

'Such a shame.'

'—and sank without trace.'

'The yacht company?'

'Keeled over.'

'Canoe maker?'

'Up a creek with no paddle.'

'Then we bought that ferry company.'

'You were sold down the river.'

'Helicopter division?'

'Never left the ground.'

'The firework company—I suppose you'll call that a damp squib?'

'Not at all. Indeed, at first it threatened to go off like a rocket.'

'Excellent. And then?'

'It blew up in your face.'

'The casino?'

'Had its chips. Even the celebrity hairdressers took a haircut.'

'Well, these have been challenges, I will admit, but not failures because we've never had failures here. And there have been far more positives to balance them out.'

'I can't think of a single one.'

'This corporation was once like a vast California redwood dominating the heavens and with roots extending for miles in every direction. And now it's merely got rid of all the dead wood to be reborn as a vigorous, lithe, young sapling ready to face the winds of the world.'

'I see it as something a trifle more modest. Not so much a sapling as a desiccated old stick.'

'And its future?'

'It could stir paint or make a half-decent budgie perch.'

'That reminds me: we had an eco-friendly green paint company. That brightened the balance sheet up. Record profits in its third year.'

'Indeed. Then it fell into the red in the fourth and went to the wall in the fifth.'

'This is such negative thinking.'

'It's called reality, my friend.'

'It's people with such problematic thinking and pure bad luck that got us into this... temporary sub-optimal situation. Take the volunteers. Think of the dedication it takes, working for free because they love and believe in the brand. If we could only harness that love...'

'I think it's more sheer boredom. They want something to occupy their minds.'

'Why are you here anyway? Not a fake doctor are you?'

'The company has received an offer to buy it, and the rest of the board have asked me to approach you for your agreement to sell your shares.' The gentleman produced his business card. He was a lawyer.

'But I could sell my shares on the open market if I wanted to.'

'You could, but you'd get next to nothing.'

'So what are you offering?'

'A dollar for each share.'

'Are you serious?'

'It's very generous. But it must be completed today.'

Frank grumbled, but was about to sign when a young female voice shouted 'Don't!'

It was Gloria. 'What are you doing here?' said Frank.

'This is a con. Don't sign anything.'

There was an argument, but Gloria made clear she had a buyer prepared to pay five dollars for each of Frank's shares. The lawyer asked for proof. Gloria then produced an email ostensibly from Lily.

'Really?' said Frank. 'Lily wants to buy into the company? I always knew that kid was smart. There's no slack in her rope. I always wanted her on the board.'

It was at this moment Gloria's phone rang. 'Hey, Maggot, what's up? No, don't worry. We'll talk later. Trust me, you won't have to.'

'Was that your prospective buyer?' said the lawyer suspiciously.

'No,' Gloria lied.

'Tell your buyer, "No",' said Frank looking at the lawyer,

'You'll be voted off the board,' came the reply.

'OK. But you'll still need my shares.' Frank then indicated it was time for his nap and told the disgruntled lawyer to leave.

88

Lily was worried she might end up buying the company by mistake. Gloria had assured her there was nothing to worry about and it was just for show to put off the lawyer. Lily wanted to trust her but still hardly knew her. She was even more anxious when, early one morning, she received a call from someone claiming to be Frank. Lily wondered why he was phoning and even how it was possible. Why hadn't Gloria warned her? 'How did you get my number?' she said.

'I found it on Gloria's phone. She doesn't know. They all think I'm feeble in the mind, but I like to play possum. I just wanted to speak to the person who's been so vital to this company's progress and now wants to own it. I'm glad you're buying the controlling interest. Those vultures would dispose of the assets, although in reality they'll make sure their "consultancy fees" wipe out the value of them. The business is still very much alive. They claim it's not walking but hobbling, not breathing but wheezing, like an old slowpoke, but the way I see it, the brand is immortal, constantly rejuvenating itself, and will soon be flying high, proud and strong as a condor, whereas even you, angelic as you are, can only get old. So will my destroyer, that is, my saviour, speak?'

She decided to play along but act tough as well. She was suspicious. 'Only anyone soft in the head is going to buy it,' she said.

'Harsh.'

'You should be grateful. I would only want it for the blueberry flip smoothie plant. It would cost me plenty to get that going again.'

'But what of the pets division? I received word this morning that it's doing well.'

'It's still in business at least. But if you're not careful, you'll end up like all the other flops. All the other companies that refused to say sorry and then went bust. Companies never learn.'

'I can say sorry now.'

'Doesn't it occur to you that it's too late?'

'I wanted to say it when you first wrote to me. It was a joy to hear from such a valued customer.'

'Then why didn't you?'

'Lawyers. You know how it is. My lawyers wouldn't let me apologise.'

'That's the most pathetic excuse ever. At least none of the others said that. You ought to ask a few of them. There's a few would like a word with you. Some of your rivals you hated so much.'

'But we never hated.'

'Really? Well, they'd certainly love to get their hands round your throat.'

'But I've got big plans for Retchingham. I thought we could be partners. You could help the Retchingham redevelopment project.'

Retchingham? Lily thought, surely Frank would not make that mistake. 'What plans?' She pretended not to know. 'What redevelopment project?'

'A shopping mall, a stadium, a...'

'All nonsense. Completely impractical. You obviously know nothing about the town. No wonder the company went bust with your ridiculous ideas.'

'But these are ambitions. We're not bust. I wanted to offer you an exciting opportunity...'

'Instead of buying your shares? What are you up to?'

'Up to? I'll sell you half my shares at three dollars.'

'No thank you. I know you need to get out of the company because you failed.'

'Failed? There has been no failure, only challenges.'

'A child could see it. An eight-year-old. You couldn't stop buying. It was like an obsession with you. A sick compulsion.'

'It wasn't as simple as that, I assure you...'

'I'm sorry, but my grandma's calling me...

'Grandma? That old...'

'We're making a caraway cake. It's my new favourite thing.'

'Not blueberry smoothies? You were such a fan.'

'Blueberry *flip* smoothies. It shows how much you know. They're not being made anymore.'

'Perhaps we could start a new division making fancy cakes.'

'Perhaps, but not with you.'

89

Gloria phoned Lily to assure her she had not acquired her father's shares in the company, either by accident or fraud. The lawyer who visited her father was a fraudster hired by one of the other board members who'd been voted off. Lily told her about the weird phonecall she'd had from the person claiming to be Frank, saying she believed he was also a fraudster.

'This is not a great advert for running a company,' said Lily. 'Not if you have all that to contend with. It's difficult enough making money in the first place.'

'Oh, you do protest too much, Maggot. How exactly did you make your first million? By essentially doing nothing. You did not drink that smoothie, it did not make you ill, you did not join the Friends group, you didn't do anything at all except phone Ernie Topp. And whose suggestion was it to look in the *World's Toughest Lawyers* book? No, Maggot, I do not think you can complain about making money from hard work.'

Lily was defiant: 'Point taken, Glowie, but it's the wrong point. It was my single-mindedness led to my luck. I made it. Clever people know how to succeed without killing themselves with work. So, anyway, what is your father up to now?'

'He's talking to the manager of the one profitable product line, namely...' But she was gone suddenly. Lily only hoped she hadn't been kidnapped.

Later, Gloria told her about another weird situation involving her father. When he was back in his office he was again visited by someone suspicious. Fortunately, it had been recorded: 'Who are you?' said Frank.

'Lex Disher. I'm the head of the one profitable division remaining.'

'Profitable? I like the sound of that. *One* of the profitable divisions you say?'

'No, I said... oh, never mind.'

'Things are on the up. How many years have you been in profit?'

'Three months. It was the last deal the product acquisition director made.'

'Product acquisition director, eh? Fancy name. Didn't know they'd left. Or even that they'd joined. But we can build a great success from this. What field are you in? Let me guess: something cutting edge, ahead of the curve, the great green future, space, new forms of travel, new ways of being. AI? Rejuvenation? I can feel it. The blood's tingling. It's electric. So which division are you in again?'

'Canine hygiene.'

'Sounds cool. What does it mean? What's its main product?'

'Dog diapers.'

'Say again. It sounded like "dog diapers"?'

'That's right. You heard correctly. Luxury diapers for high-end dogs.'

'Sounds disgusting.'

'They are extremely useful. The discerning dog owner loves them.'

'Well, I own a dog. He doesn't wear diapers. Nor will he ever, and I'll sell that dog diaper business off the first thing I do. That and the ridiculous dog hotel.'

'The lovely luxury dog hotel? And the pooch fruit facials?'

'Yes, them too. So how did we get into dog diapers, in a manner of speaking? Or is it better not to know?'

'It was a subsidiary of a garden centre chain we bought out.'

'That's aspiration for you: ending up big in dog diapers. I wonder what the dear creator of this great company, as an artisan baker, would have made of that outcome. So what brings you here today?'

'Someone wants to buy the division.'

'Who does?'

'Tek Spurtmann.'

'That jerk? Who used to be with us, babbling to me about workers' rights one time?'

'He's got his own operation now. Making lots of money. More money than this company.'

'Temporary, I can assure you. We'll blow him out of the water. But maybe, on reflection, diapers could be the cornerstone of our big future. Let's expand. We must always move forward.'

'How do you mean?'

'I'm thinking: what about diapers for horses and camels? Llamas maybe... kangaroos...'

'I don't think...'

'Then do think. Think big in diapers. Think elephant diapers. Think rhino. Think blue whale diapers. Think...'

Lex left before Frank could finish his sentence.

90

Gloria received a letter from Lily. Unlike her letters to the company, Lily sent it as an attachment to an email:

Dear Gloria,

I guess you're right. I'm lucky. But that fact doesn't mean I'm lazy. I deserve my luck. My mum had it rough. She would want me to do well, and I do feel I'm blessed. Maybe some force is protecting me. So I don't feel guilty but grateful. Is it so wrong that I have been lucky? And what of you? You live in a luxurious mansion whereas I grew up in a modest house. My grandmother had to borrow money to pay for my tuition. Did your dad? No.

Lily

Gloria wrote back:

Dear Lily,

I did not intend to upset you as I obviously have done. I don't begrudge you your success. How could I? You do not need to be defensive, especially when I hold you in such regard.

Oh Lily, please do not be angry with me. It would break my heart for you to think ill of me, especially when the perception it would be based on would be so inaccurate. I did not mean you to think I believed you lazy. I'm sorry I have been the cause of annoyance to you. The thought that you might wish to become more distant from me, psychologically as well as physically, destroys me.

Gloria
PS The mischief here continues.

The 'mischief' Gloria referred to was an attempt to unseat her father from the board. It failed. Frank's opponents then threatened to resign en masse. Frank announced he would issue a positive statement about the company, which is what he did all the time anyway, and then resign. He would sell them his shares in return for ownership of certain assets including the drinks division but not the much-touted canine hygiene division. This was agreed.

91

Cerise & Lily expanded their business to include private investment. Cerise's dad, Mr Pitcairn, who'd made a killing on buying and selling shares since he'd started tutoring her, put in two million pounds, and Lily matched it. They set up a small office in London.

One day, the summer after turning nineteen, Lily found out from Facebook that Mack was at university in London. Lily hadn't seen or heard from her in years. She messaged her and suggested meeting but found her reluctant. Eventually, Lily was able to persuade her to meet off campus.

They met in a quiet wine bar one evening. Mack looked tired and uncomfortable and older than her years. 'I feel like you're someone from my distant past,' she said. 'Why did you contact me? You must know there's no future for us. I used to think about you all the time. Then you told me you shagged Brian Panker. I couldn't believe you were so desperate. Why did you even tell me? You must have known it would upset me.'

'I wanted to make you jealous.'

'Like that worked! I confess I hated you over it.' She reached out to hold Lily's hand. 'But I don't now.' She gave her a mischievous grin. 'So, tell me, I have to ask: what was sex with Brian even like that time?'

'Brianish.'

Mack started laughing. 'Like what? Where did you do it? Oh, Lily, I've missed you so incredibly much!'

'In my bed at Grandma's.'

'The same bed we spent those chaste nights in? You absolute slut! So why was it Brianish?'

'Because when he was getting into it with me he suddenly heard a noise downstairs, turned ghostly white, jumped up, and hid behind the bed.'

'Romantic or what?'

'Then he quickly dressed, stuck his head out of the door, and ran off.'

'So was Grandma even home?'

'No, it was the dog in the kitchen trying to steal a cheese roll.'

Mack's face was a picture of happiness. 'Oh, Lily, I love you every bit as much as I ever did!'

They got drunk. On the walk back to the campus Mack suddenly stopped and embraced her. 'Marry me one day, Lily.'

Lily said nothing. It was too early to be thinking about marrying. She attributed Mack's proposal to her being drunk and ignored it, but Mack thought the lack of response was from another cause: 'You're in business with Cerise Pitcairn, I noticed. She looks a cutie. Quite a partnership.'

'Don't be jealous.'

'I'm absolutely not. No, really, I'm not.'

Lily was reassured. She liked her old friend to feel jealous and seek to hide it.

For a few nights they stayed at Lily's flat together. They made love, but Lily could not hide her indifference to it, and Mack sensed this and was hurt, unimpressed by Lily's pretence at enjoying it to please her. In the following weeks, Mack returned to other lovers, more passionate and playful. She gradually abandoned Lily in favour of these more exciting partners.

There was silence from Mack for months, apart from the occasional text to let Lily know she was OK and asking after her. Lily began missing her deeply. Above all, she felt disappointed with herself: Mack wanted her as the love of her life, but she had let her go again without revealing the strength of her own feelings, and now it was too late.

As in other times of disappointment, she threw herself harder into her work.

92

Gloria wanted Lily to buy her father's part of the business for three million dollars and said she would then buy it off her. Lily was reluctant, and finding the cash meant selling some investments. She said, 'How could you possibly afford it?'

'Borrow it.'

'From whom?'

'My dad, if necessary.'

'What!?'

'And why not?'

Lily declined to be involved. She was naturally cautious and content with her Cerise & Lily venture and her stocks and shares trading. She needed no distractions.

Gloria had different ideas. She decided to visit Lily and persuade her. One afternoon, she appeared unannounced at Lily's office in London. 'So finally we meet, Maggot,' she said.

Lily melted: Gloria was tall and dark, with the glamorous looks and presence of a young Latina film actress. Lily's feeling of being overwhelmed was made greater by the element of surprise. 'Why have you come?'

'I'm here to assure you there's nothing wrong with what I'm suggesting,' said this fiery-eyed Mexican-American goddess.

Lily took her into a small private office. After pleasantries and casual chat over coffee, Lily said, 'Please don't try and bamboozle me. I'm easily confused, so I tend to dig my heels in.'

'I couldn't do that. And I wouldn't try.' Gloria explained how her father's mental health was deteriorating. She wanted to take the business over from him, but he wouldn't agree, so the plan was for Lily to buy it and sell it on to her.'

Lily stiffened. 'And what do I get out of it?'

'Besides knowing you've helped a good friend?'

'You're not *that* much of a good friend.'

Gloria was clearly miffed. 'Alright, I've obviously upset you.' She began gathering her papers. Lily sensed finality—real finality, not an act. She felt sympathy for Gloria and her father. 'Stay,' she said.

'I've come all this way to ask a favour. I should have stayed at home. At least the weather's better there.'

Lily pleaded with her to sit down. 'Let's go to dinner,' she said.

'If the answer's "No", I need to find someone else to help me.'

'The answer's "Let's talk about it."'

Lily took her to a restaurant selling traditional English food. In the end, Gloria agreed to pay an additional two hundred thousand dollars in the acquisition deal. 'That's to cover your expenses,' she said. Apart from legal fees and transaction costs on the investments, which should not be anywhere near this amount, Lily was at a loss to know what these expenses might be, but she had won the day.

And to the extent it mattered to her, she'd also won Gloria, who was impressed by Lily not backing down easily but agreeing in the end to assist a friend. After business they talked about relationships. Gloria was interested in Mack. 'So do you think you'll marry her one day?'

'I don't know. I love her to bits, but it's too early to think about it. I want kids, but it's too early for them too. But she's gone anyway. I don't know.'

Gloria said she'd never found satisfaction in romantic relationships. Guys either just wanted sex or they were controlling or self-absorbed. 'And I'm not lesbian.'

'Nor am I,' said Lily. 'But I love Mack so I want to make her happy—even if I fail.'

Lily sensed Gloria was about to say something in response but was holding back and so Lily said, 'Can I ask you: why have you helped me so much? There was no reason for you to do so.'

'There was,' said Gloria. 'I don't know how much I've helped you, but to the extent I have, in all honesty, guilt has been a big factor. Guilt for the way I treated you in the early days. If guilt was a fuel, it would power the world for ever.'

'It wasn't so bad,' said Lily. 'I've had far worse.'

'No,' said Gloria. 'It was wrong and stupid and I will never forgive myself.'

93

Gloria was true to her word and the deal went through satisfactorily. Lily was glad she'd put her trust in her.

After that, Lily didn't hear from her for a while. Eventually, Gloria wrote to her, 'I'm sorry I haven't been in touch lately, but my father has been very ill. His mental health deteriorated to such an extent that, for the wellbeing of himself and everyone else, I've had to invent a pretend company and make him head of it. I realise that sounds crazy, but it seems to be working. Everything is set up to look real, and he makes real decisions but about pretend things. He has people send reports to him, and he sends emails and records speeches. He knows the only companies he can buy and sell are fake, but thinks it's for some higher purpose—the breaking of an international cartel. He's happy enough, less stressed than he was in the real world, but it's so sad.'

Gloria said her father's disillusionment began when he tried to speak to God once. 'I don't think I ever told you. It was back when he was running the real company and looking for a financial saviour.' Gloria recalled that her dad was sceptical: even criminals prayed to God but only so they'd get away with their crimes. No, a dream, he decided, would be better. In it he would appeal to God to save the company. As CEO he knew the company had done nothing wrong. It was a deserving case. All it had done was over-stretch a little. Who hadn't done that at least once in their lives? A mild case of buying-shopping disorder at worst. Therapy would help cure that. God would give him the hope to inspire the company to greatness again.

One evening, he ate a plate full of different cheeses to give him dreams, as well as a couple of vitamin B6 tablets for the same purpose. Unfortunately, he consumed too much and had to drink a cherry brandy to get off to sleep. After all that, however, the dreams were so bland he woke up from sheer boredom. For the rest of the night he felt drowsy, unable to return to sleep, and when he got out of bed he was unable to fully wake up. It was when he was in the bathroom shaving that, frustrated at being unable to reach God in dreams, he said out loud: 'Is God even at home these days, I wonder?'

Gloria said, 'Then God answered him. And it so surprised Dad, he accidentally cut himself. As he tried to stop the bleeding he said, "Who did I hear speak just then? Could that be God? It sounded like someone muttering and grumbling in the background. God, are you really there?" And God said grumpily, "Yes! What do you want, loser!?"'

Gloria described how Frank became all humble and God snapped, 'Get on with it, you schmuck!' So Frank said the company had always got on well with God, even though it had more money.'

'Did he really say that?'

'Yes but God just told him to hurry up, and then pointed out the disclaimer, saying the lawyers insisted on it, it being such a litigious world, and if Dad wanted to read it, he needed to check out God's website. Otherwise, he would be deemed to have accepted its terms. So Dad, trying to get on God's right side, said, "I'm sure it's very reasonable," and God replied that it wasn't reasonable at all: "Just like your lousy company with all its ridiculous disclaimers and warranties and stuff no-one even understands—especially the whackadoos who drafted it. But I can give you the short version of the disclaimer now: If you don't like it, tough!"'

'Oh dear!' Lily exclaimed.

'Then God said, "There's more humans than ever before in this world and most of them have their begging bowl out, bleating about the weather and viruses and a host of other things. I've never been so busy with all their prayers and petitions and whatnot, with people wanting contradictory things and seeking to do each other down with their petty disputes, and now you come creeping me out. I wish more people were atheists. Then they wouldn't bother me with their idiotic, selfish requests. Except they would. The worst are the ones who hedge their bets. They get all high and mighty about how belief is only for the ignorant masses, then start wailing to me the moment something goes wrong..."'

Lily thought, for someone so busy and impatient, God did seem to gabble on an awful lot.

'"...They don't want to keep their part of the bargain: going to places of worship and asking for forgiveness and so on—oh no, always too busy for that—but they still want all the good stuff: saving their asses from fire, or helping them secure a loan they'll never pay back. They'll take the plum all day, thank you very much, but not the duff. I've heard it all. Every excuse."'

'Your poor dad.'

'Then Dad asked for God's blessing for the company to achieve greatness again and God declined. Dad ignored this, thinking God maybe misheard, and said God would know from personal experience that a brand can have problems with a tarnished image, and God was furious: "I'll have you know that before me people believed in any old tripe. There were more gods than there were people. None of them were any good. I soon cleared out that filthy stable, I can tell you. I burned out the lot of them, and since then I've had uninterrupted success. Tarnished indeed!" Dad then suggested a partnership, helping each other along, stressing the company would play the junior role. God rejected that, saying, "Your pathetic company can rot."'

'Oh no!' Lily felt bad for Frank.

'So Dad said it was obviously a bad day to call, and God said, "You're not as dumb as you look. Every day's a bad day." Dad suggested ringing back, and God told him to forget it, saying the stuff the company made was rubbish, and all the bosses had been greedy wretches. God said, "You've ripped the world's population off, made their lives miserable, and made them unhealthy. You deserve to end up in the dustbin with all the garbage you made. And, by the way, the company has *never* had more money than me." Then God disappeared.'

'So what did your dad make of it all?'

'He thought it must have been an impostor he'd been talking to. He didn't try to talk to God again.'

'Poor Frank.'

Lily phoned Gloria regularly after this, inviting her to talk about it all. She felt sorry for Frank who'd tried so hard to make the company a success. He had a vision, albeit a cracked one, and he'd been kindly disposed towards her and never blamed her for the antics of the Friends.

94

One night after a business dinner, Lily arrived home to find she had received a letter from America:

Dear Lily,

It is many years since you wrote the letter which was to change all our lives. I guess you never did receive the apology you requested from the company. Not in a letter anyway. I felt you deserved another letter.

I would like to invite you to come to visit me in the States. I did ask you before and you said you would consider it another time. I feel that time has come.

There are plenty of rooms in this house and you can stay here as independently (or not) as you wish. The truth is, Lily, that I want you to play a bigger role in my life. There is no reason why you should want the same of me. I was mean to you in the early days and I have apologized for that and apologize again now. But I feel I can trust you. There are not many I can say that of. And I ask nothing of you. But why would I suggest you visit? Because I am lonely? Yes, but more because I simply wanted to reach out to you with affection. I am nothing special. You, by contrast, have some quality that cannot be defined. It is a mystery to me. I'm sorry if this sounds weird (there, I apologized again!). If so, it is because I am not always good at describing what I want to say or what I feel. If you come and stay, it would be an honor for me. There are some cool places around here I can take you to. If the weather's good, and it usually is, I think you will have a nice time. And I am easy company. You can stay for as little time or as long as you want. If you wish to, you can even stay for ever! Just joking. Or am I? If you want to stay in the States, with me or not, I will make it possible. Anyway, think about it. I won't pressure you by suggesting it again. On the other hand, the offer is always open. At least, for as long a time as my poor brain can contemplate! All my life I've been a winner, or so I've been told. But I feel like a loser and have for a long time. If I had you more in my life, I would feel like a winner.

Above all, stay just as you are, just as lovely.

All my love,
Gloria

Later, Lily looked at Gloria's Facebook page, at her photos, her posts. Here she was with her parents, there with her brothers, here on a fishing trip, there playing soccer. Lily had once dreamed of a life in America. Now the chance had come. She knew what Gloria meant. She did not need to spell it out.

Lily would sleep on it. She would talk about it with Grandma, and with Cerise. She would debate with herself about how long to stay for, although in a sense it made no difference what she decided. Looking over her life to date she felt most of it had been based on false hopes and self-deception. She would talk to Gloria about all this. She believed Gloria would understand it. And she could talk openly to her about Mack and know she would not feel jealous, for she was the real thing. The question she hurt herself with, as before, was whether she deserved the real thing, but at least she now understood, in her mind if not her heart, that the question itself was worthless.

She decided she would go ahead and visit Gloria—she would celebrate her twentieth birthday with her—and she made arrangements accordingly.

95

One Saturday, Lily went to Retingham sensing it would be the last visit for a long time. What impressed her was the vibrancy of the town. There were brand new shops—interesting independent ones—and no boarded-up premises. She noticed a traffic sign advising the route to the new Robin Hood theme park, and another mentioning the town was twinned with Irvine, California. Retingham's relationship with the company had brought success for it. That was the lesson: you aimed high and worked for it, and maybe you didn't get what you aimed for, which might be unachievable, but you could still do better than anyone thought possible.

She went into Bashetts' shop. Bashett himself had passed away. He'd had a heart attack after some kid queried her change and didn't back down when Bashett tried to chase her away. Lily would have bought a smoothie, but they didn't sell them anymore. On the cover of the local newspaper, she noticed a face she recognised from years ago but couldn't place. She bought the paper and sat in Saviour Park reading it. She realised the face was of the

Runt, now a successful model and singer. In the accompanying interview she was asked about her inspiration. Her reply was that bullying at school was the main spur: 'There was one blonde girl in particular. She beat me up twice but counselling helped, and the next time she tried it I was ready for her.'

Also in the paper was an update on progress on the new school, which was to be called the Frank Salesman High.

She went to see Grandma and they talked about where Grandma might like to live. She was in good spirits and reluctant to contemplate new surroundings yet, so they talked about how much Lily would earmark for sheltered housing, or at least a new bungalow. Grandma said, 'By the way, you proved Auntie Gwynne wrong and no mistake.'

'What happened to her?'

'She got scammed, she tracked the scammer down, tried to kill him, and is now in prison. That's what watching too much crime TV does for you.'

Grandma gave her blessing to her going to the States, even if it turned out to be permanent, though Lily stressed this was unlikely. 'You must write, though,' she said. 'Proper letters like you used to.' Lily promised she would write often whether she went to live abroad or not.

She went to the cemetery. There was a strong breeze and it blew tree blossom onto Jane's grave. She talked to her mother about Gloria, and about the powers. At first, she wasn't sure her mother was listening, but as she came away she was struck by the thought that if you used the powers they could rebound on you, and perhaps that was the reason Jane had died in a car crash. This had never occurred to her before. She turned round. 'No,' she said in defiance. She felt shocked at herself denying the influence of the powers. She had no need of them now. Did it mean she was therefore denying her mother? No, she assured herself it did not.

In the market square there was an event taking place, with a singing group miming and a dance troupe. The MC was a young woman with a familiar face. 'Hey Lily!' she heard as she left. Maybe it was the Runt. She'd heard enough and didn't turn to see who it was.

She rang Sally Peacemaker but the line was busy. She left a message, wishing her and her parents well. She said she'd send her a Facebook message.

She visited Ted. There was a training session on. She watched until it finished. She noticed that Ted was embarrassed when she looked him in the face. It was because he desired her. She was used to it: frustrated teenage boys, lonely old drunks in parks, even suave, married businessmen. Now it was dear, sweet Ted. Except it wasn't her he desired but the Jane he saw in her. And perhaps the Jane in her would have responded, had she been less self-aware.

They had a brief, pleasant chat, then she held him tight and said, 'Thank you, Ted, for all you did for me.'

He smiled. 'You did it, Lily, not me.'

'OK, but you know what I mean—without you it wouldn't have been possible...' Her sentence tailed off as she left. No need to say more.

96

The following afternoon, Lily was in the flat preparing her travel case when she received a call from Mack: 'So you did it then after all this time. Well done.'

'Long time, no hear. Did what exactly?'

'Fixed the Bizzells.'

'Eh? I'd have liked to but...'

'You did it. Julia and the girls all dead. The hex worked.'

'Seriously, I don't know anything about it.'

'Seriously, I need to see you. Not to talk about that.'

'I'm going to the States tomorrow. Let's get together when I'm back.'

'No, tonight. I must see you while I can. Will you be at the flat?'

'Hotel. I'll send you the address. Mack, I never did a hex.'

'I know. So where are you staying in the States?'

'My friend Gloria's.'

'I see, is she your...' It was Mack's reassuring jealousy.

'No. It's not like that.'

'Not like me, you mean.'

'That's not what I meant.' Lily rang off, already impatient with Mack's insecurity.

When she met Mack in the hotel lobby she found her looking ragged and desperate. Her jacket was torn, her jeans dirty. Her face was pale, her hair a tangle, and she smelt of booze. Their hug gave Lily little pleasure, sad as she felt at her friend's demeanour.

Once in her room, Lily challenged, 'So what's it all about, Mack? Something drastic's happened to you.'

'Can we go for a drink?'

'Haven't you had enough already?'

This annoyed Mack: 'Don't be a prissy little bitch. If you're going to be prissy, I'll go. I'll fuck off right now.'

Lily grabbed her arm. 'Calm down. Have you eaten yet? You've come to see me and you're not going to walk straight out.' Mack pulled her arm away, but Lily snatched her hand and lunged forward to kiss her repeatedly on the neck. Mack did not resist.

She took Mack to a vegetarian restaurant she thought she would like. After they'd ordered, Lily said, 'So what's the matter?'

Mack was nervous and did not want Lily looking into her face. 'I'm not the person I was, OK? Things have happened to me these last few months. And you're not the same person either. You're even more up yourself than ever.' Seeing Lily's discomfort at this she half-smiled and said, 'But you've always been up yourself and that turns me on. But you don't need to be up yourself to reject me.'

'I promise I won't.'

Mack gave her a look that conveyed innocent trust. 'So I got into a relationship with an older woman named Marlene. It was good, it was wild, it was passionate, but it burned me up. She was a sex addict and she turned me into one.'

'How could she?'

'I would have done anything for her but she was insatiable. And as part of her domination of me she introduced me to drugs. Like you, I've always stayed clear of them, but she made it impossible to avoid. Mainly coke. I couldn't resist it, and I couldn't resist her. I was obsessed. But then I found out she had other girls and I was one of several and I became disillusioned. And I became desperate to see you, believing you could help me, but you were never there. Always so busy...'

'When?'

'Unattainable. Up yourself as you are.'

Lily was annoyed: 'When? When did you even try?'

Mack ignored her. 'I got away from her, and I tried to cut out the coke, but I couldn't, and I started drinking more—cider mainly but whatever was cheap.'

'You should have told me. You know...'

'And I thought you wouldn't...'

'For God's sake, Mack, will you listen!?' Her friend, shocked, fell silent. Lily continued, 'If you ever feel this way, you must tell me. I don't believe you tried to contact me. But, anyway, why are you telling me all this now?'

'I just wanted you to know that your...' She made an effort to look into Lily's eyes. '...your favourite has fallen...' She blushed.

'From your perch?'

'So now I'm not the stronger one like I used to be.'

'You were never the stronger.'

'Yeah I was. I'd wrestle you now except we're in here, but even if we weren't, you'd win this once, even though I always used to.'

'No you didn't.'

Instead of replying, Mack leaned forward, took Lily's hand in hers, and kissed her on the underside of her wrist. She looked into Lily's eyes and said, 'I fucking love you, Lily Upshire, and I always have. Even when I cut you off to punish you, I wanted you so bad. I thought about you every day and night. I pretended I didn't care, but I was lying to myself, and I knew it.'

Back in the hotel room, Mack wanted to catch the TV evening news. On it there was a report that a car had driven off a bridge into the Trent. Five members of a family killed. They were not named. Lily said, 'How do you even know it's the Bizzells?'

'It has to be. What other family did you curse?'

'Don't.'

'I can imagine them on the way home from an expensive dinner, all drunk after celebrating the Runt's latest success. Probably the boys travelled separately so survived. You maybe didn't curse those two.'

'Stop it.' Although no details were given, Lily suspected Mack was right and it was the Bizzells. She could even believe she'd done it. It would mean she'd mastered the hex game now that she no longer wanted it. She hadn't cursed them or anyone else for a long time. Surely a curse she'd made couldn't survive that long. She felt bad.

Mack knew how Lily's mind worked. 'Stop beating yourself up,' she said.

'But...'

'But nothing. The way that family treated you they deserved to burn to death. Drowning was too kind.'

'Stop it, Mack. Please.' She told herself there was no hex. No, it was an illusion.

That night, any last resistance on Mack's part was broken, and she made sure Lily knew it. Lily could feel the desolation in her friend. She knew she'd won but did not want any thought of victory. Not even victory at life. As soon as you thought you'd won you got knocked down—boxing had taught her that.

As they lay in bed in the soft light their eyes were locked in a mutual gaze. If there could be a screenshot to remember all their lives, they would both choose this moment.

When they were lying side by side holding hands Mack said, 'Tell me, when we make love does it mean nothing to you?'

'I just love to look in your face when you come.'

'And?'

'And there's nothing I can't learn. Even that.'

'Even that? Oh Lily, you're so funny—so awkward talking about love. But don't get mad at my being amused.'

'I won't,' said Lily tenderly.

'Tell me it isn't the last, whatever.'

'Whatever.'

A few hours later, the alarm on Lily's phone sounded. She switched it off. She needed a little more time. Mack was stirring. 'Will I do as a c-word?' said Lily.

'Do? You're the only c-word I want now, even though I have to learn to share you with Gloria.'

'As I said, it's not like that with her.'

She kissed Mack. She held her tight, but when she released her, Mack nudged her away. 'You'd better get ready,' she said.

Lily slowly got up and stood at the window, looking at the streets under the lights, and then her gaze drifted to the edge of darkness. She checked her phone. There was a text from Gloria: 'Looking forward to seeing you.'

She was tempted to respond, 'Me too,' but it did not feel right. Instead, she sent a text to Mack, 'I'll always be there for you. I'll be back sooner than you know.'

She returned to sit on the bed, tempted to slip under the covers. She went into the bathroom to shower. She took her time, wishing Mack would join her, but Mack was not awake, flickering in and out of sleep. Once dry, Lily dressed quickly.

Mack had thrown off the covers. Fully clothed, Lily lay on the bed and snuggled up to her naked body. She closed her eyes, listening to Mack's breathing that she imagined as the sound of waves upon the shore, imperceptibly louder with each breath. For a moment she was looking down upon herself beside her lover. She knew, whenever she heard the ocean, or even imagined it, she would think of her, and feel the soft warmth of her body in this moment before parting, so bittersweet.

THANK YOU

Thank You For Reading My Book!

I really appreciate it.

Please leave a helpful review on Amazon letting others know what you thought of the book.

Thank you so much!
John Holmes